DARK COVENANT

H. L. RANDALL

Dark Covenant
H. L. Randall

Universal Battles Books RPG

Alliance, Ohio 44601
Universalbattles.com

First published by Universal Battles Books RPG 2016

ISBN   978-0-9862928-2-8

Dedication

This book is dedicated to fiction lovers everywhere.

Acknowledgement

I would like to thank my editor Colin Tripp for his valuable contribution to my book. My appreciation also goes to the designer of my book cover, SelfPubBookCovers.com/FrinaArt.

Contents

PROLOGUE

For over a century the land lay barren until the witches came. The ground was dead—full of decaying trees and slimy mud that covered the carcasses of animals like a foul-smelling blanket. The witches had escaped from North Berwick, Scotland, following the harsh enforcement of the 1562 Witchcraft Act.

Many of these witches traveled to the New World. Crammed into three small wooden ships for months, they rocked with the turbulent waves of an angry sea until reaching the quiet shore of what would later become Illinois. They brought with them centuries of earth knowledge through healing salves, medicinal plants, herbs, spirituality, and magic.

The witches cultivated the land into a livable masterpiece and named it New Berwick. They chose a portion of the land and built a large community that they named Falcon Haven after the birds that made its trees their homes. A hundred years passed and humans also settled there, but the witches kept their identity a secret.

Legend has it that the earth spirit Asase Ya had appeared before their high priestess in the form of a spider to make a covenant with them—payment, the spirit had said, for their restoration of the land. Asase Ya vowed to be their protector and benefactor for as long as they worshiped her and obeyed the covenant rules.

But Corina Brewer, a headstrong young witch, ignored the rules. She abused her powers and led other witches to consort with the dead, a practice forbidden to covenant witches.

Corina was rebellious even as a child. In the winter of 1810, she, her younger sister Holly, and her best friends Gunner Lenox and Amber Moore found an old bat cave. They sat cross-legged in a circle on the stone ground and held hands. An ancient spell rose from their lips and beckoned the darkness.

They chanted until the lit candles they had placed before them floated several inches off the ground and a chilling wind stirred inside the cave. The candle flames glowed in the breeze like fiery red eyes. Holly's mouth stiffened as she shook nervously and spurts of urine warmed her thighs. Amber's heart pounded—she squeezed Corina's hand until the magic ring Corina was wearing sliced into her own finger. Yet Corina felt nothing as her green irises rolled to the back of her head and the whites shone like two tiny boiled eggs.

A huge snake-like stream of black smoke swirled several times around them. A pale figure with no arms or legs emerged from the thick blackness and hovered above them. It had no face, just wavering grey fog inside the slits where eyeballs should have been. The top of its head popped back, and a dark forked tongue slid from the opening. Holly screamed and tore her hand away from Gunner. The figure shot back into the smoke and the cave walls sucked it in.

"Damn you, Holly. You idiot!" Corina shouted.

Gunner had tried to grab Holly, but she was too quick for him. She bolted from the cave screaming, and never stopped running until she reached home.

*****

"Corina is the evil one," the senior witches once said of her. Though she proved a thorn in the coven's side, the local council refused to banish her because they believed she was worth saving.

"She's young—a little patience is all the girl needs," Hilda, an elder witch said to the members of the local council. Hilda was short and stout in a grandmotherly fashion; the student witches considered her their advocate. Whenever they got into trouble, they would run to her because she treated them as if they were her own children.

"Oh, that girl will be the ruin of us all if we don't do something," Harriet said, slamming her palm down on the conference table. Harriet was tall and thin. She had a thick nose that sat in the middle of a thin, wiry dark face with dark, close set eyes. Her mousey brown hair was generally pulled back in a bun. She despised Corina and resented her for getting away with mischief that witches in Harriet's day would have never dared. Harriet constantly snooped around trying to find anything she could on Corina and her fellow delinquents.

As young as thirteen, Corina had proven dangerous around unsuspecting humans, especially those in the public school she attended. She had a gift for being charming and sweet yet deathly cold at the same time. She had a stare that seemed to burrow into your soul.

When she was sixteen, Brad Crawly, a mortal, dumped her for the new girl, a pretty redhead. Corina appeared civil enough and asked Brad to meet with her one last time to bring closure to their relationship, as she told him. The next day in art class, Brad's demeanor suddenly changed from his usual bubbly and outgoing self to someone almost unrecognizable. And, as if he'd snapped into some hypnotic trance, he got up from his seat, walked to the front of the classroom, stood next to Mr. Carter, the schoolmaster, and slit his own throat from ear to ear.

The blood splattered in a jagged line across Mr. Carter's face. In shock, Carter stumbled back against the wall and slid down to the floor. The children thundered from the classroom like a spooked herd of cattle, some screaming and others stopping to vomit in the hallway. Still other students, who'd reached outside, huddled together on the schoolyard grass shaking and crying.

Gunner and Amber watched as Corina just stood in the classroom doorway observing Brad lying on the floor, his head nearly severed from his body. Her cold eyes traced the stream of blood from his throat as it pooled under the desk and around the legs of the chairs. She cocked her head as if fascinated. Her stare seemed lifeless, and her eyes like marbles peering through the wooden face of a mannequin.

As a young adult her powers had grown stronger and her personality more sinister. Over the years, she and her small group of followers continued rebelling, and Harriet's snooping finally paid off. The group was tight lipped and remained loyal to Corina. However, Holly and a few others broke under intense interrogation, which included forcing their heads under water while chained crocodiles snapped their massive jaws just inches from their faces.

Harriet looked like the cat that ate the canary. "I knew she'd bring trouble. But did anyone listen to me?"

"Yes, yes, we know," Hilda answered, "but you often made those accusations without merit."

A small group of council members searched the defiant witches' quarters and found evidence of forbidden arts: books with covers made from human skin, vials of blood, small animal parts, a severed hand, daggers with skull and cross-bone handles,

9

and voodoo dolls that resembled a few of their human school teachers who had suffered unexplainable sicknesses throughout the year. Not even Hilda could save the renegades as they stood before the Witches of Darmieth—the supreme high council of dead witches—who sat in midair with the tips of their red and gold trimmed velvet cloaks barely touching the white marble floor.

Holly was no longer the quiet, silly, shivering little girl she'd once been. Though she broke under interrogation, she had hardened over the years, and her only weakness was her fear and loyalty to her sister.

"You have disobeyed the rules of the sacred covenant made by Asase Ya," said Isadora, high priestess.

"You have broken your vows," said another.

"Shamed your families," a third council member said.

"Ushered darkness into your community," said the fourth.

"And defiled Mother Earth with forbidden magic," spoke the last.

When all five had spoken, Isadora announced the sentence to the fallen faces of many witches but to the delight of Harriet. "The Witches of Darmieth," Isadora began, "find Corina Brewer, Holly Brewer, Amber Moore, Gunner Lenox, Isabella Wrighthorn…,"as she read off the names, Holly felt as though she were floating above the room with Isadora's voice sounding far away. Her body hovered over the tops of windows and skid across the surface of the high walls, up to the colorful, artistic ceiling of humans sacrificed to sacred dragons and up through the roof to the pale blue sky where she sailed on a cloud before being carried away by a swift wind. Then an angry gasp from her sister forced her back to the dark reality and she heard the last few names on the list, "… Rosie Stevenson, John Pepperwill, and Wendell Higgins have been found guilty of necromancy—and are hereby banished from The Mystic Circle with all coven rights and magic permanently terminated."

"You think this is the end of me, you dead bitches?" Corina shouted as the other outcasts hurried past her.

"Careful, girl," Hilda warned after seeing the sudden fire in Isadora's eyes.

"Come on!" Holly said, pulling Corina by her arm.

Corina stumbled sideways and looked defiantly over her shoulder, wanting to say more. But Holly continued pulling her until they reached outside where horses and coaches waited with their belongings.

No longer under the protection of the covenant, the outcasts settled in Necropolis, a cemetery world where the worst of evil was buried and the undead roamed restlessly. After decades of failing in the dark art, Corina and her followers finally regained supernatural powers by absorbing all the magic from the dead bones of the most powerful sorcerers of the ancient world. She founded a kingdom and called it Ironforge; for not even magic, outside of her own, could penetrate her fortress.

In the early 1900s, after getting wind of Corina's powers, the covenant witches cast a spell that put a mystical shield around Ironforge so that Corina was confined within her fortress; however, if humans ignored the signs that warned to stay away from her castle and instead ventured too closely, the wall pulled them into the stone and mortar like a magnet. Human flesh made the mystical wall stronger as if each person were a sacrifice.

To the mortal eye, it appeared as just a huge wall; only witch eyes could see the invisible horror—thousands of people embedded in the wall from the waist up, their middle and lower extremities fused with the mortar. Each was clothed in rags of their own century, their terrifying faces silently screaming and their arms flailing and struggling to pull free.

The covenant witches realized that Corina's powers had grown dangerously stronger. More disturbing, her anger had followed them into the twenty-first century.

*****

In a modern world, still confined to her fortress, Corina stands looking into a large ancient cast iron pot that lingers inches off the floor in midair. A green fire burns under it. Inside the pot, a brown liquid substance bubbles noisily as a mini, transparent tornado swirls two feet above the liquid. Within the swirl, she can see all of New Berwick: Falcon Haven, Greyscott Falls, and Sheerfield. Like the news flashing from one part of the region to another, she watches people walking about, vehicles bustling, deputies directing traffic, children playing on school grounds, bikers and joggers, sailing ships, and low-flying helicopters. "My new playground," she says. Then, within the mystical swirl, Falcon Haven appears more clearly. Several witches are busy toiling on the ground. Corina swells with delight at the very sight of them. "Ah, there you are.., the covenant bitches of Berwick." Her green eyes narrow and glitter like those of a coiling snake. "Yes, go on with your pointless lives. I will escape and then you'll l know the true power of darkness."

As she stares into the swirl, Holly, Amber, and Gunner look over at her, their ears perked like ravenous dogs—waiting for her command, their black hearts pounding with sinister anticipation.

*****

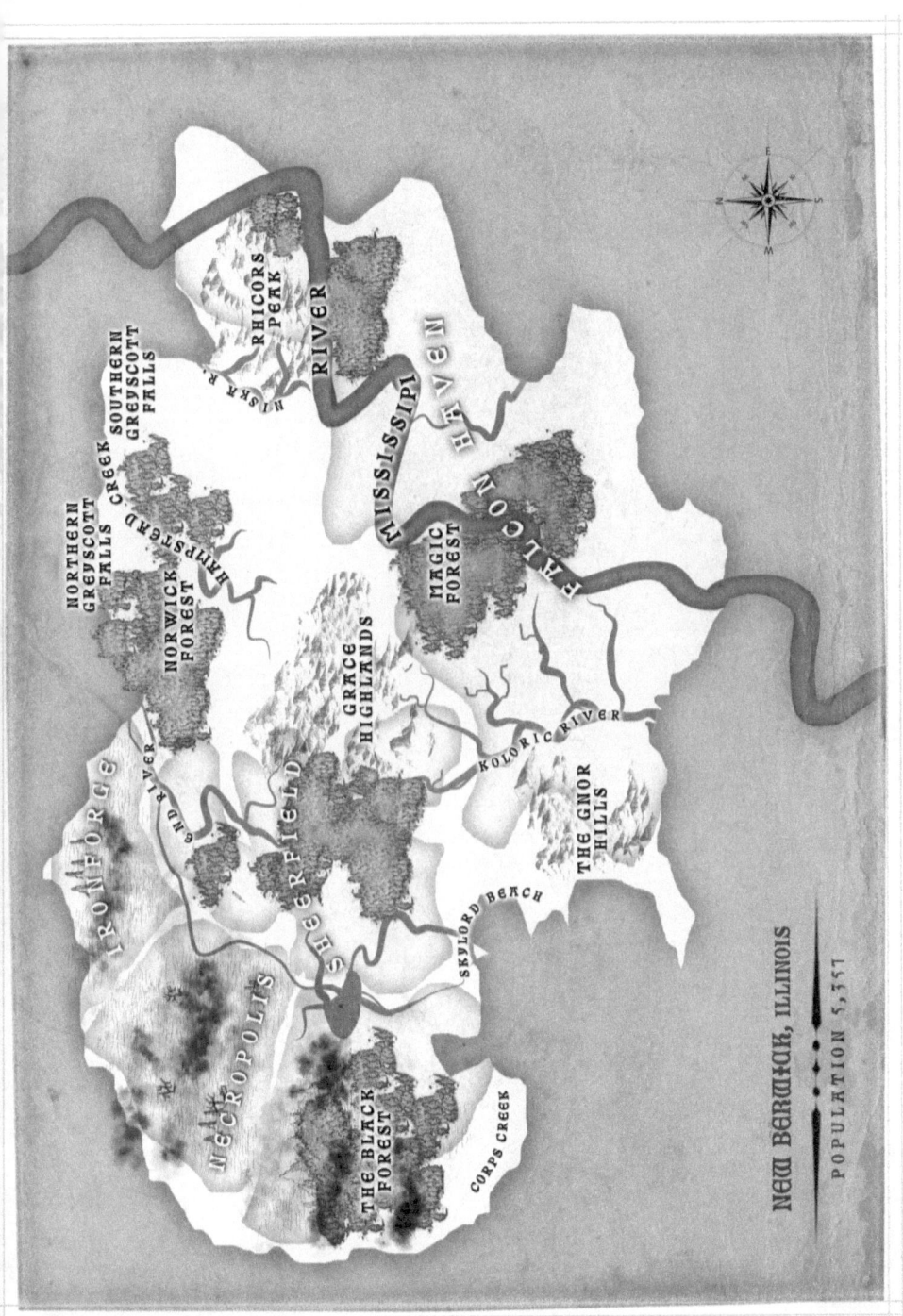

NEW BERWICK, ILLINOIS

POPULATION 5,357

13

Chapter One

Northern Greyscott Falls—population 411

Killing his infant son was the hardest part. Leaving him to rot among the stone statues—making that long journey home with the sweet scent of his little body still upon him, completed that sleepless nightmare. But this was a task expected of all fathers of his kind, something much needed and long overdue. He was doing what his father and his father before him were too cowardly to do. River Porter's deep brown eyes peered down upon the babe. Could he go through with it? Would he be able to run the six inch dagger through the tiny heart until the light went out of its dancing blue eyes? Could he, once again, stomach hearing the faint gasp, witness the flailing arms and legs go still as the blood pooled around the lifeless thing that would have been his son?

Really, it was the wish of his people that these babies were sickly so as to claim a mercy killing. But fate would not have it so. Sick or healthy, they must all die. River would follow this law and be damned for it.

*****

"Is Daddy going to be all right this time, Mom?" Becca Porter asked, trying not to let the cream-colored porcelain bowls slip from her hands.

She was nine—the youngest of four girls and was given menial household chores because she was so clumsy. Her mother attempted to change that by entrusting her with delicate things. Her father loved her and her sisters, but also resented them at times. Jewel looked up from the book just long enough to give Becca a sharp stare. "Just set the table," she said.

"All right." Becca dropped her head and moped back to the dining area.

Jewel Porter had lived in New Berwick all of her life. So very beautiful, she had captivated River the first time he laid eyes upon her. Six months later, they were married. Jewel served as a historian—called a Sencha, for one of the local covens. Putting her spell book aside, she brushed her dark raven hair from her cheek with her delicate white hand. The long wavy locks brushed against the fluffy pink pillow on the cot where she rested. Jewel was very protective of her husband and resented the daunting task that tormented him—that tormented all of the husbands and fathers of her community.

She had given birth just hours ago but had dismissed the midwives. Not wanting to appear weak and sickly when River returned, she thought it important that the household function as usual—as if their infant son's blood was not screaming upon his hands.

Jewel bled heavily and the pain tore into her loins. "I'm not going to cry this time," she said softly. She forced the sea back into her eyes; it burned and blurred her vision. The room spun around, and her breathing deepened.

Chelsea, seventeen and her eldest daughter, stood in the shadows of Jewel's bedroom. She gasped at the sight of her mother who looked pale and weak.

"Mom, are you all right? You don't look so well." She walked briskly across the room to Jewel and felt her forehead.

"I'll be fine, honey," Jewel said, placing her hand on her own abdomen.

Chelsea could see her mother's chest rising and falling rapidly. "Shall I send for the midwives?" Before Jewel could answer, Abby and Dria, Chelsea's younger siblings, rushed to Jewel's side, bumping the cot so hard it moved an inch or so. They had overheard Chelsea's concern for their mother.

Abby frowned. "Mom, what's wrong?"

"Watch it!" Chelsea shouted, "And don't crowd her!" The two stepped back immediately at her command—just as they were taught to do. Dria, the quiet one, stood glassy-eyed with her hands to her mouth. Suddenly, a crash that made them jump came from the kitchen.

"Really, Becca?" Chelsea shouted.

"I'm sorry," Becca's timid voice screeched as she fumbled to pick up the broken dishes.

*****

After River had cleaned up the blood, he wrapped the limp body in a blanket lovingly crafted by Jewel and placed it in a tomb beside the other four infant brothers. He stood looking at the five coffins, his eyes filled, and he sighed heavily. He had daggered the oldest son in 1994, the second in '99, the twins in'03, and now this one. Five nameless and lifeless little bodies lying in a row like cartons of eggs on the bottom shelf of a run-down grocery store. He tucked the red velvet knife case under his arm and pulled the heavy crypt door closed. After locking it, he made his way to his car that was parked just outside the tall, black iron gate.

River steered the silver SUV recklessly toward home. Above him hung a third-quarter moon surrounded by glittering stars that winked down at him. Once he attempted to drive right through the steel railings and end his heartache only to slam on his brakes at the last seconds of that senseless thought. But who else could do the killings? Jewel? No, not my sweet, her heart is too pure—and certainly not the girls.

The winding road seemed endless as he tried desperately to make it home to the warming arms of his wife. As he drove, the smell of honeysuckle, the region's perfume, kissed his face from the opened window. He remembered the many stories his grandfather had told him about New Berwick: the place where his ancestors had married, built homes, fished, hunted, and planted trees and gardens. The land was full of forests, woods, and creeks. Giant mountains loomed over the steep hills and valleys. There were barns, small ranches, and mansions. Some mansions took up many acres and looked like small, elegant castles. Beyond the swell of hills rose apple, pear, and peach trees. The stretch of blue-green grass held plants of every floral color in nature's bounty. Everywhere were white, sparkling waterfalls.

The sky housed a host of indigenous and migrating birds while the forests embraced medium and small, fluffy breeds. Silver threads of river snaked throughout the region and ensured life for every species. As River's eyes scanned the road-side portion of the territory, it was hard for him to believe that this land had once been a lifeless swamp.

*****

When River entered his house, the smell of his favorite dish, lamb stew, permeated the air. Becca saw him first and nearly knocked the pitcher of iced tea off the table.

"Honestly, Becca," Dria blurted.

Becca ran to him, grinning. "Daddy!"

River held out his arms and she fell into them. After hugging Dria, River looked towards the cot where he was certain Jewel lay. He walked into the next room and, to his surprise, found her standing and looking radiant, dressed in dark slacks and a long-sleeved soft blue blouse that matched her blue eyes. River walked to her and gathered her in his arms. He kissed her lips then pulled back a few inches and frowned.

"Honey, should you be up so soon? Remember the last time—"

"I'm fine, sweetheart, really." Then she said in a low voice, not wanting the children to hear, "I drank a potion."

He nodded and looked over his shoulder to be sure she wasn't overheard. "Jewel, you know that's not only forbidden but it's dangerous."

"It was just a little bat blood," she said, toying with him. "The bat hardly noticed. He flew away as happy as a lark." She grinned and pecked his nose.

Before he could scold her, Chelsea burst into the room quickly followed by Abby. "Mom, you're up. Look at you," Chelsea said, her eyes wide.

Abby looked Jewel up and down. "What happened? A moment ago...I don't understand. Mom, you, you look wonderful."

"Dad, she was so pale, and, and we were so scared..." Chelsea stammered.

"Your mother is fine. Okay? Stop worrying." He kissed Chelsea and Abby on their foreheads. "I'm going to go wash up for dinner." He left Jewel's side and walked across the room to the bathroom. The children gathered around Jewel, each kissing and hugging her neck. With the girls holding on to her on either side, Jewel managed to walk to the dining area and over to the dinner table.

River finished drying his hands on a towel and joined them. "Okay, let's eat," he said, rubbing his hands together. He pulled out the chair for Jewel and did the same for the girls, then took his seat next to Jewel at the round table.

Abby wasted no time after sitting down before blurting, "Dad, can I get a tattoo? Mom said I could if you said yes." She fidgeted in her seat while waiting for a response.

"I'll think about it." He inhaled deeply through his nose. "Wow! Everything smells so good." River spooned lumps of lamb, carrots, and potatoes from the large crockpot and placed it in his bowl.

"I cooked, Dad," Chelsea said.

River put a spoonful in his mouth. "Um," he nodded his head with approval at Chelsea.

"Becca set the table," Jewel said with chest-inflating pride. Becca smiled while twirling the spoon in her stew.

Abby's eyes shot up at the ceiling as her mouth formed a smirk before she spoke. "And she only broke four dishes, a bowl, and one of Mom's favorite tea cups." Chelsea frowned and elbowed Abby while Dria giggled.

Jewel glared at Abby. "That wasn't very nice Abby. And I hated that tea cup anyway," Jewel said, looking sympathetically over at Becca. "You did fine, honey."

"Yes, sweetheart," River said, "the table looks really nice. And I hated that old tea cup, too. Good riddance." He smiled at Becca and stuffed his mouth.

River was a thoughtful, kind husband and father. His goal, like most Porter men, was to have a son to carry the family name. He adored his girls, though sometimes he was bothered by their flashing bright eyes and sunshine smiles, their giggles, the long white legs moving under them and their pale, thin arms that would wrap around him whenever they greeted him at the door. These were all the things he'd never know from his sons whose bodies lay in a crypt.

Jewel looked over at her tall, husky husband. She reached up and brushed a dark brown lock of hair away from his forehead. He smiled at her with the oil from the lamb sauce still on his thin lips. He and his brother, Dex, had inherited their father's wealth, but they had also inherited his good looks and had evolved from a hearty stock of tough fighting men.

Their great-great-grandfather, Merchant Porter, his three older brothers, and nearly a hundred other young men were the security force for the covenant witches in 1842. They were highly skilled fighters and were nicknamed Moon Crawlers because they could blend with the shadows and were famous for their almost-invisible presence and feather-like movements against any given enemy. Many said they could ease past a nest of snakes without getting hissed at.

The Moon Crawlers once destroyed an entire zombie unit that Corina had created to attack the covenant witches. They entered the camp before her mystical hounds could scent them out. Corina was enraged—after gazing over the ashes and bones of her defeated demonic army, she sought revenge.

It was nearly sundown, and the evening spewed its familiar scent of jasmine in the air. Merchant Porter, his brothers, and a few other Moon Crawlers were enjoying the night off by celebrating one of their men's marriage to a local beauty. Corina sent a shapeshifter to impersonate one of the young girls responsible for bringing and serving a special dish. Only this dish was prepared exclusively for the Moon Crawlers.

The shapeshifter slaughtered two wolves, chopped up the meat, and mixed in the human portions of a young boy. She emptied a vial of blood taken from the girl as she lay unconscious. After adding a mystical herb, water, and goat's milk, the concoction was placed in a cast-iron oven to bake. The dish was served to the bridegroom first, and after serving it to the other Moon Crawlers, the shapeshifter vanished.

Hours later the girl, who was still unconscious, was discovered lying by the roadside with little memory of what had happened. She swore it wasn't her they saw serving the food. As the hysterical girl began to recover some of her memory, they noticed a deep cut in the palm of her right hand. The girl told them that on her way there she had been chased by something that emerged out of thick, black smoke with crystal-like eyes and long, bony fingers. They believed her, knowing how Corina operated, but had no idea what it meant.

Two weeks later, in the evening, all the Moon Crawlers, to the horror of their families and the witches running for their lives, one by one, and sometimes in groups of threes and fours, began to turn into huge, vicious wolves. The witches managed to escape safely to a sacred cave where a spell protected them, but the humans weren't as fortunate. They were ripped apart and left with throats that had become gaping red holes and staring eyes that still held the terror of their death.

The early morning sun was the first to witness what the full moon had done. It beat down on the men as they lay sprawled, naked, and horrified. They were covered in blood with human flesh still stuffed in their jaws or hanging from their teeth. Many woke in their homes beside the bodies of their wives, children, and parents. The groom, who was still on his honeymoon, found his bride's torn headless body in the next room. The sheriff and several townsmen carried him away screaming, "I didn't do it. I swear to almighty God. You gotta believe me. I'm innocent!"

After being found guilty of butchering his wife, he was placed in solitary confinement and scheduled to be hanged. But during a full moon he escaped. At daybreak, lawmen found pieces of the guards scattered on the floor, on shelves, and on top of a desk and filing cabinets. There were multiple bullet holes, all in the direction of the cell. The iron bars had been splintered like twigs, and there was a large bear-sized hole where the door had been.

The curse only affected the males. Over the years, the werewolf population grew until they had to acquire their own region. They settled in Greyscott Falls.

The covenant witches were powerless to undo the spell because it required the death of a young child. And this was against everything they stood for. However, before every full moon, and with the men heavily chained, the witches would send a thick mist that included fake growling noises to mask the howling of the wolves and to frighten away any humans who might venture too far into the region.

But River and the other fathers felt this was not enough. They decided on a more permanent solution. "The best course," an elder wolf said, "is to end the curse by letting it die with us." That meant all male children had to be eliminated at birth until the last werewolf died. Abortions had no effect—only a silver blade through the heart could kill an infant werewolf.

Many in the pack couldn't agree at first. River fought it as long as he could. It was even harder, almost impossible, to get the women on board. But after years of witnessing the horrors their men and boys faced with every full moon, they too agreed that the curse had to end.

However, not all of the wolf pack agreed with the law. Tempers flared, lives were threatened, and civil war seemed imminent.

Chapter Two

Falcon Haven—population 1, 652

Beatrice Taylor was a direct descendant of the original witches who founded New Berwick. Beatrice served as the Master of Magical Chants, called a Cainte, for her coven. She had been widowed for several years and lived with her only child Barbara Morrison, son-in-law, Pete, and adorable seventeen-year-old granddaughter, Kayla.

In the middle of dinner, Beatrice realized she didn't have much of an appetite, so she excused herself and decided to settle down for the evening. But a phone call from Jewel put having a glass of wine and curling up with a 1662 Norwegian spell book on hold. She urged Beatrice to meet her at an underground library located on the outskirts of Greyscott Falls. It was run by a pale, blue-eyed, elderly man who dressed like a gypsy.

It was dark when Beatrice set out. She barely found the place because it stood far off from the main road behind a cluster of trees. Jewel's Mercedes S-Class stood out among several cars and pick-up trucks that were parked in front of the building.

When she entered the little library, she found it lit by hundreds of candles that hung midair a few feet below the high ceiling. Multicolor, faded books filled a floor-to-ceiling bookcase that ran the length of the wall. Only a few odd people were seated at the round wooden tables. The man dressed as a gypsy stood behind the check-out counter. He had a creepy look in his eyes, but he flashed a yellow smile that Beatrice showed right back.

Jewel spotted Beatrice looking around for her and waved her over to where she was sitting. Jewel sat at one of the wider tables with books spread out all over it and in piles. They were mostly old, worn books with strange bindings. Beatrice smoothed her fingers over one of the books and discovered it had a strange texture.

"What on earth was so urgent?" Beatrice asked. She sat across from Jewel and placed her handbag on one of the piles of books.

23

Jewel's eyes were wide with excitement. "I really think I'm on to something," she said.

"On to what?"

Jewel didn't answer but opened the large ancient spell book. It was bound in human skin and written in Hungarian. She read a spell in the language and interpreted it for Beatrice in English. When she finished, Beatrice's eyes were beaming.

"Does this mean what I think it means?" Beatrice asked.

"I may have found a way out of the infant killings."

"Great Jupiter! You think it'll really work?"

"It has to. I can't bear burying another son. And what it's doing to River, well, it just has to work, Bea. But I can't do it alone, I'm a historian. I can do average spells, but this requires real knowledge, the kind you have." She looked at Beatrice pleadingly.

"Well, of course, silly. Did you think I wouldn't help?"

"Thanks, Bea. But, you can't tell anybody about this book."

"I won't say a word. Coven's honor," she said, spreading three fingers over her heart.

*****

Southern Greyscott Falls—population 309

"What do you want, Uncle River?" Matthew Porter, tall, husky, and dark-haired like his father stood wide-legged with a rifle in his hand.

"You're not going to shoot your old unc are you, Matt?"

"I don't want to, Uncle River. But if you take one more step I'll have to follow my dad's orders."

"I understand, son. But I just want to talk to your father."

"He ain't here."

"Know when he'll be back?"

"Nope."

"All right. Tell him I'll stop by later."

"Wouldn't do that if I were you."

"I'll take my chances. Nice seeing you, and tell your mother I said hi."

The teenager kept his rifle in both hands pointed down at the ground and never took his eyes off River until he pulled out.

Matthew Porter was the son of Dex Porter, River's younger brother. Dex and some of the wolf pack split years ago and move closer to the hills. They had refused to kill their sons, instead preferring to simply ride it out and wait for the curse to be broken, even if it took a thousand years. They hated River and the other fathers who had made it law to kill male infants. The southern pack, where Dex was from, called it murder, while River, along with his northern pack, felt it was more cruel to allow their sons to live under a curse, never able to have a normal life.

A few years after the law had gone into effect, one-third of the pack still opposed it. They were threatened with raids on their homes and the kidnapping and killing of their sons if they didn't do the deed themselves. River had refused to go along with the raids and tried to talk his brother and the other holdouts into accepting the law, but Dex threatened to kill anyone who came near his home. River told Dex he would never harm his nephews and that he'd die before he let anyone else harm them as well.

"You'll die sooner than that," Dex had told him, "if you don't get off my property." Dex had said that as long as River was killing his own sons, he was no brother of his. This not only put a strain on the brother's relationship but also their wives who happened to be first cousins.

*****

River drove around for a while to make it seem like he had left, but instead of turning onto the main road he exited onto a small dirt road and eased into the shadow of a tall oak tree. He was right—Dex was home. His truck was parked near a pile of lumber. "Well, my lying-ass nephew…but you were just doing what you were told," he whispered.

River made his way back around Hampstead Creek and cut through Norwick Forest. He slowly pulled up to the house and parked. He sat for a while before getting out. When he finally emerged from the truck, he kept his eyes peeled for Matthew. As he started up the long walkway, he spotted Dex and Matthew walking quickly out of their front door. Both were holding rifles across their forearms, their faces stern. River flashed a smiled as he approached them but wasn't surprised to see their faces not mirroring his.

"Dex," River said, nodding.

"This is very brave of you, River," Dex said.

"Or stupid," replied Matthew.

River continued walking slowly towards them, then stopped and raised both arms out to the side and held them there. "I'm unarmed," he said, letting his arms flop at his sides. "I just want to talk, brother."

"Don't call me that."

"What do I call you then? We both had the same mother and father." Just then Dex's wife, Jan, came to the door with their youngest son, a seven year old, and a bigger boy, about ten, at her side. River waved at them. Dex followed his brother's eyes over his shoulder and saw them standing there.

"Go back in!" Dex shouted at his wife, then turned his head back to stare at River. "You need to go, River. I mean it. I'm not going to tell you twice." Matthew looked at his father, then back at River, and raised his rifle.

River threw his hands up in front of him. "Wait, Dex. I know you're angry with me, with all of us. But there's something I need to tell you."

"About what, Uncle? About kidnapping and killing me, my two little brothers?"

"Matt, look at me. You know better than that."

"I don't know anything, Uncle River, except you need to go."

"Dex," River said, looking to him to disagree with his son. Dex just stood there with his rifle raised, his eyes cold and defiant. River took several steps back and said, "All right, Dex."

He slowly turned and walked back down the path to his truck, his head down watching his feet. Before getting in, he looked up and caught Dex's eyes. *My brother really hates me.* River got in and pulled off. In his rearview mirror, he watched Dex and Matthew entering the house. River's eyes glazed over.

He wanted to tell Dex the good news about Jewel's new spell and how it could stop the killings. He had thought Dex would be happy, perhaps even forgive him for the past killings and welcome him back as his brother. But River now guessed this was just an empty dream.

He thought about how close he and Dex had been growing up. Once as young boys they had disobeyed their father, turned into werewolf pups, and strayed too far into the woods. A young black bear attacked River and would have killed him had it not been for Dex's quick action. As tiny as he was, he jumped on the bear's head and dug his little claws and fangs into one of its eyes. The bear roared in pain, shook Dex off its head, and fled.

River hated that he couldn't tell his parents of Dex's bravery that day without revealing their disobedience. But it was an event that bonded them for life—that is, until the Killing Law arrived.

Chapter Three

Sheerfield—population 2, 753

Fifteen-year-old Tiara Winters was missing. Her parents had last seen her three days ago when they locked her in her bedroom as punishment for her involvement with a local boy.

The next morning the maid found the room empty and the French window pushed opened.

"This isn't the first time we've had to deal with a rebellious teenager," Sheriff Wayne Tilbert had stated earlier to a Sheerfield Bugle reporter. "Whatever it takes, we'll find her," he concluded. Rose Tilbert, Wayne's wife, sat across from him at breakfast, absorbed in the morning news.

"Isn't it just awful about that Winters girl?" Rose said, shaking her head.

"We're not giving up just yet," Wayne answered.

Their seventeen-year-old daughter, Veronica, playfully punched the arm of her fourteen-year-old brother, Christopher. They sat at the table giving each other teasing stares; then, like little angels, they closed their eyes and bowed their heads while Wayne said grace.

"Mighty and merciful Father, we thank you for this food we are about to consume for the nourishment of our bodies. We thank you for this land, the plants, and the animals upon it. Bless the farmers, the merchants, and the hands that prepared this meal. In Jesus' name."

"In Jesus' name," Rose and the kids repeated in unison.

Wayne and many Sheerfield residents were descendants of the Dominions, the last human group of immigrants to settle in New Berwick, a little over two hundred years after the witches. This group came to escape religious persecution and settled in the middle of the region, founding Sheerfield. The group got the name Dominion from their late founder, James P. Tilbert, who had said God told him to dominate the earth with the word of God, and that there was only one God and one book for the world, but that all other religions should be tolerated because people deserved the right to make their own choices.

Nevertheless, newcomers, or troublemakers as they were sometimes called, were discouraged from practicing paganism. They were also warned by the authorities to stay in Sheerfield and away from the neighboring areas where use of strange rituals was suspected.

Halfway through breakfast, Wayne's phone vibrated on his waistband.

"Yeah, Ken," he said, getting up from the table and walking a few paces away to talk in private.

"Bad news," Deputy Ken Carter exclaimed.

"The Winters' kid?"

"I'm afraid so, sir. Looks like some kind of wild animal just ripped that poor kid to shreds."

"Wild animal? There hasn't been anything bigger than a jackrabbit around here for decades."

"I know, but bears and wolves have been known to travel for miles looking for food."

"Where was she found?"

"South of Greyscott Falls, in Norwick Forest."

"What the devil was she doing out there?"

"You got me," Ken said.

"Dear God!"

"Kids…who knows why they do anything these days," Ken snapped.

"Ok, bring her into the coroner and let's find out what did this. And keep this quiet until we're sure it's her. If it is, I don't want the girl's parents hearing this from anyone else but me. Make that clear to everyone."

"Will do, sir! But it's her all right. We know by the description of the clothing Mrs. Winters gave us."

"All the same, let's make it official," Wayne said. He snatched the phone from his ear and then quickly spoke back into it. "….and thanks, Ken." Wayne clicked off and rearranged his face before turning around. He stopped by the table and took one last sip of coffee.

"Is everything all right, Dad?" Veronica asked.

"Yes, sweetheart." He kissed Veronica and Christopher on the top of their heads and went around to Rose who searched his eyes, then frowned. "Have a good day, dear," she said, lifting her cheek to his lips.

"I will," he responded. He gently touched her chin with his finger—a gesture that meant he appreciated her not asking about the phone call. Official business, you know.

*****

While walking to his car, Wayne tried to force Ken's description of the young girl's body from his mind. As he drove, he made a face like he was going to be sick. There hadn't been any kind of killings by people or animals in Sheerfield that he could remember. He had attended funerals of people who had lived good lives and simply died of natural causes, sickness, or accidental deaths, but not killings. He made a few official stops along Kingston Road before reporting to duty. The long, quiet ride gave him pause to reflect on how best to handle breaking the news to Mr. and Mrs. Winters. He had fantasized about being the hero after finding the girl—perhaps finding her somewhere pouting after a quarrel with a boyfriend— and returning her home to grateful parents.

After twenty minutes of driving, the quiet ride suddenly changed as Wayne turned the corner and was within blocks of the sheriff station. He saw absolute chaos in front of the building. Wayne pulled up to the station, turned off the car, and slumped down in his seat. A large group of people flocked to his car and surrounded it.

"What the hell?" he said to himself.

Wayne pushed the door open and forced his way through the crowd. His every push was accompanied by town-folk yelling—microphones pushed in his face from every angle, and questions flying from more than two dozen reporters' lips.

"I have no statement!   Please!" Wayne yelled as he forced through the crowd and got within a few feet of the sheriff station's steps. One of his deputies cracked the door as he got in range, and hands reached through the slim opening to grab several parts of his clothing and pull him inside. The deputy quickly slammed the door in the crowd's face. Wayne leaned against the wall and panted heavily. He turned around, spotted Ken, and quick-stepped toward him. "Did you—?"

"No!" Ken interrupted, "And don't ask me how they found out." Ken paused, looked down, then slowly back up at Wayne. "I know you said you wanted to be the one to tell them. But they called and I had no choice."

"Who called?" Wayne asked, resting his butt on the edge of his desk.

"The Winters," Ken answered, his expression asking, who do you think?

Wayne sighed. "How did they take it?"

Ken lowered his head.

"God help them," Wayne said. He flopped down in his chair and tossed his car keys on the desk. Wayne watched the faces of his office staff as they continued their duties in sad silence.

*****

It had been twenty-four hours since Tiara Winters's body was discovered. Close to midnight, Dex Porter heard several hard bangs on his back door. He stumbled barefooted down the back stairs to the kitchen, clicked on the light, and opened the door. Three of his neighbors stood like clay statues.

"What's going on?" Dex asked, his voice gravelly.

Bret, Pete, and Jim rushed by him and stood near the kitchen counter.   Bret's hairline was beaded with sweat, and Pete and Jim had deep frown lines across their foreheads.

"Sorry to wake you at this hour, Dex. But this can't wait," Bret said.

Pete and Jim nodded in agreement.

Dex pushed the door closed. "Ok, let's have it."

"It's about that Winters kid," Bret said.

Dex shrugged. "What about her?"

"It was no animal attack."

Dex bit his bottom lip and searched Bret's face.

"It was Debra Carter's boy, Raymond." Bret waited for a reaction from Dex.

"Keep talking," Dex said, looking at him from under his eyelashes.

"Debra is an alcoholic, everybody knows that. She ain't been right since her old man drove a silver dagger through his own heart some while back. She can't be trusted to see to it that that boy of hers is chained down during a full moon."

"This ain't the first time he ran free after his transformation," Pete weighed in.

Dex's voice rose. "What the hell do you mean this is not the first time? He's killed before?"

"No!" Bret said quickly. "Before it was just farm animals. People thought it was bears or mountain lions that crossed into our region. Of course we knew better, but like I said, it was only animals. So—"

"Great Jupiter!" Dex said, running one hand over his face and pulling his chin. "How many others know this, and why wasn't I told Debra wasn't chaining the boy?"

"Because it was only animals at first."

"Dammit! You had to have known something like this could happen," Dex said, looking from one face to the other.

Matthew was standing at the top of the stairs in his t-shirt and briefs listening. He could have easily gone downstairs and filled in the blanks. Debra Carter was, indeed, drunk the night of the full moon. But Tiara's murder was not entirely her fault. Raymond and Tiara had fallen in love—or so they thought. Raymond had revealed to her that he was a werewolf. But to his and Matthew's surprise, she said she didn't care; in fact, she thought it was pretty cool. Tiara swore to keep the secret, but Matthew seriously doubted that she took Raymond serious. She giggled a lot and made jokes. Raymond thought it was cute that, when on a date, she had pulled a fake silver bullet from her purse.

Matthew told Raymond he was fooling himself if he thought he was no danger to her. Raymond said he would never harm Tiara.

"But it won't be you harming her," Matthew had told him, "but the thing you will become, the thing we all become."

This strange fascination Tiara had for the dark side of her lover must have compelled her to meet Raymond in the forest that night. Perhaps he frightened her and she ran, but not far enough and certainly not fast enough. Matthew had tried so hard to talk Raymond out of meeting her that night, to the point of barely making it back in time to be chained himself.

Matthew shook his head while listening to them trying to figure things out. He went back to his bedroom and closed the door.

*****

The men grew nervous by the minute. Bret shook his head. "Something has got to be done about that boy, Dex."

"Yeah, and what happens if the Northern pack finds out?" Pete grumbled.

"You boys go on back home. I'll think of something," Dex told them, looking puzzled.

"Well, I hope you do. The Northern pack's been waiting for something like this to happen," Jim warned.

"Don't worry. You boys go on, now. I said I'll take care of this."

The men mumbled their thanks to Dex for agreeing to handle the problem as they filed out of the kitchen and onto the grass in the backyard.

Dex stuck his head out the door. "And remember: don't say anything to anybody about this."

Pete never turned around, but threw up a hand in acknowledgement of Dex's warning.

After the dark SUV pulled off, Dex eased the door closed and flipped off the light. He stood staring into the black with his back to the kitchen door and forced his head back hard against it. "Raymond, you stupid bastard," he said through his teeth.

Chapter Four

Jewel stood wide-eyed after opening the front door. "Dex?" she blurted.

Dex had not set foot inside of Northern Greyscott Falls, let alone his brother's house, in nearly a decade. "Plea...please come in," she stammered. Jewel awkwardly stepped aside, and Dex walked into the family room. The shock on her face turned into a frown when she thought better of his sudden visit. "Is everything all right with Jan and the children?" she asked, putting a hand to her chest.

"Jan and the kids are fine. I just need to speak to River. I saw his truck, so, I assumed..."

"Oh, yes, he's here. I'll get him." Jewel hurried off, taking the back stairs up to their bedroom.

Dex stood with his hands in his pockets and shifted from one foot to the other. He looked around, surprised at how little the place had changed since his last visit. A few pieces of new furniture here and there, but time hadn't erased the warmth he always felt when he entered his brother's home. On one wall hung a group of pictures, and Dex half-smiled when he noticed the colorful portrait of the two-brother family on its far end. They were so happy then. But years of feuding seemed to overshadow any love he felt for his older brother.

River rushed into the room looking like he'd seen a ghost. "Dex?"

Dex turned.

River's face lit up as he walked towards his brother, but there was no warm greeting from Dex. Instead, he said rather coldly, "Is there some place we can talk more privately?"

River's smile faded and he gestured toward the den. He followed Dex into the room and closed the door.

"Sit. Ah, please."

Dex took a seat on the sofa, and River sat in the big armchair across from him.

"Would you like a drink?"

Dex shook his head and then spoke. "I'm going to make this quick. I prefer you hear this from me." River focused attentively. "That Winters girl wasn't killed by any animal," Dex began. "She was killed by Raymond Carter...that's Debra Carter's boy."

"I know who Raymond is, but why would he do such a thing? Did the girl do something?"

"Well, according to Matt, the girl and Raymond were lovers. He was stupid enough to trust the girl with our secret, and she was stupid enough to believe he wouldn't hurt her after his transformation. Matt feels just awful about—"

"Whoa! What do you mean after his transformation? Raymond killed her after turning?" River shot up from the chair and stared at Dex. "You mean he was running loose?"

"River, hold on."

"Holy shit!" He paced back and forth in front of Dex. "River, don't freak out on me. I need you to sit down and hear me out."

River stopped pacing and exhaled hard; he took a few steps towards the chair and flopped down.

"Like I said, Matt feels bad about this."

"Why should he feel bad? Did he help kill the girl?"

"No! Matt didn't kill anybody," Dex said impatiently. "He's upset because he didn't warn us that an outsider knew our secret and that Raymond was unchained that night."

"Great Scott!" River said, looking down at the floor. "I know this sounds cold, but I hope he killed her before she told anyone."

"I don't know."

"What else did Matt say?"

"Nothing, except that Raymond feels terrible."

"As well he should. He's going to feel a whole lot worse with a silver dagger sticking in his goddamn heart."

"Now let's not go there," Dex said. "He's just a boy."

River chuckled nervously. "You think the Northern pack is going to care he's just a boy? What did the little son of a bitch have to say for himself? Have you talked to him?"

"Matt's got him hidden some place. He won't say where."

"Now look: Matt's my nephew and I love him, but he's heading for real trouble if he's helping that boy."

"I know, but they've been friends since they were tots. He was the only one Raymond called after he transformed back and realized what he'd done."

"Stupid little prick!"

Dex continued as if he hadn't heard his remark. "Matt said he was talking out of his head and begged Matt to meet him at this little shack located off the edge of the forest. He said he found Raymond naked and bloody, cradling the girl's dead parts and crying his eyes out. He had to fight the boy to take her severed head away from him. Matt buried the body parts deep in the forest and covered the spot with leaves then he got Raymond the hell out of there."

"Who else knows about this?"

"Pete, Bret, Jim, now you. But they don't know where he is either."

River peered across at Dex. "After all the years of avoiding me, why did you come to me?"

"Because this mess won't stay hidden forever, and the Northern pack listens to you."

"And you're hoping when it gets out, and things get ugly, I'll be able to stop whatever..."

"Exactly."

River scooted around in the chair and wet his lips.

"Dex, I got to tell you...the best thing all around is for this not to get out. This is exactly what the Northern pack was afraid of., the very thing they said might happen—that a younger generation couldn't handle this curse...that one night one of your immature sons or nephews would kill a human and it would bring the Dominions and outside hunters down on us."

Dex stood up, and River followed suit. "If you think this incident is going to make me sorry I didn't murder my sons, you're sadly mistaken," Dex said loudly.

"I don't give a rat's ass if you're sorry or not. You made your choice, and I made mine." River shook his head. "This could mean war between the packs—with the Dominions waiting around to wipe out the victors."

"The question is, brother, which side would you be on?" Dex spat the word "brother" like he had a bad taste in his mouth.

"I'd protect my family same as you," River said in defiance.

Dex's jaw tightened, he brushed past River, opened the door, and walked out. River followed him all the way to the front door.

"Dex, wait!"

Dex froze but kept his back to River.

"I'll do what I can," River said, sounding more sympathetic, "but I can't promise anything. Just know whatever happens, I'll do everything in my power to keep Jan and the kids safe."

"I don't need you to keep my family safe." Dex grabbed the doorknob.

Jewel, oblivious to the new tension between the brothers, shouted a cheerful goodbye from the top of the stairs, but Dex gave a quick wave as he bolted from the house. River watched him drive off. He wanted to kick himself for not taking advantage of his brother's visit; it had been a perfect moment for him and Dex to reconcile had River said all the right things. Now River felt he had just made things worse.

*****

Saint Paul's Christian Academy: High School Study Hall

Veronica Tilbert's phone buzzed among the books that were spread out over the long square table. She tossed her reddish brown hair to one side and put the phone to her ear.

"Kayla Morrison, where are you?" she demanded. Christa, Veronica and Kayla's best friend since third grade, stopped writing and looked up at Veronica.

"I'm not coming," Kayla said, throwing her backpack and purse on the passenger front seat of her red Chevy Malibu.

"What do you mean you're not coming?"

Christa spoke up after hearing Veronica's side of the conversation. "What does she mean she's not coming? This is a group project, we need her."

"I'll be home in time to turn my part in." Kayla backed out of the driveway.

"But we were supposed to do it together." Veronica was shushed by Mrs. Kendell, the study hall monitor. "You need to be here," Veronica said, lowering her voice.

"I'll call you and compare notes when I get back," she said, pulling onto Kingston Drive.

"What could be more important than acing this project?" Veronica asked.

"We'll make an A, don't worry. I've done most of it, and I'll finish the rest when I get back."

"Back from where, Kayla?"

"Stop being nosy. I'm not ready to share that right now." Kayla took a left on Pledgemere Road, which connected to Key Highway.

Veronica walked out from among the tables and entered the hallway. Christa followed her as Veronica pushed opened the door of the girls' bathroom and settled in a corner so she could talk more freely. "Okay, who is he? Is he cute? Have you done it yet? And was it good?"

"Holy crap!" Kayla said, chuckling.

"Don't answer, Kayla—she has you on speakerphone in the girls' bathroom."

"What the hell, Ronnie?"

"Chill! I was going to turn it off as soon as you got to the juicy parts."

"Like hell you were," Christa said loudly, leaning in to hear better.

"Just do me a favor, both of you. If my mom calls..."

"...You were with us at study hall. Yeah, we know!" Veronica said.

"Thanks, bffs," Kayla said playfully and clicked off.

A twenty-minute drive brought Kayla to the big road sign of Greyscott Falls, and her face melted into a smile. She had come here before by accident when she'd gotten lost. He frightened her at first—coming out of the woods the way he had. But the delight in his eyes when he saw her in tight jeans and a sweatshirt, her honey-blonde hair flowing over her breasts, made her know she could trust him. She couldn't get the dashing young man out of her mind. He was tall, dark, and oh so hot. She hadn't spoken about him to anyone; Kayla wanted the sweet memory all to herself.

Turning south, she pulled onto Moonhawk Road and got out of the car. She walked a few feet away from the car and just stood there, looking off. This was the place where the crackling leaves under his feet had startled her, where his tall, handsome frame had glided toward her so smoothly and controlled, where his dark hair blew in the soft breeze, where he gazed at her with those sparkling blue eyes, and where his luscious tan lips parted to give her directions back to the main road.

Kayla kept coming back to this spot where she had first met him. She didn't know his name, where he lived, or what he was doing that day alone in the woods. But she kept returning in hopes that he'd drift by again.

She had written in her diary: *I come back many times, but can never find my dark handsome stranger. How I dream of him touching my breast, his hands up my thighs, feeling his hot breath on my cheek and his gorgeous mouth on my lips...*

Her continued reminiscing of that night became nearly six pages. And after writing in it, she stashed the book in its usual place—well out of sight of their nosy housekeeper.

Though she appeared deep in thought, her eyes widened as if she sensed a presence behind her. She closed her eyes, hoping to see his tall, husky body. She swallowed hard and hesitated to turn around, but eventually did so slowly. She stopped dead, and a gasp stuck in her throat. She gazed at something worse than any nightmare she'd ever had, more horrible than any movie she'd ever seen or any scary story she'd ever read. She stood paralyzed and gazed into its milky white eyes.

Breathing rapidly, beads of sweat lined her forehead, and her head bobbed nervously. It was huge with a head twice the size of an average wolf. It was nearly as tall as a bear, and its paws were huge with claws as sharp as knives. She looked over at her car. Her eyes seemed to wonder if she could make it. Her feet felt like lead sinkers, and her mouth was like a dried fig. The silver and black wolf glared at her with eyes as lifeless as road-kill. Its partly open mouth shone white fangs like icicles that were as thick as her thumbs.

"Don't move," a soft male voice whispered behind her.

The wolf stood there looking to its right, then back at her, looking over its shoulder, then back at her again as if it were trying to decide whether to eat her or something more filling over in the brush. A smaller wolf could eat half its own weight in a day. Kayla was five-foot-six and weighed 116 pounds—a satisfying meal only if it ate her clothes as well.

Her legs grew weak and she weaved slightly. Finally, as if something had called to it from beyond the trees—or perhaps it scented a more prized prey—the menacing giant swiftly pranced away and disappeared into the thick darkness of the forest. Kayla was so shaken that she didn't bother to find out who had called to her from behind, or why. She dashed to her car and quickly locked herself in. As she fumbled for her keys, she jumped when a knock came on the passenger window. A man, who looked to be in his late forties, was tapping.

"Are you all right?" he asked.

She nodded and started the car. He kept trying to get her to lower the window, but she continued backing up until she got to the road. She then turned and took off at top speed. Her hands were shaking so badly she couldn't steer. Finally, she pulled over to the side of the road and rested her head on the steering wheel. A truck sped up beside her. She gasped when she saw the same man getting out of the truck. Then another man, on the driver's side, got out and followed him toward her.

Both men stared at her through the driver's window. She heard the older man's muffled voice through the glass.

"Are you all right, Miss?"

"Yes," she said after cracking the window just enough for him to hear her clearly.

"My name is Dex Porter," he said, "and this is my son, Matt. Didn't mean to frighten you. We were just concerned."

Kayla finally calmed down and suddenly seemed eager to show her gratitude. She opened the door, her legs still weak, and nearly tumbled out of the car. Kayla thanked Dex but kept her eyes glued to Matthew.

"So, your name is Matt?" she asked. Matthew nodded. "You...you probably don't remember me..."

"I remember," Matthew said. "You were lost."

"Yes, ah...stupid me," she said awkwardly.

There he was, standing before her, her dark prince. He was even hotter in the bright sunlight. He wasn't wearing a jacket this time, and his shirt was tightly pressed against the bulk of his muscular body begging to break free. Was it *his* sweet voice she'd heard back there telling her not to move?

"You look a little peaked," Dex said. "Would you like to come back to our house? It's just a little ways back. My wife could maybe fix you a drink of something."

It was music to her ears. She moved to stand beside Matthew and gazed into his blue eyes.

"Yes...I think I could use a drink or something." At that moment, she faked being lightheaded and swooned, but the wrong man caught her.

"You better let me drive," Dex said, handling her like a delicate flower. He helped Kayla to the passenger side of her car and fastened her seat belt. He pointed the car south to his home off of Cooncan Road with Mathew following behind in the truck.

Chapter Five

Hours passed, River stood by the window, still wanting to kick himself for not making better use of his meeting with Dex.

"Honey, what happened?" Jewel asked, walking over to him. "Why did Dex run out like that?"

River reached out and held Jewel gently by her shoulders. "Baby, Dex is the least of our problems right now. Something we've always dreaded—a showdown with the Southern pack."

"No. That can't happen. You and Dex won't be the only brother against brother. It would destroy whole families."

"I know," he said, sweeping a lock of her hair away from her cheek.

"What did he say when you told him about the spell?"

"I never got that far."

"You didn't tell him? But, that could have solved everything. The packs wouldn't dare strike each other once they know about the spell."

He dropped his hands to his side. "You sound as if you already know what this is about."

"I've known for days. Jan was awakened by Bret banging on their door that night. She overheard the whole thing then she phoned me."

River stepped back and frowned at her. "You knew about Raymond killing that girl and never said a word to me?"

"I wanted to, but Jan felt this incident would force Dex to turn to you. She thought this dilemma would bring the two of you together, and I went along with it."

"Jewel, we've never kept secrets from each other. How could you go along with this?"

"Honey, I know. It was killing me not to tell you. But the thought of you and your brother putting an end to this feuding...working together... and...I'm really sorry."

"Well, you and Jan's little plan didn't work, did it?" He stalked off.

"River, River!" Jewel's shoulders dropped as she watched River walk slowly up the stairs. Becca stuck her little head out from behind the bookcase. Jewel gasped. "Becca, what on earth are you doing there? Why aren't you upstairs doing your homework?"

"Are you and Daddy fighting?"

"No, sweetie. Come here."

Becca walked swiftly over to Jewel and held her around the waist. Jewel bent and kissed her forehead. "Daddy's just upset about something. It's nothing. Everything is fine." Becca appeared satisfied; she squeezed Jewel's waist then scurried up the stairs to her room.

*****

After Jewel allowed River a couple of hours to calm down, she took the back stairs up to their bedroom. She found him resting on the king-size bed, looking up at the ceiling, his hands folded behind his head. She spoke to him. "I know you're angry. And you're right. I shouldn't have kept that from you—no matter how good my intentions were." River just stared upward. She continued. "I don't know what else to say except I'm sorry." He didn't answer.

"Talk to me, damn it."

River sat up, swung his feet off the bed, and scooted to the edge. "You're right. You shouldn't have kept it from me. But I overreacted. I was upset with myself for not using that time to reconnect with Dex. Instead, what did I do? Piss him off more. I had no right to take it out on you."

"Oh, sweetheart." She walked over to him.

He looked away from her. "I'm the one who's sorry—a sorry excuse for a brother."

"Now, stop it." She slid beside him and put her hand on his shoulder. "Dex is just as much at fault as you are. I've watched you, over the years, time after time reach out to your brother and all he ever did was threaten you, pushing you further away." She pulled his face to hers and kissed him on the mouth. "It's time the women took over," she said.

46

"What do you mean?"

"I told Jan that I knew a way to keep peace between the packs even if the truth got out about Raymond."

"You told her about the spell?"

"No. I didn't want to tell her over the phone. But I did guarantee that if she got Dex and Matt over here tonight, there'd be no war."

"Honey, are you sure about that? You feel that strongly about the spell?"

"I do."

At six o'clock that evening Jewel sat nervously wondering if Dex would swallow his pride and show up. But she didn't have to wait long; Jewel's face lit up when she saw the silver SUV drive up. She greeted them at the door then led them into the den. After everyone was seated, Jewel gestured to the finger food she had prepared. "Help yourself," she urged.

"Thank you," Jan said politely. She fixed two small plates and handed one to Dex while Matthew fixed his own.

River poured bourbon. He brought the tray of drinks over to the group and stood while they emptied the tray—all but one. Jewel sat with her drink. After everyone had taken a few sips and appeared relaxed, she cleared her throat and spoke. "I've discovered a spell that can stop the infant killings."

Ice stopped clinking in the glasses. The sudden silence made the quiet ticking of the clock seem loud. Dex, Jan, and Matthew sat motionless like they didn't quite believe what they had heard. River glanced over at Jewel and she glanced back at him.

"Did you hear what she just said?" River asked them.

"I heard," Jan said, "but I don't quite know what to think. After years of living with this curse, can this be true?"

Jewel gestured to River. "Hand me the book."

He walked over to a mahogany table and lifted the heavy, thick book that he had to carry with both hands, then placed it on her lap.

Jewel rested her hands on the book and spoke directly to Dex. "I can get rid of the moon curse, but I can't repair the damage between our two families—that's for you and River to figure out."

No one moved or spoke.

Jewel sat back with a stern look on her face and folded her arms. "I can wait."

"Dex," Jan said, her eyes pleading with him.

Dex hesitated but stood. River got up and took a few small steps over to him. They shook hands, but River was overcome with emotion and pulled Dex to him and hugged him tight. Dex, red-faced and awkward, slowly raised his arms and gave River a quick squeeze, then pulled away and flopped down on the sofa. Jan patted his arm and Matthew beamed a smile as wide as his face.

Satisfied, Jewel leaned forward and opened the book to a page she had tagged. "This book is not just any grimoire—it's called The Grand Grimoire, an ancient book of spells as old as the Bible. There are only a few of them in the world, and they contain the most powerful spells this realm has ever known. In the wrong hands, they can have catastrophic consequences."

Matthew nodded to the book. "That book really holds the spell that can break the curse?"

"Yes," she said, patting the human-skin cover.

Dex looked bewildered. "How long have you had it, and why haven't we known about that book until now?"

"Not long, and I was lucky to find it," she said. "But, I have to tell you, it doesn't really break the entire spell."

"If it doesn't undo all of it, Aunt Jewel, then what good is the spell?"

"You'll still be wolves and will continue to turn at will—I haven't found anything that can undo the spell itself. But I can stop the forced turning during a full moon. I can stop the unconscious killing spree you all have to endure."

"I can live with that," Dex said excited. "That means we'll have total control and no more damn chains."

"How does it work, Aunt Jewel?"

"Let me say this first," River interjected, "Jewel is taking an awful risk by doing this. She could be exiled from the Mystic Circle, or worse, she could have her magic taken permanently."

"It's this book," Jewel said, touching it like it was something to be frightened of. "It contains spells that require the summoning of the dead in addition to human sacrifices. These kinds of spells are forbidden to covenant witches like us. Just having this book in my possession could get me charged with necromancy. The penalty is, like River said, being stripped of my magic; but in ancient times, it was death."

"To our knowledge," River said, "modern witches don't believe in the death penalty."

Then Dex spoke up. "If this spell keeps us from having to chain ourselves down like animals—we'll keep your secret."

"Thank you Dex," Jewel said. Then she leaned back. "Now, Beatrice and I have discovered exactly what was used in the two-hundred-year-old spell. It was something in the meat pie served at the wedding to your male ancestors. The pie consisted of wolf meat, the flesh of a young village boy, a mystical herb, whose name I can't pronounce, and, I think, the blood of the witch who cast the spell."

"Oh dear goddess! You'd have to kill a child?" Jan blurted, looking around for a similar reaction. But she found everyone staring at Jewel as if hypnotized by what she'd said.

Seeing the look on their faces, Jewel said quickly, "I'm not going to chop up a child, if that's what you're thinking. I'm not a monster."

"We don't think you're a monster," Dex said. He looked at Jan and Matthew to give Jewel reassurance. Jan and Matthew nodded quickly in agreement.

"I'm not in favor of hurting some kid, but I've got to tell you, the idea of not turning every full moon..." Matthew broke off, nodding his head as if he desired that more than anything.

Jewel smoothed her hand over pages of the book. "But, that's just it. We don't have to kill the child to make this work—not really.

If the child dies with the saliva from a werewolf bite in his system, I can resurrect him."

"But he'll be a werewolf!" Jan snapped.

Jewel snapped right back. "Well, I never said the spell was perfect, did I?"

Matthew smacked his knee and stood. "I don't give a damn—I say we do it!"

"Not so fast, Matt. One of us is going to have to keep an eye on this kid as he grows up, especially in his teen years. He won't know he's a werewolf. Everyone around him would be in great danger." Matthew flopped down on the sofa.

Jewel quickly looked at all of their faces, but no one spoke up.

"All right, I'll be responsible," Matthew said finally.

Dex reached across Jan's lap and touched Matthew's knee. "Really, Matt, you'll do that?"

"Sure, why not? I mean—the kid won't know it, but he'll be giving up his mortal life to save ours. It's the least I can do."

"That's a big responsibility, son," Dex said. "Are you sure?"

"Look, if this spell works, I'll be the kid's second daddy, okay?"

Jewel pushed the heavy book aside onto the sofa. "Oh, it'll work. All we need now is the kid. But who?"

Minutes ticked by with the group presenting only vague ideas. They called out various kids' names, but no one could agree. Finally, Matthew said, "If I'm going to be responsible for this kid, then I get to choose him." He pondered, then said, "He's got to be someone strong, but not a bully...he's got to be smart, no juvenile delinquent, someone...someone from a close and loving family. He has to be outgoing, pleasant, and gets along with others." After a couple of tugs on his ear, Matthew snapped his fingers. "I've got it, the Sooner kid."

"The Sooner kid?" River asked.

"That's right...the little Sooner boy...Russell Sooner," Jewel said grinning. "I think they call him Rusty. Yeah, I think he's perfect."

"Anybody object or have a better person in mind?" River asked looking over at Dex, Matthew, and Jan.

"Is he really all those things?" Jan asked.

"He's in Dria's class," Jewel remembered. "All the kids like him. I think Dria even had a little crush on him at one time."

"Then I guess it's settled," Jan said. "Little Russell Sooner it is."

Dex stood up. "I believe this calls for a celebration."

They all mumbled in agreement. River poured more drinks and brought the tray of half-filled glasses over to them. Everyone grabbed a glass and held it up in the air—Dex worded a toast and the sound of clinking glasses filled the room; but before the bourbon touched anyone's lips, Jan said, "Wait! Who's going to kidnap this kid and bite him?"

Everyone lowered their glasses and gazed at Matthew.

Chapter Six

Forty-nine-year-old Bob Wilson pressed his foot down on the brake, bringing the black Jeep Renegade to a complete stop as the light flicked to red. Serving as Sheerfield County's coroner for a little over twelve years, he had seen his share of mysterious deaths.
He and Sheriff Tilbert had a close friendship that dated back to the early 1990s. Bob's ex-wife, Jenny, was still an alimony pain in the butt, and his adult daughters hardly called anymore. He and Jenny still cared for each other, but, as some would say, they had just grown apart.

The light blinked green and Bob eased the car into the twenty-five m.p.h. speed limit required for Baker Hill's quiet residential area. He ran his tongue nervously over his bottom lip and rehearsed the disturbing report he was about to give Sheriff Tilbert; something he should have told him months ago, but needed more medical proof before he could. After years of fact-finding, only Bob and the victims knew the darkness of the truth. Yet, he was reluctant to say anything without tangible evidence.

Bob pulled up to the sheriff's station and found that the only parking spaces left were reserved for personnel. He parked two blocks up and made short work of the distance with his long strides, thanks to his six-foot-three frame. Seeing unsuspecting Sheerfield County folks driving about and walking to and fro made him even more anxious about his report. Eighty-two-year-old Mrs. Paddington could still walk her dog at her age.

"Good morning, Bob," she said in her scratchy voice, "lovely day isn't it?" She stopped and cracked a yellowish smile while letting her little mutt crap on the sidewalk.

"Good morning, Mrs. Paddington, yes it is."

She bent over wide-legged and scooped the poop up in a small plastic bag. "Bye now."

"Goodbye, Mrs. Paddington."

Brushing by an officer coming through the door, he stepped into the bustling atmosphere and gazed about looking for Wayne. A loud scuffle erupted not far from him. A staggering drunk had taken a swing at a female deputy, and she, along with two male officers, was all over the guy.

"Hey, Bob, I'll be right with you," Wayne's voice rose from across the room. He pointed his finger, and Bob nodded that he understood. Bob walked into Wayne's office, took a seat on the guest side of Wayne's desk, and waited for him to finish up a short meeting with several of his deputies.

After about ten minutes, Wayne walked in and greeted Bob with a handshake. "Sorry about that, Bob," Wayne said, walking around and taking a seat behind his desk. "I know I said I'd be free around this time, but ever since the death of the Winters girl, these phones have been ringing like mad. People are starting to get paranoid."

Bob wormed around in his seat, wanting Wayne to shut up so he could tell him of his own findings, but Wayne rambled on...

"Nobody wants to believe it was an animal," Wayne said, "People got their own theories, you know. They call up here swearing they saw wolves walking on hind legs, red eyeballs staring through their windows, witches flying around." Wayne chuckled. Bob faked a grin and Wayne kept talking...

"I'm telling you, they've got my deputies hopping like little bunny rabbits. I've never seen the town like this before. Oh, but listen to me going on and on. So, what exactly brings you here today, Bob?"

"Werewolves."

Wayne jumped slightly in his seat. "What did you say?"

"You heard me. Werewolves."

"Are you kidding me? Have you gone mad, too?"

"I'm sorry, Wayne. But the people here in Sheerfield *should* be jumpy. Oh, I'm not saying they're really seeing those ridiculous things. But they sense something, and their senses are not wrong."

"Bob, I don't need this nonsense from you...not from you."

"I'm telling you no animal killed that girl."

"Keep your voice down," Wayne said sharply. He shot up, walked briskly over to the door, and closed it. "Why are you doing this to me?" Wayne dragged back behind his desk and eased down into the chair.

"What killed Tiara Winters was neither animal nor human."

Wayne shook his head. "If this was coming from anyone but you, I'd toss them out of here on their rear end. You're a man of science for God's sake. You can't believe this. What's happened to you...you been working too hard?"

"Oh, cut the bull, Wayne. You know as well as I do what's been living around you your whole life. But, you're right about one thing—I am a man of science, and one thing that's certain in your profession and mine is to recognize a pattern before drawing a conclusion. Right?"

"I'm listening." Wayne settled back in his chair.

"When I examined Tiara Winters, it wasn't the first time I'd seen such evidence. Remember the two tourists who were found ripped apart three summers ago? Remember just recently, farm animals that were reported missing and the uneaten parts that were found?"

"Yes...and...?"

"It was said they were attacked by an animal then, too. I examined the bodies, what was left of them, each time the same results...not animal, not human."

Wayne quickly leaned forward. "But you confirmed each time that it was an animal!" He pointed a finger at his filing cabinet. "I have your reports right there!"

"Lies!"

"What?"

"Lies. Because I didn't want to start a panic and have those demon killers or whatever the hell they're called start a war with our neighbors. I had to be sure—now I am."

"This is absurd. I'm not listening to this." He ran his hands over the numerous papers and files on his desk. "You see all this work I've got here?"

Bob just stared at Wayne as he continued talking.

"I'm up to my butt in werewolf and ghoul sightings, people boarding up their windows afraid to come out of their homes…neighborhood events cancelled. Now you come in here with this bull crap."

Bob continued to stare at him without blinking. He knew Wayne was stalling.

Wayne looked off and concluded, "Damn, half the towns' gone crazy and you with it."

Then after a few seconds, his eyes met Bob's and Wayne fell back in his chair like he was defeated. "All right." He breathed a long sigh. "They're called Shadow Hunters. They hunt all things evil, mostly demons," he said in a low, soft voice. "Yeah, I remember," Wayne continued. "People started a rumor that werewolves had killed the tourists, and there was talk of hiring the hunters to come and clean out the region where they were attacked."

"It's funny how your memory has suddenly returned," Bob said sternly.

"Well who wants to believe this werewolf shit?" Wayne spat at him.

"Wayne, you and this whole town have lived in denial for years. As hard as you're pretending, you know I'm right, don't you?"

Wayne put his elbows on his desk and ran his bent index finger back and forth under his chin. Then he placed both palms on the desk and sat straight up in his chair. "Are you certain of this? I mean, really certain?"

"I'm positive."

Wayne sat silently for a moment to gather himself before he spoke again. "As a boy, I'd heard grownups talking about it a lot; everything in me doesn't want to believe it. If it's true, how the hell are we supposed to fight these things anyway?"

"Did they ever say how many there were?" Bob asked.

"Not that I can recall, but wolves are not loners—they run in packs."

"Um—that's right…packs."

But Wayne was so preoccupied with his thoughts that he didn't hear Bob's answer. "What happens when people around here get wind that their sheriff even half believes this stuff? What am I going to tell my deputies? They'll think I'm a lunatic."

"Then we won't tell them. We'll go and find those hunters and let *them* destroy the monsters. Have them bring back a dead one as proof—they'll believe us then."

"But, I don't know who they are, or where to find them," Wayne tried to reason.

"I'll help you." Bob reached across the desk and touched Wayne's wrist. "I see you've come to terms with this, Wayne. No more denying?"

"I can't refute your evidence, Bob. And if there *are* packs of these creatures existing among us, God help us, we've got to do something."

Chapter Seven

Beatrice speed-dialed Jewel after she stepped onto the balcony for more privacy. She couldn't stop shaking. "Jewel, I think we're in trouble," she said, her voice trembling.

Jewel tried to keep her phone from slipping between her cheek and shoulder while she bent over to put groceries in the trunk of her car. "What kind of trouble? And who is we?"

"You and me, silly. It's that book."

"No. The council couldn't have found out about the grimoire. Could they?"

"Well—kind of, yeah."

Jewel fumbled with her seat belt then checked the rearview mirror before backing out.

"I...I mentioned it to Naomi...I was so excited," Beatrice said. "I swear I didn't know she'd blab."

Jewel hit speaker and tossed the phone on the passenger seat. "Great Jupiter, Bea. Naomi is a high-level witch. She has friends on the council. What were you thinking?" She pulled out of the mall parking lot into traffic.

Beatrice kept looking over her shoulder to make sure she wasn't heard. "But she swore she would never say anything."

"Dear goddess. And you believed her?"

"Okay, don't panic—let's suppose she did tell them. No crime has been committed as long as you haven't used the spell," Beatrice said.

"You fool! Just having possession of that book is a crime itself. I told you that."

"I know, but you could say you found it or something."

"Great Jupiter! The council isn't stupid. They know the Grand Grimoire is no ordinary book just lying around waiting for someone to pick it up. There are those who have sold their souls to get their hands on one of these. Damn! I can't believe you did this."

"I'm...I'm sorry...I...I didn't mean to ...forgive...me...so stupid...I... "

"All right! Breathe. Calm down. Tell me exactly what Naomi said."

"She…she said that…the council wants to meet with us."

Jewel mumbled several inaudible curse words. "Did she say what it was about? Where? When?"

"She just said she wasn't certain, but that she'd call later with the details. Oh, Jewel, I'm so sorry. What are you going to say?"

"The truth… what else? Then I'll throw myself on the mercy of the council."

"But the council *has* no mercy when it comes to breaking Tenet rules, you know that."

"You better hope they do, because if I go down, so do you. I gotta go."

"Jewel! Don't you dare hang up on me. Jewel! Dammit!"

*****

A cool wind from the opened window parted Sheriff Tilbert's brown locks and whipped the collar of his shirt as he held tightly to the steering wheel. Bob sat on the passenger side staring out the window as the car rounded the curve on the dry, dusty road. A few rays of sun peeking through the dark clouds were the only hint that it was still day. Dead leaves swirled around the car like huge flies, and a tough, sudden breeze blew from the east, causing a windmill to squeak like a rusty, old door hinge.

"This place looks like something right out of a Frankenstein movie," Bob said, straining his eyes to read the numbers on the old wooden houses.

"This was your idea," Wayne said with a smirk.

Bob had succeeded in talking Wayne into finding the Shadow Hunters, the locals called God's Angels—a group of kick-ass tough guys whose specialty was fighting against witchcraft and supernatural entities. During the several weeks of their investigation, Wayne and Bob talked to about seventy people. Some stories about the hunters sounded believable and some sounded down-right cartoonish; people hailed the hunters as everything from angels sent by God in human form to a hard-nosed biker gang turned vigilantes on a mission to save humanity.

Some said that, when the Shadow Hunters were needed, they would suddenly appear out of nowhere, and when their job was done, they'd vanish without a trace. Wayne got goose bumps listening to the locals' endless rants about the demons the hunters had encountered. No one was sure as to who the hunters were or where they came from. Although the stories conflicted, one thing remained constant throughout their investigation: Warren Campbell's name kept popping up. He seemed to be the one man who knew how to get in touch with the hunters.

The houses were all on their right. Though wooden, they were sturdily built and mystery crept from each house as flickers of dim light streamed through the cracks of faded window shades. The grounds surrounding the houses were mostly dirt and stones with a few patches of faded grass throughout.

Scattered trees filled with large black crows stood on the other side of the road. Behind the trees was a small, gloomy graveyard full of grey wooden crosses with white chalk markings on each one. Just beyond the graveyard a thick forest lurked with shadows of movements within the trees and on the ground. The wind whistled about them like a mystically sweet song.

"That's the house there," Bob said, pointing to a three-story grey frame.

The banging of both car doors seemed the only sound other than the wind as Wayne and Bob made their way up the walkway to a red painted door. Wayne pulled the odd-looking door knocker up—it was a cupped bronze hand with the large head of a nail in its palm. A horrifying, high-pitched cry swept from behind the door, making Wayne freeze.

"It's probably the TV," Bob reasoned.

Wayne banged the knocker lightly at first then pounded loudly and more vigorously after there was no answer. A shadow quickly appeared through the curtains at the window. Then the shadow disappeared and the door opened a crack. A tall, slim figure stood with a dim light at its back.

"Can I help you?" said a graveled female voice.

"Good evening, ma'am. I...I'm Sheriff Wayne Tilbert," he said, trying to get a good look at the face, "and this is Dr. Bob Wilson. We'd like to speak to Warren Campbell."

"He's not here," she said and closed the door. The two looked at each other and Wayne banged on the door and called to her several times before giving up.

"Why, that rude old crone," Bob said.

Halfway to the car, Bob looked over his shoulder and saw a shadow larger than the old woman who'd opened the door. It stood still behind the thin curtains. Bob got into the car, but kept his eyes peeled to the shadow in the window. Wayne pulled off, leaving behind a long trail of dust.

"Well, genius, what do we do now?" Wayne asked, squinting at the road ahead.

Before Bob could answer, a dark figure of a man wearing strange sunglasses that had tiny blue lights blinking on either side of the frames appeared. He was draped in a long black leather coat and wore black leather boots with metal on the toes. He stood still and wide-legged in the middle of the road, the shadows of his hands at his side.

"What the hell...?" Bob blurted.

Wayne mashed on the brake, coming within inches of hitting the guy. With long, slow strides, the man made his way over to the passenger side of the car. Bob glanced quickly over at Wayne who slid his hand under his jacket and placed it on the handle of his gun. Wayne nodded an okay, and Bob lowered the window a tiny crack.

"Howdy," Bob said.

But Bob's pleasant voice didn't match the wariness in his eyes. The stranger bent over and a long blonde lock of his hair fell over his shoulder and stood out against the cold dark leather.

"What do you want with Warren Campbell?" he said in a soft but sinister Clint Eastwood voice. The whiteness of his clenched teeth stood out within a tight-jaw and an olive face that was covered with a five o'clock shadow.

Bob looked deep within the glass frames and saw no eyes. "Are you Campbell?"

"Follow me," he said

"Just tell us where he is," Wayne said, his hand still on his gun handle. "We can go there on our own."

"Without me there's a slight problem," the man said, his dark glasses fixed on Wayne's face.

"Yeah, what's that?"

"You'd be dead before your foot cleared the floor of your car."

Bob glanced at Wayne, Wayne bit his bottom lip, and there was a short pause. Then Bob's sudden movement to stick his hand inside his jacket made the stranger quickly fall back. With his left side facing Bob, the man grabbed his coat and flipped it over his right hip exposing his gun and placed his hand on the handle. When Bob pulled out a name card, the man took his hand off the handle of his gun, allowing the coat to fall back into place.

"If you see Campbell, tell him it's urgent," Bob said, poking the card at him.

The stranger stepped forward. He took the card in his leather-gloved hand and glanced down at Bob's name and phone number. He stepped back from the car and slid the card in a deep pocket on the outside thigh of his tight leather pants. He said nothing, but stood there and watched the car disappear in a grey cloud of dry dirt and swirling dead leaves. When Wayne looked into his rearview mirror, the man had vanished and the sky was dark with the flapping wings of black crows.

Chapter Eight

Every month, Matthew Porter and his cousin Rick, who was two years younger than Matthew, went deer hunting in Norwick Forest. For years this had been a dangerous undertaking because the northern and southern wolf packs were enemies and both hunted there. Many clashes had taken place on the very path Matthew and Rick were traveling. With Jewel's discovery of a moon cure, and River and Dex burying the hatchet, it seemed only a matter of time before the other wolves settled their grievances. There seemed hope for the packs to be as one again.

The forest was overrun with sweet, succulent deer. The bears and ordinary wolves were long gone from the area; the werewolves saw to that. Walking through the forest, Rick continued to pester Matthew: "So, let me understand this," Rick said, "the girl you didn't want to have anything to do with for the past few months is now banging away at your heart strings?" He had tried for weeks to talk Matthew out of seeing Kayla. Members of the wolf packs had always been weary of outsiders discovering their secret.

Matthew appeared annoyed. "I told you at first I didn't want to get involved with Kayla because of what Raymond had done to Tiara. But now there's a moon cure."

"But what if it doesn't work? No one's ever done it before."

"It will work. It has to..." Matthew's voice trailed off as he deliberately smacked his shoulder against Rick's—almost knocking Rick off balance as Matthew pushed past him. He rushed ahead of Rick who managed to catch up. "I didn't mean to sound pessimistic. I just think you should take it slow with this girl. I mean, you know the risk of anyone finding out about us..."

Matthew stopped and turned to him. "I know the risk. I'm not stupid. You...you know, it's none of your business. I'm sorry I even told you." He whirled around and walked off. Rick had to walk briskly to catch up again. "Matt, I'm your friend as well as your cousin. I'm sorry. I didn't mean anything. Kayla's a great girl, really."

Matthew didn't answer. His attention was fixed on something else. But Rick forged on. "Look, as I said, Kayla is a great girl and all, it's…"

Matthew shushed Rick. "Deer, two o'clock," he whispered.

Rick ducked down and slowly turned to see.

The deer stood majestically and quietly. Its caramel-colored coat glistened beneath the sun; its keen ears flickering at the slightest sound, dark eyes darting for danger.

"Is it yours or mine?" Rick asked in a hush voice.

"It's yours, cousin. Take him."

Rick stayed bent down. He slowly moved behind a bush, stripped naked, and got on all fours. His skin turned a deep brown, and large hair bumps arose upon it. His body shook as if lightening had shot through his bloodstream. The bones in his back rippled, and his biceps bulged. Eighteen years had made his shape-shifting quieter. His bones cracked, outstretched, and dislocated with ease. Grey and silver hair spurted out all over his body like a Chia Pet. His nose elongated, his ears shot upward to points; his fingers and toes stretched outward, his palms and heels lifted off the ground; his long fangs and claws were as sharp as a razor's edge. His brown eyes rolled to the back of his head like someone had pulled the arm of a slot machine, and he zeroed in on his prey with new, wolfish light-grey eyes. A spike-like organ shot out from his rear-end, quickly growing outward and filling into a bushy silver and grey tail that positioned itself for balance.

Rick lowered his ears to the side of his head so the deer couldn't see their points. He kept his head down, and his paws were as quiet as socks on a plush green carpet as he eased forward. The deer kept grazing, looked up momentarily then went back to pulling and chewing.

Strong, muscular hind legs propelled Rick forward as he swooped in for the kill, but the deer bucked and kicked Rick in the ribs so hard that he landed on his side. Rick shook off the pain and bolted through the woods after the deer. They ran side-by-side for a few seconds then the deer cut to the left, leaving Rick tumbling on the grass. Back on all-fours, Rick caught up to the deer, careful to avoid its hooves, but the deer cut right causing Rick to tumble nose-down.

Matthew shot out of the bush and overtook the deer. He inched up to it but was careful not to get too close to its hooves; no matter how many times the deer cut to the left or right, Matthew stayed dead on it.

The deer was running for its life, but it all seemed like a game to Matthew. The two galloped out of the woods and across a wide-open field like racehorses to the finish line—their thundering hooves and paws muffled by the soft grass. Matthew appeared to be running out of steam. There was a thicker patch of woods up ahead, and it seemed a way for the deer to clearly escape. Once it got into that thicket, he would lose it for sure. The deer's long strides and high jumps put several feet between it and Matthew and dinner looked like it was going to be fish tonight, when suddenly Rick flashed in like a cannon straight out of hell and side-swiped the deer; it tumbled uncontrollably, kicking up enough dirt and grass as if to dig its own shallow grave. Before it could gather itself and recover, Rick pounced on it, sunk his fangs deep into the back of its neck, breaking it. After the cracking sound, the sweet scent and taste of its blood made Rick euphoric.

He and Matthew flopped down hard on opposite sides of their prize, blood oozing from the deer's mouth, its ghostly eyes staring upward. Rick coughed and tried desperately to catch his breath. It had been years since they had shapeshifted while hunting. Matthew lay with his mouth wide open, sucking in all the air around him and sweating profusely. They both lay on their backs human and naked.

"Next time, I'll be more...more in shape," Rick managed to say between breaths.

"Next time, I'm...bringing a...a damn gun."

*****

It was a special evening, and Kayla smeared a fresh layer of pink across her plump lips. She flipped a blonde curl with her finger and flashed her long lashes at her rearview mirror. She and Matthew were dining at the family's cabin that stood on a hill just a few yards from the Porter mansion. Veronica and Christa had ambushed her into promising to brief them on her intimate evening with her handsome stud.

Kayla pulled up to the cabin and smiled when she saw Matthew standing in the doorway with a bouquet of flowers. He glowed when she walked up to him. She wore a strapless soft-blue dress and black high-heel pumps. Sparkling blue earrings dangled against her long neck. A heavy dark shawl covered her delicate white shoulders. Kayla took the bouquet. "Matt, they're beautiful. Thank you," she said, pecking him on the cheek.

He took her wrap and led her across the shiny hardwood floor that had beautiful Persian rugs scattered throughout the room. She stopped and gestured to a large wedding portrait hanging above the cold fireplace. "Who are they?" she asked.

He stood proudly beside her in front of the portrait and looked up at it. "My paternal great-grandparents. Great-grandmother got her dark complexion from her Egyptian roots."

"She was very beautiful," Kayla said, her eyes sweeping across the room. She ran her hand over the dark velvet sofa and seemed to admire the mahogany tables and antique lamps.

On the far side of the room stood a decorated table with two white candles in tall silver candleholders, sparkling dinnerware, and a colorful flower arrangement in the center. Soft music set the mood as its melody rose above the flickering candlelight.

"You seem impressed," he said. She nodded approval.

Matthew took her arm, escorted her over to the table, and pulled out her chair. She laid her flowers aside as he busied himself like a high-class, polished waiter, pouring Mourvèdre into two glasses, and handing one to her. Then he put on mitts and lifted a large faux-silver insulated platter from the hostess trolley, placing it on the far right of the table next to her. He then mixed a green salad and placed it on the other side of Kayla before taking his seat. She spooned the salad dressing, which was an old family recipe, and made a yummy sound after sampling it.

"Matt, everything is so wonderful: the table setting, the music, the food. Did you do all of this yourself?"

"Pretty much, except the food. My mom did that, of course."

Kayla lifted meat onto her plate next to her baked potato. "Um, this is delicious," she said after tasting the meat. "What is this?"

"It's venison medallions with whiskey, mushrooms, and horseradish cream sauce," he said, placing a serving of the meat on his plate.

"Oh my!" she said after swallowing. "It's...it's...," she couldn't find the words.

"I know," he said, flashing a smile, "my mom is an excellent cook." As they dined, Matthew gave her a short run-down of his family's history, omitting the werewolf part of course, and she gleamed with delight after hearing that there could be some ancient Egyptian royalty lurking in the Porter's background, which Matthew didn't mention wasn't proven.

She took a sip of her wine and placed the glass at the head of her plate. "Tell me about yourself, Matt. I've learned so much about your family but almost nothing about you."

"There's really not a lot to tell." He forked his salad. "Um, let's see," he said chewing. "Aah, you already know that my father inherited my grandfather's lumber mill. Well, I manage the sites and make sure the right materials are delivered to the right places at the right times. Overseeing the workers, stuff like that. Sometimes I'll replace a worker when we're short-handed."

She looked impressed as he continued.

"My dad insisted that I be general manager. I told him sitting behind a desk was not my thing."

"So, you're an outdoor kind of guy."

"Basically," he said, cutting his meat. Kayla was surprised by his European style of eating, keeping his fork in his left hand with his index finger on the back neck of the fork after cutting his meat with the knife in his right. She watched him cut, fork, and bring the meat up to his mouth several times as he answered her questions.

"So, you turned down a cushy job behind a desk for a job getting a little dirt under your fingernails."

"Didn't say I turned it down. I just don't sit in an office all day."

"You are actually general manager of your dad's company?" Matthew nodded yes and blushed. He appeared uncomfortable talking about himself.

"And you are how old?" she asked.

"I'll be twenty at the end of the year."

"That's awfully young for a general manager."

"My dad's been grooming me since I was thirteen. Enough about me." He leaned forward. "What do you do besides look incredibly beautiful over a candlelit dinner?" He slid his hand over and gently squeezed hers.

Kayla gasped at his sudden boldness. She lowered her eyelashes and smiled. Then she cleared her throat. "I'll graduate from the academy this year, and I thought I'd work for a year or so before attending college. You know—give my head a break."

"And such a lovely head," he said, squeezing her hand. "Where are you going to be working?"

"I don't know. I haven't thought that far."

"I could get you something at the mill. What's your major?"

"Accounting."

"Accounting, huh? We could use you in our front office."

"But, what would your dad say?"

"My dad? I'm general manager, remember." He held onto her hand and stared at her.

"I don't know what to say."

"Say you accept."

"I do. Thank you." His sparkling blue eyes were hypnotizing. She stammered to find something else to say and ended with, "The food was...was delicious."

He smiled at his making her nervous. "Shall we take our wine into the next room?" he said. She nodded and he stood, swooped around, and pulled out her chair. Then he took both glasses of wine and led her into the adjoining room. He handed her the glass of wine and set his on the table near the sofa. "Do you mind if I remove my jacket and loosen my tie a bit?"

"No. Please do," she said, taking a sip of her wine.

The evening had been everything Kayla had hoped for, and for

Matthew it went deliciously according to plan. They slow-danced to a long Kenny G solo, and then stood gazing at each other. He couldn't get enough of looking at her. Kayla by now exhibited a buzz from her third glass of Mourvèdre. "No more for you, young lady," he said gently prying the glass from her hand. She playfully pouted and put a fist on her hip.

Matthew turned to set her glass down on the table; he loosened his tie more and opened the first few buttons of his shirt. When he turned to face Kayla, she noticed a tiny, strange animal tattoo on his throat. It was a black winged animal she had never seen before.

"What's this?" she asked, reaching up and smoothing her finger over the tattoo. She pulled open his shirt collar to get a better look.

His face brightened as if her soft touch on his throat had lit a spark in him. "It's just a mythical creature I drew when I was a kid. I liked it so much that I had a tattoo made of it."

"You have quite an imagination. I like it, too," she said, letting her finger slide slowly down his chest.

Matthew's blue eyes narrowed, and he moved in close. He put one hand on her back, the other hand grabbed her hair and he pulled her head back gently. He pressed in hard and kissed her passionately, forcing her mouth open with his tongue. She moaned and moved her soft body against his muscular frame. They continued to kiss while she unknotted his tie. It fell to the floor and lay at his feet like a motionless silk snake. He slowly unzipped the back of her dress; it slid over her plump hips and pooled around her high heels. She stepped over the dress then kicked it away and unbuttoned his shirt, guiding it past his muscular arms until it fell over the tie. He kissed and bit her neck while unhooking her bra, and she fumbled with the zipper of his pants.

His pants dropped to his ankles. "Um...no underwear, I like that," she said, sliding her tongue over her bottom lip. He grinned and kicked away his pants, slipped his feet out of his shoes and bent to pull off his socks. Matthew stood gazing at her in her panties and stilettos, her breasts looking like two scoops of vanilla ice cream with pink cherries pointing right at him.

"You're beautiful, baby." He swept her up in his arms and carried her before the fireplace, laying her on the thick bear rug. He removed her panties and eased between her legs. She kicked off her heels. He positioned himself on his elbows and forced her mouth open once again with his tongue. She moaned with her mouth full of his tongue, and his erection pressing against the soft, pink mound of her sex. He kissed her neck and ran his tongue slowly down to a nipple to suck it, then ran his tongue in little circles around it. She combed his hair with her fingers as he sucked each nipple.

Rolling her hips and panting, Kayla gently guided his head downward. He ran his tongue over her abdomen, placing little bites along the way before reaching the ultimate pink bud of his desire. He circled it with his tongue and sucked it until she moaned and twisted uncontrollably.

"No," she gasped. "Not this way. I want you inside me."

He stopped and looked up at her. Her eyes were little slits of passion, her breathing deep and heavy, and her face flushed from months of wanting him. He pulled up and rested back on his knees. Her eyes widened when she saw how beautifully long and hard he was.

He touched her skin with the tips of his fingers—tracing her long neck down to her breast bone—circling one pink nipple, then squeezing it between his fingers until her cheeks flushed a bright red. He spread her legs wider with his knees then lowered himself on top of her. He slid into the wet sweetness of her body. She gasped, crossed her arms around his neck, and closed her eyes—her mouth sucking in the air.

He took her mouth into his. She gasped when his massive erection sunk deeper inside her. With the floor at her back, her mouth full of his tongue, her body full of his erection, there was no place to go but ecstasy. Moments seemed like hours as she buried her face in his neck while he stroked slowly and gently inside of her. She threw her head back, panting heavily. Soft music echoed in the background as the pumping of his hips had her head bobbing to and fro. He sped up the rhythm. She arched her back and said his name many times in a hushed voice. She tossed her head from side to side, her blonde locks sweeping the floor. Her beauty and passion released the beast in him, and his thrust became harder and more intense. She felt a sting on her neck. "You're hurting me," her voice trembled. He ignored her and drew a red line across her neck with his razor-sharp fangs. His eyes turned a misty grey, and his masculine moan deepened into a mild growl. "No, no," she told him. But he retraced the line again and again, deepening it with his fangs until a small trickle of blood oozed from her neck. He lapped it up like a cat licking its milk. The pain on her neck and the heat in her groin seemed to heighten her passion.

"More," she pleaded, sucking in her breath. Her eyes closed tight, her nails raking his back.

He obeyed and repeated the erotic biting until her voice rose as he quickened his rhythm—thrusting harder and harder—rocking them both into an emotional frenzy with inaudible utterances that needed no interpretation. Matthew fell to the side of her, both of them panting and smiling widely.

"That...was un...believable," she said breathily.

"A...mazing." Matthew grinned as the shine on his sweating body defined every muscle of his torso.

She giggled and put her head on his pounding chest. They kissed periodically while her phone played tinkling music every time her best friends left a text. And it rang constantly as her mom wanted to know where the hell she could be at this time of night. She ignored the phone and kept her head on his chest as he played with her hair. They talked for hours then kissed once more before getting up and dressing.

"Oh Matt, I'm never going to forget this night...never," she said, her heels clicking against the concrete as they walked arm-and-arm to her car.

Stopping at the car door, she turned to him and he held her by her shoulders and kissed her. When they broke apart, he smiled down at her and brushed a honey-colored curl away from her cheek.

"Call me so I'll know you're not lost again," he teased.

"I won't get lost," she said, playfully hitting his arm with her fist. He opened the door and she slid in. He bent down and gave her one last smack on the lips before she started the car and drove off. He stood until the darkness swallowed all but the two red lights as her car disappeared into the dark of the road.

Chapter Nine

The room was dimly lit, with only a few basic pieces of furniture: a couple of chairs, a sofa, lamps, end tables, and a watercooler in the far corner. The shades were drawn, and the white painted walls were bare save for one large framed picture of the council leaders. Their shadowy faces and haunting eyes appeared to follow Beatrice wherever she stood. She gazed at the portrait as if those lifeless stares bore stark evidence of events to come.

"Why haven't we heard anything? Why are they torturing us?" Beatrice blurted. She seemed unable to tear her eyes away from the portrait.

Jewel frowned. "Worrying isn't going to help, Bea," she said. "Just sit down."

The room was nicknamed the White Room. Some said it was used like the biblical *White Throne of Judgment because* witches were summoned to the White Room to be judged fit to remain in the Covenant

Jewel and Beatrice had sat for two hours wringing their hands, darting their eyes, and jumping at the least bit of noise outside the room. Before leaving her house, Beatrice had tried to reach Naomi numerous times, but she never picked up or returned Beatrice's calls.

Events couldn't have been worse for the duo. The weather outside began to match their obvious doom. River, Dex, and Jan begged to come along and help with their defense, but Jewel told them that she and Beatrice would face whatever they had coming— that she didn't regret one bit trying to free all of the men from the dreadful moon curse. Still, River's mind raced as he waited breathlessly near his phone for word of the council's decision.

In the long hours of their waiting, only one person had come to see about Beatrice and Jewel. The woman said nothing, just stared at them and talked quietly into her cell phone before leaving. She did this twice. Each time, Beatrice would sink a little more in her seat while Jewel sat calmly but quickened whenever the door opened.

"I wish they would just get it over with," Beatrice said, getting up from her seat and walking over to the watercooler. "Great!" her voice rising as she threw up her hands. "More torture. My throat is dry and no damn cups."

"Bea relax. Upsetting yourself isn't good for either one of us."

"How can you be so calm?" Beatrice asked, moping back and flopping down next to Jewel.

"We'll make our case and hope for the best."

"I sure wish I had your confidence."

Another hour ticked by. Jewel closed her eyes and sat quietly, resting her head back against the wall. Beatrice paced back and forth cursing the *no-cup watercooler* under her breath. Suddenly, the door swung open for a third time. Jewel looked up, her eyebrows lifting when she gazed upon the murky faces of two men. One was short and stocky, the other of average height and thin. Beatrice rushed over and stood next to Jewel who had now jumped to her feet. The men walked around and faced the women, and with not a word spoken grabbed Jewel and Beatrice and wrestled them to the floor.

"Take your hands off me, you bastard," Beatrice screamed, her foot nailing the groin of the man who was holding her.

The thin man cupped his crotch and fell to his knees. Agony spread across his face. "You bloody cunt!" he forced through clenched teeth. He backhanded Beatrice across the face. Blood spewed from her mouth as one side of her face smacked the floor.

"Bea, don't fight!" Jewel pleaded.

Beatrice bit her bottom lip but heeded the warning, allowing the man to flip her over face down. She stiffened while he straddled her and pulled her hands behind her back. A tiny string of blood connected the bottom of her chin to the floor. After both were gagged and tied up, they were taken to an underground garage and forced onto the back floor of a truck that quickly sped away. Lying back-to-back, Jewel used her fingers to comfort Beatrice during the long and jerky ride.

After what seemed like an endless journey, the car rounded a mountain three times. Each completed round took them a level higher until they nearly reached the top of the mountain. The wheels spat gravel for several yards before coming to a complete stop. The women were taken from the car and hustled through the mouth of a cave where they were made to stumble blindfolded up a flight of stone stairs into a deeper part of the cave. There, they were shoved onto the hard grey surface and left to shiver in the cold. Beatrice began moaning loudly through her gag until someone came and pinched her nose, cutting off her air.

*****

Night turned into morning but not inside the cave; there, night remained as one huge shadow that hung over the women.

"Bea...Bea," Jewel whispered while shaking her. Beatrice's eyelids fluttered open and her squint fell on Jewel's no-longer-bound naked body. Beatrice sat up and grabbed her head. "Oh my head," she said, and, with a look of confusion, examined her own nakedness. "Who untied me? Where's our clothes. Oh Jewel! What are they going to do to us?"

"I don't know. Just try to stay calm."

"Will you stop saying that? Aren't you scared? I am."

"Of course I'm scared: The very thought of never seeing my girls or River again terrifies me. But, Bea, I've got to stay hopeful. I've got to believe that the council will listen to reason." Jewel sighed heavily. "Poor River. He must be beside himself by now."

"Poor River...what about poor us?" Then Beatrice dropped her head. "Oh, let's face it—nobody's worried about me. My daughter and just about everyone I know thinks I'm a crazy old coot anyway. They're probably saying...*good riddance.*"

"Don't say that, your daughter loves you—and what about Kayla? She thinks the world of her grandmother."

"Well, maybe Kayla." Beatrice's forehead suddenly wrinkled as if she'd remembered something important. "Wait a minute," she blurted. "You know they nearly killed me last night. Someone held my nose until I blacked out. I thought I was a gonner."

77

"You *were* making quite a ruckus. I guess they just wanted you to shut up. Anyway, after they'd left, I crawled over to you and heard you were still breathing."

"Oh, thank you, Jewel," was all Beatrice could say before bursting into tears.

Jewel reached over and pulled Beatrice against her chest to hold her. "Now don't. We'll get out of this somehow."

"I'm so sorry. This is all my fault," her voice trembled.

"Shush," Jewel said, "we're in this together." She rocked Beatrice. One by one, Beatrice's tears rolled off her chin and raced down Jewel's bare back.

*****

Hours later, with bare feet slapping against the cold hard surface, Jewel and Beatrice were led naked through a long tunnel-like hallway and up a spiraling stone staircase. The staircase had no banister or railings. The higher they climbed, the more Beatrice whimpered. Jewel looked up at the enormously lofty ceiling that was draped with beautifully crafted spider webs and loaded with spiders.

"Eeeek!" Beatrice squealed as she smacked a huge one that hung from a silver thread just inches from her cheek.

"Don't hit them," a male voice scolded, "they're sacred and protected by the goddess."

Jewel and Beatrice continued the seemingly endless climb toward an undisclosed destination. Finally, the journey came to an abrupt end, and another mouth of the cave welcomed them, but this time they would not be alone. There in the darkness, as multiple lit candles floated twenty feet above them in midair, a hundred fellow witches stood draped in long black cloaks—their faces buried deep within their hoods. Each held a single lit candle and chanted in ancient Greek. The fire wavered above the wicks as puffs of air left their lips.

As the cloaked figures eased into new positions, shadows on the walls parted, revealing epic stories of an ancient coven. Bold earth tones depicted bullheaded men, dancing young girl figures, and bulls with long, pointy horns. There were different farm animals, mostly cattle, and as well as birds and snakes. Some of the figures looked to have been stabbed or beaten with a stick. Better-crafted drawings of dagger-mouthed dragons covered the ceiling and appeared to glitter above the flickering candlelight.

Jewel looked behind her and saw that the men had disappeared. Beatrice trembled as she held tightly to Jewel's arm.

A figure clad in a red-hooded cloak stepped from the darkness. "Come forward!" the booming female voice demanded.

As the women obeyed, the crowd parted like the Red Sea and a new line of cloaked figures emerged from the shadows, but they did not hold candles. Jewel swallowed hard and urine streamed down Beatrice's legs when they spotted the figures grasping knotted cat o' nine tails with tiny silver balls hanging from the ends. The chanting rose, and the cloaked figures raised their whips as the same voice demanded that the women walk toward them.

"Please!" Beatrice cried out. Though Jewel's body shook, she spoke boldly. "We demand a trial," she said, her voice cracking.

"Silence!" yelled the red-hooded one. "Move forward!"

The chanting rose to near-deafening levels. Then Jewel's face turned ash-white when Beatrice, with a defiant look—as if welcoming her death—suddenly straightened and strutted ahead of her. Jewel reached out and grabbed Beatrice's arm, but Beatrice snatched it away and continued her pace. Jewel followed her; they reached the line and waited. The black cloaks circled them, and the chanting stopped. Beatrice stood with her chin raised, her lips tight. Jewel took a deep breath. She whispered each of her girls' names and closed her eyes. She strained to remember River's lips upon hers.

Suddenly, the deafening chanting began again as if the hooded figures were cheering from the sidelines. The first blow buckled Jewel's knees. She screamed as Beatrice stumbled over her because of several lashes striking Beatrice's torso simultaneously. Another whip wrapped around Jewel's neck—when the figure pulled it back, the tiny spikes on the balls nearly slit Jewel's throat. Beatrice began to fight but was kicked in the stomach and held down by several black-booted feet and whipped mercilessly. Jewel managed to get to one knee but was beaten down with lashes coming from every direction. Each whip sliced opened backs, buttocks, arms, thighs, and legs that reddened and bled as the women's pleas were ignored. The silver balls glittered in the candlelight as whips were raised again and again, thrashing down and turning delicate white flesh into oozing raw meat.

"Damn you!" Jewel yelled. She reached out for one of the descending whips; it cut a deep gash in her hand when she grabbed it. She pulled the whip so hard the dark figure tumbled down into the circle. Jewel appeared to be winning at wrestling the whip away until several fists pounded the back of her head. Jewel cried out and doubled over but wouldn't let go of the whip. Finally, it was snatched out of her hand, leaving a three-inch gash in her palm.

Beatrice leaped from her knees and tried to run out of the circle, but a strong hand forced her back. She spit out a front tooth after someone slammed her face into the concrete. She lay semi-conscious, protecting her face while the silver balls rained heavily down upon her.

Jewel curled into a fetal position to cover her head, her teeth clenched. Blood flowed from every part of her body. The flogging seemed endless until the cloaked figures abruptly stopped all at once, as if they had been counting the licks. At the command of the red-hooded one, they all stepped back into a perfectly straight line, the whips down by their sides, the balls still swinging and dripping blood onto the cold stone floor.

Jewel and Beatrice, who appeared too weak to move on their own, were helped off the floor by yet a different group of cloaked figures and led to another mouth of the cave. Lying in their own blood—half-conscious, pieces of flesh hanging from every part of their bodies—their moans filled the enclosed space. They lay for several minutes, both drifting in and out of consciousness.

Beatrice slowly peered through puffy eyelids. The right side of her face was double in size. "Jewel, are you all right?" she slurred, slobbering blood.

"I...I can't feel my legs," Jewel said. "Is it over?"

"I think so."

"You...you sure we're not dead? I feel dead," Jewel moaned, passing out again.

Beatrice didn't answer but managed to raise herself. She crawled over to Jewel and placed her ear between her torn breasts. Jewel's chest barely rose and fell. Over in a far corner sat an antique bathtub, something right out of the nineteenth century Old West. Beatrice pulled herself to her feet. Unable to fully straighten herself, she stood slightly bent and stumbled over to the tub, steadying herself by holding onto the side of it. She dipped her hand into the murky water then pulled it out and sniffed her fingers. "This is a familiar scent. I suppose they want us to bathe," she mumbled to herself. She looked over her shoulder at Jewel who was still lying on her back, her eyes closed. She eased over to her, sliding a mangled foot behind her, and tried to lift Jewel. "Can you hear me?" Beatrice asked.

Jewel peeked up at her through purple swollen eyelids and nodded. Then Beatrice helped her up and the two staggered over to the tub. Beatrice helped her into the water then she climbed in across from her.

"This scent is so familiar," Beatrice repeated with a frown.

There was no room in the tub for them to stretch out their legs, so they sat with their knees drawn up to their chins and water lapping at their necks. Beatrice splashed her face. She did the same to Jewel, patting her cheeks gently with her wet hand, but Jewel flinched when Beatrice's finger touched her swollen lip.

They lingered in the bath, tilting their heads back and closing their eyes. The strange aroma permeated the air. After a short while, Beatrice managed to get out of the tub first. Jewel soon followed. The bath seemed to have revived them. Jewel sucked in her breath every time the towel touched a wound, and there were numerous ones all over her face, neck, breasts, lower torso, and extremities. Beatrice looked up from toweling herself off and froze.

"Where did that come from?" she asked, pointing to a six-foot mirror encased in brass lion paws with a brass lion's head in the center of it at the top.

Jewel gazed at the mirror out of her good eye. "Wasn't it there before?"

"No," Beatrice assured.

"Well, may as well make use of it," Jewel said, limping over and standing before it. She was examining her bruises when Beatrice heard her gasp.

"What is it?" Beatrice asked, looking over at her.

Jewel stared as if something terrifying within the mirror was staring back at her. "Bea. Look. Hurry."

"What?" Beatrice asked again, dragging herself as fast as she could to Jewel's side.

"Look!" Jewel repeated frantically.

Beatrice watched, and her mouth slowly dropped open. Her eyebrows stretched upward so they nearly touched her hairline. She stared as each cut and bruise slowly disappeared from Jewel's body: all the way from her head, neck, torso, and down to her feet. Hanging flesh vanished as new flesh appeared. As both stood spellbound, Beatrice's body did the same. Not only were the bruises, cuts, and discoloration gone, but also the pain and swelling.

"What do you make of it?" Jewel asked, her voice barely a whisper.

Beatrice slapped her thigh. "I knew I recognized that scent," she said. "It's Dragon Root—the most powerful magic healing herb." Beatrice moved closer to the mirror and drew her lips back. Her knocked out tooth was back and not even loose.

"Bea, I don't get it."

"I don't care. We're still alive. Perhaps without our magic, but we survived."

Just then, a head poked in through the doorway, which made the women jump. "The council is ready for you," the woman said in a pleasant voice.

Jewel and Beatrice gave each other a solemn look.

"Let's get this over with," Jewel sighed.

She and Beatrice slowly re-entered the place where they were nearly beaten to death. The mystery of the cloaked figures was revealed, and Beatrice sucked in her breath when she saw her friend Naomi among the crowd. There were no blood splashes on any of the cloaks, and no one held whips. There was no way of knowing just who had been involved in the flogging.

Beatrice and Jewel were once more ordered to stand naked in a circle. They seemed to sigh at the same time and took a big breath. The witches surrounded them, and Jewel nearly choked on her own spit when one by one each of the witches kissed them: on feet, knees, genitals, breasts, buttocks, and lips as the local high priestess read from an ancient stone tablet—then the priestess stopped, looked over at Jewel and Beatrice, and announced.

"By unanimous decision, you, Jewel Anastasia Porter and Beatrice Rena Taylor, have been added to the Third Level of the Mystic Circle." Then she began reading from an ancient book. "There are three great events in the life of mankind: love, death, and resurrection in a new body. And magic rules them all." She continued to speak the sacred words as several women brought special attire to the circle.

Naomi came over and put white frocks on them. Another placed new shoes on their feet. Still another wrapped them each in new black cloaks. Then Naomi, with a grin as wide as could be, led them around the Mystic Circle as the high priestess proclaimed to the great goddess, Asase Ya, that two new witch queens had been consecrated for her glory. Two magic knives, called Athame, were dipped into a silver chalice of wine, and onlookers were informed, "That as the woman is to a man so are they to the Athame."

The Priestess had Jewel and Beatrice swear an oath of secrecy about what went on at the ceremony. "You are now married to your ceremonial dagger—the most powerful tool of our trade," proclaimed the high priestess as she handed each their customized blades. "You are both free to start your own covens. For you are now bonded to a powerful circle. It enables us to combine our magic no matter where we are—living or dead. Congratulations," she ended and kissed both women on each side of their faces.

The cave erupted in applause, flashing smiles, and cheers.

"Start the celebration!" a top council member shouted.

Dozens of men in chef attire streamed through every opening of the cave with silver trays of vegetable dishes, fruit dishes, and pastries. Wine bottle corks popped and crowds gathered around Jewel and Beatrice like no flogging had ever taken place. Not one face gave away who actually did the beatings. And Jewel, as well as Beatrice, seemed reluctant to ask.

The celebration had moved into its second hour when Beatrice suddenly spotted Naomi again and pulled her away from a small gathering.

"Bea, what the hell?" Naomi said, trying to keep her drink from spilling.

"Why didn't you tell me this was about our initiation?" Beatrice scolded.

"Didn't you hear the priestess? No one ever tells—it's tradition."

"But Jewel and I've been worried sick for weeks. We thought you told them about the grimoire."

"Shush!" Naomi hustled Beatrice over to a dark corner. "Don't mention that book here. Are you crazy? You trying to kill us both?"

"Oh, relax. No one heard me."

"Great Jupiter! Don't you know where you are?" Then Naomi tapped her own forehead with the palm of her hand. "Of course you don't. I forget. Bea, this place is loaded with magic. The walls will write whatever they hear if asked by the right spell." She grabbed Beatrice by the shoulders. "Don't say anything you don't want known. Do you understand? And for goodness sake, don't mention my name if you do."

"Yes...yes, of course. I... I'll be careful. I'm sorry."

Then Naomi's eyes softened. She hugged Beatrice. "Now honey, go on back and enjoy your party and remember," she said releasing her shoulders and putting a finger to her own lips. Beatrice nodded, and Naomi scurried back to her little group. Beatrice eased her way through the cheerful crowd and looked for Jewel.

Chapter Ten

Gunshots echoed across the southeastern sky of Greyscott Falls as members of the southern and northern packs hid behind barricades with rifles blasting.

"Give him up, Dex!" shouted Crane, one of the northern men. "You haven't got a chicken's ass chance in a fox den."

"Let's talk about this, Crane!" Dex shouted.

Crane answered with a shotgun blast that whisked past Dex's head. Dex ducked down as the blast ripped through a nearby tree. Hundreds of rounds thundered from both sides. One of the southern men cried out as a bullet tore through his shoulder. With lead flying, Dex was unable to help one of his wounded men who lay unprotected half outside the barricade.

"Wait!" Dex yelled. "There's no need for this. Let's have a sit-down...talk like men."

"Nothing to talk about. Give us the boy and we'll go."

Dex took advantage of the sudden halt—he ducked out to grab the wounded man by his boots and pull him to safety. The man growled in pain as blood leaked from his shoulder and dripped off his hand. One of the pack members smartly grabbed a rock, wrapped it in a pocket handkerchief, and applied pressure to the wound.

"Killing each other isn't the answer," Dex yelled. "There's no reason to harm the boy, either. He won't do it again. I've been trying to tell you, there's a moon cure."

"Don't know nothing 'bout no moon cure! Accept that Raymond is the one who killed that Winters girl!"

"Killing the boy is useless," Dex shouted.

"Dex is right, Crane!"

"River...is that you?" Crane yelled, peeking out from behind his truck.

"Yeah!"

"Always knew you'd be a traitor if it came to this. I'm really disappointed in you, River!"

"Can't let you shoot my brother and nephew, Crane. Besides, the sheriff already knows it was a werewolf that killed the girl! There's talk up in Sheerfield about summoning the Shadow Hunters!"

A hush fell over the northern men. The very sound of that name made hairs stand up on the back of Crane's neck.

"We're no match for those hunters, you know that," Dex yelled to Crane.

Crane's mouth suddenly went dry, and he could hardly speak. He lowered his rifle and looked around at his men who stood frozen. They lowered their firearms and began to grumble among themselves. Crane eased out from behind his truck with the barrel of his gun pointed down at the ground. Dex waved to his men, who also lowered their rifles, but stayed behind the barricades. "We're coming out!" Crane shouted. "Don't shoot!" Four of Crane's men joined him as Dex, Matthew, and River came out to meet them in the neutral zone.

Crane spit out a mouthful of tobacco. "Why didn't you tell us about this so-called moon cure and especially about the Shadow Hunters?" Crane demanded of River.

"You didn't give me much of a chance. Jewel only discovered the cure a few weeks ago."

"That was plenty of time to tell us," snarled one of Crane's men.

"How was I to know you had planned a damn war? Before I could tell you about the cure, the council discovered my wife's use of black magic—she could be in a lot of trouble as we speak."

"Have you heard from Aunt Jewel, Uncle River?"

"No. It's been three days, and she's not answering her phone."

"What's this about your wife missing?" Crane blurted.

"It's some bullshit witch thing. If Jewel hadn't been called to some council meeting, she would have used the spell by now, and there would be no way anyone could find out about us. But the way it stands now, all the Dominions have to do is wait for the next full moon and track us to where we'll be chained down. Then they'll have all the evidence they need to come down on us...all of us," River warned.

"So, you see, if we start killing each other, there won't be enough of us left to defend ourselves against the hunters," Dex weighed in.

"What about the Raymond kid?"

"I'll see to the boy personally," Dex said. "I promise. I'll chain him myself until Jewel comes up with the cure."

Crane spit out a mouth of tobacco and looked around at his men. Their once hard battle faces were now etched with fear after hearing the name Shadow Hunters. Crane turned his attention back to Dex.

"All right," Crane said, his eyes blazing. "You make sure that kid is chained. If another one of your spoiled brats do something like this again...no one," his eyes zeroed in on River, "and I do mean no one," he looked back at Dex, "will talk us out of coming back here and finishing the job. I hope I make myself clear," he said looking over at Dex's men.

Dex stepped forward. "We don't take too kindly to threats, Crane," he said.

Crane stared at Dex. "You don't seem to understand the seriousness of what that kid did."

"I know all right, but you don't seem to understand the devastation it will cause if you take the boy. It will start a war between the packs and leave us all exposed."

Crane spit out another mouth of tobacco and wiped his lips on the wrist of his sleeve. He looked as if he were in deep thought. He said nothing, then turned and motioned his men to leave. River watched Crane and the four men walk quietly back to the group. The group spoke among themselves for a few moments then Crane's men got into their trucks and headed off.

"Whew! That was close," Dex said, turning to River.

River slapped a hand on Dex's shoulder. "Damn close. But we did it, bro."

The southern pack appeared relieved as they all moved out from behind the barricades. They looked kindly toward River and nodded. He had sided with them and his brother against his own northern pack. One by one they climbed into their vehicles. Dex and River waved them off.

"Thanks, River," Dex said. "This could have gotten pretty ugly. I appreciate you stepping in."

"You don't have to thank me—we're brothers, and nothing or no one will ever come between us again."

Dex lowered his head like the little boy River knew as a kid, and Matthew, who hadn't seen his father and uncle that friendly in years, was lapping it up with a smile as wide as his face.

"Let us know if you hear from Jewel," Dex said before climbing into his truck.

"I will."

*****

River returned home to a worried Chelsea who had allowed little sister Abby to go out on her first date, and now couldn't reach her by phone.

"I'm sure she's fine. I'm going up to take a shower. Has your mother called?"

"No. Dad, where can Mom be?"

"I'm certain both Mom and Abby will be home soon," River said, trying not to let on that he was also worried. He turned to her after reaching the top of the stairs. "Call me when you hear from either of them."

"Okay."

The dark outline of clouds blazed against the sky with every flash of lightning. The rain beat down heavily upon the windowpane. Chelsea paced the floor. Abby had called an hour ago saying she was on her way home. Chelsea debated with Dria if she should drive out looking for her. Just then a car rolled up; it was not Abby but Benjamin Casey.

"What on earth is he doing here," she wondered out loud. Before Ben could knock, Chelsea opened the door. Benjamin stepped inside. His brows were raised and his eyes unblinking as their intensity fixed on hers.

"Chelsea, I've got to speak to your dad."

"Is it Mom?" she asked. Her breathing quickened.

"No, honey—this isn't about your mom. I'm sorry."

"Go get Dad," she ordered Dria. Dria hurried up the staircase. Chelsea stood looking at Ben and tried to read his face. Ben seemed careful to stand on the mat as water dripped from his shiny raincoat. Chelsea struggled to make small talk until her father came down.

"Ben?" River said frowning as he hit the last step. "Let's go in here," he said, leading Ben to the den. Chelsea watched the door close. She tried Abby's cell phone again and continued watching for her at the window.

"River, I know I should have called, but I was in the vicinity so I decided to stop in—tell you in person," Ben said.

River handed him a glass of scotch. "Here, this will warm you up." Ben took a big gulp and made a face.

River poured himself a drink then gestured for Ben to sit.

"No. I don't want to get your sofa wet," Ben said, taking another gulp. He lowered his glass and spoke. "The Dominions are planning a raid on us during the next full moon."

"How do you know this?"

"I was shooting pool with a couple of them over at Renzo's tonight and I heard them talking."

"What the hell are you doing being friendly with Dominions? That's dangerous, Ben."

"They don't know I'm a wolf, and someone has to make friends with outsiders. How else are we to know what they're up to?"

"That makes sense," he said, draining his glass of scotch. "We've got three days before the full moon to find a more secure place to chain down."

"Have you heard from Jewel?"

"No, nothing."

"But where are we going to find a place that can hold all of us?" Ben asked.

"I don't know. Damn! I wish Jewel were here. She'd know what to do."

"What about the other witches? They might help."

"I doubt it. Right now I think they're pretty pissed at Jewel for having that damn spell book."

"Then it's hopeless."

"Nothing is hopeless. Look, we still have three days," he said, putting a hand on Ben's shoulder. "I'll think of something."

"I sure hope so, River," Ben said, shaking his head. He threw his head back and drained the rest of his scotch. River walked Ben to the door, then stood in the doorway and watched him scurry through the pouring rain to his car.

*****

Just a few minutes later, Abby entered the house and big sister Chelsea was all over her, shouting and finger-pointing.

River stepped between the girls. "All right you two, settle down." He turned to Abby. "Why didn't you answer your phone? Your sister was worried sick."

"I forgot to turn it on," she lied. "I'm not a baby," Abby said, rolling her eyes at Chelsea.

Younger sister Becca came downstairs to see what all the fuss was about. Suddenly, the door opened and Jewel walked through, thrilling River and the girls. There was a considerable amount of confusing chatter among them as they all hugged her and tried to talk to her at the same time. River finally managed to quiet the girls so Jewel could explain her strange disappearing act of the past few days.

Jewel dutifully repeated the lie she and Beatrice had cooked up for her to tell the girls—that she and Beatrice had gotten caught in the storm with a flat tire and had to shack up in an old empty cabin where there was no cell signal. "Thank goodness I had snacks and bottles of water in the trunk of my car or we'd have starved."

"But mom," Chelsea said, "three days?"

"Well, dear, after the storm let up Bea and I managed to walk a little ways from the cabin where we were able to get a signal and call for help."

Satisfied with their mom's explanation and her safe return home, the girls each hugged her and started up to their rooms with Chelsea and Abby bickering all the way up the staircase.

River looked down lovingly into Jewel's eyes. He knew his wife so well. "Now, what really happened?" he asked, half-smiling. As he listened, he was overjoyed to hear that she and Beatrice had been elevated to the level of Witch Queens and were in line to have their own covens. The elevation had made Jewel more powerful. Being elevated also meant more freedom and independence from having to check in with the council about everything she did.

With only a few days left before the full moon and the Dominions' plan to raid the pack, Jewel couldn't be sure if this was enough time to prepare the moon cure. There was only one ingredient missing: the blood of the little Sooner boy.

Chapter Eleven

As Sheriff Wayne Tilbert prepared for the night raid, Bob Wilson was beside himself. Bob circled the floor nervously while Wayne sat on the corner of his desk cleaning his semi-automatic rifle.

"Wayne, for the last time...this is a foolish move."

"We've been over this," Wayne said quietly, inserting a thirty-round magazine into the chamber.

"For the love of God, man, they're not human, they're beasts. You're going to get yourself and your deputies killed."

"Will you relax? You've seen me with this baby," he said, patting his gun. "I can hit a deer right between the eyes at a hundred yards."

"Yeah, but that deer's not coming at you thirty-five miles an hour to rip your brains out of your freaking skull."

"Look, there'll be at least fifty of us with shotguns and rifles. Stay here if you're scared."

"Scared? Is that what you think? Wayne, this is not about my being scared. It's about you committing suicide and getting those poor men with families ripped apart and—"

Wayne slammed the rifle down on the desk. "What the hell do you want me to do, Bob? We tried it your way. We spent months looking for those damn Shadow Hunters and got nowhere. We had to bury that sweet young girl with no limbs and no head. Her parents are still grieving out of their freaking minds; the whole town is in a panic. We're going to bring closure to that family's suffering tonight," he said banging his fist on the edge of his desk. "I've made up my mind, and this is going down tonight! End of discussion." Wayne snatched his rifle off the desk and flopped down in his chair.

"All right, Wayne," Bob said in a hushed voice. He lowered his eyes to the floor and gently bit his bottom lip.

Back at Greyscott Falls, Jewel and Beatrice could not complete the spell in time. They would have needed, at least, another week. So, it was left up to the women to protect their men. They found an old mine shaft and double-bound the men with chains—carefully sealing the opening of the mine to silence the howling. The hardest part for the women was leaving their young boys whimpering and shaking with fear—having experienced the gut-wrenching pains of shape-shifting only a few times.

The full moon lit up the night sky. The glare of it made Wayne's fifty or so deputies and volunteer gunmen a bit weary. The fog was thick and fast like a moving cloud, and a long train of vehicles eased through it. The lower heaven seemed to tremble under the bright sparkle of the moon—as if it knew the evil that it harbored.

Wayne had rejected the idea of asking a judge for a warrant to search the wolves' premises because his reasons would have been laughable. There had been too many fake werewolf sightings over the years to convince any Sheerfield judge to take Bob's theory seriously, which prevented Wayne and his men from gang-busting into their home. However, Wayne did have a plan. They would simply plant themselves throughout the wooded area and wait. If they encountered the beasts, they'd have enough fire power to take them down.

As they crossed into Greyscott Falls, the men turned off the headlights and motors so as not to advertise their presence. They would make the rest of the journey on foot. Wayne eased out of his truck and signaled to his men to take their positions. The thick forest separated the road from the pack's residential area, where parts of Tiara Winters were found among the leaves. Owl hoots and small night creatures spooked the men, and gleaming eyes of small predators competed with the flashlights held by the men as they crept through the infamous Norwick Forest. They responded to each other's birdcalls that pinpointed their stations. Wayne became frustrated when he noticed unwarranted movement within the shadows. It was Ben, one of his deputies, moving quietly but fast out of his position.

"Ben, where the hell you think you're going? Get your ass back to your station," he commanded.

"My flashlight went dead. I got batteries in the truck."

Wayne okayed him and watched Ben's dark figure disappear in the fog. Minutes ticked by.

Steve, one of the deputies, got antsy. "I don't think these wolves are anywhere near here. I think they're hiding somewhere. But where?" he asked rhetorically. "We're going to have to move deeper into the woods if we want to find them."

"I know. As soon as Ben comes back. I don't want to leave him behind."

More minutes ticked by. Wayne kept watch over his shoulder, waiting for Ben to return. Wayne had just made up his mind to go look for him when shots rang out. Everyone's heads jerked in the same direction at the same time.

"Who was that?" someone called out.

"It came from over there where we parked."

"That's where Ben is. Ben, you all right?" Wayne shouted. "Ben?" He yelled again.

"I'll go check it out," one of the deputies said.

"I'll go with him," said another.

Wayne and the others waited while crouched down in the dark—a menacing moon lurked overhead and thick fog covered them with its viscous grey. Some of the men nearby got edgy, and Wayne softly called for them to stay calm.

"I don't like this," Pete whispered.

Wayne breathed hard. "We'll give them a few more minutes."

Finally, when Ben and the two deputies didn't return, Pete and Steve volunteered to join Wayne in looking for them. They eased through the woods, cringing at every step. The little bit of light that filtered in through the thickness of the tall trees illuminated the smooth metal on the rifles and even the buckles on their boots. Every rustling sound of a bush or tree caused their heads to snap around and their bodies to jump. After several minutes of walking, Pete stopped abruptly.

"Wait!" Pete ordered.

"Wait, what?"

"We're too far up. We parked back there," he said.

"What do you mean back there? The vehicles are up ahead," Steve insisted.

"No. I'm telling you, we passed it. I remember that tower," he said pointing.

Everyone looked back at the tower and began walking toward it. They stopped, and Wayne looked around, his face studying the situation. "Holy cow, he's right," Wayne said. "This *is* where we parked."

"Then where the hell are our vehicles?"

"There're gone," Pete said, turning in a circle.

"We can see that, genius," Steve snapped.

"Who the hell took twenty cars, vans, and trucks without us hearing it?"

"Someone or something strong enough to move them, that's what."

The men eyed the empty spot where the vehicles had been. They glanced around with a look of wonder in each of their eyes. Pete's face had an overwhelming urge to run written on it. Only his macho bragging rights prevented him from scrambling like a little pussy.

"There's no sense looking for them in this fog," Wayne said.

"What about our vehicles?"

"No sense looking for them neither. We better head back," Wayne ordered. "Whoever took our rides could be watching us right now."

"Right—there's safety in numbers," Pete said, stepping quickly and peering nervously over his shoulder.

It took the men just minutes to travel back to the group where Wayne broke the bad news.

"What the hell are we supposed to do way out here in the dark without a way back?" one of the men blurted.

"Someone could be trying to scare us," a deputy reasoned.

"Hell, it's working on me," answered another.

"Me too!" the words rose sporadically among several men.

"Oh, come on—you sound like a bunch of girl scouts," Pete said. "As soon as day breaks, we'll find the men and our rides and get the hell out of here. But right now, we must focus on what we came to do."

"Pete's right," Wayne said. "We'll just camp out here. Keep your eyes sharp and your guns ready. There's a lot of little night creatures roaming about, so don't go shooting at the first thing that moves."

The men agreed and took their places among the bushes and trees.

Dark clouds moved across the face of the moon; the fog thickened and rose several more inches. Some of the men's eyes grew heavy, and they drifted off to sleep. Others took little cat naps, hugging their rifles to their chests.

As the long hand of the clock moved beyond midnight, a haunting presence swept through the trees. An odd scent, distant snarls, and outlines of strange figures formed in the shadows. A long and oppressive shadow disturbed a bush then an eerie silence fell upon the night. Panic settled among the men when some didn't return their night calls. Sleeping men's eyes flashed open—hands tightened on rifles. A large owl, like a warning, hooted loudly; it bolted from a branch, wings spread across the sky then disappeared into the black.

Pete appeared to sense that something was wrong. He peered around nervously like he was being watched. He pulled his rifle close to his body then upward. His eyes darted around then rose to the sky. He gulped a swallow of air when his eyes fell upon a monstrous silhouette high up in a tree. Its yellow eyes blazed back at him. Pete lifted his fire arm and aimed for the widest part of the creature. Without the aid of light, the scope was useless for a head shot. He squeezed—the shot rang out over the fog. The beast let out a scream that cut through the night like a wounded hound from hell. But being injured didn't stop it from swooping down on Pete. Though it had the strength of ten men, Pete fought ferociously for his life—enduring fatal bite after fatal bite—blood squirting from his face and neck until the beast struck a stentorian blow that tore

Pete's head clear from his body.

Pete's head bounced off a tree and rolled unnoticed into the fog near a deputy's foot. The deputy tripped over it and missed a shot at a dark figure rocketing toward him. Its fangs tore into the deputy, nearly ripping his face off before he could even scream. A gun shot blast struck the creature in the shoulder when it was spotted with the deputy's lifeless body still hanging from its mouth.

"Over here! Over here!"

Hundreds of gun blasts sounded in the creature's direction. Panic struck throughout the darkness with loud growls like roars of thunder.

"Over there! Over there!"

"How many are there?"

"Just shoot damn it!"

More body parts sailed through the air. Chaos reigned: piercing death screams, gunfire from every direction, several men dropped and many scrambled to find solid cover behind trees, large rocks, or under fallen comrades. Wayne's calls for order were ignored as he was knocked to the ground and trampled by fleeing men.

"Wayne! Pete! Where are you?" Steve screeched.

"Save yourself! Get to the road! I'll be right behind you!" Wayne shouted.

But Wayne had lied. He wasn't just trampled underfoot—he was shot and coughing up blood. He tried to keep his head above the fog even though the cool mist kept his mind clear. He flopped down on his belly, and his wounded body remembered his early Marine training of crawling under wire, in the mud, while under fire; he gritted his teeth and pulled himself as hard as he could over the gravel in the direction he'd seen all the shadows of his men go. Gunshots peppered the sky and footsteps thundered past his face— heavy boots striking him as he desperately tried to crawl clear of the forest.

Feeling half-dazed, it seemed to Wayne that he was moving much too fast to be sliding on his belly. Two shadows appeared on either side of him, each holding one of his arms and pulling him through the fog, over bumps in the path— perhaps rocks—

perhaps dead deputies—maybe Ben. Blood poured from his chest wound. Wayne's head bobbed back and forth then went down for the last time and he was out cold.

Wayne's arms were released and he fell limply on his face. The coolness of the ground caused his eyelids to flutter. He had slowly turned over on his back and was gritting his teeth when a bolt of pain flashed through his chest. He looked up into the faces of two women he'd never seen before. They were covered in black-hooded cloaks and were staring down at him with little or no expression.

"Who are you?" Wayne asked in a strained voice.

"You're safe now," one of the women assured. "There'll be no more trouble as long as you all stay out of the open until morning."

"We can't...can't," Wayne coughed, blood dripping from his lips.

"He's trying to tell you some assholes stole our vehicles," Steve said. He bent down and supported Wayne's head with his hand.

The women stood majestically, said an incantation, and waved their hands in a circle three times. There was a loud gasp from the crowd of men when their cars, trucks, and vans suddenly appeared. When Steve looked back at the women, they were gone.

"Witches! I knew it!" someone shouted. "They're the ones who did this."

"Yeah, let's get 'em!"

"No!" Wayne said faintly. "If they'd wanted to hurt us, they would have."

"I still think we should go after them!"

"Seriously, Joe?" Steve smirked. "You really want to tangle with creatures that can wave their arms and twenty vehicles appear out of nowhere?"

Joe's chest deflated and he looked down at his feet like a pondering fool.

The men stood gazing at their rides like they were trying to process what they'd just witnessed. They talked among themselves for a few moments then dispersed to settle into their trucks and cars and waited for morning.

The witches were right; whatever attacked them didn't return. And whatever magic they'd performed also worked on Wayne. He had stopped coughing up blood, and the hole in his chest had closed. All that remained of his injuries were his blood-soaked shirt and crusty blood stains on his chin and mouth.

*****

The daylight brought grown men to tears after having seen the horrible way their fellow deputies met their ends. As they walked around, they saw blood-covered, twisted bodies—severed heads with wide eyes staring up at them, and guts, brains, and limbs hanging from tree branches. Broken rifles and hundreds of shell casings sparkled among the stones on the ground.

"Wayne, over here." Steve called. With his eyes glassy, he stood over Pete's headless body, his metal name tag splattered with blood.

Wayne took his time, stopped, and sighed. "He just had a new baby. How the hell am I going to tell his wife this?"

"I gotta find his head," Steve said, his lips trembling.   He looked around on the ground.

"I think it's there—over there," Wayne said, pointing.
Steve walked a few feet, spotted Pete's severed head, and brought it back where he gently placed it beside the body. Then Steve's eyes widened when he saw Pete's hand gripping something. Steve could see a part of it showing through Pete's fingers. He pried open the cold hand and took the object. It looked to be a piece of an animal ear—black and silver fur. He brought it up to his nose and sniffed. Forcing back the tears, he smiled at Pete's last ditch effort to leave a clue. "A cop to the bitter end," Steve said, his voice cracking.

Wayne stood, pulled his phone from his waist, and dialed. Bob's phone rang.

"Hey, Bob, I'm bringing a sample over for you to analyze....No, not good.... I don't want to get into any details right now. Just wanted to be sure you'd be in the lab....Ah...about an hour....Okay.... Right.... Right.... See you then."

Chapter Twelve

As Illinois state police tried desperately to control the media frenzy outside of Saint Paul's Church of the Dominions, hundreds of mourners packed the pews. Caskets draped in American flags lined the front of the sanctuary, and a large gold-plated cross towered over the pulpit.

"Mommy, which box is Daddy in?" three-year-old Myrah asked Lilly Neilson, Pete's widow. Lilly tearfully whispered the answer in the tot's ear, pointing to Pete's picture near the casket.

But the child's question sent Wayne over the edge. He hopped up from his seat and hurried off to the men's room where he locked himself in a stall. He gritted his teeth as his gut-cry shook his body so that he struggled to catch each small breath.

The bereaved loved ones had insisted that the service be kept short. And at the end of it, the families slowly filed out onto the street and into black limousines. One middle-aged woman fainted while her grandchildren clung to her bewildered daughter-in-law. Spectators were overcome as bagpipes played "Amazing Grace," and Pastor Randall spoke comforting words from a passage in the New Testament.

At the burial site, a five-man rifle party gave the three-volley salute to the fallen deputies. The five men lined up with muzzles pointed over the caskets and shot blank cartridges into the air three times. After the flags were folded, white-gloved officers brought the flags and handed one to each surviving spouse and parent. Pete's widow held hers tightly against her breasts and wept.

*****

Later that afternoon, Bob called Wayne about the piece of ear Pete Neilson had ripped from his attacker.

"It's an animal all right, but no animal God made."

I don't know how long we can keep a lid on this thing, Bob. There's talk of werewolves buzzing all over the city. Before there's an all-out panic, I think we need to give the search for the Shadow Hunters another try."

"Now you're talking. When do we leave?"

"I'll get back with you soon," Wayne said, ending the call.

The day had been long for everyone: the frightened townsfolk with their superstitions, the loved ones of the fallen officers, the surviving deputies, and, of course, Wayne, who blamed himself for leading his men to their deaths. Why hadn't he listened to Bob? Where were those damn Shadow Hunters when you needed them? He sat alone, still grasping the phone. Lilly and the kids were out serving food and bringing comfort to the mourning families of the fallen. Thanks to him, Wayne thought, there were now orphans, some the same age as his kids. Wayne examined the many family pictures placed around the room and on the walls, as if imagining the pain his family would have felt had it been *his* detached head and body that were buried. The guilt and pain in his heart said, perhaps, it should have been him. He laid the phone aside and picked up a picture of his wife and children. He took a deep breath and stared at it, then exhaled as his eyes filled.

*****

"Sooner!"

Russell's ten-year-old playmates yelled his last name from the sidewalk in front of his parent's home. Inside, Russell gulped down his milk, grabbed his baseball mitt from the floor by the leg of his chair, and ran from the dinner table.

"Later!" Russell yelled back. It was a play on his name, "Sooner or Later." Ever since kindergarten, it was how he and his best friends, Mark and John, greeted each other. It started as a tease then became a personal greeting. No other kids were allowed to use his name. That is, not unless they desired one of Russell's fists against their noses.

"Don't stay out too late," his mom yelled as Russell hit the door. "Did you hear your mother?"

"Okay, Mom. Okay, Dad." Russell ran up to his friends, and they started for the baseball field.

The day was cool, but the sun was bright, and it lit up the shine on Russell's dark-brown hair. He was an "A" student and very well liked in his school and neighborhood. Rusty, as he was called outside the classroom, stood tall for his ten years and was very athletic. He was the only child of Tray and Caroline Sooner. Russell had a twin who died during childbirth. He'd always wanted a brother, and Mark and John more than doubled that void.

Halfway to the field the three picked up enough kids to overflow onto two baseball benches. Russell kept looking around and over his shoulder.

"Why are you always looking around?" Mark asked.

Russell hunched his shoulders. "Ah…nothing," he said.

But for several weeks, little Russell had had a strange sensation that someone was watching him, perhaps even stalking him. But when he'd look around, whatever it was had vanished. He never mentioned it though it gave him the creeps.

*****

Late one night while Russell slept, a noise woke him. He sat straight up in his bed and saw that his bedroom window was open. Russell hit the light; he reached for the sword that hung over his bed and pulled it from the mounted sheath on the wall. It was a real sword his father had bid on and won for him at an RPG festival. It was said to have been used by a leading actor in a dragon-slayer movie. He tiptoed around the room, his puppy dog brown eyes scanning every corner. He opened his closet door and began poking around with the dull blade then he turned and flicked it several times under his bed. Appearing satisfied, he closed and locked his window before climbing back into bed. He placed the sword by his pillow and slid under the covers.

Outside, across the Sooners' backyard, Matthew, who had been surprised by the suddenly awake child, hopped away on one foot, having landed wrong when he leaped from the child's bedroom window.

"Damn! Little asshole," he said, dragging his injured foot across the gravel to his truck. He leaned against the door and pulled on his twisted ankle. "Aah!" he yelled out, hearing the bone snap back.

On the drive back, Matthew needed to come up with another excuse. Certainly, being surprised by a ten-year-old with a dull sword wasn't something to tell an impatient witch. Jewel could be a real pain in the ass if things didn't go her way, and she had been on Matthew's back for weeks about Russell. Matthew had never bitten a child before and had several arguments with Jewel when he tried to back out of it. As he pulled in front of his home, he saw several cars and trucks parked in the driveway. One of those cars belonged to his uncle River. "Now what?" he mumbled. There was shouting coming from behind the door. When he opened it, the shouting stopped and all eyes fell on him. Matthew limped across the floor.

"What happened to you?" Jan asked.

"I'm fine, Mom. What's going on?"

His cousin Rick stood next to Raymond and his mother, Debbie. Everyone seemed angry at each other, and Rick kept his eyes on the floor.

"Is it true?" Dex asked Matthew.

"Is what true, Dad?"

"Rick said it was you, him, and Raymond who attacked the sheriff and his deputies."

Matthew glanced over at Rick and said nothing. He looked around as if to gather his thoughts so he could speak. Before he could, Rick blurted..."I had to, Matt. They were talking about taking Raymond out and shooting him. I...I had to tell them it wasn't just him."

"What I want to know is how did you get loose?" River asked.

Debbie looked over at River. "I'm afraid *I* did that. And I'm not sorry. The Dominions vowed to kill you all. I simply prevented it."

"By turning our boys loose?" Dex yelled at her. "You could have gotten them killed!"

Debbie grinned. "Oh, I knew those idiots were no match for our boys when I found out they were going to use plain bullets," she said.

"No match, except your son has half an ear," River said sharply.

One of the northern wolves spoke up. "Gee, I wonder where the other half went?" His smirk turned to anger. "Now they know our secret...you stupid bitch."

Straightaway, Raymond jumped forward with a right cross that sent the man thudding to the floor. "Nobody talks to my mother that way!"

The man quickly hopped to his feet, but River stepped in front of him while Dex held Raymond back.

"That's enough," River snapped.

"I guess that's it," Dex said. "We've been exposed."

Jewel weighed in. "Maybe not. I can break that curse. I know I can. If..." she said sarcastically, looking over at Matthew, "...I can get that certain little ingredient I need to complete the spell."

Matthew sighed. "I'm working on it."

"You've had weeks," she said.

Matthew appeared agitated. "Okay! I'll have it."

"So this spell...it will really work?" A southern wolf asked. "What is this ingredient? Maybe *I* can get it."

"No need. Matt is going to take care of that. Right, Matt?" she asked, widening her eyes at him.

"Yes, Aunt Jewel." Matthew limped into the kitchen, grabbed a beer from the fridge, hopped over to a corner, and flopped down in a high-backed chair. He swilled his beer and pulled on his sore ankle.

To break the tension, River sent out for more beer, liquor, and barbecue spare ribs. Later, when the delivery man arrived with their food and drink, the crowd began to mingle and chatter. While everyone seemed to enjoy themselves, Jewel grabbed Matthew by the arm and pulled him up from the chair and into the kitchen. He limped along making a pained face with every hop.

"What the hell, Matt? And what's up with that limp?"

"Look, the kid's not stupid. I think he suspects something. The little bastard pulled a real sword. I think it was silver."

"You couldn't wrestle a sword away from a ten year old? Shit! You're a werewolf, damn it."

"Wrestle the…you know what silver does to us."

"I need that kid." She looked under her lashes at him. "You're stalling."

"No I'm not. I just need more time."

"There *is* no more time. There's another full moon coming soon. Get that kid."

"All right! I'll have him by the end of the week," Matthew said, lifting the bottle of beer up to his mouth.

Jewel grabbed his wrist and yanked the bottle down from his face. "Don't give me that shit."

"Aunt Jewel, chill. I said I'll do it. You have my word."

She turned him loose, and he threw his head back and guzzled down the whole bottle of beer. He belched loudly and smiled, waiting for her reaction.

She playfully smacked him upside the head before walking off to join the others. Matthew grabbed another beer from the fridge and stood alone in the corner. Scotch on the rocks flowed heavily as laughter replaced the earlier angry shouting. Matthew ran his fingers through his silky dark hair. His deep blue eyes darted back and forth menacingly. If Matthew's deep thought expression was any indication, Russell Sooner's days as a normal little boy were about to end.

Chapter Thirteen

Mid-April marked the beginning of Little League in Sheerfield. The sky was cloudy, and a slight chill permeated the baseball diamond at Merryfield Park; parents sat in their winter jackets and cheered on the home team of ten to twelve year-olds. The crowd's roar filled the air. Russell Sooner played center for the Sheerfield Cubs. His pals, Mark and John, were first baseman and star pitcher respectively.

Most of the crowd was on their feet. John leaned forward on the mound then did a full wind up for the pitch.

"You can do it, Johnny!" his father yelled.

John shot a low pitch that the catcher had to practically scoop out of the dirt.

"Ball one!"

The batter's relatives yelled encouragements as the Cubs supporters held their breath. John nodded to the catcher, then the wind up and the pitch. The ball barely made the catcher's glove.

"Struuuike!" the empire yelled.

"Booo!" bellowed the guest crowd.

John leaned forward. Silence fell over the field. Birds flew quietly over the crowd. John stood a few seconds, observing the signals from the catcher. John gave him a nod—then the wind up and the pitch.

The batter swung. It was a high fly ball to center field. Russell Sooner went back, and back, and back, and then a one-hand catch brought the crowd to its feet. The guest crowd shouted disappointments as the Cubs crowd went wild.

Mr. Sooner jumped so high that he nearly fell off the bleachers. Mrs. Sooner hopped up and down, her blonde ponytail whipping and cutting the air, and the Cubs dugout resounded with ultimate glee.

"Two down and one to go, honey," Mr. Sooner told his wife. "Way to go, Rusty!" he yelled.

"That a boy, Rusty!" his mom yelled.

The next batter was up. A hush spread over the park—and for good reason. It was the bottom of the ninth with two outs, the Cubs led by one run, and an earlier batter was still on base. The first win or loss of the season usually set the tone for the remaining season. Everything was riding on this game. The batter had struck out earlier, so the pressure was on.

The first two pitches were strikes followed by name-calling aimed at the umpire by the guest crowd, then a death-like silence. The kid took a deep breath. He drew his bat back and glared at the mound. John, looking more serious than ever before, nodded at the catcher. He leaned forward, the ball in his right hand resting against his knee. Then the wind up and the ball rolled off his fingers and flew toward the batter. It was on the outside, the catcher had to lean, and it was definitely a ball call, but the kid stretched and got a good piece of it on the end of his bat that sent the ball flying high into the outfield. The ball flew a little to the right; the right outfielder moved in.

"I got it! I got it!" Russell shouted.

The right outfielder backed off. Russell went back, and back, and back, but the ball soared over his head, over the fence, and into the woods. The guest crowd went ballistic as the batters rounded the bases. The final scores was guest team six, Cubs five. Russell's shoulders sagged as he stared at the spectacle of heroes being hoisted onto shoulders and carried off the field. He noticed a small hole in the fence and squeezed through it.

Slowly walking over the chilled grass, he found the woods eerie and dark with streaks of light shining through the tops of giant trees. Russell didn't really want to search for the ball. He needed time to get over the pain of losing the game, though he knew the Cubs would win many more. He scooted down by a tree, his knees up to his chest, and his hands between his legs lightly punching the inside of his baseball mitt with his fist. Suddenly, the white of the ball caught his eye. It stood out within the shadow of a thick bush. As Russell rose and made his way toward it, he thought he heard something.

*****

Hours ticked by. The stars were out, and the temperature had dropped significantly.

"I promise you, we are doing everything we can to find Rusty," Sheriff Tilbert told a hysterical Mrs. Sooner as her husband held her. "We have every deputy and hundreds of volunteers searching the woods right now."

"Please. Please find our boy," Mr. Sooner begged before breaking down and hugging his distraught wife.

"I will," Wayne said. He turned and walked out of their home.

Wayne had driven a quarter of a mile back to the station when his phone rang. He clicked speaker. "Hey, Bob. I could use some good news right about now."

"I'll let you be the judge of that. You remember that strange man we encountered that day when we were out looking for the Shadow Hunters?"

"Sure."

"Well, he contacted me. I told him about our werewolf problem, and he said the Shadow Hunters can't help us."

"What! I thought they were supposed to be these bad dudes that went around battling evil?"

"He said hunters only deal with supernatural evil, like vampires, demons, or witches, and that werewolves are not evil—they're just a group of innocent men who were in the wrong place at the wrong time and pissed off the wrong witch."

"Holy Jesus! Not evil, huh? You mean ripping off the heads and limbs from a fifteen-year-old girl and a half dozen deputies not evil? Is that the not evil he's talking about?"

"I'm just the messenger."

"Great! Son of a...so, what do we do, just let them run loose until they kill us all?"

"No. Here's the good part."

"Oh, my. There's a good part. Well, let's have it."

"Wayne, Buddy. Chill. Now, this guy claims we can defeat them ourselves. Get this—silver nitrate kills werewolves deader than a doornail."

"Silver nitrate?"

"Yep."

"How does that work?"

"After I got off the phone with the guy, I found this strange website and did some research of my own. According to this mysterious scientist whose name I can't pronounce, you drill a hole in the bullet head, pour in the silver nitrate, and seal it with wax. Once fired, it will hit the target and the wax will melt from the heat to release the fluid."

"Hm. Sounds simple enough."

"Actually, when the bullet explodes inside the body, silver nitrate is injected into the blood stream, damaging vital organs and causing instant incapacitation and a quick, agonizing death."

Wayne's face lit up. "Okay, so...so, where can we get our hands on this stuff?"

"That's the sweet part. They're going to help us the only way they can. They're sending us a whole truckload of everything we'll need, including armor and special weapons."

"Who? Who's sending it?"

"Wayne, you sound like an owl. The Shadow Hunters, that's who. He said to expect, you ready for this one, the Death Dealer in a couple of weeks."

"Death Dealer?" Wayne chuckled. "He actually said that?"

"I'm just the messenger," Bob said with a snicker.

"Aah, man. This is too weird. Should we believe this guy? I mean, you think this is a joke?"

"You saw the man, same as I did. He didn't strike me as the court jester type."

"Yeah, he did remind me of The Crow."

"So, are *we* feeling better?" Bob teased.

"Heck yeah! I'll have to try and take this all in, of course. But, hey, Bob. Good job, my man."

"Look, I didn't do anything. The guy called me."

"Keep me posted."

"Definitely."

Wayne clicked off and immediately dialed his acting top deputy who had replaced Pete. "Carl, contact every deputy, on duty and off; drag them out of bed if you have to—but tell them to meet me at the station. Pronto....yes, NOW!"

It had been four days and four nights since Russell Sooner was reported missing. Mr. Sooner sat in a big armchair next to the fireplace, his head bowed. He held a glass of scotch in one hand and an empty scotch bottle in the other. Mrs. Sooner, who hadn't spoken a word in days, stood like a statue by Russell's bedroom window and stared out into the darkness.

*****

Deep in Norwick Forest, Russell Sooner lay semi-conscious with a high fever and a nasty bite wound to his neck. The boy had put up quite a fight four days earlier after Matthew had turned human and pretended to rescue him minutes after the wolf allegedly ran off. He had kicked Matthew in the groin and cracked him on the head with a rock when Matthew tried to force the boy to go with him. Since time was of the essence, Matthew eventually put the feisty little tiger in a sleeper hold and carried him off.

Several minutes before the full moon, Jewel stood with the grimoire opened to the moon cure spell, while Beatrice prepared the sacrificial altar. Farther away in a mine shaft, the women double chained all the males and left, sealing the opening of the mine behind them.

Russell groaned and softly called for his mommy. Under normal circumstances, the child's plea would have proved heart-wrenching for Jewel, but his sacrifice was too crucial for the survival of the wolf pack. The wound on his neck had begun to fester. His baseball uniform was replaced with a white ceremonial garment that was drenched with sweat from his fever. The child shivered and moved his head from side to side. His neck wound pulsated like the beating of a human heart, and pus streamed onto the base of the altar. The smell from the wound choked the air.

"Beatrice, it's time," Jewel instructed. "Prepare the child."

Chapter Fourteen

As Russell moaned, Beatrice dipped her finger into a tiny pool of her own blood and drew an ancient Greek symbol upon his forehead, *doma*, meaning "gift."

After Beatrice prepared the boy, Jewel lifted her Athame and held it up to the sky; the blade began to glow and tiny currents flowed along the length of its six inches. She brought it down, slit the palm of her hand, and allowed her blood to spill into the wooden cup of a prepared potion. She passed the cup to Beatrice who placed it to Russell's resisting lips, holding his nose and forcing him to swallow. Beatrice cleaned the Athame and returned it to the red velvet case.

Jewel opened the grimoire to the spell that was written in Greek. She and Beatrice held hands and chanted the incantation.

*****

Deep within the mine shaft, the howling of the chained wolves echoed against the stone ceiling. The women were warned to stay inside their homes. In the wolves' advanced state of transformation, they never recognized their women. They would just as soon rip their daughters, mothers, or wives apart as they would a deer or a wild steed. But Kelly, Rosa, and Delveen said they had faith in Jewel's spell and were determined to witness the end of their menfolk's long suffering. Kelly found a way to pick the lock, and they entered the noisy darkness of the cave. Shining their flashlights, the women's eyes widened at the toll the full moon had taken—the wolves thrashed about pulling against the chains so hard that each rusty link dripped with their blood.

Frightened, the women huddled against the wall as they watched the ones they loved snarl, baring two-inch fangs at them, their irises turning a yellowish hue. Delveen begged to leave, but Rosa and

113

Kelly wanted to stay, thinking they could greet their men once the spell was broken and welcome them into their new life.

The women held fast against the near-deafening howls that chilled their bones. Yet when they heard the tinkling sounds of chains spilling to the concrete floor, any illusions Rosa and Kelly had suddenly faded when everyone bolted and raced to the only exit out of the cave.

Once outside, they chained and locked the door then parked their van closely against it. Minutes ticked by as they sat in the van holding hands and praying to the goddess, but they were interrupted when several wolves violently shook the mine door and caused the van to rock. Then one by one, screws popped out of the door hinges. The women broke hands and screamed for Delveen to take off. The tires screeched and created a mini-dust storm when the van jetted away.

Delveen's hands shook as the van wove back and forth across lanes and Rosa's paranoia of seeing wolves at every turn didn't help. Delveen eased on the brake while rounding a sharp curve, but lost control of the wheel when she swerved to avoid hitting a dark figure that stood in the middle of the road. She crashed into a tree and was knocked unconscious. Kelly opened the door and jumped out of the back seat. She tried opening the driver's side, but it was jammed. She jerked on it several times before it opened. "Don't just sit there, help me!" she yelled to Rosa.

Rosa sat staring like she was frozen. Kelly reached across the unconscious woman and slapped Rosa across the face. Rosa came around, scrambled out of the car, and hurried to the driver's side to help. They dragged Delveen out and lifted her onto the back seat. Rosa scrambled back to the passenger's seat, while Kelly got into the driver's seat and turned the key—nothing happened. She tried numerous times, but the engine continued to choke.

"I think I saw something!" Rosa said, looking into the right-view mirror.

"What? What?"

"May....Maybe I didn't. I'm not sure. Can we just go? Please!"

"I'm trying to, damn it!" Kelly snapped. After a few more tries, she leaned back. "I think it's dead."

"No! This can't be happening."

"It's...it's going to be fine."

"Fine? It's not going to be fine. No one knows we're out here, and even if they did, no one will come for us. Oh, why did I listen to you? Why?"

"I'm sorry." Kelly paused. "Look, I got us into this. I'll get us out."

"How?" Rosa snapped. "You said there was no way they could get out of those chains."

Before Kelly could answer, Delveen eased up into a sitting position, blood streaming down her face. "What happened?" she asked, grabbing her head.

"We're going to die, that's what," Rosa said, chuckling coldly.

Kelly looked over disapprovingly at Rosa. They sat quietly in the dark with Delveen weaving from side to side in a daze.

*****

Jewel and Beatrice's chanting became louder and more intense. The spell formed into a green mist, rose, and hovered over the altar. Suddenly the clouds parted as if the moon had blown them away. Jewel's irises rolled to the back of her head and remained. They looked like white marbles in their oval slits. A thick fog gathered at the foot of the altar, and the boy, flat on his back, rose several inches in the air. Lightning cracked the sky. Thunder roared like lions locked in mortal combat. Rain—heavy as stones, tearing branches from trees—came pouring from the sky. But the sacred altar remained dry. The green mist acted as its rooftop—hard as concrete and slick as a duck's back.

Little Russell ascended several feet. Lightning lit up the sky as bright as daybreak. A tree caught fire and split in two. The child moved into a standing position in mid-air, his body stiff as a board, his hands tightly at his sides, fingers pointing downward. His eyes flashed open—first all white then totally black. He grinned sinisterly, showing tiny, sharp fangs. Then the rain turned to blood;

it colored the clouds that moved across the moon, making it appear a crimson red. Another roar of thunder and a flash of lightning blew a car-size hole in the dirt a few feet from the altar. A red mass like a man-size blood clot rose out of the ground and formed into a body with no face. It floated over to the boy. Without eyes it appeared to read the child's forehead. Then the child willingly opened his mouth, and a hole in the creature's face widened and sucked his soul like it was vacuuming white smoke from a chimney.

*****

Kelly and Rosa sat like statues and chanted to the goddess as the blood-rain beat hard against the van, tinting the windows. Delveen had passed out a second time and lay on the backseat.

Suddenly, something hit the van hard like a ramming bull. The jolt knocked the women against the dashboard.

"What was that?" Rosa shouted.

Kelly said nothing—just peered nervously around the car, not able to see out of the windows. Then the van rocked back and forth, shot up in the air ten feet, and slammed to the ground.

"It's the wolves! They're out! Great goddess, help us!" Rosa bellowed.

Massive paws wiped the blood from the windows. Fangs and yellow eyes gleamed in front of the windshield, and snouts flattened against the glass on all other sides of the car. Kelly was a minor witch and didn't have strong abilities, but she said an incantation that enchanted the van, protecting the doors and windows. The wolves surrounded the van and struck hard blows against the panes, trying to rip off the doors, but the spell protecting the van held.

"Are we safe now?" Rosa asked.

"Not really! It will only hold a short while."

"What?" Rosa asked loudly. Her eyes grew wide as she stared into the beastly faces, their snarling mouths dripping saliva. "Oh Kelly, we were fools to come out here. I don't think the spell worked."

Kelly reached, opened the glove compartment, and pulled out three silver knives. "Here, take this. This will buy us some time."

"O...okay," she stammered.

"You crawl in the back with Delveen. Any part of them that comes through a window, don't hesitate—just stab."

Rosa nodded nervously. She put the passenger seat back as far as it would go and climbed over and onto the back seat. She gently shoved Delveen to the floor. The blood-rain continued to pour like every blood bank in the world had exploded over Greyscott Falls. Rosa kept looking quickly from window to window, holding the knife up in her hand and making little practice stabs in the air.

Kelly straddled the center console, holding knives in both hands. She looked straight ahead, letting her peripheral vision take care of the driver and passenger windows. The wolves saw the knives but were too bloodthirsty to back off—they would simply have to feel that sting of death. Not being able to get to the women enraged them and they started beating on the glass again. The banging went on for nearly twenty minutes like bombs bursting in rapid succession, but the windows held.

Lightning struck a tree and sent it crashing in front of the car. The burning tree was totally ignored by the wolves that were too focused on wanting to devour the women. Suddenly, a tiny crack etched into the windshield.

"The spell is fading. Get ready!" Kelly said, panting heavily.

Rosa's lips quivered as a small crack pierced the window to the right of her. "Mine's cracking too," she said in a child-like voice.

"Okay, just do what I said."

Rosa watched tiny cracks slowly snake across the window like someone had sped up a video of an invisible spider spinning a web. "It's crac...king," Rosa said, the words sticking in her throat. Then the window turned into a poorly constructed roadmap. "It's really crac...king," Rosa cried.

Kelly said nothing, but stared straight into the beastly faces as they pounded the windshield. Every window began to look like crushed ice, and the women held their breath and tightened their grips on their daggers. The spell was still holding, but only by a thread.

Suddenly the back right window caved. The blood-rain splashed through, blinding Rosa temporarily. Her eyes wide, she jumped back, exposing the unconscious woman.

Only one wolf at a time could fit through the windows. A huge dark paw shot in. It could barely reach Rosa, but the tip of its claws raked across her face. She gritted her teeth and stabbed the paw, sending the wolf howling backward like an injured pup. Another paw reached in and took a swipe, attempting to knock the knife out of her hand. Rosa sliced the paw open. Another window caved. Kelly braced herself and cut the first snout that forced through the window. One by one the other windows followed suit, and a wolf appeared in every opening. The women lay on their backs and fought for their lives like cats battling a pack of dogs. Their silver blades glittered as they sliced and stabbed in every direction. Each cut from the silver blades sent the wolves retreating in devastating pain. The women were bleeding badly as the wolves delivered numerous slashes on their legs, face, arms, and hands.

"Awe!" Kelly screamed as fangs sank into her shoulder. She drove the blade into a yellow eye, sending the wolf howling to the ground. She quickly whipped the blade around and caught another in the throat. In the backseat, Rosa swung her blade feverishly as claws ripped at her head and feet. Her blade sliced into a paw that had dug its claws into her leg and tried to pull her through the window.

Then everything stopped and the wolves retreated. The injured ones lay on the ground in fetal positions, shaking from the effects of the silver. The women were ankle high in blood-rain that continued to pour through the shattered windows. Partly blind from the blood, Kelly wiped her face with the back of her hand. She kept blinking as she waited for another attack. The wolves looked upon their fallen brothers then slowly turned their heads to glare at the women—baring the full length of their fangs.

"Shit!" Kelly said. "All we did was piss them off."

"Here they come!" Rosa said. But this time, she snarled right back at them.

Several wolves rushed toward them. The women readied themselves. But the wolves lifted the van over their heads—tilting it then shaking it violently so the women would fall out through the windows.

"Hold on!" Kelly yelled. She dropped one knife so she could grab the steering wheel. Quickly grabbing the wheel with the other hand caused the second knife to fall as well. She heard it ping when it hit the concrete.

"Delveen! No!" Rosa yelled as she helplessly watched Delveen's limp, unconscious body slide through the window and spill onto the ground.

Rosa screamed Delveen's name again and deliberately let go, viciously slashing a wolf on the way out as she fell. Rosa landed on top of the beast and rolled off. He lay howling in pain. Every muscle in Kelly's arm quivered as she tried to hold on, but her fingers weakened and she tumbled out. The wolves tossed the 4,500 pound Dodge Caravan aside like a toy, then slowly surrounded the women, snarling loudly, their yellow eyes all aflame, strings of saliva dripping from their opened mouths. Rosa held the dagger out in front of her and stabbed at them but was attacked from behind. One sunk his fangs into her shoulder while another slashed her arm with its claws, causing her to drop the blade. A group of wolves descended upon Kelly. She lowered her head and cracked her face to cry, their hot, foul breaths just inches from her head. She looked over at Rosa who was covered in wolves. Kelly tightened her jaw and waited for the first bite, when suddenly the blood-rain turned to water and washed the blood out of her eyes. The wolves, still inches from her face, suddenly froze like some mysterious mechanism had switched them all off at the same time.

The wolves looked up at the sky with amazement. A red cloud slowly parted, revealing a sparkling white, glorious moon. They lost interest in the women and backed away from them. Some turned about in a circle like they were confused, while others closed their eyes, letting the rain wash against their faces. When they opened their eyes, their irises were brown, blue, and green again. Rosa pulled away from her now bewildered attackers. Rosa, her hair bloody and flesh torn, scrambled to Delveen on her hands and knees and gathered her up in her arms. Kelly crawled to Rosa's side. The women sat huddled and held each other as the beasts appeared to be mesmerized by the moon.

The wolves stood on hind legs with their paws in the air—then on feet with hands in the air. Their naked bodies were free of fur. Their bones cracked, connecting back into the shapes of men. Their opened-mouth smiles welcomed the full moon for the first time. They swallowed the rain as if it could cleanse their souls from a century of bloodlust and shame. The thunder and lightning stopped. The rain poured like a spring shower as the blood washed into the earth and disappeared.

Chapter Fifteen

The Ford Explorer rounded the curve then picked up speed. Matthew Porter's elbow rested leisurely on the black rubber lip of the opened window. The cool wind parted his thick, dark hair. The noon sky was full of birds as if nothing strange or unusual had happened nights before, as if no blood had fallen from crimson clouds—no thunder or lightning—no werewolves, no demons, no child sacrifice, and no innocent women fighting for their lives. But it *had* happened. And Matthew, along with all the other wolves in Greyscott Falls, was damn better off for it.

He looked up into the powder-blue heavens and smiled. Then his forehead wrinkled when he checked his speed after noticing red and blue lights flashing in his side-view mirror. The white patrol car with Sheerfield County Sheriff Department written in big green letters sped up beside him.

"Pull over!" Deputy Steve Heller yelled from the patrol car megaphone.

Matthew hesitated.

"I said pull over damn it!"

Matthew looked to his right before crossing the lane. He flashed his signal, and the driver in the next lane, observing Matthew's dilemma, politely fell back so Matthew could cruise over and onto the arm of the road. The flashing patrol car lights made it easier for Steve to cruise over every lane. He pulled the patrol car behind Matthew and scrambled out with his gun drawn.

"Turn the car off and put your hands where I can see them!" he yelled with both hands on his gun, his arm straight out.

Matthew turned the key in the ignition. He kept his eyes on the deputy in his side-view mirror and slowly clicked off his seatbelt.

Steve eased up to the driver's window and motioned with his gun. "I said keep your hands where I can see them."

Matthew placed both hands on the steering wheel. "I was just unhooking my seatbelt."

"Now, keep your right hand where I can see it and unlock the door with your left hand. Now!" Steve shouted, pushing the gun closer to Matthew's face.

"All right, all right," Matthew snapped. He slowly brought his left hand down and unlocked the door.

"Keep your right hand on the wheel...open the door and get out of the car!"

Several patrol cars suddenly appeared and skidded to a halt. Doors flew open—one patrol car faced Matthew's van, the others blocked one of the lanes, causing miles of traffic to slow to a crawl. Motorists stopped to observe what was happening.

"Keep moving people," an officer commanded, waving the motorists on.

Matthew stood facing Steve. "Turn around and put your hands behind your head!" Steve ordered.

Instead, Matthew took a step toward Steve and attempted to reason with him. This misinterpreted action sent fellow officers into a frenzy.

"Step back!"

"Get down on the ground!"

"Get your ass down. Now!"

"Don't move!"

"I'll blow your goddamn head off!"

Matthew freaked out and hit the ground hard—throwing his hands behind his head and tightly locking his fingers. Although lead bullets couldn't kill him, they could cause considerable damage.

The deputies' faces were flushed with adrenaline, and their sudden action had kicked dirt in Matthew's face as they surrounded him with their guns drawn. More patrol cars rolled up, and the sound of a helicopter roared above them.

Steve holstered his gun and bent over Matthew to search him. "You got any weapons on you?"

"No."

"Any drugs?"

"No."

"Anything in your pockets that can stick me?"

"No."

Steve turned Matthew's pockets inside out and smoothed his hands up and down Matthew's jacket and faded jeans then squeezed the top of his boots.

"Any weapons in your car?"

"Yeah. A rifle…hunting rifle."

Steve stood up. He brushed past one of the officers, walked over to the van, reached in, and popped the hood. A stout officer walked to the back of Matthew's car and raised the hood of the trunk to search it. After pushing aside a blanket, some hunting knives, and other non-incriminating objects, the officer yelled, "Got it!" and held a Beanfield Sniper up in the air like he had won a trophy.

A tall female deputy scurried up to the front passenger side of Matthew's van and pulled open the door. Russell Sooner sat buckled in—dressed in his baseball uniform, with a dripping vanilla ice cream cone in his hand. "Hey little guy, are you all right?" Her stern sheriff face melted when he flashed his baby blues and nodded.

*****

When Mr. and Mrs. Sooner got the call, they rushed to Sheerfield Holy Cross Medical Center where Steve had taken Russell for a routine victim examination. Minutes before the Sooners got there, Russell had sat quietly in the examination room in a teddy bear and balloon hospital gown, eating a cookie with several medical personnel at his beck and call.

Mr. Sooner, who hadn't shaved in weeks, ran up to the nurse's station. Mrs. Sooner, no make-up and wiry blonde hair hanging raggedly down her back, fell in beside him.

"We're here for our boy, Russell Sooner," Mr. Sooner blurted, panting heavily.

The nurse looked up from noting something on a chart. "Oh, yes of course, Mr. and Mrs. Sooner. Russell is in room 316," she said, pointing. They ran down the hall where they encountered an officer stationed outside the room. He looked at them sternly.

"We're Russell's parents," Mr. Sooner said.

The officer's eyes softened and he stepped aside. The Sooners entered the room where Russell sat on a tan hippo with pink toenails, a smiling face, and big brown eyes. The top of the hippo was the exam table. The walls were light-purple with a dark-purple wall border smattered with little yellow daises. One wall had a painting of a green-leaf tree filled with blue jays the other had a painting of a toy doctor's kit. There were multi-colored chart holders on the doors of the wall cabinet. A male nurse who had just finished taking Russell's vitals for the third time watched the boy's face light up when his parents appeared in the doorway. They ran in and grabbed him, smothering him with hugs and kisses, tears flowing down their faces. The nurse stood back and let loose a beaming smile.

"My baby," Mrs. Sooner cried. Her eyes flashed up at the nurse. "Is he all right?"

"He had a slight temperature when he arrived, but it's normal now."

"Oh sweet Jesus," she said, kissing Russell's pink cheeks. Mr. Sooner joined in with a squeeze.

The staff on the children's wing was said to have cheered loudly after learning of Russell's safe return. After a few moments, the doctor entered the room and appeared to enjoy the Sooners' celebration. "Don't mean to interrupt, but I'm Doctor Lorac," she said, smiling and extending her hand to Mr. Sooner. He shook it then she reached past him and shook Mrs. Sooner's hand

"Doctor Lorac, I was just telling my husband that Rusty seems fine. And the nurse says his vitals are normal. Is there any reason why we can't take him home today?"

Doctor Lorac, looking quite serious, pulled up a chair and opened Russell's chart. Mr. Sooner scooted next to his wife and cupped her hand. Russell sat with his legs folded under him, sipping a juice the nurse had given him. The only noise was the wheels of a nurse pushing a blue elephant medicine cart as it rolled by.

Matthew sat handcuffed to a chair at the sheriff station. Sheriff Tilbert and Deputy Heller sat across from him while several deputies watched from a two-way mirror outside the room.

"Now, let's start at the beginning, shall we?" Wayne said, attempting to wear Matthew down until he got the truth.

Matthew dropped his head and stared down at the floor. "I'm not telling that story again. Either charge me with something, or let me go."

"You're not going anywhere you pervert piece of shit," Steve said, hopping up and walking over to Matthew with his fist clenched.

Wayne grabbed Steve by the arm and pulled him back. "No call for that." Steve stepped back after he and Matthew exchanged dark looks.

"Now," Wayne said, "after you found him wandering by the side of the road, then what?"

Matthew exhaled hard. "I told you. I asked the kid if he were lost. He didn't speak at first, just looked at me like he was in a daze or something. I asked him his name and where he lived, and he told me. He agreed to a ride home. On the way there, I ran into you guys...and now I'm here. End of story." Matthew flopped back in the chair.

"You want us to believe this kid willingly got into your car...a stranger...someone he's never seen before?" Steve interjected.

Matthew said nothing. He tapped his handcuffs nervously against the side of the chair.

"Stop that!" Steve ordered him.

Matthew stopped cold and stared off in the distance.

There was a long pause. Steve studied Wayne's face. Matthew scooted around in his chair and swallowed hard. Wayne stared at Matthew, then sucked his teeth and said, "Let him go."

Steve's heavy voice hit a high note. "What?"

Outside the two-way mirror, hands went up in the air and mouths dropped.

"You can't be serious."

"Look, the boy doesn't remember a thing. The doc says there's no physical evidence that the child's been harmed in anyway. And this guy doesn't even have a freaking parking ticket. So, what the hell am I supposed to do?"

"The kid doesn't remember anything because Mr. Dirt bag over there probably drugged him or something."

"We don't know that."

"Holy Moses!" Steve smacked his palm with his fist and glared at Matthew.

"Let it go, Steve. I mean it. If the kid remembers anything, and we need to arrest him, we know where he is. Oh, by the way," Wayne said, turning to Matthew, "Don't leave town." Turning back to Steve he said, "Now, get his ass out of here." Wayne walked out of the door and into the gazes of disappointment. They stared at him as if he'd just turned Jack the Ripper loose in a whorehouse.

"Anybody got something to say to me?" Wayne announced, his fists on his hips, his eyes blazing over their faces.

The staff broke and scattered in multiple directions. Wayne stormed into his office and slammed the door so hard a picture of the mayor slid off the wall and smashed on the floor.

Chapter Sixteen

River Porter couldn't get enough of the bright full moon, which marked the beginning of a series of new nights for him and his pack. Families of wolves camped around a crackling fire roasting lamb, guzzling beer, singing, and rejoicing in their newfound freedom from the curse while their children played night-ball nearby. It was the first time the pack had witnessed what other creatures had known for centuries—just how beautiful and glorious the full moon could be without the dread of bloodlust.

River took a deep breath and closed his eyes. The night air filled his lungs with a natural fragrance that embodied ecstasy and joy. Jewel joined him on the patio and placed her head against his shoulder.

"I'm pregnant," she said softly. "The goddess has forgiven us and has granted me a son."

This was music to River's very soul, and a tear formed in the corner of his eye. Merchant, his grandfather's name, rolled over in his mind. *It is a good name for my son*, he thought. Without looking at Jewel, River slipped his arm around her waist and held her at his side. They stood and gazed at the moon. He kissed her forehead many times as they listened to the high-pitched laughter of their neighbors and the playful screams of the children. For the moment, words seemed insignificant because the gentle touch of their hands said it all.

*****

On the edge of Norwick Forrest near Hamstead Creek, the young adult wolves, along with some local beauties, held their own party away from the prying eyes of their parents. Interpol's rock classic "All Fired Up" defined the mood as a young brunette scurried by and shoved fresh cold bottles of beer into the hands of Matthew and Kayla, then hurried off to shove one into each remaining reaching hand.

The night wind lightly brushed against Kayla's honey-blonde hair. Matthew threw his head back and downed his beer in one gulp, then tossed the empty bottle into the trash basket. He grabbed Kayla and roughly pulled her to him. She let the half empty beer bottle slip from her fingers to the grass. He parted his lips and took hers into his mouth. She moaned and wrapped her arms around his neck while the torrid sounds of the rock album helped them lose themselves in the sweetness of their own world. He kissed her long and passionately. She broke away momentarily and rested her cheek against his chin, then pulled back a little and noticed his gaze.

"Why do you keep looking up and smiling?" she asked. "You act as if you've never seen the moon before."

Matthew choked on the truth, "Oh, be...because I'm standing under it with the most beautiful girl in the world," he stammered, still gazing up.

"Then...shouldn't you be looking at me," she teased, cocking her head to one side.

He grabbed her by the waist and lifted her above his head. "You're right," he said, smiling up at her. She giggled as he brought her back down then playfully wrestled her to the ground, tumbling on top of her. His body pressed against hers, and he smothered her neck and shoulders with multiple kisses. She ran her fingers through his dark hair and tightened them around the locks. She pushed him away playfully and pouted her plump lips like he'd been naughty.

"I've missed you," she said. "For weeks, I thought you were avoiding me."

"No. I just had some urgent family matters I had to deal with. I'll make it up to you, I promise."

She looked over at him and frowned. "I hope nothing too serious."

Nothing too serious? he thought. He envisioned the severed head of Tiara Winters and a hysterical Raymond hugging it to his chest. He knew that would never be him and Kayla—not now, not ever, thanks to Aunt Jewel.

Matthew sat up and she joined him before sliding next to him. The light of the moon, mixed with the park lights, loomed above them. Earlier, Matthew had explained to his cousin Rick why he wanted to tell Kayla he was a werewolf, but Rick angrily advised against it. He told Matthew that humans simply couldn't be trusted with a secret—especially one as delicate as theirs. Matthew disagreed. He would wait for the right moment, he told Rick. Matthew was sure she'd understand. Their feelings for each other were stronger than any secret. Rick told him he had no right—that it wasn't just his secret, and that he'd be endangering them all. Matthew promised not to implicate anyone else. "If you insist on doing this," Rick had warned. "I will have to tell the others." Matthew promised, "I won't say anything without first talking it over with my parents." But Rick scolded him, "You'll talk it over with the pack. We're not leaving our fate in the hands of your parents."

Kayla snapped her fingers. "Hey, earth to Matthew. Come in," she joked.

Matthew looked over at her. Kayla fell back onto the grass—he fell beside her and stroked her hair.

"Where were you just then?"

"I was lost in the beauty of your love," he said, clowning.

"Liar." She playfully smacked his face, and they rolled about on the grass wrestling and kissing. Later on, while Kayla giggled, Matthew threw her over his shoulder and carried her deeper into a thick area of the forest. He laid her down upon the cool ground where they spent the next hour naked in each other's arms.

*****

It was 11:45 and Doctor Lorac was just about to have a nightcap when her doorbell rang.

"Who the devil is that at this hour?" she thought out loud.

She walked briskly to the door and peeked through the peep hole. It was Charlton Daniels, the young pathologist from the medical center. She unbolted the door, undid the night chain, and opened it.

"Charlie?"

"Doctor Lorac, I apologize for stopping by so late. May I come in? It will only take a minute."

Doctor Lorac moved aside. "Of course," she said. "Come in."

He wiped his feet before stepping onto the shiny hardwood floor. She closed the door then gestured to him. "Please, have a seat."

She followed closely behind him as he turned and walked over to the multi-colored sofa. "Can I get you a brandy? I was about to have one myself," she asked.

"Yes, thank you. And make mine a double if you don't mind," he said, giving the living room a good looking over.

Doctor Lorac walked over to the Brookfield bar and poured brandy into two snifters. She walked back and handed one to Charlton. After placing his palm under the glass and giving it a few swirls, he sipped the brandy and leaned forward to gaze down into the glass as if he were searching for what to say. She eased herself down into a high-back chair that faced him and took a sip of her drink. He looked up at her.

"Doctor Lorac, you've known me a long time. I...I mean at least a few years." He stopped and took another sip. Doctor Lorac sat watching him under her dark lashes—her eyes fixed on his worrisome gaze. He continued. "What I'm about to tell you is going to sound unbelievable, I know. But I...I beg you to hear me out."

"Charlie what on earth has gotten you so spooked?"

"Just hear me out," he said, then sipped more of his drink. "You know the Sooner boy's blood sample you sent me?"

"Yes. What about it?"

"Well, I lied about the results."

"What do you mean, you lied?"

"Two of the blood collection tubes had missing labels. I'm not sure what happened. I checked the list and saw whose labels were missing. So, I went down to the children's wing, found the two kids, and drew their blood again. Both hated being stuck a second time, by the way. If their little pouts could kill, I'd be dead right now."

"Okay, but you stated that Sooner's results were normal. Now you're telling me you lied? Why?"

"I didn't know what else to do." Charlton looked at her sternly without batting an eye. "The truth is, the blood is not human." He quickly threw up a hand. "Now, I know that sounds crazy, but I tested it three times to make sure, and...and, I'm telling you, it's not human. I'm going to take it to the state lab and get their opinion, but I wanted to run it by you first." Charlton took a deep breath and waited for her response.

"Charlie, that's absurd. If the blood isn't human, then what is it?"

"That's just it. I don't know."

"I'm sure there's an explanation. Did you check the equipment?"

"There's nothing wrong with the equipment," he said a bit irritated. "I told you, I tested it three times. And the other child's results were fine."

"But, that doesn't make any sense."

"I figured you wouldn't believe me. That's why I'm taking it to the lab."

"Have you...shared this with anyone else?" she asked squinting at him.

"No. Of course not."

Doctor Lorac stared at him while slowly placing her drink on the glass end-table before standing up. "Charlie," she said, walking swiftly to the door, "I think you should go home and get some sleep. And I'd remain silent about this if I were you. I wouldn't want anyone questioning your mental state." She pulled open the door and stood with the knob still in her hand.

Charlton looked down at the floor then rose, walked to the door, and stood facing her. "What I've told you may sound ridiculous, but I can assure you..."

"Good night, Charlie," she interrupted, avoiding his eyes.

The night air breezed through the door as she held it open. Charlton lowered his head and eased by her. "Goodnight, Doctor Lorac. Sorry I bothered you." He walked slowly out into the night. She closed the door behind him then casually walked over to the kitchen nook, picked up the phone, and dialed. She drummed her fingers on the counter as it rang.

A ringing broke through the dark silence of a bedroom. A sleepy Jewel rolled over from beneath the arm of her husband. She lifted her head from the pillow, turned on the light, and clicked the phone. "Hello," Jewel said in a whispery voice.

"Wake River. We've got a problem."

Chapter Seventeen

Jewel blinked several times to clear her eyes. She swung her legs from under the covers and sat on the edge of the bed. The fluff of the scatter-rug slipped between her toes when she placed her feet on the floor. River quietly snored behind her. Half-awake now, Jewel switched the phone to her other ear. "What do you mean we've got a problem?" she asked.

"Charlie Daniels, the pathologist at the medical center, was just here. He was all pale and looked as if he'd seen a ghost," Dr. Lorac said.

"You're waking me at...," she looked over at the clock, "...twelve o'clock at night to tell me you had a visitor?"

"Jewel, please. Don't be ridiculous. Just listen. Charlie has discovered the Sooner boy's inhuman blood and..."

"What! You were supposed to take care of that."

"I did, damn it. I switched in a tube of my own blood."

"Then what happened?"

"Somehow the labels fell off two of the collection tubes—one was Russell Sooner's and the other another child's. Charlie went back to the children's rooms and drew their blood again. So..."

"... Are you telling me that this pathologist actually tested Russell's blood?"

"I'm afraid so. Jewel, I'm sorry. I really thought I had it covered."

Jewel's shoulders slumped. She left the edge of the bed, walked across the room, and stood in front of the bedroom window. The temperature of the floor chilled her bare feet and woke her more. "It's not your fault," she said, running her fingers through her hair. "What are the odds that his blood sample would be in one of the tubes with a missing label?"

Dr. Lorac strolled over to the chair and sat down. She leaned back and crossed her legs. "I'll do whatever you want to make this right," she said, grabbing her glass of brandy from the end table. "Just tell me what you want me to do." She drained her glass and waited for Jewel to answer.

"No, you've done your part. As I said, it wasn't your fault. I'll tell River, and we'll take it from here."

"You'd better hurry then. I told Charlie not to mention it to anyone, but from the looks of him a few minutes ago, I don't think he can sit on this. He said something about taking the sample to the state lab."

Jewel turned quickly from the window and slowly walked back toward the bed where River stirred. He lifted his head from the pillow and widened his eyes at her. "Who the hell is that at this hour?"

"Just a minute honey," she said, crinkling her nose up at him. "He's got to be stopped, Sally."

"Sally? Who's got to be stopped?" River asked, yawning.

Jewel shushed him then asked Dr. Lorac, "When is he taking it to the state lab?"

"He didn't say exactly. They're closed on weekends, so he can't do anything until Monday anyway."

"Thank the stars for that. It gives us just enough time to stop him. Thanks for the warning, Sally." Jewel clicked off and laid the phone on the night table. She flopped down on the bed and faced River.

River sat up and put his pillow behind his back. "Now, can you tell me what's going on...and what Sally wanted that's gotten you looking so pale?"

"You're not going to like this," she said.

"Shit! Now what?"

"Something happened with the switched blood sample and Charlie, that's the pathologist, tested Russell's blood."

"How the hell did that happen?"

"Does it really matter?"

"And now he knows." River said, avoiding her eyes. "Anyone else know?"

"I don't think so. Whoever he tells is not going to believe him. But Sally thinks he might be planning on taking the sample to the state lab Monday morning."

"Like hell he will."

"That's my baby. Problem solved," she said, patting his hand and sliding under the covers.

"Oh, just like that, huh. I get to clean up the mess?"

"It's so nice to have a wolf around the house," she joked.

"Yeah, especially when witches screw up."

She turned to him sharply. "You take that back."

"Make me," he said with a chuckle.

Jewel quickly sat up, grabbed her pillow, and hit River over the head several times until he, all the while laughing, apologized. He pulled the pillow from her hand and placed it back behind her. She clicked off the light. He gathered her in his arms, and they slid down and huddled together under the covers.

"What are you planning on doing?" she asked, snuggling up to him.

"I'll call Dex, Rick, Matt, and a few other wolves. See what we can come up with."

"You're not going to hurt him?" Her voice was somewhat poignant.

"That depends on him."

"River, promise me you won't hurt him."

River sighed but said nothing.

Jewel's voice rose. "Riv...ver."

"All right," he said. "I won't draw blood."

"Is that the best 'yes' you can give me?"

He kissed her on the forehead, rolled over on his side of the bed, and pulled the covers up over his shoulder. In a matter of minutes, he was fast asleep.

*****

The next afternoon, Dex, Matthew, Rick, and six other wolves gathered in River's house, in the clubroom, where they had been summoned earlier that morning. The girls were at the movies, and Jewel was out with Beatrice baby shopping. The men sat on the dark u-shaped sectional sofa—each nursing a cold bottle of beer. River stood in front of them, leaning against the bar. He took a swig of his beer then placed the bottle on the marble counter. His forehead wrinkled and he gently bit his lower lip before speaking.

"This better be good, River. I gotta get my trout home for dinner," Dex said, smelling like a fish market.

"I have bad news. And I need you guys' help."

"Oh damn!" Dex blurted. "What is it now?"

"Sally, Dr. Lorac to most of you, called Jewel last night with some depressing news." The men sat listening, swilling beer, their faces turning grim as River slowly spilled the details about the pathologist.

"So…where do you want the body buried?" Rick said with a smirk.

"Negative. Jewel made me promise not to hurt him."

One of the other wolves spoke up. "You think this guy's gonna just hand the tube over? What do you mean, don't hurt him?"

"Of course we may have to hurt him. But I promised Jewel I wouldn't draw blood."

"You always do what your wife says?" a young wolf blasted him.

"If I don't want to be turned into a little green frog—yeah."

"Haaah!" the men's laughter filled the room.

"I'm sure glad witchcraft skipped over my wife," said another wolf.

"Yeah, but it landed on your mother-in-law pretty good. Isn't *Mommy Dearest* still living with you and Nancy?"

More laughter and lots of high-fives ensued at that remark. Everyone knew his mother-in-law called the shots.

"No wonder you're home promptly every night," Rick teased.

"And all this time I thought it was Nancy making you toe the line," Matthew joked.

The room erupted with more laughter and hand slaps. The young wolf took the teasing on the chin and cracked a half-smile.

"All right, all right. Let's get back to the problem at hand," River scolded.

But then an older wolf took a stand. He stood with his chest out—his dark hair frosty with grey. "See, that's what's wrong with you young pups today. You're not real wolves. Now, in my day, a wolf ruled his home. Take my wife's mother. She lived with us for a while. And one day she opened her mouth once too often. I grabbed her by the neck..."

"And did you snap it?" a young wolf asked eagerly.

"Well...no. But she knew I could have."

"Awe!" The wolves yelled, followed by loud laughter, jeers, and hands waving the old wolf to sit down.

River banged his fist on the bar several times. "Okay, guys, guys, settle down. Now, this is important. This blood tube thing could affect us all. Please, fellas."

"River is right," Dex said. "And no more beer until the meeting is over."

"Nawh!" the men growled with disappointment, but Dex finally got them to sit quietly with ears tuned-in. River laid out his plan, while other wolves offered suggestions. Nearly an hour passed, and a little scheme was drafted. After guzzling more beer, the wolves left and went their separate ways.

*****

The weekend faded quickly. Monday morning rose with a bright orange sky. Charlton Daniels sat seven floors high in his luxury condo sipping a cup of freshly brewed coffee while sitting at the table on his balcony that faced a quiet creek. He kept twisting the tube of blood between his thumb and fingers, looking at it like it held some deep, life-altering secret. The ringing of his phone startled him out of his deep thought. He laid the tube by the sugar bowl and clicked his phone. He frowned when he saw the name. "Doctor Lorac?"

"Charlie, good morning. I...want to apologize for the way I acted a few nights ago and to tell you that if you insist on taking the blood sample to the state lab today, there's a shortcut that can get you there faster. I know you don't welcome a two-hour drive."

"Thank you. That's very kind. I wasn't aware of a shortcut."

"It's a backroad behind Norwick Forest. Not too many people use it. I doubt many even know about it."

"I…think I know where that is."

"With your GPS system, you shouldn't have a problem finding the lab from there."

"Thank you again. Awe, actually, I was just about to leave…"

"Oh, of course. I don't want to hold you up. We'll talk later," she said.

"Sure thing." Charlton clicked off and drank the rest of his coffee. He put the tube in a small brown envelope and slid the envelope inside his sports coat pocket. He walked from his balcony to the back of the kitchen where he stepped into his private elevator and rode down to the garage.

Dr. Lorac immediately phoned River who was standing by.

"River?"

"Yeah."

"He bought it."

"Good, we're on our way."

Chapter Eighteen

Charlton pulled out of the garage onto the quiet street. Up ahead, the caution light had been yellow too long for him to beat the red. He eased up to the light and stopped, his left elbow resting on the black rubber of the open window. The light changed, and he drove a block before making a left on Kingston Road. He drove several more blocks and made a right on Moonhawk Drive. Twenty minutes into his journey, his phone rang. He clicked speaker. "Hello," Charlton said without checking the ID.

"Charlie," a husky male voice responded.

"Ben. I heard you were back. How was your trip?"

"Oh—just fine."

"That's good."

"I...ah...called your office and they said you weren't coming in until late. Doctor's appointment? You're not sick or anything?"

"Oh, no. I'm taking a blood sample up to the state lab."

"Boy. You're in for a long drive. No wonder you took the morning off."

"Not really. Doctor Lorac told me about this shortcut behind Norwick Forest ..."

"Norwick Forest? Doctor Lorac told you that?"

"Yeah."

"You sure you understood her correctly? Sally's lived here all her life. There's nothing back there except a swamp and some dead trees. Doesn't take you anywhere."

"Are you certain?

"I'm positive. That's why folks around here call it the dead-end forest. Check with her again. It's probably just a miscommunication. Anyway, I've got to get to a meeting. But the only way to the state lab from Sheerfield is I-83 north—straight shot."

"Eighty-three north. Got it. Thanks, Ben."

"My pleasure. Talk to you soon."

Charlton, his face now devoid of expression, clicked off and laid the phone aside. Coming to a stop sign, he mashed on his brake. While several pedestrians crossed, he sat staring through vague eyes—he flinched when an impatient driver hit her horn. He spotted a 7-Eleven a couple of blocks away, drove there, and parked. He sat drumming his fingers on the steering wheel and watching people stroll in and out through the glass doors. He picked up his phone and placed his thumb on Dr. Lorac's number but laid the phone back down. He smoothed a hand over his flaming red hair and sighed hard. Then, as if someone had pinched his bottom, he jumped forward and started up the car, pulling out of the parking lot and back onto the street—heading for the road Dr. Lorac had suggested. He didn't know why, but he just had to see for himself if Ben was right. *Maybe a new road had been built, and Ben didn't know about it. Yeah, that's it,* he thought. *Ben is so busy traveling around the world, he wasn't aware of recent developments in Sheerfield. Sure. And Dr. Lorac, well, she's just being kind—knowing how a four-hour drive to the lab and back would tire me out. Besides, I'm needed back at the lab and this shortcut would get me back sooner.*

He endured numerous red lights, stop signs, old folks jaywalking with their metal canes, drivers stopping suddenly without signaling, slow-moving farm trucks, sharp curves, and deer crossings until he found himself on a long, dark, and silent stretch of a road lined with tall trees. He slowed the car to a near crawl, turning his head right and left. There was nothing but blackness beyond the trees and a stench like dead animal permeated the air.

A deep-seated curiosity seemed to be pushing him on. He drove deeper and deeper behind the forest. As he rounded a fourth dirt curve, he noticed a red Dodge Caravan with the hood up, and a very attractive young woman bending over it. The tight jeans she wore parted her butt cheeks well. Charlton stopped. The woman looked up and waved at him. She pushed her long blonde hair away from her face and smiled. "Hey there," she called. "I seem to have made a wrong turn then the damn thing just cut off on me. Sure could use your help."

Charlton looked around him before he spoke. He stuck his head out the window. "Looks like I did the same. Awe...made a wrong turn, that is. Haven't you called someone?"

She shook her head. "Phone's dead."

"You can use mine." The blonde beauty just stood there, her green eyes gazing at him. "I can, maybe, give you a ride," he said. "Where are you trying to get to?"

She put a fist on her curvy hip. "Grundy County."

"You really did make a wrong turn."

"Tell me about it," she said, posing in six-inch heels.

Charlton struggled to gather his words. "Actually, I'm not very good at fixing things. I'll be more than glad to drop you somewhere."

"It's my dad's car and he'd have a hell of a fit if I left it out here. Sure wish you'd take a look at it," she said, her green eyes dancing as a long blonde curl sat in an s-shape on one of her full breasts.

Charlton sighed heavily. He looked right and left again before checking the side and rearview mirrors. The young beauty's eyes widened when she saw him backing out. "Hey! You're not leaving me here?"

"I'll...awe...send someone back for you," he yelled at her as he turned and tore out of there. Her obscenities echoed above the squeals of his tires as he roared off. After he'd driven about a quarter of a mile, he hit speed dial then speaker. Dr. Lorac's phone rang.

"Hello."

"Why the hell did you lie to me?"

"Charlie, calm down. What's happened?"

"What was supposed to happen? You tell *me*." Dr. Lorac answered but Charlton wasn't listening. Something in his left mirror had caught his eye. It was the red Dodge and it was speeding up on him fast like a shark after its prey. "Shit!"

Dr. Lorac's voice faded as he tossed the phone and mashed the accelerator. Rounding a bend, Charlton braked just in time to make a sudden sharp left turn. The wheels screeched loudly like a dog in pain while dust flew up and hit the windshield, nearly blinding his view. Two hundred feet behind him, the red Dodge swerved around the same curve with ease, creating a mini–dust storm.

A straight patch of road lay ahead. Charlton was doing eighty with the red Dodge still in close view. Charlton braked and went around another curve, but the car swerved out of control. He held the steering wheel, though every vein in his hands was popping up. The car shot across the lane and off the side where the wheels spat gravel until he managed to guide the car back onto the road. He looked at his side mirror and the red Dodge was right on him. He had a head start, but could he keep the lead? Could he hold on to it until he was clear of this godforsaken place—clear to see street lights, houses, live animals, people again?

Charlton increased his speed but couldn't shake the Dodge. "Damn it!" he growled.

The red Dodge was coming, no—blazing. The two hundred feet became one hundred feet, fifty feet, twenty-five, a few feet, a few inches—then so close, like a dog sniffing another dog's ass. Suddenly, the Dodge fell back and shot from behind. Charlton swallowed hard—he was finally face to face with his pursuer—Matthew and Rick, both dressed in black and wearing dark shades, but no green-eyed blonde. Side by side, the two drag raced, dust and dirt swirling around both cars.

Charlton was leaning forward with both hands tightly on the wheel—his eyes glancing back at the teen wolves. His breathing was heavy: beads of sweat poured from his forehead, and the blue veins in his temple were pulsating as he watched the red Dodge inch closer to him.

"What do you want?" Charlton screamed at them. Rick, who was in the passenger seat, waved for him to pull over.

"Go to hell!" Charlton yelled, and he surged ahead of the Dodge.

Matthew roared up and rammed him, forcing the car off the road and into the dirt, but Charlton fought the wheel as the car bounced up and down over rocks and animal carcasses. His jaw tightened as he soared back onto the road. He slammed his car into the Dodge, catching Matthew off-guard. Matthew swerved but maintained control. The two cars rammed each other back and forth—whipping through turns like twin cars on a rollercoaster track. Another hard ram from the Dodge forced Charlton onto the dirt, but this time his car rolled into the path of a dark wooded area, missed several trees, then finally side-swiped a huge stump before coming to a halt. Charlton sat dazed for a moment, dust and dead leaves flying all around. He managed to unfasten his seatbelt, but the damaged door wouldn't budge. He kicked it open and bolted.

Running through these woods was like a blind man stumbling through someone's backyard. Only the sunlight streaming through the top of the trees provided any visibility. Panting hard, he stopped and turned but saw nothing—nothing chasing him, just the darkness all around covering him like a ghastly sheet of black.

Then, suddenly from beyond the blackness, came a sound like something moving fast. He spotted a giant hollow tree. He ran and ducked inside the hole of the tree, covering his mouth to muffle his loud breathing.

River's wolf vision made it easy for him to scan the darkness. A wicked grin etched across his face when his gaze fell upon the hollowed tree. "Hey Charlie!" he called from across the distance.

Charlton's body grew stiff, and his breathing deepened. He stuck his head out and took a quick peek to his left, then snatched it back inside the tree hole.

Hushed laughter surrounded Rick's voice pouring from the shadows. "Chaaar...leee," Rick sang out.

Mathew cupped his mouth like a megaphone. "Come out, come out wherever you are."

Charlton whipped his head to the right. Nothing but the dark met his gaze. His pulse pounded in the veins of his neck. His lips quivered.

"We can smell you, Charlie."

"Did you piss yourself you naughty boy?" Charlton heard a chuckle that became menacing in the darkness.

Charlton's eyes rolled back and forth. His forehead wrinkled as he slid a shaky hand to his crotch. It was wet. "Damn," he whispered.

"Funny thing about wolf noses, Charlie," Dex said, striking a pose just outside the hollow tree where Charlton was hiding. Dex leaned around. "BOO!"

Charlton's spit caught in his throat at the sight of Dex's shadowy face, and his legs weakened beneath him. "Jesus Christ!" He said in a high pitched voice. "Who *are* you people? What do you want?"

"Just give us the tube," Rick said.

"And...we'll let you go," said Matthew, raising his arms out to the side. He and Rick stepped into view and stood ten feet in front of Charlton, with a stream of sunlight at their backs.

"You! Both of you!" Charlton pointed his finger at Matthew and Rick. "You're the ones in the red van that ran me off the road. You could have killed me."

River eased into a stream of light. "Nobody wants to hurt you, Charlie," he said in a calm voice. "Just give us the blood."

"But, what do you want with it? It's just blood." He nervously laughed. "I...I mean—"

"You know what's in that tube," Dex said. "That's why you're taking it to the state lab. So, don't play us stupid."

River clenched his teeth. "Hand it over, Charlie. Now!"

Charlton stood straight up and stepped out of the hollow of the tree. He kept his thighs tightly together to hide the pee stain and attempted to look defiantly at them. "Or what?" he said, staring right at River.

"Did...did he just say, 'Or what?'" Rick asked.

Dex pulled on his chin. "I believe he did."

"You've got guts. I give you that," River said. "It's a shame—in about five seconds they're going to be hanging from the mouths of our friends over there." He nodded to his left.

"What do you mean?" Charlton asked, squinting. "What friends?"

Six men withdrew from the blackness. Piece by piece, they stripped off their clothes.

"Wha...what are they doing? Why are they removing their clothes? You...you're not going to let them rape me? Jesus Christ!" Charlton broke. He got in three good steps before River dashed, grabbed him, and shoved him hard against a tree. "You try that again, and I'll cut your eyeballs out," he said, mashing Charlton's nose with the flat side of a blade.

Charlton stood, not so brave now, and looked past River, keeping his eyes glued to the men. A lump rose in Charlton's throat. River turned, and his face brightened. Aroused by what was about to happen, his chest rapidly rose and fell as he watched his six brethren go down on all fours, their eyes turning a deep yellow. Their skin darkened as fur grew out and covered their razor-bump skins. Bones cracked like trampled tree branches, and faces elongated. Six-inch fangs and claws sprang into place like fruit rapidly growing on a vine.

"Holy Mother of God," Charlton said, making the sign of the cross.

The wolves' howls scattered the buzzards out of the trees, and land scavengers shot in all directions. The wolves' huge paws slowly inched toward Charlton. He slid down the tree like every muscle had left his body. Trembling with his knees drawn up to his chest, he reached into his inside jacket pocket, pulled out the brown envelope with the tube of blood, and held it out to no one in particular.

"You think we should let him off that easy?" Dex joked, turning to River.

"Naw." River grinned. "How about making him play fetch?"

"Yeah. I'll throw him and we'll let one of the wolves go fetch him."

"Don't!" Charlton pleaded.

The wolves stood, saliva hanging from their mouths, the yellow balls of their eyes glaring at Charlton through tiny slits.

"Let's just send one over to pick up our little package," River said.

Charlton jumped forward. "No! Here." He placed the envelop far from him on the ground and jumped back.

"Go and pick it up," River ordered. "Or I'll have them rip your face off."

"All right! All right! No need for that," he said. He crawled over, picked it up, and scrambled back to the tree. He stretched out his arm with the envelope in his hand.

One of the wolves, his black fur streaked with silver, pranced over. He stopped in front of Charlton's outstretched arm and stood. Charlton turned his head and shut his eyes tight. The wolf bypassed his arm and moved in a few inches from his head. He leaned in, curled back his lips, and ran the tip of a fang across Charlton's face. The red line thickened, and a thread of blood ran down his cheek. Charlton's body shook. "Please, please. I don't want to die. Just take it." His eyes were still shut tight and a terrible smell rose from his trousers.

The wolf sniffed him in disgust, stepped back, took the envelope in his mouth, and trotted away into the darkness, closely followed by the other five wolves.

"Remember, we know where you live and work," River said. He, Dex, Matthew, and Rick strolled off into the forest, leaving Charlton alone and shaken.

Back where the red Dodge and other vans were parked, River stopped and opened the brown envelope he'd taken from the wolf. He pulled out the tube of blood, let it fall to the ground, and smashed it under the heel of his boot. He tossed the envelope and raked his heel across some brush to clean off the blood. Then he turned to a naked teen wolf getting dressed and smacked him upside the head.

"Hey! What the hell?" the young wolf yelled.

"I told my wife I wouldn't draw blood. You made me break that promise."

"You said to scare him."

"He *was* scared! Don't you know human shit when you smell it?"

"Haaah!" The other wolves laughed.

Then one said, "That crazy bastard really thought we were going to rape him."

"After he saw what we were really capable of, I bet he wished we had," said another wolf, grinning.

There were rounds of laughter and lots of kidding. Car doors banged, and the sounds of tires crushing gravel died into total silence.

*****

Chalton, disheveled and bruised, resembled Frankenstein's monster with his arms outstretched, blindly stumbling and feeling his way through the darkness. At one point, frightened by his own shadow, he ran, fell over a stump, and got quite a bump on his forehead. Then, after a short walk, he saw his car up ahead. "Thank you, God," he said. He ran to it, smacked the hood with a wet kiss then jumped into the car. He turned the key several times, but it choked and went dead. Charlton reached for his phone and called Ben. But within seconds of talking to Ben, who wanted to know every detail, he dropped the phone from his ear. He twisted his mouth at Ben's rapidly firing questions squeaking out of the phone. He yelled down at it. "Damn it! Just come get me!"

"All right, awe...pants, underwear, and adult wipes. Gotcha!"

Chapter Nineteen

It was late in the afternoon when Ben drove off 49 south and onto the dark road leading to the dead-end forest. He remembered the area well. As a boy, after being called a scaredy-cat by his friends, he had joined them there on a bike ride one Halloween night—a night that haunted his childhood for many years.

Ben squinted, looking left and right through the sun-beaten windshield. All he had gotten from a hysterical Charlton was that he'd been run off the road by some fiendish characters. Ben slowed down and searched for skid marks as a clue to where Charlton could be waiting. A few more minutes, and it was checkmate; he observed dark tire markings leading into a forced path in the woods. He pulled off the road and followed the artistic tread marks through the soft ground and dead leaves, gravel crunching under his own tires. As his car inched deeper into the wooded area, it was as if the sky had blinked from day to night. Ben's jaw dropped as he peered through the sudden darkness. He swallowed hard and mumbled to himself. Then a stream of sunlight lit fresh scrapings on several trees that acted as arrows pointing him to a stump. He sighed in relief after seeing Charlton's damaged, grey Buick sitting like an abandoned junk car. Ben eased up and parked.

When he got out of the car and walked up to the Buick, he found Charlton sitting with his forehead resting against the steering wheel. Ben's tapping on the window caused Charlton to jump. When Charlton saw it was Ben, his shoulders eased down and he opened the door.

"Ben, thank God. I wasn't sure you'd find me."

Ben wrinkled his nose at the odor escaping from the car. "You...you all right?"

"Yeah. Did you bring what I asked?"

"Yes. I'll get them."

Ben hurried back to his car. He reached over the driver's seat and brought out a dark cloth shopping bag. Charlton was standing on the outside when Ben returned and handed him the bag.

Charlton walked to the back of his Buick and Ben looked away while Charlton pulled off his pants.

"I know you have a lot of questions," Charlton said, tossing aside his soiled underwear. "I'll try to explain on the way back."

"Sure thing, Charlie. I'll go start the car." Ben walked swiftly back to his car, holding his breath as Charlton stood naked from the waist down and peeled open the pack of adult wipes.

Ben slid into his car, started it, and rolled down all the windows. Charlton scrubbed himself then slipped into the fresh underwear Ben had brought him. After putting on the pants, he walked over to Ben's car and got in. Ben started the car and slowly backed out. Charlton stared into the blackness where he'd been held captive by the wolves. To block out the memories, he shut his eyes until Ben was clear out of the woods and back onto the road.

The beginning of the drive was spent in many minutes of total silence. A bad reception spot on the road made it impossible for radio or phone signals to get through. Ben looked over at Charlton several times but neither spoke. Ben tried to whistle, but only air and spit came out of his mouth.

"I know something happened," Ben said. "And I'm trying to be patient. You call me scared out of your mind. I drop everything to come to this God-awful place. Find you dirty, your face bloody and smelling like piss and shit, and you're just going to sit there and say nothing?"

Charlton tapped his knee with his fingertips but didn't answer. Ben took his eyes off the road. "I'm in the dark here, Charlie. Help me out," he said in a high-pitched voice. Ben had to focus back on the road and the sharp curve that was coming up ahead. There was another long silence. Ben's jaw tightened and he shook his head. Charlton stopped tapping and stared, then said, as if he were in another moment of time, "I had living proof about something people had been speculating about New Berwick since I came to this town."

"What's that?" Ben asked eagerly.

"About the strange inhabitants living around us. Now the evidence is gone, thanks to your Dr. Lorac."

"What evidence? What did she do?"

"I'm sure it was no mistake, her sending me to this fake shortcut. I should have listened to you, but I just couldn't believe Dr. Lorac would lie to me. So, I decided to check it out."

"I don't understand. She deliberately sent you in the wrong direction, but why? I've known her for years. It doesn't sound like something she'd do. What could have been her motive?"

"I can't explain it, Ben. I'd tell you more, but it would only serve to make you think I'm crazy. Plus, I'm so embarrassed to have you, my friend, see me like this." His eyes filled. "I really appreciate you, Ben. But what little I've told you is all I can say right now."

"Christ, Charlie. It's no need to feel embarrassed. You've seen me at my worst many times. Remember when I got drunk that time at my tenth wedding anniversary and puked all over everybody? Remember?" Ben forced a laugh but noticed that Charlton's face remained stony. "Just tell me this," Ben said in a more serious tone. "Are you saying there's a connection between Dr. Lorac and those bastards who ran you off the road?"

"Yeah, they wanted what I was taking to the lab. But that's only the tip of the iceberg."

"What were you taking to the lab?"

"I can't tell you."

"Who were these people? Were they from around here?"

"You don't want to know."

"Damn it, Charlie!"

Charlton glanced over at him. "I'm not dragging you into this. It's too dangerous."

Ben turned his head slightly to look at him. Charlton's eyes were glazed, and his face was grim and pale. "Whatever it is, you don't have to carry this burden alone. You know that."

Charlton looked down at his lap. *How the hell can I tell him that I saw six men turn into wolves the size of bears right before my eyes.*

After no response from Charlton and a long silence, Ben turned

151

his full attention back to the winding road and said, "Okay, if you want to handle this alone then I guess I'll just have to respect that."

The rest of the journey was again quiet, so Ben clicked on his favorite music station. Twenty minutes later, he pulled up to the front of the residential building and Charlton got out. "Thanks Ben," he said then walked away from the car.

Ben watched him a little ways then leaned and yelled through the open passenger window, "Oh, Charlie, don't worry about your car. I'll have it picked up in the morning." Charlton never turned but threw up his hand as a sign of thank you.

A well-dressed doorman flashed a smile before opening the door. Charlton walked in and Ben drove off.

Inside his condo, Charlton tossed his keycard on the mahogany antique desk in the bedroom and made a beeline to the shower. He clicked the shower knob then shed Ben's clothes. Under the heat and steam, he closed his eyes as the water flowed down his hair and face, his chest and stomach, his buttocks and thighs—turning slightly brown at his ankles and swirling into the drain. He lingered there under his private waterfall like he needed to wash River and the wolves off of his skin—as if the steam could erase the yellow eyes burning into his, the wet snout on his forehead, the coarse fur brushing against his brow, and daggered fangs scraping across his cheek.

He stepped out of the shower and stood naked before the mirror. He smoothed a finger across the red line the wolf's fang had made. He jumped at the sound of his phone. He grabbed a towel and put it around his waist as he walked to where his phone lay. His top lip curled when he saw Dr. Lorac's name. He hesitated, then picked it up and clicked on.

"Go to hell, you bitch!"

He clicked off, placed the phone down on the desk, walked over to his bed, and tossed the towel aside. He plopped down, put one hand behind his head, and closed his eyes. In his sudden slumber, he shifted his body many times—eyelids fluttering, head snatching left and right, and body jerking. He sprang up to a sitting position, inhaled a noisy gush of air into his lungs, and looked around his bedroom wide eyed. The phlegm in his chest made his cough sound like a choked car engine. He eased his head back onto the pillow. Goose bumps peppered his body because the central air had kicked on while he was asleep and lying naked on top of the bedspread. He had been asleep for several hours yet it was still light.

*****

Dr. Lorac called Charlton multiple times and left messages, but none were returned.

Weeks rolled by, and Charlton had not reported for work. Dr. Lorac inquired and learned that he had called out sick. A few weeks later, Charlton walked into the office of Dr. Brighton, the chief of staff, and presented his resignation. Charlton had accepted a prestigious position at a leading hospital in another state, but asked the doctor not to disclose his whereabouts. Dr. Brighton agreed in writing that he would not release that information. Ben was the only non-relative Charlton trusted to know his new location.

In a phone call to Jewel, Dr. Lorac became distraught when she learned how the wolves retrieved the blood sample from Charlton. She made an excuse to get off the phone, then ran to the bathroom sink and splashed cold water on her face. She looked up, stared into the mirror, and hated what she saw.

Weeks later, after Charlton had left town, Dr. Lorac still couldn't shake her guilt for helping the wolves at his expense. She rarely left the house except for work and to attend church. Other times she'd mope about her house sipping a glass of brandy.

One night, at around eleven o'clock, she closed her diary and rested her back against a fluffy pillow. She had just wiped a tear from the corner of her eye when Beethoven's "Fifth Symphony" rang from her phone. She quickly picked up. "River."

"I hope I didn't wake you," River said.

"No, not at all."

"I never thanked you for the heads up. This could have been disastrous for the wolves."

"Oh…yeah…glad I could help. But I feel just awful about

Charlie. Did you really have to go that far?"

"He wasn't taking us seriously, Sally. We tried just asking, then demanding. But he was pretty stubborn…even got defiant at one point."

"Okay."

"We had no choice. But, we weren't really going to hurt him. We just—"

"I know," she interrupted. "I guess it couldn't be helped." She sighed and placed her hand on her forehead. "My head is really killing me. I've got to get some sleep. Is Jewel still up?"

"She's in the shower."

"Tell her I said good night."

"I will. And Sally, try not to worry. I'm sure wherever he is, he'll be fine."

"Yeah."

"Goodnight, Sally."

"Goodnight."

Chapter Twenty

New Berwick remained uneventful for many months. That is, nothing out of the ordinary seemed to happen. People went about their lives: working their farms, operating their businesses, taking care of their families. Then a heavy rain, unusual for the summer season, fell steadily for nearly two weeks. But it stopped as suddenly as it had begun. Strangely, though, no rainbow formed above the clouds—only darkness and a slight chill in the breeze. Mystery invaded the hours as birds disappeared, leaving their nests full of dead chicks. Dogs barked at the sky. Cats developed unusually bad tempers, and people flooded the emergency center with injuries from squirrel attacks. "Squirrel attacks?" an emergency personnel asked, chuckling.

Even forest animal behavior was reflected in the change; many hikers kept to the path and away from wooded areas. People stayed indoors, wrapped in their superstitions—only leaving when they had to and even then being extremely cautious. Residents of Sheerfield County wore wooden crosses that were blessed and passed out to parishioners during church services. Others carried silver snuff boxes stuffed with smelly herbs to ward off evil. The witches had seen these changes in nature before though not for many decades. Still, they were worried. And when witches worried, it was definitely not a good time to be human.

Several nights came and went, but one particular night a young man lay dreaming. Alone in his bed, he tossed and turned—first mumbling something inaudible then flipping his head from side to side. "No. No," he said loudly with his closed eyelids fluttering.

Then the covers mysteriously rolled from his chest to the foot of the bed, and his t-shirt pulled up to reveal his tan muscular frame. A force made small impressions on the soft spots of his abdomen like invisible lips pressing on him. A captive of his slumber, he smiled and moaned throughout the night.

Jessie Carter leaned forward at his work station and yawned. On his desk were a computer, monitor, a phone and headset, family pictures, lamp, a business card holder, and lots of pens and yellow scratch pads. His large cup of coffee with a lot of cream and sugar was lukewarm. Above his desk hung a framed copy of a Luxury Retailer Achievement award and to the far right of it a motivation sign in bold capital letters that read, ATTITUDE, APPROACH, EXPECTATION. Jessie had been a top real estate agent for Blue Hurst Realtors for more than six years.

Karl Burgess, a fellow employee, walked up and rested his arms on the partition. "Hey, Jess—rough night?"

"Ah, man," he said before yawning again. "I'm not sleeping well. I keep waking up in the middle of the night. Never had trouble before."

"You look beat." He grinned. "Okay, who is she?"

"No. Karl, I'm serious man. It's not that. I'm...I'm having these weird dreams."

"What kind of dreams?" Karl turned his head quickly and looked over his shoulder. "Shoot. That's my phone." Backing away he said, "We'll talk about those dreams later."

"Okay."

By lunch time, Jessie's tired look was very noticeable. His supervisor thought Jessie's yawning was embarrassing to customers, so he took Jessie aside and suggested that he should go home to get some sleep. Jessie apologized and swore it would never happen again.

On the way home, he couldn't stop thinking about his dreams that were in pieces and quite fuzzy in his head. He thought out loud, "Oh, no. I can't go to sleep." He had forgotten that his girlfriend, Rebecca, was coming for dinner. He couldn't postpone it. He could say he was sick. But her being a nurse, she'd want to come anyway and take care of him—even spend the night. There was only one thing to do: take some No Doze.

As soon as Jessie got home, he washed down two pills, changed his clothes, and started cleaning the apartment. He prepared the steaks and broke apart leaves of lettuce and spinach, added other ingredients then carefully blended a family recipe for the dressing.

When the doorbell rang, the apartment was spotless. The table was set, including beautiful crystalline candle holders that cupped white candles; their aroma filled the air. He opened the door and, as soon as she stepped in, she lifted her cheek for him to kiss it.

"Hm," she moaned, coming into the living room. She looked around, her eyes sparkling. As she talked about how wonderful the place looked, he handed her a glass of wine and told her to be seated while he finished preparing the sauce. The kitchen was separated from the living room and dining area by a wide picture-frame counter and bar stools. They could still see each other and talk.

"Sorry it took me so long to invite you over," he said while measuring a tablespoon of butter, "but the place was a mess and things at work—well, it's been really busy lately, which is a good thing. I'm not complaining. Busy means money." He chuckled.

"This makes up for it, honey. Everything is lovely." She took a sip of her wine as she sat and crossed her shapely legs. Her six-inch heels made them all the sexier. She smoothed her blonde hair away from her face and watched as Jessie busied himself in the kitchen.

"You know...there's something hot about a man up to his elbows in flour," she teased.

He looked up and grinned. "All done." He lifted the bowl, brought it to the table, and set it down. "Come and get it," he said.

"Hmm, smells good," she said, standing and taking a whiff of the air. She laid her glass aside and walked over to the table. He pulled out her chair, but before he sat down said, "I forgot something." He walked over to his CD collection, pulled out an Isaac Hayes love album, and loaded it into the player. He scurried back and sat facing her.

They ate and toasted each other—drank, talked, and laughed. And Sir Isaac, as Jessie and Rebecca playfully called him, soon set the mood for what was to come shortly after dinner: shoes, heels, panties, shirts, briefs, bra, and other articles of clothing made a trail from the dinner table to the master bedroom. Isaac's deep baritone voice, an empty wine bottle, and half-filled wine glasses marked the end of one part of the evening, but all had definitely contributed to the next phase taking place just a few feet away.

Rebecca, on her knees in the middle of the bed, struggled to see through the blur caused by the wine.

"Come to papa," Jessie teased.

But as her vision cleared, the color of her cheeks changed from rose to a pale, lifeless hue.

"What the hell is that?" she snapped

"What?" he asked, lying comfortably on his back.

"That," she said, pointing at his body. "And that?" she said again, pointing to his neck.

Jessie jumped up from the bed and, with his back to her, checked his body in the mirror. "What the hell?" he blurted, looking at the hickeys and bite marks all over his abdomen and neck. "I don't know where these came from."

Rebecca hopped off the bed. "And I guess you don't know how you got those scratch marks on your back either."

"What?" He turned his back toward the mirror and his mouth swung open. "I...I don't understand."

"You don't understand? You bastard." She walked around naked, snatching up her clothes. First putting on her panties then struggling to snap her bra. When she was fully dressed she snatched up her heels and walked to the door barefooted.

Jessie, naked from the waist up, scurried after her. "Honey, I swear to God, I don't know where these marks and scratches came from. It's not what you think, I swear."

Her face was fully flushed, and her eyes filled. He tried to block her from going out the door, but she shoved him aside, swung the door open, and stormed out.

He watched her stomp down the hall and turn the corner. Then he closed the door and went back to the bedroom to examine his body again. But when he looked, the hickeys, bite marks, and scratches were gone. "Wa...what the hell?" The phone ringing made him jump. He picked up.

"Hello," he said.

"Hey, Jess, sorry I was so busy at work today, I didn't have time to get back to you. Now, you said something about some dreams?"

"Man, forget the dreams. Something weird is going on with me. I...I don't know if I'm going crazy or what."

He told Karl everything that had just happened between him and Rebecca and about the marks on his body.

"Damn, that's some strange shit."

"I swear I haven't been with another woman and that's the truth."

"Wow. You think this has anything to do with the dreams?"

"Man, I don't know."

Karl said, "I have an uncle who's into a whole lot of paranormal stuff: dreams, nightmares, tarot cards, Ouija board, you name it. He might can tell you what it means. He claims God told him over twenty years ago that he was to devote his life to fighting evil. When I was little, I remember our family treating him like a leper. If you're up to it, I'll give him a call and we can go over there tonight."

"I'm so confused right now. Your weird-ass uncle sounds good to me."

"You want me to pick you up, or you want to meet me there."

"Is it far?"

"It's on the other side of Metcalf."

"I'm not familiar with that area."

"Okay, I'll be there in thirty."

*****

When Karl drove up, Jessie was pacing in front of his apartment building smoking a cigarette. He dropped the butt and crushed it under his foot, then climbed in the front seat.

"You sure your uncle can help me?"

"Well, I told him as much as I could over the phone. He didn't say he couldn't."

Jessie cracked the window and pulled a cigarette from the pack. He lit it and was careful to turn his head towards the window when he exhaled. It was nearly ten o'clock at night, and the ride became bumpy as they crossed the railroad tracks leading to the rural area.

The longer Karl drove, the fewer houses became visible from the roadside, until one house far away, sitting all alone with only a thick wooded area as part of its backyard, appeared. It sat high, and it looked like a lighthouse all lit up and shining over a vast sea of dirt and gravel.

Karl drove up and parked. He got out and walked around to the side. But Jessie just sat, hesitating to exit the car. Karl threw him a puzzled glance, and Jessie opened the door and slid out. Jessie stood by the car examining the outside of the house.

Karl said, "You going to stand there with your thumb up your butt, or are you coming?"

The men walked up to the door, and Karl knocked lightly. The door opened and a slightly balding man of about 5'8", fat and round, stood grinning.

"Come in, come in," he said, stepping aside. "Just have a seat anywhere you think is comfortable."

He closed the door and followed Karl and Jessie into a little room that looked like a gypsy palm-reading parlor. A round table sat in the middle of the floor. It was covered with a round beige table cloth, and a porcelain lamp with a worn pink lampshade sat next to it. The two dark wooden chairs had carvings of strange angelic creatures. Different colored bean bags were scattered throughout the room. Over in the far corner was a reader's end table, and, above it, a wall book shelf lined with tattered, cloth-covered books.

"Uncle Ward, this is Jessie—Jessie, my Uncle Ward."

"Glad to meet you, sir," Jessie said, extending his hand.

"My pleasure," Ward said shaking it. "Karl told me of your problem. And I understand there are some dreams?" Ward said gesturing for them to sit.

Jessie told Ward about his strange dreams. After he'd finished, Ward pulled on his chin and paced a bit in front of the table. He stopped, glanced at Jessie, and paced again. Finally, he stopped and spoke.

"This is more serious than I thought. Have you ever heard of a succubus?"

Jessie looked at Ward with a frown. "No, can't say that I have."

"It's a female demon, traced back to medieval legend," he said walking over to the bookcase and pulling a book from the shelf. "Up until now," he said, "I didn't think it really existed."

Ward walked back to the table and placed the opened book before them. He turned it so Jessie and Karl could get a good look at a sketch made by an artist who claimed he'd seen a succubus—although Ward and other paranormal experts were skeptical.

"That's really a succubus?" Jessie asked, pointing his finger at the page.

"No one truly knows what one looks like—only that it appears in dreams in the form of a beautiful, voluptuous woman in order to seduce men…usually through, but not limited to, oral sex. The male counterpart is the incubus." Ward raised his eyebrows then said, "Sex with one of these things is said to be quite intense."

"Far freaking out," Karl blurted with a wide grin.

His grin soon faded when he looked over at Jessie who had flopped back in the chair stone-faced and with his mouth open.

Ward frowned at Karl. "For God's sakes, this is not funny."

"I'm sorry Uncle Ward, I didn't mean anything. I just thought—"

"Why is this thing after me?" Jessie asked.

"I don't know, son. But that's what we need to find out."

*****

An hour ticked by, and after exhausting every possible explanation, Uncle Ward saw Karl and Jessie to the door and promised Jessie he would find out all he could about the nightly visits from the succubus. When Uncle Ward closed the front door, Jessie and Karl stood outside looking at each other in amazement because of the many clicking sounds they heard coming from the different locks Ward used to secure his home. After hearing the final click, they turned and slowly walked to Karl's car and got in.

"Dude, that was some creepy shit my uncle just laid on us. I can stay the night if you want," Karl said, buckling his seat belt.

"I don't mean to sound like a pussy, but would you? I'd appreciate it."

"Make that two pussies. That shit freaked me out too."

"You know," Jessie said. "I don't remember hearing all of those locks when your uncle first opened the door."

"Come to think of it, neither do I. Maybe your story creeped him out too."

"I guess."

The ride back to Jessie's apartment was silent. Karl had glanced over at him several times during the drive and found him quite occupied with his thoughts. Karl wanted to make conversation, if only to discover just what Jessie was thinking, but thought it better to hold back until he could, at least, contribute some answers to the mystery of the succubus and its tormenting of Jessie. Um, some torment, he thought. He couldn't get the image of a voluptuous she-demon performing mind-blowing oral sex on a spell-induced sleeping man out of his head.

Back at the apartment, they said little to each other with the exception of some small talk. After brushing his teeth, Jessie bid Karl goodnight and went into the bedroom, leaving Karl to slumber on the living room sofa. The sofa was a bit uncomfortable, and Karl found it hard to fall asleep. He turned on the TV for some late night entertainment and soon dozed off.

The next morning when Karl woke, he rose and walked into the kitchen to make coffee. He stood in the doorway yawning and scratching his butt and observed Jessie staring out the window.

"Good morning," Karl said after a wide-mouthed yawn.

Jessie never answered, but stood like a statue as he continued to stare out the window.

Karl walked over to the kitchen sink and reached above it for the cabinet knob. "How was your night?" Karl asked while looking around in the cabinet for the coffee can. He took the can down from the shelf then half-filled the glass coffee maker with water. As Karl measured the coffee grounds and added the desired amount to the filter, he continued looking over at Jessie. Karl pushed the *on* button, took down two coffee mugs, and placed them on the counter.

"Hey, you all right?" There was a pause.

"Why shouldn't I be?" was the cold and almost robotic response.

Karl walked over and placed his hand on Jessie's shoulder, gently pulling him around to face him. Karl was taken aback, and he swallowed a lump in his throat at the sight of Jessie's face: it was dark with eyes as lifeless as a shark's just before it sinks its teeth into its victim.

"For God's sake, dude, what's up with you?" Karl snapped.

Jessie's lips moved, but another voice, gruff and whispery, said, "I'm not your dude."

Next door, Mrs. Bingham, after listening a few seconds with her ear to the wall, phoned the sheriff while her husband stood at her side.

"What is your emergency?" the dispatcher asked.

"Send officers to 200 Forman Avenue—ah...ah apartment 723. No. Not for me—it...it's my next door neighbor, ah...ah Mr. Carter...ah, Mr. Jessie Carter."

"Okay, ma'am, calm down. What about Mr. Carter?"

"It's...it's awful. Oh, dear God," she said, turning toward the sounds coming through the wall.

"Okay, ma'am...ma'am. I need you to focus on talking to me. I'm sending help as we speak. But I need to know what is happening."

Mr. Bingham grabbed the phone. "It sounds like someone is killing him! We can hear furniture crashing and glass breaking and, Jesus. I've never heard a man scream so."

"Do you know who's in there with him?"

"No. But please, he needs help. I'd go in myself, but my wife..."

"Absolutely do not go in there," the despatcher warned. "Law officers will be there shortly."

"No, I won't," Mr. Bingham said.

"Don't leave your apartment. And lock your door."

"Yes, we will, but please hurry."

"Help is coming, sir."

As soon as Mr. Bingham clicked off, he and his wife placed their ears to the wall but heard only groaning.

"Hear that?" Mr. Bingham said to his wife, "I think he's still alive."

"Thank God," she said.

Five minutes later, several officers filed down the hall with the building manager behind them holding the master key to Jessie's apartment. First an officer knocked and called out then, when no response came, the manager used his key to enter the apartment. The Binghams peeked out then entered the hall only to be told by a deputy to stay back. By this time, several neighbors had gathered in the hall and were commanded by an officer to go back to their apartments until officers found out exactly what they were dealing with.

Mrs. Bingham poked her head out of the door. "I think he's still alive. We heard groaning," she said.

"Please, ma'am, let us do our own investigation," an officer cautioned her, "and stay inside, ma'am, please."

But no sooner had the officer entered the apartment than the Binghams and other tenants crowded in the hallway and stretched their necks to see what had happened.

The kitchen was in shambles, appliances on the floor. The table overturned, chairs scattered around the room. The coffee grounds and black coffee mixed with blood on the floor. And there was blood on the walls and ceiling and splatters of it on the stove, cabinets, and refrigerator. There were broken dishes and shattered glassware everywhere. In the middle of it all was Karl. His face was bloody and twice its normal size. His eyes were swollen shut, and there were deep slashes on his face, neck, and torso. Karl's legs and right arm were twisted. He held his side with his good hand and seemed to jerk with every breath he took. His t-shirt and underwear were ripped—soaked with blood—and his left shoulder looked like it had been through a meat grinder.

"Who did this to you, Mr. Carter?" a female officer asked.

"Not...Carter," Karl wheezed with blood bubbles forming on the side of his mouth.

"You're not Carter?" asked the female officer. "Then who are you?"

"Did Carter do this to you?" another officer asked.

Karl gagged, coughed up dark-red blood, and blacked out.

The officers were not certain of how many people besides Carter were involved in the attack. The statements detectives got from the Binghams and other tenants on the floor were quite similar. That is, Jessie Carter had lived there for over two years and that he was a very nice and quiet young man. "Don't know why someone would want to hurt him," said one of the tenants. "He's such a nice young man."

"Never had a moment's trouble out of him the whole time," the tenant manager told the detective.

"Coming through, coming through," the paramedics shouted to officers who backed up against the wall and got out of the way of the fast-moving gurney.

Mrs. Bingham got a quick look at the unrecognizable battered man. "God be with you Mr. Carter," she said.

"We're all praying for you, dear," a female tenant said.

The sheriff department, that routinely kept details of a crime from the public, allowed the tenants to continue to think it was Jessie Carter on the gurney until they could get a statement from each person who lived on his floor.

The paramedics worked feverishly on Karl, inserting IVs, administering oxygen, and checking his vitals. He would need a lot of blood, and they had to get him stable before reaching the hospital for him to have even a slim chance of surviving.

At the hospital, Karl had to endure five and a half hours of surgery just to stop the bleeding and repair his many broken bones, with more surgeries to come. Doctors were puzzled as to why he hadn't died given the damages to his organs. The surgeon told his family that he probably wouldn't last the night, but that they were flying in an expert that had had success with patients in near-death conditions. The doctor told them to pray.

An APB was put out on Jessie. His picture was placed in every county sheriff's department and Illinois police station with a statement: "Armed and Dangerous." The media made a plea to the public: "If you see Jessie Carter, do not, we repeat, do not, try to apprehend him, but call 911."

People who had been interviewed by the detectives before began to do an about-face once they knew it was Karl and not Jessie that was attacked.

"I knew there was something fishy about him," said one of the tenants on his floor.

"The quiet type, they're the ones you've got to watch," another concluded.

"I could tell the minute he handed me his deposit and first month's rent and I handed him the key that he was going to be trouble," said the same manager they'd questioned before. "I should have listened to my gut," he said, patting his protruding belly.

Where was Jessie Carter? And why had he so viciously attacked his best friend? Karl's Uncle Ward believed he knew. Now, finding Jessie before the law did was crucial.

Chapter Twenty-One

ICU, New Berwick Memorial Hospital

"Honey, please wake up," Karl's mom pleaded. Tears dripped from her cheek and fell upon Karl's fingers while she held his hand tightly against her quivering lips. After enduring hours of surgery and receiving multiple pints of blood, Karl was placed on a ventilator so his body could rest and better heal. He was badly swollen from his elbows to his hands, around his torso, and from his thighs to his ankles. The IV served round-the-clock medication as well as fluids and nourishment.

Karl's eyelids fluttered often, and though there was evidence of brain activity, he gave no response when spoken to. Only immediate family members were allowed to visit one at a time. Detectives Joe Moss and Donald Reading had come by the hospital earlier but left disappointed because Dr. Covington refused them access to Karl for questioning. Since Detectives Moss and Reading were familiar with similar cases involving victims like Karl, they were under the impression that he could communicate information to them through the movement of his fingers. But Dr. Covington had sternly assured them that, given Karl's extensive injuries, any type of communication was impossible.

Karl's sister-in-law, Lois, and his nephew, Rodney, were patiently waiting to see him next. Lois wanted Karl's mother to have all the time she needed.

Little Rodney scooted around in his seat then asked, "Mom, why is the hospital so cold?"

"Hospitals have to maintain thousands of pieces of life-saving equipment, honey, that function better in lower temperatures. If they kept it too warm, the equipment could malfunction."

"Oh," the child answered.

"I have a jacket in the car. You want to go and get it?" She rummaged in her handbag for her car keys.

"No. I'm good."

A hospital housekeeper tip-toed into Karl's room to empty the trash. She didn't want to disturb Karl's mom who had knelt by his bed holding an open Bible and praying.

Quite inexplicably, the hospital had received an unusual amount of emergency patients in just three days. Karl had become their 405th patient. Unlike larger hospitals in Illinois, this was a strange occurrence for the small New Berwick region. People were basically health conscious, and major accidents and crime were practically non-existent.

*****

At about 2:15 pm, Jewel's phone rang. River and Dex had gone deer hunting, and the girls were hanging out at the mall.

"Hello," Jewel answered.

Ward Burgess hesitated a moment then replied. "Jewel, it's me, Ward."

"I know—long time. How've you been?"

"Ah—well—"

"Never mind, I know that tone. What do you need? You know I'm always here for you, Ward."

"And never think I haven't appreciated your help all these years, dear." He sighed, "God, where do I begin?"

Ward told Jewel about his nephew Karl's friend, Jessie, and the night the two came to see him about Jessie's dreams. He told her about his theory on it being the work of a succubus but said he never dreamed the demon would move on Jessie so quickly. He also told her what had happened to Karl and the extent of his injuries. He said he'd wish he had been more aware of the dangers so he could have warned Karl to stay away from Jessie. Ward needed to find Jessie but didn't know where to look.

"Ward—great goddess. Honey, I'm so sorry."

"I have to find Jessie before he hurts anyone else. But I haven't a clue where he could be."

"I wish you had called me sooner."

"I thought I could help him. I let Karl down. God, if he dies—"

"Now, hold on, I might can fix this."

"Oh, Lord, Jewel, can you? I don't know why this is happening to him."

"Sounds like the entity wants into our world and is using Jessie to get here."

"That's exactly what I thought. But why?"

"That's what we need to find out. I can cast a locating spell on Jessie. Get him back here and question the demon. But I'll need you to get me some things."

"Sure, sure," he said anxiously. "What do you need?"

"Some personal items of Jessie's: a brush, a sock, shirt. Think you can get me those things?"

"I can try. I know where he lived but don't know if I can get into his apartment without his key. I'm not a relative, so I don't think the manager will let me in."

"I can get you in. Just get over there then call me."

"Okay, I'm leaving now."

Ward clicked off and grabbed his truck keys from the dining room table. He took considerable time unlocking all the locks on the front door, then bolted to his black and silver Lincoln Navigator parked in the garage. On the way over to Jessie's apartment, Ward put in a call to his sister-in-law, Nancy Burgess, and Karl's mom, hoping to hear good news. Nancy whimpered on the phone and told Ward that Karl was still unconscious and that the experts sounded to her like they were giving up on him. Ward told her to hang in there, keep praying, and that he'd check back later.

When Ward arrived at Jessie's apartment building, it had begun to thunder and rain heavily. This was never a good sign to those like Ward who dealt with the affairs of the supernatural. The doorman smiled and held the door open for him, and Ward nodded and approached the desk where the security guard looked up from a book and smiled.

"Afternoon, sir, can I help you?"

"Good afternoon. I'd like to see the manager please."

"Okay, is he expecting you?"

"No. Tell him I'm the uncle of Karl Burgess and I have to get into Jessie Carter's apartment to get some items he left there."

"I don't know. Detectives from the Sheriff's department are still going in and out of there. They said they didn't want anybody up there. But I'll try."

The guard picked up the phone and spoke with the manager for less than a minute then hung up.

"I'm sorry. The manager said a detective instructed him not to let anyone in the apartment. I kind of knew he wouldn't. Carter's brother came by a couple of days ago, and he wasn't let in either."

"Thanks for trying."

Ward turned and walked away from the desk. "Shit," he said under his breath. He phoned Jewel.

"Yes, Ward. Are you in?"

"Hell no I'm not in. The damn manager says the detectives don't want anybody in the apartment. So, now what do I do?"

"I said I'd get you in there didn't I? Now go back and insist on seeing the manager."

"What?"

"Trust me."

"Okay," he said with a sigh.

Ward walked back to the desk where the guard had gone back to reading his book.

"Sir," the guard said, looking at Ward from under his glasses.

"Tell the manager I need to see him. It's really important."

The guard appeared reluctant, but called and relayed the message. He hung up the phone. "His office is down the hall to your left," he said pointing. "But it won't do you any good."

"Thank you." Ward turned and speed-dialed Jewel while strolling down the hall. She answered. "Jewel, I'm about twenty feet from the manager's office. What do I say?"

"Nothing—just hand him the phone."

"Hand him the phone?"

"Hand him the phone, 'Ward'."

Ward walked up to the door and knocked. A bald chubby man opened it and stood in the doorway. A whiff of garlic hit Ward's nose. The man was chewing and swallowed quickly so he could talk. "Can I help you?" the manager asked, sucking whatever out of his teeth.

"I'm Ward Burgess, Karl's nephew. I need to get into Jessie's apartment and get my nephew's things.

"I can't do that, sir. I'm under strict orders from the sheriff department."

Ward handed him the phone and stood there dumbfounded. The manager frowned and asked, "Why are you handing me your phone? Who is it?"

"It's important, sir. I think you should speak with her," Ward said without a clue of what Jewel was up to.

"Hello?" the manager said. Seconds into listening, his whole expression changed. His eyes appeared wide and fixed. Holding the phone at his ear, he turned and slowly, like he was in a trance, walked over to a wall, pulled a key from it, turned, walked back, and faced Ward. "723," he said like a recording and handed the key to Ward.

Ward grabbed the key, shaking his head and smiling at Jewel's awesome abilities. He walked down the hall, boarded the elevator, and rode it up to the seventh floor. He read the numbers on the wall with an arrow pointing right. Jessie's apartment was around the corner and third from the far end. Ward opened the door to darkness and a foul odor. He hesitated for a moment, wondering if the demon was still in the apartment. He swallowed a lump in his throat and straightened his shoulders. Walking softly, looking around, and passing dark rooms, he tried walking swiftly past the kitchen—not wanting to see where Karl had nearly lost his life— but stood a few moments anyway, his eyes glassy. Then he made his way to the bedroom. He walked past the bed and gasped loudly when he saw his own reflection in the mirror. He quickly recovered, holding his stomach, and continued walking to a chest of drawers where he picked up a hairbrush. He also bent down and grabbed a sneaker and the t-shirt lying next to it. He put the brush inside the sneaker, wrapped the sneaker in the t-shirt, and stuffed it into his jacket pocket.

He looked around the bedroom and turned to leave, but thought he heard something and froze. He listened to the loud beating of his own heart and jumped when, from the corner of his eye, he thought he saw something large and shadowy move in the open closet near the window. He couldn't move. Then he *could* move—running past the kitchen, a dark room, another dark room, through the living room, and out the door. He rounded the corner and waited for the elevator—squirming in place like a child needing to go potty. When the door opened, he hopped inside.

The slow ride down to the first floor helped to settle his nerves. Once he got back to the office, he saw that the manager was still standing in the doorway stone-faced with the phone to his ear. The man couldn't let the phone go, so Ward took the man's hand and put the phone to his own ear. "Jewel, I have them."

"Okay, put the phone back to his ear."

Ward slid the key into the manager's shirt pocket then returned his hand. After slowly handing the phone back to Ward, the manager suddenly snapped to himself and the frown returned to his face. "Look, mister, I can't let you in the apartment. That's final. You'll just have to take it up with the sheriff's department."

"I quite understand, sir. Sorry to have bothered you."

The manager closed the door, and Ward chuckled as he made his way down the hall. Before he got to the outside door, the guard called out, "Sir, you need to sign out."

"But I never signed in," Ward said walking out the door grinning. "Jewel, baby, I love ya," he said to himself.

The guard looked at the sign-in sheet then scratched at his mustache.

Chapter Twenty-Two

Jewel held the phone to her ear with one hand and pulled aside the window drapes with the other. "Ward, where the hell are you?" she asked, peeking out the window.

"I've just turned onto Raven's Court."

"What's taking you so long? You left Jessie's place over an hour ago."

"I stopped by the hospital to look in on Karl. He's no better, Jewel. My sister-in-law is a wreck."

"You don't sound like you're doing so well yourself."

"I'm hanging," he said. "I should be there in a few."

"All right."

Jewel clicked off and walked into a special room that was set aside for spell preparation. She unfolded the map of Illinois on the table and ran her hands over it to smooth out the creases. After lifting the heavy grimoire from her desk, she placed it on the map then opened it and thumbed through the pages until she found the spell. Jewel repeated the ancient spell over and over in her mind. Casting spells was a delicate matter, and she knew how easily things could go awry if even a single word of an incantation was omitted or misspoken.

Twenty minutes later, Ward pulled into Jewel's driveway and parked. Walking to the house, Ward squinted because of a stream of sunlight peeking through the clouds. He didn't see the pair of skates lying in the path of the front steps. He stumbled over one of them, causing his feet to end up where his head used to be.

"Shit!" he yelled, looking around to see if his embarrassing dilemma had been noticed. After picking himself up, he snatched up the skates and stomped up the steps.

Ward gave the door three swift kicks. Jewel walked to the door and looked through the peephole. She opened it to Ward standing and gripping a skate in each hand.

"You know I almost broke my ass on these damn things?" he said brushing by her.

"Dear goddess! Are you hurt?" she said, taking the skates from him. Her eyes scanned his body.

"No. Just my pride," he said, pulling the small bundle from beneath his coat.

"I've told Becca a dozen times about leaving her skates all over the place. Are you sure you're all right, Ward?" her eyes still checking him.

"I'm fine. Here," he said, handing her the bundle.

"Wait, let me put these away." Jewel walked over to the closet and placed the skates inside on the floor. She walked back, took the bundle, and told him to follow her into the dimly lit prepared room.

Jewel sat at the head of the table, and Ward sat at her left. She unwrapped the t-shirt and placed the hairbrush and tennis shoe on the table with the shirt. Four candles had been placed on the map—representing north, south, east, and west.

"What if he's not in Illinois?" Ward asked.

Jewel didn't look up from her task. "Then we'll use another map," she said. "We have to start somewhere." She collected a few strands of hair from the hairbrush and dropped it in a bowl that had colorful ancient markings on it. With a pair of sheers, she snipped the shoestring in half and cut small pieces of fiber from the t-shirt, dropping everything into the bowl with the hair. She lit all four candles with a silver lighter that carried a strange gold marking.

Jewel picked up her ceremonial blade. "Give me your hand," she said, extending her own to him.

"What!"

"I need your blood."

"Why *my* blood?"

"Because you're the one who's looking for him."

Ward hesitated but put his hand in hers then turned his head and squeezed his eyes shut.

She lifted his hand and held it over the bowl. With her blade, she cut across his palm then cut back in the same line.

"Aah," Ward forced through clenched teeth. He opened his eyes and watched his blood flow into the bowl as Jewel chanted words in Hungarian.

After Jewel had finished repeating the words, she handed Ward a towel. "Here," she said, "put pressure on it." Ward pulled back his hand, placed the towel over the cut, and pressed until the bleeding stopped.

Jewel took one of the mystic candles, lit the bloody items, and placed the candle back in its place. Then she placed both her hands above the bowl and said an incantation—her face turning white as chalk. Blue veins rose on her temples and wormed down the sides of her face to her neck. Ward's eyes widened at the sight of her. Then he gasped when the items in the bowl made a loud sizzling sound and blue smoke rose and hovered over the bowl. The blue smoke formed into a tiny, multi-colored serpent that crawled from midair onto the map that was spread over the table. Jewel ended the incantation, and watched the serpent slowly slither across the map, heading straight to Ward.

"Whoa—what's it doing?" he said, jumping back from the table.

"Relax. It has your blood. It won't harm you."

The serpent continued inching toward Ward. It stopped, reared up like a miniature cobra, and hissed at him before turning and crawling south of the map. It traveled slowly—straight lining and swerving until it reached a certain area. It stopped, froze, then burst into flames and disappeared, leaving a bloody symbol on the spot.

"There!" Ward said, pointing his finger.

"I know that area. It has lots of unexplored caves. No human can survive there."

"Then we better get going if we want to help him," Ward said.

Jewel's eyes seemed to smile at him. "I'm impressed. After what he did to your nephew, you still want to help him."

"That thing isn't Jessie. I don't believe he'd ever intentionally hurt Karl. And I feel responsible for not being able to help him when he and Karl came to me that night."

"I know how you feel, but it's going to take more than just you and me to go out there and get him."

"Can't you conjure something up?"

"Ward, I'm a witch not a goddess. These things take time. I can't just pull stuff out of thin air."

Ward's face drooped, and he flopped back in his chair. Jewel walked over to him and placed her hand on his shoulder. "I'll get River and Dex to gather up some of the wolves. They'll find him and bring him to me. Then I'll be able to cast out the demon."

Ward looked up at her, and his face appeared to brighten.

"But first," she continued, "let's see what I can cook up to help your nephew."

Ward's smile nearly took up both sides of his face.

*****

Two nuns walked slowly past the hospital rooms talking and clenching their rosary beads. A new mother beamed, holding her baby close to her breast as a proud dad rolled her wheelchair onto an elevator. A doctor strolled down the hall with his eyes squinting at a chart.

On the fifth floor—room 502—Karl coughed up yellowish mucus. Despite that, he was showing great improvement thanks to a smelly brown liquid Jewel had given Ward to pour under Karl's tongue. Because ICU patients were constantly monitored, it was impossible to get near Karl unnoticed, so Jewel made Ward an invisible cloak to wrap around him. After visiting hours, he had entered Karl's room and administered the potion.

Ward enjoyed the invisibility. However, the magic was only good for ten minutes after he'd wrapped himself in the cloak, so the timing had to be perfect. He had performed the task in about seven to eight minutes. With a two minute window left, he was tempted to plant a wet one on the lips of a cute nurse he'd seen on his way out but thought better of it.

Karl sat up in a daze about an hour after Ward left. Nurses immediately called the doctors who were equally as astonished as the ICU staff. Karl was coughing up an awful lot of mucus, but continued to improve each hour. What they didn't know was that the substance wasn't just mucus, but infirmities pouring out of him. The staff assistants worked steadily throughout the night changing Karl's wet hospital gowns, bed sheets, and covers. By morning, the excessive mucus had diminished, and Karl had completely recovered.

Ward pretended to be ecstatic when Nancy called him the next day with the good news. He had his nephew back, and his sister-in-law had her sanity back. Now, if he could only find Jessie, the world would seem so much nicer.

A team of doctors, buzzing among themselves, left Karl's room and went back to their separate units. Karl's recovery was the talk of the hospital. Two of his doctors—Dr. Covington, a surgeon, and Dr. Stover, a general practitioner—headed for the elevators. It was the end of a long day for them both.

"This is definitely one for the medical books," Dr. Covington said, pushing the elevator call button.

Dr. Stover shook his head. "I've been practicing medicine for nearly twenty years and never seen a recovery like this."

"I was on my way home," Dr. Covington said, "before I was called to Mr. Burgess's room. But now I think I could use a drink on the way. Care to join me?" There was a six second silence. "All right, I'm buying," Covington said, folding his lips.

Dr. Stover grinned. "Then I guess I'm drinking." The floor number over the elevator lit up and the metal door parted.

*****

River and Dex picked up the last of the wolves who had eagerly volunteered their services in the search for Jessie. River pulled his black Durango SXT out of the driveway, followed by Dex in a red Chevy Silverado. A train of several cars and trucks lined up behind Dex and headed for a place where no humans had ever gone. No one knew how Jessie could survive such a place, but River promised Jewel that he and the wolves would save him. The location was near Ironforge, and it was a demonic place called Necropolis, a cemetery world of the frozen dead and undead. The only difference between the two was that the frozen dead stayed put; if you didn't disturb their graves, they didn't bother you. The undead, however, needed no incentive.

The long caravan journeyed through black mud and thick, foot-high fog, crushing dead animal bones and human skulls under its wheels as they traveled closer to the dark caves. The stench caused Dex to roll up his window and place a handkerchief over his nose and mouth. He turned to Matthew who sat in the front passenger seat. "Damn, evil stinks," Dex said.

Matthew stretched his eyes and fanned the odor away from his face.

By midday, the wolves had traveled well inside of Ironforge and parked their cars and trucks several hundred feet from the nearest cave. There were seven caves within fifty feet of each other. Doors swung opened, and each wolf got out with a handkerchief tied over his nose and mouth—giving them the appearance of 1800s western bandits. Many carried ropes as a safety precaution and pepper spray for possible encounters with reptiles, large wood rats, or bears. Because of the spread of civilization, many animals had made those dark underground dwellings their home. The wolves were instructed to be mindful of sink holes and discouraged against squeezing through tight openings inside the cavern. Sometimes it was easier to squeeze through, but often impossible to squeeze back out.

River waved his arm at them. "Spread out in groups of threes or fours and search each cave," he said, his words muffled by the cloth. "If you see anything, one of you come out and fire a spark into the air."

Spark guns were their only means of long-distance communication because phones were useless in that area. One of the older wolves was to stand by the vehicles and wait for the signal that indicated Jessie had been found or that someone was in danger. Then he was to run in and get River.

Dex, Matthew, and River entered a cave together. The entrance was engulfed by impenetrable blackness. River watched their shadows dissolve into the black, and the musky taste of the air clogged his throat. He and Dex carried old fashion bronze carbide lamps that had been used decades ago by miners. Matthew wore a light mounted on his helmet.

The red dirt path snaked a quarter of a mile into the

underground. The cavern that had never witnessed sun or moon looked as if time had stood still within it. Its shape was ovoid—the walls smooth from the floor to a ceiling that stretched a hundred feet up where giant stalactites perched and bats roosted. River's boots hit against loose stones that littered the floor; stale air filled his lungs. Yet, the darkness beyond his senses felt intriguing. Water dripping into water and crickets chirping surrounded him like a noisy blanket as the chilling gloom appeared to swallow everything within. Large cones hung from the ceilings, and even hard hats were no guarantee against injury from falling rocks.

As they journeyed farther, they came across frigid pools of stagnant water. River wondered what was around the next boulder, and just how far the path went. Under Dex's boots, loose stones shifted, making the noise of the disturbed rocks echo against the stone walls. Their lights caused some parts of the cave to come alive—snakes dashed under rocks, insects scattered, small mammals scurried, and the light bathed the path up ahead in a glimmering orange glow.

Then a great shout that startled them came from behind.

"River! River!" the old wolf yelled out of breath. "Come quick, they found that guy Jessie, and he's meaner than a grizzly bear disturbed from a nap."

River, Dex, and Matthew sprinted toward the shouting man, passing him near the exit. River came to a halt and saw the wolves pouring into one of the middle caves. "In there," the old-timer said pointing.

River ran in with Dex and Matthew right on his heels. A little beyond the mouth of the cave, mounted lights on the wolves' helmets flickering against the cavern walls made Jessie's shadow look like a ten foot black monster. The wolves had him surrounded, and he was growling like a dog and hissing like a pissed off cobra.

Before River could give a command, one of the wolves charged Jessie who stood wide-legged, his body leaning forward, arms bent at the elbow and fingers spread apart. When the wolf came within reach, Jessie lifted him over his head and hurled him against the stone wall. Other wolves charged and, one by one, were batted high into the air; some went crashing into the hanging cones, many landed hard on giant boulders, and others were sent skidding across the jagged rock floor.

River's voice had been drowned out by the commotion. Now that many of the wolves lay nursing their wounds, the other would-be attackers heard him clearly yell, "Cease your attack!" He inched toward Jessie with his palms facing out—a no threat sign. Jessie stood foaming at the mouth, his eyes blood-shot and wild, following River's every move.

"Jessie. No one's going to hurt you. We're here to help you."

River began to move in closer, but Jessie shot into a fighting stance and River backed off.

"Okay. Jess. Okay. I'm going to stand right here. But I need you to listen to me. I know you're still in there somewhere, Jess. This thing isn't you."

"There is no goddamn Jessie!" several voices echoed from Jessie's mouth.

"You're in there, Jess. We know you're in there. And we know you want to come out, but you've got to fight it, Jess. You've got to fight it."

"THERE IS NO GODDAMN JESSIE!" the voice thundered against the walls causing the entire cave to tremble like there had been an earthquake and the wolves to tumble over like duck pins. Giant cones and rocks fell from the ceiling, injuring some wolves and barely missing others.

Recovering from the fall, River started to rise but flopped back down and gasped at the sight of Jessie's face beginning to melt. His nose washed into his mouth, and his eyes oozed out of their sockets like lava. His head waved into his neck and his neck into his shoulders and torso, followed by his legs and feet, until he was nothing but viscous goo. Then an eerie silence hung in the air, and all eyes remained fixed upon the pool of goo. Suddenly, a woman slowly rose out of it and stood majestically. The wolves gasped as they gazed at her.

"Who the hell are you?" River shouted.

"No need to get up," a male voice rang out from the blackness.

A man and two women strolled into view.

"Yes, at her feet is where you belong," said one of the women.

"You pathetic two-footed beasts," said the other woman. "Look upon the Queen of Darkness…the one who gave you your piteous existence."

"YOU!" Dex blurted, pointing at Corina. "You're the witch who cursed us!"

"But, how did you—?" River's voice froze in mid-sentence. No one could have escaped such a spell, he thought. River's face grew pale.

Corina smiled widely.

Gunner, Amber, and Holly strolled over and stood next to Corina who appeared the very image of her tall, slender shadow. She was dressed in long, flowing black—from her neck to her waist to her feet and out into a long train. The threesome glowed with sinister ambition. Corina raised her hand, the cave magically lit up like a day sky, and behind her, fifty feet away, stood a vast army of the undead—their eyeballs a fiery red—the stench of their decayed flesh filled the air. The twenty-nine inch silver blades made a deafening hissing sound when the undead's bony fingers pulled them from black leather sheaths.

River's face dropped. "Holy shit!"

Chapter Twenty-Three

Shrieking cries like dogs being butchered echoed across the noon sky. Many headless wolves lay at the feet of the demons, and countless dead meat fragments were scattered on the stone floor after massive paws had lifted and hurled several demons into the air, causing them to smash against the cavern walls. A gruesome fight to the death had the wolves at a ten-to-one disadvantage.

River swiped off his opponent's head, but the demon continued wielding his sword with precise accuracy, forcing River to back up and slicing into his chest and paws. River yelled out in pain and doubled over on the floor. The silver burned his skin as if his wounds had been seared with a red-hot poker. The creature stood over him with its sword raised, but River was too weak to get out of the way. The blade came down, but fell, along with the arm, at River's feet when Dex ripped off the demon's shoulder and grabbed its exposed ribs with his mouth, shaking his own head violently until the rest of the creature broke apart and the decaying pieces slid across the floor. Dex turned and saw Matthew in trouble: three demons swinging and barely missing him. With his father at his side, Matthew tore off the sword-wielding arms of each. Together, Dex, Matthew, and Rick defeated many demons with thunderous swiping of their paws, sending a host of them crash landing and scattering across the cavern floor.

River, lying helplessly on the floor with silver burning in his veins, saw that the wolves couldn't win even though they fought gallantly. There were only twelve wolves left and still numerous demons. Seeing the hopelessness, River shouted, "Retreat!"

Dex and Matthew grabbed River off the floor and ran with him—meeting up with Rick and the other eight wolves as they turned and shot toward the only exit out of the cave. But Corina bellowed a magic word—the opening disappeared and became a continuation of the wall. Corina curved her back and laughed, as did her admiring trio. She stopped laughing, squinted, and yelled, "Destroy them all!"

The demon soldiers, with their blades sparkling under the light, quickly advanced, the sound of their boots loudly stomping against the stone floor. The wolves had nowhere to run. River ignored his pain and he, along with the other wolves, prepared to die like soldiers. In their stances, the wolves bared their fangs in most hideous grins, so much so that beneath their noses nothing but teeth were visible. Above their noses, the yellow orbs of their eyes looked like tiny blazing suns. With their snouts nearly to the ground, their backsides up, their tails positioned for balance, and their growls sounding like a thousand motorcycle roars, the wolves were prepared to charge when suddenly a strong wind entered the cave. It swirled above the wolves, circling them several times, then soared past the wolves, lifted the demons, Corina, Holly, Amber, and Gunner ten feet into the air, and blew them hard against the cave wall, holding them there. The wolves raised their heads in puzzled amazement.

Back at Northern Greyscott Falls, Jewel stood over a bowl of mystical water. While she incanted, a stream of blue mist, like a mini-hurricane, poured into the water. She had used the bowl for a locating spell to find River and had observed the wolves battling for their lives against Corina and her demon army. The stream continued while the glare from her eyes focused on a spot on the cave wall where the door had been.

Inside the cavern—while the undead, Corina, and her cronies were held by the wind—a mysterious fire, searing through the wall, burned an outline of a door. Then the door-like chunk fell outward, and the wolves bolted through the opening. Instead of shape shifting and getting into their vehicles, they remained wolves and tore past the caves and through the forest—their paws eating up the ground until they reached Greyscott Falls and stumbled into the safety of their homes.

Jewel staggered into the living room and flopped down in a nearby chair, exhausted from performing the spells, among them one that placed a stronger boundary spell on Corina and her followers. The spells had taken her strength because each was to have been performed by two or more witches but there had been no time to call Beatrice. The clear mystic water was now dark, as if someone had switched off the light inside the bowl.

Thank the gods the children are out of the house, Jewel thought. She sat back, rested her head against the soft cushion, and closed her eyes. Moments later, while she catnapped, something soft and cool pressed against her lips. She flashed open her eyes and saw River's grim face pull back from kissing her. She mustered up strength, shot up from the chair, and threw her arms around him, squeezing him so tightly he could barely breathe.

"Oh, honey," she said. "I knew something was wrong. I just knew it." She pulled away and examined him. He was still naked, and his skin was a pale blue because of the silver that was contaminating his blood. She made him lie down on the sofa. "Here, drink this. I had it already prepared." She gave River the potion and watched him make a face as he drained the cup. He put his hands behind his head and closed his eyes. Jewel grabbed a blanket and spread it over him, then bent and kissed him—leaving him to sleep while the potion evaporated the silver from his blood stream.

Back at the cave, a furious Corina seethed over what had happened to her perfect revenge. When the wind had ceased, those who were held against the wall crashed to the ground. Of course Corina, her sister, and friends were only bruised, but the interference broke Corina's spell and her demonic army vanished in a puff of black smoke.

"That wind wasn't conjured by any covenant witch," Corina fumed. "I know their strength and what their feeble magic can do. That was black magic. There's strong witchcraft in New Berwick, and I've become its bull's-eye. "Very well then...we'll bide our time," she said, looking over at her partners. "Then we'll find those bitches and make them pay." A wide grin spread across Corina's face, and her black eyes twinkled as if she'd thought of something quite extraordinary. "We'll throw a party," she said. "Yes. There'll be music and dancing. We'll use their guts for guitar strings," she sinisterly joked. Holly, Amber, and Gunner laughed, then Corina spoke a spell and a circular portal, the size of a quarter, opened about six inches off the cavern floor and stretched six feet high and wide; the foursome stepped in one at a time. The portal shrank then disappeared.

*****

Beatrice, finally learning of the wolves' dilemma and fully aware of Corina's escape from the spell that the covenant witches had placed on her over a hundred years ago, rushed to Jewel's side. Beatrice took over caring for River and was pleased to oversee the running of the Porter household until Jewel recovered.

Jewel opened her eyes, looked up into Beatrice's sunny face, and inquired in a voice barely above a whisper: "The baby?"

Beatrice placed her ear on Jewel's baby bump and heard the strain of the baby's heart beating. She immediately placed her hand on Jewel's abdomen and spoke an incantation—the baby's heart resumed beating normally and his breathing improved. "There," Beatrice said. "You will have a strong son. But no more spells, though...your body can't take the strain."

"River..." Jewel said breathily.

"He's fine. You just rest and think about having a healthy baby boy...something you and River have been wishing for since I can remember."

Jewel yawned, and her slurred words were inaudible.

"Shush, now," Beatrice ordered.

Beatrice lifted Jewel's feet and gently placed them on an ottoman. She sat in another chair across from Jewel and watched her chest quietly rise and fall. Though she spoke comfort to Jewel, deep lines spread across Beatrice's forehead because, behind an invisible barrier, was a sulking, angry, and conniving sorcerer—more powerful and dangerous than any being living or dead. Her hunger for blood was unsatisfied, and her thirst for revenge unquenched. Beatrice knew that Corina, given enough time, could challenge any spell placed on her. That she had proven well enough.

Beatrice sat looking over at her dear friend as she slept so peacefully.

Chapter Twenty-Four

Jewel examined every finger and toe of the newborn. She saw that little Merchant Dexter Porter was perfect in every way. He had the kind of beauty all babies possess plus an inch-long widow's peak that would be kept shaved to hide the tell-tale marking of a werewolf. River sat on the edge of the bed while the dark-haired, blue-eyed babe squeezed his index finger with a strength unfound in human babies. As the small pink lips eagerly suckled, the once long-suffering father planted several kisses upon Merchant's forehead.

Outside the bedroom, the upstairs hallway was packed with gleeful spectators wanting a glimpse of the Porter's first boy, while presents from Greyscott residents poured into the downstairs living room and dining area. The midwives were never wrong; they had prophesied months ago that Jewel would be among more than fifty northern women to conceive a son. It was a pride that the southern women unapologetically had embraced during the twenty-year pack feud.

Merchant's proud sisters Chelsea, Abby, Dria, and Becca were busy downstairs attending to the guest. Beatrice and Jan prepared sandwiches, cake, and coffee and put Chelsea and Abby in charge of serving the food while Dria and Becca graciously accepted gifts from the guests and seated them.

It was six in the evening; Dex, Matthew, and Rick were entertaining the wolves in the lower-level clubroom—serving food and alcoholic beverages and following the tradition of passing out cigars even though most of the wolves didn't smoke them.

"I think it was fitting for the gods to bless Aunt Jewel with the legal birth of the first northern boy," Matthew said. "After all, she did break the moon curse."

"I'll drink to that," Rick said, throwing his head back and draining a glass of bourbon.

"Careful, dude," Matthew warned. "That's not beer you're drinking."

"Just because you're a couple of years older than me," Rick slurred, "doesn't mean you get to te…tell me what to do."

"Holy crap, here we go." Matthew took Rick by the arm, walked out of a side door—away from the house—and stood on the grass.

"Let go of me," Rick said, pulling away from Matthew's grip. Matthew scolded him. "You know how you get when you drink hard liquor. I don't want you blabbing about anything we've talked about."

"Like what?" Then Rick grinned like a naughty child and placed his fingers over his mouth. "Ooh…I see. You're afraid I'll mention something about you wanting to tell Kayla you're a wolf." Rick stumbled backwards, and Matthew had to reach out to steady him.

"That's it, I'm taking you home." Matthew put his arm around Rick's shoulder to aid him, and the two walked over to Matthew's car and got in. During the ride, Rick continued to protest and at one point opened the car door while it was still moving in an attempt to jump out. Matthew struggled to hold onto him with one hand while he steered to the side of the road with the other—in the process cutting off a driver who laid on his horn and hurled obscenities at him.

Matthew switched off the car and turned to Rick. "Idiot! I've had it with you."

"But I don't wanna go home, Matt."

Matthew exhaled hard to calm himself. "Now…you can sit here and behave yourself, or you can ride in the trunk. I don't give a shit. Dude, I swear, you try anything, I mean anything…" The ringing of Matthew's phone interrupted him. It was Kayla. Matthew's tone brightened. "Hey, beautiful," Matthew greeted her, "you're on speaker."

"Hi…I called you several times and…"

"Is that the great and wonderful Kayla…Hi Kaylaaah," Rick blurted.

"Who is that?" she asked with a chuckle.

"Oh, that's just Rick." Matthew elbowed Rick to be quiet. Rick hunched his shoulders and grinned, then laid his head against the window and closed his eyes.

"That's Rick?" she asked.

"Yeah, he's had a little too much to drink. We just came from my Aunt Jewel's. She had her baby...and—"

"Well, congrats. Girl or boy?"

"Boy. Anyway, I'm driving Rick home now," he said. Matthew quickly checked his left view mirror then shot out ahead of the oncoming traffic. "You want to meet up later?"

"That's why I'm calling. I'm on my way to your place. Think you'll be home by the time I get there?"

"Sure. I'll be there in about twenty minutes or so. I'm five minutes from Rick's now."

"Okay, see you there. Goodbye, Rick," she said playfully. Matthew glanced over at him. "He's out...see you in a few." Kayla gave a quick okay and clicked off.

Matthew again looked over at Rick who was fast asleep with his mouth wide open—saliva dribbling down his chin. After driving several more miles, Matthew pulled up to Rick's house. "Okay, sleeping beauty, you're home," Matthew said, getting out of the car. He walked around to the passenger's side and helped Rick out. He steadied Rick all the way up to his front door then watched Rick fumble through the same pockets over and over for his keys.

"I can get 'em," Rick snapped, slapping Matthew's hand away when he tried to help. Rick finally pulled out his keys, which slipped from his butterfingers to the ground. Matthew bent, picked them up, and unlocked the door. He helped Rick inside and watched him stagger into the living room and flop down on the sofa. Matthew urged him to lie down then made sure the door was locked before leaving. He got back into his car and dialed Kayla to say he was on his way, but the phone went to voicemail.

Kayla, who had always admired the small brook behind the Porter's mansion, decided to take a walk along it. She made her way down to the brook and stood listening to the swishing sound of the cool water washing over the large grey rocks. The sky was a pale blue, and the sunlight peeked through the top of a tall tree and lit up the glow on her blonde hair. Beyond the brook was a wooded area where she and Matthew took long walks. In the summer, they would always slip away from their friends, Matthew would spread a blanket, and they'd lay immersed in each other's arms for hours.

"Hey," Matthew yelled to her.

Kayla turned and smiled as he walked toward her.

"Why didn't you answer your phone?"

Kayla frowned, searched, and then realized, "I must have left it in the car. Sorry."

"What are you doing down here? I thought you'd be at the house?"

"I love it here. Great place to stand and think, you know?"

"Yeah, I come down here many times myself. Want to take a walk?" he asked, nodding toward the wooded area.

"Sure." She grabbed his arm, and the two walked slowly toward the tall, thick trees. They entered the darkened path that was so still and quiet. Only the birds rustling the leaves on the trees and stones that their feet struck along the path disturbed the silence. Reaching a giant oak, they stopped and kissed passionately. They had been standing and talking for several minutes when Matthew's keen sense of smell picked up a familiar scent that had been long gone from that area. Wrinkles spread across his forehead, and he looked away.

"Is something wrong?" she asked.

"There's a bear nearby. They shouldn't be here," he said with a certain amount of authority. Matthew knew the pack had killed or chased off deer predators because the wolves saw them as competition. Though on occasion, a bear or mountain lion would wander in.

Kayla looked about puzzlingly. "I don't see or hear anything. How can you tell?"

"I thought I saw one," he lied. "How about we start heading back?"

She pouted. "But we just got here," she said, throwing her arms around his neck and kissing him.

Matthew put his arms around her waist but kept his eye glued to the area of the scent. She noticed he wasn't totally involved in their kiss, and she leaned back from him.

"What on earth is to matter?" she asked.

"Nothing, honey…ah, I think we better start back." Matthew got a stronger whiff of the bear because it was getting closer; he hurried her along a shortcut back to the house, but not soon enough. Kayla gasped and froze when she spotted the enormous brown bear that stood several feet from them. Its head was as tall as a horse's back, and when the bear spotted her and Matthew, it also froze and glared at them.

"Matt," she whimpered.

"Don't move," he whispered.

The two stayed perfectly still. Sometimes bears lose interest and walk off, and sometimes they attack—going from zero to 35 miles per hour in seconds. Matthew's rifle was in the trunk of his car. He could call someone on his cell, but knew any movement could spawn an attack. He felt Kayla's hand tremble inside his own. Matthew had an idea, and he mumbled it to Kayla. He would make a break in another direction—away from her, making the bear chase after him. Then Kayla would run to the car, get his rifle, and hightail it back to him. Matthew knew he could run faster than the average man even in human form, and he could give the bear quite a workout before she got back.

But Kayla was afraid she wouldn't get back in time and Matthew would be hurt. "No, let's wait it out, the bear might leave," she whispered.

"And he might not," he whispered back.

She squeezed his hand until he couldn't feel his fingers anymore.

"It's the only way," he said. "Now…on the count of three, and no matter what you hear, don't look back. Just run as fast as you can. Got it?"

"Yes," she said, in a soft squeaky voice.

Kayla's legs grew weak. She didn't want to disappoint Matthew but wasn't sure she could move when the time came.

"One," he whispered.

All the saliva in her mouth dried up.

"Two."

Every part of her body shook—except her legs. She didn't think she could move her legs.

"Three!"

Matthew broke, and the bear took off after him. Kayla took off in the direction of the house, but looking over her shoulder, she saw Matthew trip and fall; his feet tangled in some wild vines. She stopped and held her breath watching the bear swiftly move in on him. Matthew quickly untangled his foot, shot up from the ground, and tried to scramble out of the bear's reach, but the bear extended a paw. Its claw caught on Matthew's shirt and brought him down hard. He lay on his back as the bear towered over him—biting and clawing him viciously. The roar of the bear's growling was so loud the birds tore out of the trees.

"Matt!" Kayla screamed. She frantically looked around for something to throw at the bear and spotted several large rocks. She picked them up and hurled them, but the rocks did nothing to discourage the bear; it was like throwing pebbles at a dinosaur. "Matt!" she screamed again. She could see glimpses of Matthew fighting for his life on his back. She was filled to the brim with fear, but knew Matthew would die if she did nothing. She looked around for something she could use as a weapon and spotted a large branch on the ground. She lifted the branch with both hands and was running toward the bear to beat it off of Matthew when suddenly she heard another growl—deeper and more ferocious. *Oh my god, is it another bear?*

Kayla stared in total horror because she couldn't see Matthew anymore. She turned and ran, but got only as far as the tree where she had stood before. When she turned back to watch, she saw a strange animal and the bear rolling over and over each other on the ground—tearing and ripping each other with claws and bared fangs. *Where did that animal come from?* The other animal was just as tall and wide as the bear, yet it wasn't a bear. It was more monstrous looking. More like a huge ugly dog or perhaps a wolf. *Wolf,* she thought. It looked exactly like the wolf she had encountered that day when that voice behind her told her not to move. *But where is Matt? He must have gotten away.* She screamed his name. The twin growling grew deafening as if every cloud in the sky was bursting at the same time. Kayla put her hands over her ears and shut her eyes tight momentarily. She opened her eyes and started to run toward the house but stopped because she couldn't bear to leave Matthew behind. Suddenly, there was silence; she stayed still, not wanting to turn around but eventually did so slowly and saw the bear lying on its side lifeless and the giant wolf standing over it in conquest. She froze when the wolf turned its head and looked over at her—pieces of cloth hanging raggedly from its dark furry body.

She dared not move her head, but her eyes kept darting back and forth hoping to spot Matthew. Suddenly, a cracking sound came from the area where the wolf stood. She gasped when the wolf stood on hind legs and slowly diminished in width and height. She watched in horror as its fur began to disappear, its snout shortened, and its clawed paws formed into hands and then feet. Her face dropped as this grotesque thing transformed into several hideous shapes until a naked six-foot man stood staring at her. Kayla stumbled back against a tree and slid down it until her butt flopped hard to the ground. Her eyes were glazed and her mouth wouldn't close. She couldn't swallow or move a muscle.

Matthew, his muscular body covered in blood and bear fur, deep claw marks etched across his abdomen and chest—with shredded pieces of his clothes hanging from his wrists and ankles and no shoes—made his way to her as she sat trembling on the ground.

He bent to help her up, but she fearfully pulled back from his hand. He straightened up and looked down at her sympathetically.

"I didn't mean for you to find out this way."

"What...are you?" She sounded like a recording.

"I was going to tell you, but just couldn't find the right time."

"What...are...you?"

"I'm not a what!" he said indignantly.

"All right, 'who' the hell are you then? Never mind." Anger had given her strength. She jumped up off the ground and ran through the woods, but he caught up to her and grabbed her by the arm.

"Don't touch me," she said, jerking her arm away from him.

He saw fear and anger in her eyes; she saw hurt in his.

He stood looking like a small boy and said, "I'm a werewolf."

"Were…wolf?" Kayla remembered the talk of werewolves as a kid. Stupid grownups, she'd always thought. No intelligent person she knew believed it. "There's no such thing," she said. *No such thing?* she thought. *But I just saw it.*

"Please don't be frightened," Matthew pleaded. "I can explain. I 'am' a werewolf, but I'm not a monster. And I would never harm you or anyone. It's a curse that reaches back to my great-great-grandfather, Merchant Porter."

She slipped off her sweater and tossed it to him. He caught it and wrapped it around his lower torso, then tied the sleeves. Her eyes appeared to soften as he stood before her and explained fully. After he had finished, she thought, *werewolves and witches?* "Then the folk tales I've been hearing my whole life are true. I've been in love with a werewolf? Oh damn." She stepped back, resting her back against a tree. There was a cold silence.

"So, is this the end of us?" Matthew asked. He searched her face for clues.

"I don't know, Matt. I honestly don't know." She turned and walked toward the house and Matthew followed. They didn't speak for the length of the walk, and Kayla kept a distance from him. After they reached the parked cars, Matthew begged her to come into the house. He wanted them to talk before she made up her mind about them. Reluctantly, Kayla agreed not to leave before he bathed and put on some clothes.

Inside the house, after he mounted the stairs, she stood looking around the family room. But something was different now. Matt was different. She felt strange, even dirty. Something told her to run from the house, but she'd promise Matthew she'd stay, so she sat, crossed her legs, and tried to relax by placing her arm on the back of the sofa. She thought of the recent killings that people had said were caused by wild animals: those tourists three summers ago, Tiara Winters and several deputies who were so torn apart they all had closed-casket funerals. Had Matt and his people done that? Had Mr. Porter? Cousin Rick? Could Matt have participated in such ghastly killings? Or were their deaths really caused by some wild animals like that bear Matt had killed with his bare hands? Or should she say his bare paws? It was difficult for her to think of Matt with paws. Kayla suddenly got a chill down her spine and her head pounded from all she had just witnessed and learned. *What has really changed?* she thought. *He's still the kind and thoughtful person I fell in love with. He's never harmed me. Oh…but what if we married? What if we had children…what would they be?* She wanted to bathe—wash all of him off her, even from inside of her. Wash his tongue from her mouth, his penis from her flesh, his lips from her breasts and neck. But as frightened and confused as she was, something kept preventing her from running. Was it love? She thought more deeply of the times they'd been intimate. And it all made sense now—the exotic biting, the deep-throated moans, the times she'd thought his eyes changed colors. She had ignored all of those things, but now they made perfect sense. Something again urged her to stand and run. But she sat there and thought of his sweetness toward her, his kind blue eyes that seem to look into her very soul, their long romantic walks, his devotion to his family, how gentle he'd always been with her. And how could she forget how she felt those many times he'd held her and said he loved her. Suddenly she found herself not afraid—not caring who he was or what he was. *Matt wouldn't randomly kill anyone. He would never harm an innocent person—he couldn't?* He was still the man she loved, or the thing she loved and Kayla couldn't imagine a life without him. She had always wanted something different in a man—and this sure as hell was different. But not only different, it was true love. *And nothing can destroy true love…not even being two beings that are as different as we are….*

Matthew's entrance interrupted her thoughts. He stood not knowing if he should join her on the sofa. Would she pull away in fear again? He walked over to where she sat—the smell of his fresh clothes and cologne parted the air. Kayla scooted over for him to sit next to her. He swallowed hard and eased down. His eyes were as a puppy's when it thinks it's going to be punished for chewing up a shoe.

Kayla's expression softened more when she looked at him, and she touched his hand. "Matt," she said while he held his breath, "I won't apologize for my actions back there in the woods. You should have told me."

"I know, but I was afraid if you knew you'd hate me. I didn't want to lose you. It was selfish of me, I know that now, but…"
She placed her finger over his lips, leaned in, and kissed them. "I don't care," she said softly.

His eyebrows rose. "You…you don't?"
She shook her head slowly. "I love you."

A smile etched across his face—his white teeth gleaming. Matthew took her into his arms and gave her a lingering kiss that nearly took her breath away. He gently pushed her back onto the sofa, covered her with his body, and kissed her face and neck. "I couldn't bear it if I lost you, Kayla."

"You lost me for a little while," she said, looking up into his ocean-blue eyes. "But I'm back and I'm not going anywhere—ever."

Near the hour of dusk, they rose and walked arm and arm up to the family's cabin where they had first made love, and Kayla spent the night.

Chapter Twenty-Five

Months Later

A strange chill hung in the air. Animal attacks increased as people's pets continued to turn on them. Large animals such as grizzlies, black bears, cougars, and wolves—animals that had long left the New Berwick area—had mysteriously returned. Even birds swooped down and pecked at people and rodents.

Some disturbing information had alerted the local witches' council and prompted Priestess Adria to call an emergency coven meeting. The meeting brought together witches who had not seen each other for many weeks, and they loudly chit-chatted. The room overflowed with talk and laughter until Adria called the crowd to order.

"Your attention sisters and brothers...your attention, please. As you all know, there have been many strange happenings and now some recent information. The information is disturbing and, worse, involves one or more of us."

The witches suddenly looked at one another with suspicion and hunched their shoulders. Jewel, who had three-month-old Merchant suckling, sat next to Beatrice, and both women's faces turned grim. Jewel's nerves were on edge; the priestess's mouth seemed to move in slow motion.

Adria stood silently for what seemed an eternity, her light-brown eyes scanning the breathless crowd. Then her words broke through the silence like a firecracker going off unexpectedly: "There are sorcerers among us," she said coldly.

Those words plunged in their ears like daggers, and the room filled with loud gasps as witches turned to one another and looked around wondering who they could be. Beatrice turned to look at Naomi, but Jewel pinched her to keep her from giving anything away or involving Naomi who had been loyal in keeping their secret.

Adria continued speaking as she walked around the room. Several times she'd stop at a witch and everyone would think that person was the sorcerer only for Adria to walk on, with the person she had moved on from sighing in relief. It was as if Adria were toying with the guilty ones; or perhaps she didn't know who they were and was hoping to flush them out by making them sweat. Nonetheless, it was great theater that made everyone squeamish.

Naomi's heart pounded. She could trust Jewel well enough, but Beatrice could become a wrecking ball under pressure. After all, Beatrice had tried to look at her more than once. Naomi wanted to excuse herself, but feared it would draw suspicion. She had to keep her head; no innocent person would leave before finding out who the culprit was. Even though she hadn't done anything, the fact that she knew about the grimoire made her an accomplice and ensured she would share the fate of the guilty. A sudden dislike of Jewel and Beatrice rose in her stomach like black bile. *Dear goddess,* she thought, *why did I let this happen?*

Jewel couldn't stand it any longer. She had lived all year in fear of being discovered. Plus she was tired of worrying about who Beatrice would slip up and tell next. She gently inserted her little finger in the corner of Merchant's mouth and broke his suction on her nipple. With his eyes still closed, his tiny pink lips continued to mimic sucking. She buttoned her blouse and handed the baby to Beatrice who looked puzzlingly at her. "Keep your calm and don't say a word," Jewel said. She attempted to rise from her seat, but Beatrice grabbed her arm, pulled her back down, and whispered, "What are you going to do?"

Jewel gently pulled her arm free. "You'll see… just stay quiet." Jewel rose from her chair and walked to the front of the room where Adria stood speaking. When Adria saw Jewel walking toward her, she stopped talking. Jewel whispered in her ear; Adria leaned back, her expression grim. She stunned the room by calling the meeting to a close. Buzzing and noisy wooden chair legs scraping against the stone floor filled the room, but the hall emptied quickly except for Jewel, Adria, Beatrice, the baby, and the twelve local council members, which included their three officials: Mavis, Mike, and Dolly.

"Have a seat, Jewel," Adria said.

Jewel eased down in one of the front-row chairs. Beatrice pretended to play with the baby, mostly to hide her nervousness.

"What is this about?" Mavis blurted.

Adria folded her arms across her chest and responded, "Jewel has something she wants to tell us."

Jewel tried to swallow, but her mouth felt like it was full of cotton. "I'm the one you're looking for...me alone...no one else," she said, her heart pounding.

"Go on," Adria urged.

"I have a grimoire. I know it's forbidden, and I can explain. You see, the moon curse was taking a toll on the wolves...actually on all of us. I couldn't reverse the curse itself, but I could stop the shape shifting during the full moon. We were tired of killing the male children. Though my husband put up a good front...the fact is every time he'd returned from one of these killings, it just seemed it took more and more of his heart and soul. Not just River but all of our men and women. It split our pack and made us enemies. It had to end."

The council members sat stone faced, staring at Jewel.

Jewel continued and became more nervous because she knew what she was about to confess would bring her even further into highly forbidden territory. "I found out how the curse was performed: a human boy was sacrificed. Oh, I knew we weren't allowed to do that, and...and I didn't. I mean, I...I did use a young boy from Sheerfield, but he...he's very much alive. I discovered that if the boy was bitten by a werewolf, and then sacrificed, he wouldn't die. Tha...that is, he would die but come back to life. The only problem is that..." Jewel finally had spit to swallow as she hesitated.

"That?" Mavis asked impatiently.

"That... he'd be a werewolf." *There, I've said it*, she thought. Jewel did everything not to keel over from fright.

Eyebrows rose, and Dolly said to Mavis, "This is even worse than we thought."

Beatrice kept her head down and prayed. Adria looked sternly at Jewel, "You mean you turned a little human boy into a werewolf? Who is this child? And what did his parents have to say about it?"

"His name is Russell Sooner; he's ten years old, and his parents don't know." Adria and the council members looked at one another with blank faces.

Jewel continued and, seeing how her words had affected them, swallowed a gulp of air. "We…we kidnapped him after a baseball game and…"

"Enough!" Adria snapped. "Jewel, we thought we had all the facts, but it looks like we only touched the tip of the iceberg here." Adria glanced at the council members, then back at Jewel. "The council conducts locating spells frequently to make sure certain black magic items don't fall into the hands of our covenant members. Of all the years of conducting this spell, we have never discovered one item among our members…until now." She looked coldly from under her lashes at Jewel.

"You knew I had a grimoire?"

"Only this morning. But now you're telling us you've turned a human child into a werewolf?"

"Yes," Jewel said barely above a whisper.

Adria sighed. "We were hoping you'd come forth. Not that it will help you in our decision; still, we are glad that you witched up and came clean. But never in our wildest dreams did we know the extent you had taken this black magic. This is simply horrible." Adria unfolded her arms and she lifted her chin. "I'm disappointed in you, Jewel Porter. You…one of our queens. Your actions were despicable. Not only that, but you've shown a total disregard for the covenant rules and for Sheerfield's human population that we've always tried to protect against magic."

"Treason is what it is." Mike spoke the words like something stunk.

Jewel peered down at the floor in utter shame.

Mavis looked over at Beatrice. "And what of your friend?"

Beatrice's head shot up, and a lump rose in her throat. But Jewel blurted, "No! Beatrice knew nothing about this. I told you…it's me.

200

I'm the one with the grimoire. I'm the one who used the black magic."

But Mavis never took her eyes off of Beatrice during Jewel's protest. "Is that true Beatrice?"

Jewel's eyes pleaded with Beatrice. *For once in your miserable freaking life don't screw up,* she thought.

"I knew nothing," Beatrice answered innocently.

"But you don't seem surprised," Dolly said, half-smiling.

"I'm a seasoned witch...very little surprises me," Beatrice snapped. "And as I said, I knew nothing."

Jewel was proud of her. *Thank the goddesses. You didn't cave.* Beatrice hadn't fallen apart like she usually did. Though she hadn't said much, her expression and body language was so convincing that Jewel couldn't believe it was her Bea.

The council members' focus turned back to Jewel. "You do realize," Adria said, "that you'll have to face severe consequences."

"But, you don't understand, I..."

Adria interrupted Jewel. "I know the curse was hard. And I know you felt you had a good reason for using black magic. But the fact is...the rules are the rules, and they apply to everyone." Then Adria stood erect. "Your trial will be set..."

"Wait!" Jewel shouted. "Before you announce the trial date, you better hear this."

"We better?" asked an indignant Mike.

Jewel caught herself. "I'm sorry. I mean...it is crucial that you hear this."

Mavis's forehead wrinkled. "You mean there's more?"

Jewel braced herself, and Beatrice's heart thumped knowing what was coming next. Then Jewel said it, "Corina broke the spell...she's free."

"What? When? No!" Every council member blurted almost in unison, and Adria's chest deflated like a balloon. The council members twisted and turned in their seats, overflowing with outrage at the very thought.

"Wait!" Mike shouted. "Don't believe her. She's stalling. It's a lie."

"No it's not!" said a stern male voice from the back of the room. Every head turned to look. River had stood in the shadows of the room and had heard the entire conversation after the meeting ended. He hadn't told Jewel before she left, but River felt uneasy about this sudden coven meeting and decided to check on Jewel just in case she needed him. He had sat in his car across from the hall and watched the people pour out. He thought it was much too soon for the meeting to be over and couldn't understand what was keeping Jewel and Beatrice. So he decided to come inside, which is when he heard Jewel confess. It was just like his sweet Jewel to be protective and take the blame.

"River," Adria called pleasantly as River made his way up the aisle. Adria had always held River and Dex in respect because they were both great leaders of their wolf packs, and she had praised the peace River had generated between them. River glanced over at Beatrice and the baby as he passed them and stood next to Jewel.

"Corina trapped me, my brother, two of my nephews, and twenty-five other wolves in a cave just outside of Ironforge. If it hadn't been for Jewel and black magic, this whole town would be under attack by Corina and her demonic army right now."

"But how did she get loose after two centuries?" Adria asked.

"You have to remember, priestess," Jewel said. "When the covenant witches first put Corina under that spell, her black magic was in its infancy. But two hundred years is a long time to gain perfection. She was able to get past the invisible barrier by entering into a young man's dreams. At first I thought it was a succubus, but now I'm sure she entered Jessie Carter's dreams by using sex and his body for her black deeds."

"Once she was free, she discarded poor Jessie like he was a bag of trash," River said.

"Good goddess!" Adria said. "This is terrible." Adria and the council members began to grumble and fidget about. "We...we must call for the High Council. Corina could be..."

"No! Wait! Calm down," Jewel urged them. "Corina has been placed under a stronger spell. I used black magic this time. But that doesn't mean she won't break through the invisible barrier again. I doubt if any spell can hold Corina for long. It's been months since I trapped her."

"Dear goddess, then she could be free…running around out there anywhere!" said a nervous Dolly while looking through a nearby window.

Adria placed a finger against her nose. "This might explain the sudden animal attacks. Corina could have done something before you trapped her behind the barrier."

A frightened Dolly stood up, and her eyes darted. "She…she may have conjured up something and sent it to harm us, like a demonic dog, or a bear, or…" Then her eyes widened when she spotted something, and she pointed. "Maybe that…that huge green horsefly there on the wall. Eeeek," she screeched backing up. "That's the biggest fly I've ever seen."

"Oh, sit down, Dolly!" Adria scolded. "You're being silly." Adria walked over to the wall, took off her shoe, and smashed the fly, leaving a mass of shiny green, red, and grey matter the size of a golf ball on the off-white wall.

Dolly flopped down next to Mike and put her hand on her chest like her heart was hurting.

River smirked. "If only destroying anything Corina sent could be that easy."

Adria walked back over to where River and Jewel stood. "If Corina were free, believe me, we would have felt it by now."

River assumed a more serious expression. "Getting back to Jewel and this so-called trial date," he warned, "you can't punish her. I know what your rules say, but she's the only hope you've got right now. You try to go up against Corina with your white earth magic and she'll annihilate you…all of us. No one will be safe."

"We must keep this a secret among us," Jewel pleaded. "I swear to you, once I do away with Corina and her followers, I'll get rid of the grimoire and never use black magic again. Then you can tell the others and do what you want with me. I only ask one thing."

Adria raised an eyebrow, not sure she wanted to hear.

"Whoever I choose to help me, promise me you won't punish them. I can't do this alone…the spells I'll have to use against Corina are too strong for just one witch."

Adria looked over at the council members for guidance. They looked at one another and began whispering back and forth, agreeing and disagreeing. Jewel held her breath. Minutes seemed like hours as they spoke among themselves. Finally, Mike nodded to Adria.

"All right," Adria said. "We'll do what you ask." Then she looked at Jewel sternly. "But… when Corina goes, that grimoire goes. Understood?"

"Understood, Priestess Adria," Jewel said, exhaling hard. She rose and walked back to Beatrice and gathered the baby in her arms with River following close behind. They practically marched out of the hall as if they had triumphed over some conquest—and perhaps, in a way, they had.

Once outside, they separated and walked to their own vehicles. Jewel strapped Merchant into his car seat and climbed into the driver's side. Beatrice drove up beside Jewel grinning and gave her a thumbs up before pulling off.

Later that night, Jewel contacted her coven members as well as Naomi to elicit their help in a grand effort to bring down Corina and her goons—permanently.

Chapter Twenty-Six

In the following year, Sheerfield's children complained well into October that the summer had ended too quickly. Stay-at-home moms, however, were delighted the kids were back in school and out of the house for a few hours a day so they could do housework or run their businesses from home. Then, like great little soccer moms, they could be seen driving around, picking up their kids from various school practices, or dropping them off at the mall.

Christmas was two months away, and Halloween meant nothing to covenant witches. Though they tolerated the insults of pointy hats, wart noses, and broom-riding freaks, they remained very protective of Sheerfield humans.

The October days were like a Van Gogh painting: splashes of burnt orange and pumpkin-yellow leaves covering the ground, glimpses of dark-brown soil peeking between the colors. Tall red oak trees towered over all with branches that lovingly reached up to a bright pale-blue sky interrupted by streaks of white. And birds—some black, some brown, some black with red beaks, and some brown with bright orange breasts—darted about, bringing the canvas to life.

The nights, however, were a painting yet to come; when finished, it would hang crooked in the children's nightmares. Awe, midnight, why does everything happen at midnight? Evil lurks in the day well enough; human evil gladly attacks in the hours of daylight. Ghouls like to lurk in the shadows of the day until one huge shadow called night approaches, but the ghouls never leave the shadows. They become the midnight. Today, that midnight is Corina, and she is free....

"Corina is free?" River said loudly, looking over Jewel's shoulder at her computer screen.

Jewel jumped. "Good goddess, you scared me. No," she said, shutting off the screen. "It's just something I wrote to pass the time."

"Hell, you scared me too."

She gave a dry chuckle. "I'm sorry. Beatrice, Naomi, and my coven have been working so hard on spells. We've only come up with a few that may work, but nothing seem certain to put Corina out of commission for good."

"So, you decided to sit here and write about autumn leaves and little birdies. Well, that'll get rid of Corina."

"River, please, I don't need your sarcasm. I was just tired and this is what I do to relax after studying spells all damn day and night."

"Hey, I'm sorry," he said, holding up the palms of his hands. "It's just when I saw that last line it freaked me the hell out." He leaned around and kissed her cheek and said in her ear, "I know you're trying." He walked off toward the staircase. "Where are the kids? I don't want them straying too far from the house. Never know when that bitch could really break free." River turned around on the stairs. Jewel didn't answer. "You listening to me?"

"Oh, they're in their room doing their homework, and I've placed a shield around the house," she said with a faraway look.

River walked back down the steps and over to her. "You're really worried, aren't you? I don't like seeing you like this."

She rubbed her eyes, placed her hand in the middle of her back, and arched it. "I'm just tired," she said with a yawning voice.

He lifted her chin. "You're my wife. I know tired, and I know worried, and you're worried."

Jewel knew she could never fool River. The fate of everyone was counting on her to put Corina away, and she felt no closer to doing so than when she first promised the council.

"Look at me," River told her. Jewel looked into his eyes. "I know I can't do magic," he said, "but you witches are not alone. You saw how well the wolves did against Corina's demon army. We were outnumbered, but we were kicking their rotten asses pretty good until you had to save us. Now, imagine the entire wolf pack. You see what I mean?"

"Yes, honey. You guys held your own for quite a while. I was proud of you."

"We," he gently poked her chest with his finger then poked his own, "the witches and the wolves are going to defeat her. You hear me? We're going to bring her down. We're going to crush her and her ghoulish henchmen," he said with a shake of his fist.

Jewel smiled wide with closed lips and nodded.

"I mean it," he said. He bent and gave her a nice wet one on the lips, then turned and headed up the stairs to check on the children and take a shower before dinner.

Jewel slid down in the chair and placed her hand on her aching head. The spells were so difficult and consuming. Though River never complained, she hadn't prepared a nutritional meal in weeks. She'd thought of asking Aunt Vera to come and look after the children so she and River could concentrate fully on Corina. Aunt Vera was a kind witch and widow with no children. She loved the kids and had long desired to come and spend time with them. Jewel picked up her phone, scrolled down until she got to Auntie V, and touched the screen.

*****

A few miles away, Naomi was planning on doing the forbidden; she was going to contact her great-grandmother Trudy, a witch who'd been dead for more than a hundred and sixty years. The longer a witch had been deceased, the stronger her powers. Naomi believed that, with her great-grandmother's help, they stood a good chance against Corina. But one needed permission from the Gate Keeper of the Mystic Souls. The Gate Keeper guarded Elysium where the spirits of covenant witches' went to rest. Mystic Souls were not subject to the same rules as living witches—they could use any magic.

Before the Gate Keeper could give permission, the High Council of the Dead had to approve, and they had to wait for the High Council of the Living to investigate and determine if the summoning was for a good reason. And if they determined it wasn't, then they'd refuse the request.

Naomi knew she was taking a risk by going outside the jurisdiction of the Gate Keeper. Acting without the proper clearance could cause her magic to be suspended for years, but going through the right channels took weeks, sometimes months. The thought of Corina breaking free and Naomi having to wait on a decision from multiple high-up authority figures was nerve-wrecking. Naomi was going to take a shortcut and use a powerful talisman that was passed down to her by her mother. This talisman belonged to her great-grandmother Trudy, and Naomi was going to use it to contact her. However, Trudy could refuse to meet with Naomi or deny her request for help. Also, Mystic Souls were often very temperamental. Being summoned took them away from a bright and restful paradise. If Trudy became angry for any number of reasons, it was quite possible that she would kill Naomi, which wasn't a bad thing since death held a more pleasant existence for covenant witches anyway. Sometimes Mystic Souls would kill because they were glad to see a loved one and wanted their eternal company. But Naomi didn't wish to die yet; she had more living to do. Plus she'd hopefully promised her aid against Corina. So, summoning great-grandmother Trudy had a most uncertain outlook.

The talisman was a ruby and gold brooch shaped like a unicorn head in profile. The head was gold with ruby eyes, and the horn was an inch long with a needle point. The back of the brooch was flat with a latch on the side that opened the face. Naomi pressed the little latch, and the face slowly opened. Inside, neatly folded, was a piece of white cloth. She unfolded it and observed gold writing in Coptic, an early Egyptian language spoken before the seventeenth century. After Egypt was invaded during the Muslim conquests, the language changed to Egyptian Arabic, and it remains so today. As a young college student, Naomi had majored in ancient languages and was quite fluent in Coptic. She memorized the instructions, folded the cloth, and placed it back inside the brooch.

With her phone in hand, Naomi texted Jewel to inform her of her plans in case something went wrong and she didn't return. She changed into a pair of jeans, sweatshirt, and Nike shoes. She grabbed a small plastic bag containing two candles and a lighter, then went into the bathroom and closed the door. After half-filling the tub with cold water, Naomi slid into the tub fully clothed. Her soaked clothing clung to her, making her body shiver. She pricked her thumb with the horn of the unicorn, chanted in Coptic, and allowed the blood to drip into the water. Taking in a big gulp of air, she held her breath and let her head slip beneath the water—her eyes wide open. The water turned a misty grey, and Naomi disappeared.

A quiet blue river ran through the middle of a strange nowhere. Above it was no sky, only a sparkling brightness. Suddenly, there was a whooshing sound and water shot up six feet—in its midst was Naomi gasping for air. She took several deep breaths and looked around puzzled, wiping the water from her eyes. "This certainly doesn't look like paradise," she said. But then she realized that she still had to speak the incantation that would unite her with great-grandmother Trudy. Maybe that would take her to paradise. Naomi swam then walked the rest of the way through the shallow water. Walking across the grass, she spotted a flat-top rock about as big as a stool. It was the perfect spot to set up and summon Trudy. She pulled the candles from the plastic bag and placed them on the rock. After lighting the candles, she pricked her finger and let three drops of blood fall to the soil as she repeated the incantation. But after nearly an hour, nothing happened. It had failed. Naomi walked back into the river and swam to the bottom, looking for the exit. She came up for air and was ready to dive back down when she heard a voice.

"You'll never get back that way," a strong female voice said.

"Did...did someone say something?" Naomi asked looking around. A large white oval cloud floated down from the brightness and settled near the rock with the candles. It slowly faded, and a woman who looked to be in her sixties emerged.

Naomi hurried out of the river and stood before the old woman who she recognized from a family portrait. The old woman stood with a stiff upper lip and stared at Naomi with a troublesome expression. She moved in close to Naomi and raised her blue, vein-covered hands.

A lump rose in Naomi's throat. "Are you going to kill me?"

"Great stars, child. Is that anyway to greet your great-grandmother?" She held her arms out to Naomi who walked swiftly into them and embraced her.

"I'm sorry, but all my life I was told…"

"They're just rumors, child, to discourage every Tom, Dick, and Harry from bothering us. You'd be surprised at the silly stuff we get summoned for, mostly about some family secret of buried treasures that almost never exists. They don't seem to realize that the only thing that's buried is us. That's not what you're here for, is it?"

"No. I wish that's all it was."

"I didn't think so. That's why I was so worried when I saw you. What is it child?"

"It's this sorcerer, Corina, she's…"

"Awe…Corina. We locked her away a couple of centuries ago. Let me guess, she's free and running amuck and you're here to get me to stop her."

"Well, yes, sort of. She did get loose but we, that is, Jewel, this friend of mine, confined her again with a stronger spell. But Corina's a powerful witch and nothing can hold her for long. We've studied just about every major banning spell there is in the grimoire, and nothing even comes close to putting her away for good."

Trudy's eyes widened. "Covenant witches are allowed to use grimoires now?"

"No. It's a long story. Grand Trudy, can you help us?"

"First of all, you're looking in the wrong place. There's nothing in a grimoire that can permanently imprison a witch."

"But y*our* powers can, right?"

"The only thing my powers can do is confine her longer than any living witch. You can imprison her for two hundred years, I can imprison her for five hundred, six, seven, a thousand, but then the world goes on, and a thousand years is nothing to a witch…she gets free, runs amuck with her evil, and then, what, one of your great-

great-great-grandchildren comes back here and needs our help again."

Naomi's face dropped. "Then I came here for nothing."

"Well, I wouldn't say for nothing," she said, looking at Naomi under her lashes.

"Oh, Grand Trudy, I didn't mean it like that. Certainly I've always looked forward to meeting you."

"I know, child. But listen, all is not lost. There is but one power that can incarcerate her for eternity, but we don't speak the name. They don't tolerate witches, and they won't help us. But they'll help humans. You're going to have to get the humans involved."

"Humans? But they're powerless, what can they do?"

"Nothing, but when they're in trouble from evil, the name we don't mention comes running to help them. Their skills and weapons are not from magic like ours, but divine and it is imperative that witches make themselves scares whenever they show up. That's all I can tell you, child."

Naomi watched the white oval cloud appear from nowhere and float toward them. Trudy prepared to step into it. "Grand, wait! If you can't speak their name, then who do we tell the humans to contact?"

"Find Warren Campbell," she shouted before the cloud disappeared into the light.

"But...where do I find him," Naomi shouted up at the brightness.

"He'll find youuuu." Trudy's voice trailed off from a distance.

Naomi dropped her shoulders and looked off disappointed. "What am I supposed to tell Jewel? She was really counting on me," she snapped. Suddenly, it dawned on her. "Hey!" she yelled, looking up. "How am I supposed to get back? Grand! Grand Trudy! Damn." Naomi looked around eagerly then walked over to the rock, slapped the candles off of it, and flopped down. She had begun to sulk when, without warning, the rock turned into a gelatinous substance; before Naomi could get her bearing, she sank into the rock, and it swallowed her whole. She rose up in her bathtub gasping for breath. Naomi wiped the water from her eyes then jumped out of the tub. She stumbled back against the door panting and stared at the tub of water—her clothes dripping into a pool at her feet.

In the meantime, Aunt Vera moved in and had the house running like clockwork. The air brimmed with the aroma of old-world cooking, and the children flocked to the kitchen to help bake their favorite chocolate, peanut butter, and raisin cookies.

Becca grew close to her baby brother—she adored him. Jewel often found her in the nursery sitting with Merchant on her lap and reading to him for hours. She was growing up; she had shed her baby fat and had outgrown her clothes as well as her annoying habit of breaking things. Jewel had always thought it was nerves. Aunt Vera had taught Becca card tricks that strengthened her fingers and steadied her hands. A slight of hand had a way of doing that—at least, that's the explanation Auntie Vera gave.

A text from Naomi made Jewel frown. "Who the hell is Warren Campbell?" she mumbled.

Chapter Twenty-Seven

Crane Pulver, a northern wolf and father of three girls with a son on the way, was killed when the silver head of an arrow pierced his heart. He fell at the feet of his horrified hunting buddies who immediately fired their rifles in the direction of the arrows but hit nothing. Several swishing sounds filled the air as arrows struck three of the wolves, one through the chest, one through the neck, and one straight through the eye and out the back of the head. One wolf kept his rifle aimed in the direction of the arrows while the other tried to help the wolf with the chest wound to his feet.

Gagging on his own blood, he urged the others, "Save yourselves. I'm done. Tell my wife…" His head fell back with his eyes wide open.

The two wolves turned and ran as fast as they could. But seconds later, when the swishing sounds had ceased, the wolves lay dead with multiple arrows sticking out of their backs. A seventh wolf who had stopped to pee by a tree witnessed the horror. Gripping his rifle, he'd ducked down within a thick bush. He watched as heads with hair in black cornrows slowly appeared from behind trees. A regiment of tall Nubian female archers dressed in long, ancient shifts carrying recurve bows stood looking around for their next victims. The wolf recognized something…*those red lifeless eyes. No! Corina, she's loose,* he thought. Corina had wasted no time conjuring up an even deadlier ancient army, Egyptian warriors—the most notorious archers of that era. *They have the same demonic eyes as the demons we had faced in the cave.* He was one of the lucky ones who had escaped the cave. *I have to go…I've got to warn them.* But for now, he had to stay as still as an animated object.

The Nubians walked quietly like cats, stepping within several feet of where the wolf hid. One stood right above him looking around; the wolf put his hand over his mouth and would have ceased the loud beating of his heart if he could. *They must be sensitive only to movement,* he thought. They spoke not a word, but there was something else he recognized—that smell. Whatever Corina used in her magic had amounted to her evil trademark. Peeking out from between the leaves, the wolf's face turned grim when he saw the demons stopping at every bush and poking around in them with their arrows.

No! No! he screamed in his head.

The archer who stood above him extended her bow. The wolf felt the cold metal slide past his tense flesh, and he squeezed his eyes shut. Another poke and the blade sliced straight through the side of his shirt before pulling out. Beads of sweat lined his forehead—his fight or flight reflex pulsated in his brain. The archer poked her arrow a third time, and the point touched his ear. His anxiety triggered his transformation—his fangs grew out, and his eyes turned bright yellow, but something up ahead caught the demons' attention and they moved on. He waited until they were nearly out of sight before he launched into motion in the opposite direction—careful to keep low—and sprinted away.

When word of the ancient archers reached the ears of the wolves, panic broke throughout Greyscott Falls. Crane, well known for his stubbornness and fearlessness during the feud between the packs, was now known as the first noted wolf to be killed in this twenty-first century battle against a more potent Corina.

*****

The witches and wolves had agreed they needed more powerful weapons and armor to deal with the encroaching threat of the Nubians. Later that night, Beatrice and several other coven members raided one of the largest companies that sold Level IV hard plate armor. The wolves would wear them after the breast armor was mystified against the penetration of demonic weapons. Jewel had researched the ancient Nubians and found that they had been relentlessly devoted to the goddess Mut, the Mother Goddess of the Egyptians. In 2686 BC, they had guarded her temple in Karnak at Thebes. The goddess was beautiful with ebony skin, a long, broad nose, and full lips. She wore a double crown plus a royal vulture headdress made of gold and other precious stones.

Her thick black braids fell below her headdress to her shoulders and lay against her full breasts. Gold balls decorated the braided ends of her hair. Jewel located a duplicate of the royal head and put a spell on it to mesmerize the Nubian demons when they looked upon their goddess's face.

With the wolves in their mystic armor and a miniature goddess Mut in the witches' possession, all that was needed was to mystify the swords. Fighting the Nubians as werewolves was ineffective; plus, there was no way to outfit huge wolves with breast armor. They could only cut off the heads of the demons to defeat them, and for that they needed to stand upright and fight like humans. But unlike the undead army, who had continued to fight without heads, the spell was designed to cause the headless Nubians to fall limp like puppets cut from their strings.

Women, children, and elderly wolves stayed behind in a secret place while the younger wolves, weapons in hand, piled into their vehicles. Once on foot, River and Dex led the wolves with Matthew and Rick bringing up the rear. The wolves chose an open area away from their homes in hopes that Corina and her army would follow them there. Jewel and Naomi, with the duplicate head of the goddess in hand, stayed back a ways to look around for any movement in the wooded area that was several yards in front of them. The coven members stayed behind in the temple chanting—calling on the ancient spirits of their ancestors for power and protection.

Jewel observed movement from the darkness of the wooded area ahead of them. Holly, Amber, and Gunner walked out of the shadows followed by Nubian archers. Jewel and Naomi stiffened, and the wolves took their fighting stances. The trio and the Nubians stood several yards away. The scene partly resembled the gunfight at the O.K. Corral.

Gunner sashayed in front of Holly and Amber. "Pa...thetic," he said, looking at the wolves as if something stunk. "Look at you. What can you do?" He glanced back at the Nubians momentarily. "I hope you're familiar with history," he taunted. "They can shoot a fly off the wing of a vulture and not touch a single feather."

River looked unimpressed. "Where's Corina? Don't tell me she's going to miss the show. Or perhaps she couldn't bear the humiliation of seeing her henchmen reduced to dog shit."

Gunner chuckled and looked down at the ground, then up.

Holly lifted her chin. "Corina has more important things to do. She leaves the trivial stuff to us." She turned to Amber. "Destroying these bastards shouldn't take long, should it, Amber?"

"I shouldn't think so," Amber said, smirking. "Oh, I hear one of your dead wolves was expecting his first little boy. Too bad little wolfie won't have a daddy."

Red anger rose in Dex and he jerked forward, but River pulled him back. "Enough talk," River said loudly.

Gunner's face darkened, and his eyes turned black as coal. "For once... you're right."

Straight away, a swishing sound came from behind the wolves. An arrow struck one of them in the back of the head clear through his forehead. He fell face down.

"ATTACK!" River yelled.

Hundreds of arrows reverberated above them like the wings of a thousand menacing houseflies. The wolves had to split in half because they were being attacked from the front and rear. The spirits of the ancient witches embodied the wolves as their supernatural strength tore into the demons. Fifteen to twenty wolves fell dead as did fifty demons when their heads flew off in every direction. Jewel and Naomi chanted with both their hands holding the royal head of the Goddess Mut out before them. Every Nubian who glimpsed the face of her goddess became mesmerized by the green glowing eyes. When their eyes fixed on the goddess, their bodies melted into the earth as their spirits rejoined Mut in the afterworld.

The trio looked on in fury at what was happening to their glorious army. Gunner shot out his hand, and a stream of energy knocked the royal head from Jewel's and Naomi's hands. Holly and Amber joined him, and it became the battle of the witches. The five shot streams of energy at one another, knocking each other about. As soon as Naomi got to her feet, she shot back and Gunner was swept off *his* feet. Jewel, who was back on her feet, hauled Amber ten feet into the air before dropping her to the ground. Two members of the coven, observing the battle through a mystic bowl, shifted their attention to the trio. A force gripped the trio and held them, forcing their hands to become rigid at their sides and their lips sealed so they couldn't utter a counter spell. The trio was forced to stand frozen and mute while watching their army torn to bits.

Suddenly, Corina appeared out of a portal, her eyes red as rubies. She waved her hand, but the coven put an invisible barrier around the wolves and Corina's deadly bolt bounced against it with no effect. Jewel and Naomi stood unprotected but powerful because of the spirits of their ancestors. Corina was no fool.

Her eyes burned as she looked upon what was left of her army. Enraged at the Nubians' performance against the wolves, she cursed them. "Imbeciles, I banish you to utter darkness, away from your precious Mut." The Nubians fell to their knees and begged for forgiveness, but a wave of her hand tore opened the ground where they knelt; the darkness rose and swallowed them as they descended screaming. Her eyes then burned on Jewel and Naomi. "Next time," she said. She spoke an incantation, a force released the trio, and the four disappeared through the portal.

The invisible barrier came down and the wolves cheered, but the victory was short-lived. Matthew called to his father with a trembling voice. Matthew was holding Rick's dead, limp body—a silver arrow through the neck.

*****

It had been days since the battle with the Nubians. By this time, Jewel's secret was out. The entire community of witches knew about Jewel, the grimoire, and all the disobedience that went with it. Jewel had suspected that a secret like that couldn't last, but now the entire witch population was engaged in defeating Corina. And Jewel's punishment was on hold. No one spoke of it. Destroying Corina was front and center of everyone's mind.

217

The wolves' cemetery was a blue river. The witches wore black hooded cloaks; in front of them, the wolves wore black shirts and pants with red armbands—the red symbolizing that a wolf had died in battle. Rick's family stood in front of them. His mom held a black handkerchief up to her nose, and Rick's father stood next to her with his eyes fixed on Rick's body. Rick's funeral was one of many that week. He was laid out on a pyre in a small boat—dressed in black shirt and pants with a wooden sword painted gold placed in his hands. Matthew almost didn't come, and Kayla held onto him as his shoulders shook. He and Rick were like brothers; you barely saw one without the other. Matthew remembered the evening he'd taken Rick home, drunk after Aunt Jewel had her baby. He was glad that he and Rick laughed about it later. Rick had sworn off drinking hard liquor, and meant it for once.

One by one people brought grave gifts and placed them on the pyre, all to be consumed by fire as would Rick, a custom they'd followed for generations. A wolf handed a torch to Rick's father. He stepped forward and lit the pyre. Three wolves loosed the ties and gave the boat a shove, then watched it carry their brother to deeper waters. Rick's father stepped back and held his wife as their faces said farewell to their brave son.

*****

That Night
"I can't believe Rick is gone," Jewel said, lying cuddled up to River.

"Umm," River moaned. He felt her pain but his eyes were heavy.

Jewel was getting to bed earlier for a change thanks to Aunt Vera who had become a welcome member of the Porter household. She frequently helped the children with their homework. A widow who was a former world traveler, there was practically nothing she couldn't discuss intelligently. Tonight, Vera had read to Merchant and put him to bed with his favorite toy, a polka-dot stuffed elephant.

Tactics of future battles moved around in Jewel's mind like tennis balls bouncing against her brain. As she lay fidgeting in the bend of River's arm, she wondered what Corina would do next. They could match her battle for battle, but to do that would be costly to the inhabitants of the region. New Berwick couldn't survive an ongoing battle with a powerful sorcerer. There just had to be a permanent solution. *Naomi keeps going on and on about this Warren Campbell,* Jewel thought. *"But whoever he is, according to Grand Trudy, he hates witches. Priestess Adria and the coven want nothing to do with him, and neither do I.*

River lay in the dark with his eyes closed. "Honey, get some sleep. I can feel you worrying."

Jewel shut her eyes and drifted off.

Chapter Twenty-Eight

Jewel had closed the grimoire and rested her back against the soft cushion of the chair. She was sitting and sipping the spice tea Aunt Vera had made when she heard commotion in the next room and Vera say, "No, I didn't see her come in, dear. Are you sure?" Jewel heard running up the stairs then the opening and shutting of doors as if rooms were being checked.

Jewel held her breath and waited for the news to come to her. The side and back doors opened and closed several times, and Jewel saw blurry heads shooting past the window. Vera came into the room and though she smiled, the quick blinking of her eyelids proved she was trying too hard to appear calm.

"Does Becca have practice today?" Vera asked, smiling like the answer would be no big deal.

"No."

"Well, I'm sure she must have stopped somewhere at one of her little friend's houses," she said, turning to leave. Vera didn't want to stress Jewel out unnecessarily. She was hoping to stall getting her worked up if the situation turned out to be nothing serious.

Just then, Chelsea brushed by her. "Mom, have you seen Becca?"

"Not since this morning." Jewel didn't want to assume the inevitable; it was too painful. *Perhaps River picked her up from school and they're having so much fun that he forgot to call. He's done it before.* She grabbed her phone.

Dria burst into the room. "She's nowhere in the house," Dria said, frantically looking from Chelsea to Vera. "And Abby is checking the yard and garage."

"River," Jewel said, keeping panic out of her voice. "Is Becca with you?" *Please goddess.*

Vera, Chelsea, and Dria watched a look of pain stretch slowly across Jewel's face.

Abby burst in with such force that it knocked Vera and Chelsea, who were standing next to each other, apart. "Mom, someone in a dark van just threw Becca's backpack on the front lawn," she said, holding it out so Jewel could see.

Jewel looked at Becca's pink-and-white backpack with a picture of Supergirl on it. She still held the phone, but the line went dead; River had heard everything and had pushed his truck into overdrive. Soon after, the phone rang. Jewel slowly picked it up and put it to her ear. The words "Incoming Call" frightened her more than her recent thoughts. "Yes," she said, dreading the voice on the other end.

"Are you missing someone?" Gunner joked.

Every bite of food Jewel had eaten rose and settled in her chest. Her blood felt like ice shooting through her veins. Corina had kept her promise though she had never spoken it. But her burning eyes and the words "next time" from that day now had a meaning, and the reality of the words burned her brain like the scorching sun.
Jewel kept her voice calm. "Tell Corina she wins."
Vera gasped at the name.

"I'll do anything. Just don't hurt her." Jewel didn't want to sound too desperate. She knew psychopaths enjoyed the pain they inflicted, and she didn't want to add to his sick pleasure.

Gunner chuckled. "Corina always wins." Then the tone of his voice darkened. "Be at the castle before midnight, and come alone." Then a hint of pleasure took his voice up an octave. "And Jewel, don't do anything stupid if you want those baby blues to stay in her little head."

"I won't do anything."

River burst into the room as Jewel clicked off. His eyes bore into hers as he read what was so apparent within them. "No. No!" He spotted the grimoire, picked it up with one hand, and slung it at the wall. The loud thump startled the younger children, but Chelsea didn't flinch. She knew things but wasn't allowed to speak of them.

"Mom, we have to do something," Chelsea said, rushing forward.

"Chelsea, you know better," Jewel scolded. "This is a problem for adults to handle."

"I'm not a baby. I know what goes on in this house...in this neighborhood. She's my sister," Chelsea yelled.

River's mouth tightened. "Did you hear your mother?"

"Stop treating me like I'm a little kid."

"BE QUIET!" River's voice thundered.

Dria and Abby jumped at the sound because River had never raised his voice at them. Vera gathered the three girls, and they all sat quietly on the sofa.

Then River turned to Vera in a sudden panic. "Where's Merchant?"

"He's okay, Daddy. He's asleep," Dria assured him.

"Go get him," he demanded Vera. She ran from the room, heading for the nursery. "I don't want these kids out of our sight. We'll homeschool them until this matter with that bitch is settled." He flopped down on the sofa next to the kids. "How did we let this happen?"

Jewel ran a nervous hand through her dark hair then let her hand slap against her thigh. "We had strong spells around our homes, cars, our children's schools, play areas. She...she removed them."

River looked down at the floor. "Then there's only one thing to do." He paused. "I'll give myself in exchange for Becca."

"They don't want you," she said, walking across the room and picking up the grimoire. "They want me at the castle before midnight." She dusted the book with her hand, brought it back, and placed it on the table.

"That's insane," River griped.

Vera walked in with a sleepy Merchant in her arms and sat down on the sofa next to the girls. River looked over at Chelsea who was still sulking. He held her under her chin and turned it to him. "I didn't mean to yell at you, princess. I'm just angry...but not at you, honey."

Chelsea scooted over to him and placed her head on his shoulder, tears streaming down her rosy cheeks.

"We'll get Becca back," he said, "no matter what it takes."

It was four hours to midnight. The joy once felt in the Porter home hid beneath the sad reality of little Becca's dilemma. A stack of homemade chocolate, peanut butter, and raisin cookies sat untouched on the kitchen counter. The witches had been alerted to what had happened and were busy trying to come up with ideas before Jewel's deadline. They knew Corina so well—Corina would never let Jewel or Becca leave her castle alive, and that sickened them. They knew it because Corina had finally allowed them access to the inside of her castle, and a locating spell had revealed the very place where Becca was being held, which meant that Corina was hoping for a rescue mission and would ambush and kill all who came. Those were the kinds of sick games Corina played with her victims. She knew the wolves would take that chance knowing full well it was an ambush and she was right.

"River," Jewel pleaded. "Let's wait and see. The covenant members are bound to come up with a better solution."

"I'm tired of waiting," he said, fastening his breast armor. "Whatever that bitch throws at us, if we can't duck it, we'll meet it head on. Goddess knows what they're doing to our baby." He started for the door. Dex and Matthew, along with the other wolves, were to meet him at a secret location to perfect the rescue mission. Jewel threw her arms around him. "Honey, I should go with you in case things don't work out. It's me they want." He kissed her with a kiss she'd never felt before, and her heart ached because she knew what it meant. Her phone rang just as River hurried out to his truck. Hoping for good news, Jewel ran to answer it. "Naomi," Jewel said with hopefulness in her voice.

"Jewel, I believe I've got a way to rescue Becca."

"Oh, Naomi, thank the goddesses."

"Using my invisibility cloak, I can get into the castle and get Becca."

Jewel's hopes deflated. "Awe, Naomi, if that's your plan we're sunk. To Corina, that's amateur night. She won't be fooled by an invisibility cloak. Her magic will sniff you out the minute your foot enters the castle."

"I've thought of that. Listen…have River and the wolves left for the castle?"

"Yeah, he's meeting up with them now," her voice dragged.

"All right, tell them not to attack but to make as much ruckus as they can to distract her."

"So, you're hoping if she's concentrating on something else, you might get in before she notices you?"

"Exactly."

Jewel thought momentarily. "I don't know, Naomi. It doesn't sound like much of a plan."

"Don't forget, I still have great-grandmother Trudy's brooch. I can grab Becca and slip to the Mystic Souls."

"Oh, I forgot about that. Why, that's brilliant…if you can get in undetected."

"There is one problem. I can get Becca out of the castle but not back to you. Well, not right away."

"What do you mean?"

"Leaving the Mystic Souls returns you to the place you left. I was in my own bathtub when I left to meet Grand Trudy. When I returned, the trip brought me back to my bathtub. That means returning will put me back at the castle. I'll have to find a way back to you. I'm hoping Grand can help me bypass the castle. The important thing is to get Becca away from Corina…."

"….then figure out a way back that's safe.

"Naomi, this is so brilliant. I'll call River with the plan."

For the first time since Becca's kidnapping, Jewel felt excitement and hope as she eagerly dialed River. If this worked, it meant they weren't as helpless as they thought against Corina's magic. But no one dared underestimate her powers.

*****

Forty minutes to midnight. Naomi had prepared three invisibility cloaks; each cloak had a ten-minute window. She knew she would need more than ten minutes to get into the castle, find Becca, perform the spell, and get out of the castle before Corina caught them. Jewel had River and Naomi on a three-way call so she could monitor the situation. There would be no way to call Jewel if the plan worked since the journey to the land of the dead broke mobile connections. Naomi would have to wait until she reached a safe place among the living before contacting Jewel.

Jewel's heartbeat felt replaced by pins and needles as she waited nervously for Naomi to reach Becca. The wolves put on a good show by taunting, name-calling, shooting out castle and car windows, and blowing the heads off of demonic-looking statues placed in various locations on the front lawn of the castle. As long as the wolves stayed outside the gates, the guards were ordered to stand down.

The three-hundred-year-old castled had maintained its eighteenth-century Spanish beauty. It had nine bedrooms, fourteen bathrooms, and sat on thirteen acres completely gated off by a twenty-two-foot tall entry door imported from Paris.

As the castle guards were distracted, Naomi was able to get near a gate leading to the back entrance of the castle. Corina's magic could detect her but her guards couldn't. Naomi spotted a guard in a tower and ducked behind a van. She wanted to preserve the minutes on the cloaks by using some natural stealth tactics. She would wait until the guard turned his attention away from the spot where she was, then she'd scurry closer to the entrance.

Soon the guard became preoccupied with the wolves' ruckus and Naomi sensed an opening; she scrambled out from behind the van and made it closer to the servants' quarters a few feet from the entrance. The guard thought he noticed something and peered over the area. His eyes stayed there too long, and Naomi wondered if it were time to cloak up. She reached in her backpack, pulled out the cloak, wrapped it around her, and walked openly to the entrance while the guard's eyes swept over her without seeing her. It had only taken her a minute to reach the door, leaving nine minutes left in the cloak's magic.

The halls were full of undead guards with spears. And Naomi wondered if their demonic red eyes could see through her invisibility cloak. She wasn't going to take that chance. She took her phone off mute.

"Jewel," she whispered, peeking around a corner at a guard.

"Yes, is everything all right?"

"I'm in the castle, but I need your help."

"Go ahead."

"The castle guards are those corpses with red eyes. Can they see me?"

"Shit!" Jewel could kick herself for not thinking of that. She thought a moment while pacing the floor. "Put three cloaks on, you'll have triple coverage."

"That makes sense, but all three at one time will still give me ten minutes to find Becca."

"I'll direct you from the bowl, but you've got to move quickly." Naomi scurried and hid behind a tall white stone statue of a winged creature. She reached inside her backpack, pulled out the two invisibility cloaks, and wrapped both around her. She moved out in plain view of the demon guards, but they didn't notice her. Jewel directed her to a flight of stairs. As Naomi mounted the stairs, she saw something move from the corner of her eye. She turned, and the white stone statue was looking straight at her. At first Naomi thought it was her imagination, but when its eyes lifted with every step she took, she knew her fear was reality. Suddenly, it leaped into the air, flapping its wings as it slowly came toward her; she incanted with her hand extended toward it, sending the stone creature smashing into the wall. It shattered into multiple pieces, but now the guards were alerted.

Corina, who had stood on the balcony observing the wolves with amusement, jerked her body around. "Very clever." She smiled to herself, sensing that the wolves were a distraction. "It seems we have a visitor."

Gunner, Holly, and Amber snapped almost to attention.

"Split up," Corina ordered, "and bring the intruder to me."

The trio ran in three different directions, yelling out commands to the guards. Naomi almost collided with Holly when she passed her in the hallway just a few feet from the room where Becca was being held. But Holly's bracelet caught on the invisibility robe, exposing Naomi's feet and legs. Holly quickly spun around and grabbed her, yanking the cloaks from her body. Naomi's incantation drove Holly into the wall, knocking the wind out of her. Before she could recover, Naomi was in the room. She placed a spell on the door but knew it wouldn't last. Becca jumped off the bed and ran to Naomi, wrapping her arms around her tightly.

"We haven't much time. Where's the bathroom?"

"There," Becca said, leading the way to a closed door.

Bodies thundered against the door as Holly and guards tried to break in. Naomi put a spell on the bathroom door and turned on the bathtub faucet. No door under an enchantment could stop Corina; she was on her way, and it seemed the tub would never fill.

"Why are we taking a bath *now*, Naomi?" Becca blurted nervously, looking back and forth over her shoulder at the door. "Shouldn't we be leaving?" she said, hopping in place like she had to pee.

"In a minute, honey, just do what I say." Finally the tub was filled and Naomi turned off the faucet.

"Stand back!" Corina commanded Holly and the others. She waved her hand and the door flew inward, thundering against the wall. Then Corina saw the empty bed and turned her attention to the bathroom door. Becca and Naomi sat in the tub, blood dripping from both their fingers. The bathroom door flew inward, and a corner of it struck Becca's head. Corina stood in the doorway and waved her hand just as Naomi took a deep breath and went under. Corina rushed to the tub and stuck her hand in the water. Her hand went straight through the bottom of the tub and into another world—a world that couldn't abide evil. When Corina's hand touched the sacred air, she screamed and yanked it back. Her hand was black and crisp like burnt toast. She doubled over on the floor in pain. The trio lifted her and escorted her to the secret tower.

Naomi rose up out of the river, gasping for breath and holding Becca in her arms. Keeping the child's head above the water, she swam into shallow water then carried Becca and laid her on the grass. The child wasn't breathing. Knocked unconscious, Becca wasn't able to hold her breath so her lungs filled with water.

"Becca, sweetheart, breathe," she said. Naomi wasn't sure if earth magic even worked there. She held her hands over the child's torso, incanting over and over. But Becca was still. "Come on, honey." She tried CPR, but Becca didn't stir. She incanted every life-saving spell she'd ever learned and pleaded with the child to breathe. After a few more seconds, water flowed from Becca's mouth, making her gag and cough. Naomi scooped the child up in her arms and rocked her, kissing her forehead. Becca opened her eyes and looked around puzzlingly.

"Where are we?"

"We're safe."

Becca jumped and looked over her shoulders. "Is Corina coming?"

"No, only good witches are here."

Becca whispered, "We're not allowed to say witch at my house."

"I know, sweetie, but that's for your protection. Your mom and dad will talk to you more freely when you grow up. Now, there's someone I want you to meet." Naomi got up off her knees and helped Becca up. She walked over to the flat rock. "Oh no." In her rush, she had left the backpack that had the enchanted candles. Now there was no way to contact her great-grandmother.

"What's wrong?" Becca asked, looking scared.

"We're never going to get out of here. I left my backpack with the candles in it."

Becca thought for a moment. "You mean *these* candles?" She pulled the small plastic bag from under her sweater. She had seen the bag fall from the backpack and quickly grabbed it.

"Oh, Becca, bless you," Naomi said, taking the bag from her small hand. She motioned Becca over to the flat rock. "Okay," Naomi said. "You kneel there, and I'll kneel over here." She pulled out the candles and lit them. "Give me your hand. You're going to feel a little sting just like before. You can close your eyes if you want."

Becca whispered. "Are you going to do magic again?"

"Yes," Naomi playfully whispered back.

229

Becca was delighted. She was not going to close her eyes and miss this. And she'd tell her sisters everything when she got back, including stone statues that moved, dead things that walked, candles floating in the air, and strange places in the atmosphere that opened and you'd walk through.

"Okay, are you ready?" Naomi asked.

Becca eagerly nodded and held out her hand to be pricked. Then Naomi pricked her own finger and let their blood fall to the ground. She incanted and again nothing happened for nearly an hour. Becca grew disappointed until an oval shape floated down from the brightness and out stepped Great-Grandmother Trudy. "You don't have to tell me. Corina's evil is alive and well." Trudy's eyes widened. "And…who is this?" She smiled at Becca.

"Great-Grandmother Trudy, this is Becca, Jewel's daughter. Corina kidnapped her and this was the only place I could bring her."

"Oh dear child, she can't stay here."

"I know that Grand, that's why I need your help." Naomi told Trudy the entire story and asked if there was any other way, besides the way of the Gate Keeper, that they could leave and bypass returning to the castle. Naomi couldn't afford to lose her magic with Jewel needing every witch available to help banish Corina.

"There is one way, but if there's ever another emergency, I'm afraid you won't be able to get around the Gate Keeper."

"Why is that?"

"Because the only other way out of here involves that brooch. You'll have to destroy it."

Naomi looked down in her hand at the gold and ruby unicorn head. "Destroy your brooch? That's the only way?"

"Oh child, you won't really be destroying my brooch. It was stolen over two hundred years ago. That brooch isn't real. You know the portrait of me that hangs in our family home?"

"Yes, that's how I recognized you."

"Well, I was wearing my brooch when it was painted."

"But I've stared at that portrait at least a hundred times since I was a girl, and you're not wearing a brooch.

Trudy explained the mystery of the brooch and discussed it in great detail. Then she embraced them both and disappeared into the brightness overhead.

Becca aided Naomi by finding a big, heavy rock that she had to carry with both hands. Naomi took it and sat it down by the flat top rock. She placed the brooch in the middle of the rock and lit the candles.

"You ready again?" Naomi asked.

Becca nodded eagerly and held out her hand to be pricked. They held their hands over the brooch and allowed the blood to drip onto the unicorn as Naomi incanted the words given to her by Trudy. The brooch glowed and turned the atmosphere around them ruby red. Naomi picked up the large rock and smashed the brooch, which spit out yellow sparks that lit up the atmosphere. She grabbed Becca's hand, and they vanished.

Naomi and Becca became light as feathers, floating through time—back to the days of horse and buggies, then early automobiles, the 1950s, the 1980s and, finally, returning to their own time. They tumbled out of a portal and onto the upstairs floor of Naomi's home that had been in the family for generations. Becca giggled. She had landed on her butt with her legs straight up in the air. Naomi landed on her stomach and slid across the hardwood floor.

The two gathered themselves then sat looking up at the portrait of Great-Grandmother Trudy but she was not wearing the brooch. Then as they continued to watch, the gold unicorn with its ruby eyes and one-inch-long horn slowly materialized on the left side of the dark dress, just above the breast. Becca's smile was as wide as her face.

Naomi sighed in relief and pressed the mobile screen with her thumb. "Jewel, I've got someone here who wants to speak to you."

"Hi, Mommy."

"Hi, baby," Jewel said with great relief.

Chapter Twenty-Nine

Back home, away from the ears of River and Jewel, Becca held her sisters spellbound with tales of her kidnapping and rescue adventures. It was all she could talk about. The following weeks were quiet. "Too quiet," River had told Jewel. The wolves were on guard while the witches watched for signs of the unusual or normal entities mysteriously in motion. The woods were free of bears and mountain lions; they had left the area as quickly as they had come. Birds returned to the duties of their nests and pets, along with rodents, were calm again. Similarly, though not in their hearts, the wolves and witches retreated to the normal routine of farming, hunting, fishing, and enjoying family life. Theirs became a journey backward in time to deal with Corina just as their ancestors had. They had defeated the Nubian archers and rescued Becca. Corina's element of surprise was gone, or so they thought.

During early evening on a weeknight, while searching for a tidbit for her miniature dog, Chucky, eighty-three-year-old Louise Paddington noticed that her housekeeper, Dottie, had not taken out the trash. It wasn't like Dottie to forget. However, Dottie's husband was battling cancer and her concern for him had her particularly stressed: last week she'd left poor Chucky out in the rain for nearly an hour, and a few days ago an overrun bathtub had Dottie spending the better part of that morning mopping and cursing herself for being stupid. But Louise wouldn't think of scolding her for those recent blunders. *After all,* she thought, *it isn't easy working full-time and nursing an ailing husband. Besides, if I walk slowly and don't trip on anything, I can make it to the end of the yard well enough...just have to catch a few breaths on the way back.* "Chucky, you could use an extra walk, huh boy?" The little grey and black fuzz ball yapped several times, turning around and around in a circle when he spotted the leash in the old woman's hand. She had fallen and broken her hip recently and was forced to turn over to Dottie the task of walking Chucky, so this was the first time in a while that Chucky had seen his owner with a leash in her hand.

Louise opened the kitchen door and placed her foot cautiously on the steps, one step at a time, only two more to go, before tackling the long stretch of pavement to the end of the yard. With a trash bag in one hand and Chucky on leash in the other, she stood feebly on the pavement then shuffled slowly along—stopping momentarily for Chucky to sniff, pee, sniff, squat, and defecate. "Oh dear, I forgot the pooper scooper. Well, Dottie will have to get this up in the morning," she said a little out of breath. She was nearly halfway to the trash can when Chucky stood motionlessly like a stuffed toy, staring off into the darkness and growling. "Come along," she said. But the dog leapt, pulling the leash out of her hand and running off until the darkness swallowed him. It was a miracle Louise hadn't lost her balance and fallen.

"Chucky, you bad dog," she scolded, looking around for him. "Oh, he'll come back," she mumbled.

Louise finally made it down to the trash can where she lifted the top, stuffed the bag in, and then replaced the top. She sat upon the trash can gathering strength for the walk back when she heard Chucky cry out. "Chucky!" Louise yelled and saw the dog start to run halfway out of the darkness before being violently snatched back—by what, she couldn't see. Louise stood in terror as Chucky cried out as if he were being tortured. She hobbled as quickly as she could into the darkness, into the sound of the cry. A light from a nearby window flashed on. The dog's cry had alerted a neighbor. There, under the window light, squatting over Chucky, was a man yet not a man with blazing eyes. The old woman squinted at the man's bloody lips that were drawn back like a crazed animal. She let out an ear-piercing scream that brought every neighbor to their windows and doors. But as they stuck their heads out, they could see only a leash on the lawn. No one saw the man-like creature drag Louise Paddington off into the night and drain her body of every ounce of blood.

*****

Sheriff Tilbert sat at his desk with his face buried in his hands. Several residents had been found dead, their bodies shriveled up like raisins. This was nothing like before. Previously, people had wandered too far into dangerous territories and had gotten killed. These killings, however, were in their own backyards and in their neighborhoods where they lived, attended church, and watched their children play and walk to school. No one could blame these killings on bears or mountain lions that had strayed into the local forests. No, these were strange killings, even demonic in nature. *What to do, my heavenly Father...what to do.* Tilbert was drowning in his thoughts when Bob walked into his office. "What are we going to tell those reporters outside, Wayne?" Bob asked frantically. "There must be a hundred of them from all over the state."

"Tell them I'm ready to make a statement." Bob nodded and hurried out to deliver the message.

Wayne exhaled hard and straightened his shoulders. He took his time before walking outside to where reporters shoved and forced their way to where he stood at the podium.

"On November 1 at 8:25 a.m.," Wayne began, "Mrs. Louise Paddington was found dead by her housekeeper. She was lying on her lawn six feet from the body of her dog. At 10:45 a.m., the sheriff's department was called to Mr. and Mrs. Simmons's home where Carol Simmons, her husband, Mike, and eight-year-old son, Chris, were found lying in their driveway. They were all pronounced dead at the scene, and, according to an autopsy, all were killed the previous night. On November 2 at approximately 8:16 p.m., Jeff Middleton and Cornel Lubrinski, both sixteen-year-old Sheerfield High School students, were reported missing after not returning home from basketball practice. Both were later found dead on the school parking lot by the school janitor at approximately 7:45 the following morning. There are no eye witnesses at this time, but the Sheerfield Sheriff's Department is doing everything possible to find whoever is responsible and bring them to justice. Thank you."

"Sheriff! Sheriff! Sheriff!" shouted reporters. One female reporter got her way and stepped forward.

"Sherriff Tilbert, why are the autopsies being kept secret?"

"We're not inclined to release that information before we make an arrest for fear of copycat killings. It's routine department procedure."

"Sheriff! Sheriff!" bellowed reporters until Tilbert pointed to a tall man wearing thick, black-rimmed glasses. "People around Sheerfield have said this is the work of a cult...any truth to that?"

"We have no proof of that allegation."

Same reporter: "What is the sheriff's department doing to keep people safe?"

"We have implemented a plan but will not share any details at the moment for obvious reasons."

Same reporter: "Some see this as too big a problem for a small-town sheriff's department. Why haven't you called for state police?"

Tilbert fumed but kept his composure. "Our sheriff's department is quite capable of protecting its residents and has done so for many decades."

Same reporter: "But people are still dying, Sheriff Tilbert. You have no eye witnesses, you've made no arrests, and recently we've learned that you have residents with no law enforcement skills patrolling the streets. Doesn't this mean the Sheerfield Sheriff's Department is incapable of keeping its residents safe, sir?"

Sheriff Tilbert looked sternly at the reporter from under his lashes. "As I've stated, the Sheerfield Sheriff's Department is doing everything it can to catch the culprits and bring them to justice. If we should need the aid of the state police, we won't hesitate to call them for assistance."

Same reporter: "But isn't it a fact that the reason why your department is slow in finding the murderer or murderers is because you and your whole town believe this is the work of werewolves?"

A host of reporters began to chuckle among themselves and one shouted, "Well, if that's true Sheriff Tilbert, sure hope your deputies don't run out of silver bullets!"

Smiles and laughter burst forth among the journalists.

Every vein in Wayne's neck began to show. Bob stepped forward and leaned in to the mic. "As Sheriff Tilbert has explained, our highly skilled sheriff's department has a record of protecting its people. And the person or persons responsible will be caught and brought to justice. Thank you." As Bob and Wayne turned to go inside, a female reporter yelled to Bob, "Who might you be, sir?" Bob continued walking but glanced over his shoulder and shouted back, "I'm the coroner."

Excited, she yelled, "Can I ask you a couple of questions, sir? Sir!" Bob ignored her. "Is it true that the victims' bodies were all drained of blood? Sir! Sir!"

Bob closed the door behind him. "How the hell did she find that out? Think we have a leak?"

Wayne ignored Bob's question. "Smart asses," he said, looking back at the door. "I could have wrung both their freaking necks."

"All right," Bob said. "We got through that. Now, it's just you and me; what *is* your plan for protecting the people?"

Wayne walked behind his desk and sat down in his chair. "Before you came in, I was sitting here thinking we could use the church. It can only hold so many people, so I thought we could bring in the women, children, sick, and elderly. The men will have to fend for themselves or join the other volunteers and help us fight whatever this is."

"Sounds good to me. I'll put the word out," Bob said, rushing from the office with his mobile to his face.

St. Paul's Church of the Dominions was a one hundred and fifty year old wooden church built around the late 1800s. It had been renovated many times to accommodate modern comforts, including indoor plumbing, air conditioning, added steel to steady the structure in bad weather, new cushioned seats, and a large kitchen area as well as a basement—with many other improvements to come. It seated 1,200 of its 2,753 residents and, in emergencies, 1,700 with the use of the basement. It had several bathrooms and a small attached building for the pantry with room to include donated toys and clothing for the underprivileged. Those items would be removed to make room for more people.

As soon as the call went out, people flocked to the church with their belongings. There wasn't room for all the women and children. Elderly men gave up their spaces to women while many elderly women gave their spaces to the disabled. Over six hundred young and middle aged men stayed in their homes to watch over their elderly parents while many others joined the steadily growing volunteers to aid the sheriff's department in protecting the entire Sheerfield community.

Night and day the men patrolled the vast area, along with men and women of the sheriff's department. The night creatures, as the frightened residents had nicknamed them, were spotted throughout Sheerfield. Where they went during the day, no one knew; however, it became extremely common for Sheerfield residents to hear echoes of gunshots and rifle blasts from dusk to dawn. The gunshots couldn't kill the night creatures, but they could incapacitate them. The creatures would limp off to somewhere secret, recuperate, and then return with a vengeance.

*****

River paced the floor. "You know why Corina's doing this," he said, glancing over at Jewel.

"Of course. She knows how protective we are of the humans. She thinks of them as our little pets. Even using black magic, all of the powers of our ancestors are too strong for her to break this barrier we're behind."

"So she hopes attacking the humans will draw us out in the open," River reasoned.

"Yep! That seems to be the plan all right."

"Not very original," he said.

"No, but I think it's working."

"What do you mean? You're not going out there," he ordered.

"Certainly not. But for some reason, Naomi keeps saying this could be the end of Corina. So I suppose that means she's up to something....I don't know. I'm not certain of anything anymore. All I can think about these days is doing away with that evil bitch."

River walked over and gently gripped her shoulders. "I know, sweetheart. But don't stress yourself so. We've defeated her at every turn. Somehow we'll end this nightmare. You'll see."

She rested her head on his chest. "I hope it's soon. We're all running out of ideas."

Late that evening, Kayla had managed to get swept up in the mad dash to enter St. Paul's Church. At first, Sheerfield residents were naïve about the killings of Mrs. Paddington and her little dog. Again wild animal theories surfaced. Then the bodies of the Simmons family, along with the two teenage boys, were discovered and people realized the danger. Kayla, along with Veronica and Christa, were at the library when the news spread about Jeff and Cornel. The library was ordered closed immediately, forcing the teens to go straight to the church where each of their parents, except for Kayla's, was waiting. After learning where Kayla was, Beatrice told her to stay put; she and an escort of wolves would come get her in the morning.

Kayla, Veronica, and Christa tried to forget what devilment lurked outside by occupying their minds with games on their phones. The aroma of Italian meat sauce permeated the air; women openly nursed their infants; tiny fingers of small children waved back and forth with crayons on coloring books; larger kids made shushing sounds with their mouths, assuming the characters of their action figures. All the while men stood dutifully a few feet away at the windows and doors with shotguns and rifles. Everyone was assured they were safe. But Kayla wanted the safety of her own home and the protection of her grandmother's witchcraft, a secret she'd learned from Matthew and one she'd kept from her friends. With dusk soon to fall, Kayla wanted desperately to head out and beat the darkness, but Veronica and Christa begged her to stay.

Hours passed—every bench and space on the floors throughout the church was covered with bedding and pillows and blankets pulled over the bodies of sleeping people. A few snores were heard from across the room from where Kayla and her friends slept. Veronica's brother and mom and Christa's family slept nearby. Veronica's father, Sheriff Tilbert, along with Bob, was one of the riflemen guarding the door. The night was quiet except for faint sounds of gunshots heard far in the distance—an unintentional signal that another night of terror had begun.

A cell phone ring broke through the silence.

"Yeah!" Wayne answered.

"Sheriff!" a frantic voice said on the other end. "We can't hold them back!" he yelled. "There's hundreds of them…"

"I'm sending backup!" Wayne assured but couldn't hear the response through the loud gunshots. "You hear me? I'm sending back up. Hang in there…hello!" There were screams the likes Wayne had never heard before and gunshot blasts then the phone went dead. "Oh, hell! Get ready!" Wayne said to his men. "The damn things broke through the barricade, and they're heading this way."

Loud clicks of every weapon woke some people who jumped straight up to sitting positions, their faces colored with fear.

Bob woke the rest of the people and told them not to panic but to crawl under the benches. He told them to go into closets and small rooms and stay there until further notice. People grabbed their children and did what they were instructed. "Stay away from the windows and doors!" Bob ordered. There was a lot of talking and whimpering. Some children began to cry after seeing their parents' frightened expressions. Bob ordered them to keep the children quiet and to stay down. "And for God's sake don't run outside no matter what. Whatever comes inside here, we'll deal with," he warned. "Your experience in here, no matter how bad, won't be nearly as bad as what's going to greet you out there. Is that understood?" The people agreed.

Christa's mom ordered her to leave Kayla and Veronica and come with the family. Veronica hung onto Kayla, and her mom covered her little brother's body with her own. Kayla peeked out from under the bench where she lay and could see the men, with weapons pointed, peeking through cracks in the boarded up windows. Suddenly, everyone heard a crash coming from the kitchen. Wayne and Bob ran back to see what it was. Running down the aisle, Wayne and Bob were startled to hear ear-piercing screaming. When they reached the kitchen, they saw one of their men—his body half out of the shattered window and several creatures tearing out his throat and sucking his blood. Not being able to save him, Wayne shot the man in the forehead then he and Bob shot the creatures in their heads. But the bullets did nothing to the creatures except momentarily knock them back. All Wayne and Bob could do was watch them feast on their deputy's dead body. Some of his other men ran back and held off the creatures while Wayne and Bob re-boarded the window. They left two men to stand guard.

"We've got to reinforce all windows!" Wayne yelled, running back to where the people were huddled together under the benches. Extra boards flew up and almost immediately hammers began banging. A deputy was about to hit a nail when a hand bolted through an opening in one of the boards and snatched him through. Bob ran to the window and saw numerous creatures tearing at the deputy's flesh. The smell of blood brought more creatures to the feeding frenzy. Bob nearly emptied his rifle shooting them, only to see more creatures pile on. Finally, after watching the horror on the deputy's pleading face, Bob shot him through the eye then dropped his head. He then took a deep breath and continued placing extra boards over the window where the deputy had left off. The door flew open and creatures burst through. Guns blasted everywhere, and people jumped up and ran for their lives. Some were grabbed and had their throats torn out. Parents sacrificed themselves and screamed to their children to run.

"Head for the main sanctuary!" Wayne yelled to the people. The crowd took off running like a stampede of horses—trampling one another with children screaming after losing sight of their parents. The deputies managed to gather up as many straggling children as they could, reuniting them with their frantic parents who were waiting in the main sanctuary.

The mass number of creatures followed them, snarling with fangs dripping with blood. People were already in the main sanctuary, and it was quickly being filled to capacity. Many of those who were running for their lives tried to enter but were held back by the deputies who had the horrible decision of allowing only mothers with small or teen children—along with Wayne, Bob, and other deputies—into the main sanctuary. The deputies struggled to close the door, even beating their hands with their rifle butts so they could close and lock it. Tears streamed down the deputies' faces when they heard the blood-curdling screams of people being torn to shreds. Then there was silence.

No one knew what that meant. The quiet was eerie, but Wayne wasn't about to open the door. He sat back in a corner and took a deep breath. After a few moments of silence a woman gasped loudly and pointed, startling Wayne. All eyes turned to where pools of blood seeped from under the door. The people, Sheriff Tilbert, and deputies could hardly keep their composure; there was hardly an eye that wasn't glassy, but Wayne couldn't break down. He had to be strong for his family, for the people, and especially for his deputies who had to live all their lives remembering what they had done this night to protect the majority of the people.

The creatures gave them no time to mourn. The door began to peel apart as decaying fingers dug into the wood. Suddenly, arms appeared in the forced openings of the door. Then the head of a creature forced itself through a larger hole. Wayne jumped to his feet and grabbed his rifle. The deputies, wide-eyed, pointed their weapons while slowly backing up and the people held on to each other and mumbled prayers. Suddenly, the door was no more—it lay in tiny piles as if it had been through a wood chipper.

Bishop John Randall, the pastor of the church, didn't appear to be frightened; the children ran to him and lay at his feet while he stood sternly by the tall, gold-plated cross hanging over the pulpit that began to glow like a large neon sign. The bishop yelled, "You vampires, spawned from the depths of hell. The Lord rebukes you!" The creatures glared up at him and drew back their lips, showing bloody fangs with tiny strings of human flesh still hanging from them. But when one vampire's foot touched the main sanctuary floor, his entire body burst into flames and fell into a pile of ashes.

"For the love of Christ, did you see that?" Bob blurted with excitement.

"Darn right I saw it," Wayne exclaimed. "No wonder bullets had little effect…they're demons."

Bob bent over laughing and slapping his knees with his palms. "Come on in," he taunted them.

The creatures backed away from the door, snarling and staring down at the sanctified floor.

"Awe, don't leave," Bob said, grinning. "I know you're still hungry," he teased, showing off his neck. But the creatures just stood there looking down at the floor then up at them.

Wayne's face turned bright like a light bulb had lit him up. "Wait a minute, Bob. Not so fast."

"What do you mean? We've got 'em where we want 'em."

"Not really," Wayne said sighing. "There's no food or water in the main sanctuary. It's all out there…with them," Wayne said nodding toward the creatures. "They're going to wait us out."

"Crap!" Bob said. He crossed his ankles and flopped his butt down hard on the floor.

Chapter Thirty

The vampires, fearing the power within the main sanctuary, had begun roaming about other parts of the church. Many people were trapped in various places throughout the building: they hid in broom closets, a barricaded utility room, low kitchen cabinets, a walk-in freezer, and locked restrooms. Too often screams were heard coming from those areas as, one by one, the vampires discovered and killed the hidden ones. Wayne's plan for keeping people safe had failed. Those who had trusted him were being slaughtered like farm animals, which left Wayne feeling sick to his stomach. Even worse, he knew calling for state backup was useless. How could he tell state police that Sheerfield was being attacked by vampires? Wayne knew he had to implement a better plan before another night fell. *But what?* he thought, *my God, what?*

Growing weary of Wayne's bad judgment, Kayla became his biggest critic. Against Veronica and Christa's urging, she planned to escape to her car and hightail it back to Falcon Haven, into the safety of her own home.

"But it will be light in about seven hours," Veronica whispered to Kayla.

"For Christ's sake, listen to Ronnie," Christa pleaded.

"I don't care. I don't feel safe here. Before the sun comes up we could all be supper for those things out there."

Veronica touched Kayla's arm. "You saw what happened when one tried to get in here."

"And what if one succeeds next time?"

Veronica frowned. "You don't seem to have much faith in God."

"I put no faith in any gods. If my grandmother had been here, those vampires would have never gotten in."

"What do you mean by that?" Veronica asked.

Kayla caught herself. "Nothing, I...I just want to get out of here, that's all."

"But Kayla...."

"Will you help me?" Kayla asked, interrupting Veronica.

"No," Veronica erupted, shaking her head. "I'm not going to help you become raw hamburger meat for those things. No!"

"Then fine. I'll do it without you." Kayla turned, walked to the other side of the sanctuary, and sat alone. Veronica and Christa walked over to her and tried for several minutes to reason with her—even threatening to alert Sheriff Tilbert of her plan. But Kayla had made up her mind that when everyone was asleep, she'd find a way to sneak out of the sanctuary and escape to her car. The only problem was that two deputies were always on guard at the only available exit, which was where the vampires had tried to enter. Feeling defeated and sad, Veronica and Christa rejoined their families on the other side of the sanctuary.

Kayla sat alone for hours sulking. Then, later, a little past 3 a.m., she pretended to be asleep as her plan ran around in her head. If she could get to the pastor's office without being discovered, the rest was easy. Kayla knew her way around the church thanks to Veronica's endless invitations to youth group activities. This part of the church had a restroom and the pastor's office. The restroom and office had no windows, but the office had a side door leading to the church parking lot. If she could find something to pull off the boards from the door without being heard, she could escape unnoticed.

Kayla lifted her eyelids just enough to spot one of the deputies that was facing her nod off in a corner near the door. The other deputy appeared wide awake but had his back to her. *Perfect,* she thought. She looked over at Veronica and Christa and saw them sleeping quietly. She glanced around at the others, including the pastor, and all appeared to be in a deep slumber—this could be her only chance. Kayla turned over on her belly then slowly rose up on her knees. She continued to look over her shoulder at the deputies while slowly crawling towards the pastor's office. Once there, she eased open the door and crawled inside, but she was taken aback when she saw that the door wasn't boarded and a deputy sitting in a chair a few feet away with a rifle in his hand pointed down at the floor. He nodded a few times and stretched his eyes, trying to fight the inevitable. Kayla knew it was only a matter of time before he fell asleep. She crawled behind the mahogany desk and waited.

After many minutes, a distant scream rose from somewhere in the building and woke Kayla, causing her to jump and hit her head against the side of the desk. "Damn," she whispered as she snapped to and glanced at her watch. It was a little before 4 a.m.; she had accidently dozed off. Kayla peeked around the leg of the desk and saw that the deputy was snoring—his rifle still pointing down at the floor. She eased up off the floor and stood watching him carefully. She froze when he shifted in his seat and coughed, but he never opened his eyes. After he'd settled, she quietly tip-toed by him—stepping over the long barrel of his rifle. She stood at the door and kept her eyes glued to him as she quietly unlatched it, opened it, peeked out, and eased it closed behind her.

"Whew," she said with her back against the outside of the door. Looking around for any movement, she scurried to her car that was parked near the end of the parking lot then suddenly ducked down. Shadows moved all around, and Kayla slid under her car when she spotted several vampires roaming about. She stayed perfectly still as their feet moved toward her car and stopped at the passenger side. Her heart raced and thumped in her chest. Then the feet moved and dragged on slowly. Kayla remained still until she was sure the coast was clear. She slid out from under her car, nervously looking around while unlocking the door. After getting in and taking a few deep breaths, she started the car. Before driving off, Kayla thought she felt something, but when she looked around there was only the still darkness. She shifted gears and drove off.

Since her vehicle was the only one on the road, it looked as if she were driving through a ghost town. Kayla turned onto the long stretch of lonely highway. Although the crescent moon was bright, the night was darker than any she had ever seen. A breeze flowed through the trees, making the top branches sway to the rhythm of the wind. She wondered what her grandmother Beatrice would say knowing she was out on the road alone; the thought of leaving her best friends in that horrible place would haunt her for the rest of her life if anything were to happen to them. As she was well into her thoughts, a loud thump on the roof of her car startled her. Perhaps a branch had fallen from a tree and landed on top, she thought, but a dark figure suddenly sliding down her front windshield and glaring at her with blazing eyes quickly put that hurried explanation to rest. A scream caught in her throat, and her hands shook as she fought to control the wheel.

Nearly paralyzed with fear at the sight of the vampire, her driving became erratic: crossing back and forth over the white lines, zigzagging in the middle of the road, and misjudging a sharp curve that caused her to barely miss a guardrail. Her eyes widened when another vampire's face suddenly appeared upside down in the window on the front passenger side; she gasped at another squatting like a spider on the back windshield and screamed when yet another's face appeared upside down on the driver's front side. Those vampires hadn't gone and knew she had been under the car, so why hadn't they attacked her then? Was this one of their sick games? Or perhaps her screams would have brought the deputies. Driving blindly with the windows covered with vampires, Kayla mashed the accelerator then slammed on her brakes, hoping to throw them off the car, but they hung on with the traction of insects. After the plan failed, she took off speeding. She thought as long as they had to hold tight, they couldn't bust through the windows and attack her. Or could they?

"Get off damn you!" she shouted at them, but they only glared at her and drew their lips back, revealing yellowish fangs. Kayla was beside herself not knowing what to do. Then a devilish glean invaded her eyes when she spotted an abandoned tractor trailer up ahead. Mashing the accelerator, she soared toward the giant vehicle. "All right, you demonic bastards," she blurted through clenched teeth. "So you want to play?" Peeking over the shoulder of the vampire on the front windshield, Kayla pushed the car to ninety and side-swiped the trailer, crushing the vampire's body on her right between the car and the truck. Kayla looked back and saw a long smear of blood on the side of the trailer and the creature rolling like a log on the right side of the road. Her half-cocked smile turned to a frown when she saw the creature jump up as if the whole incident had been a stunt in a movie. But Kayla wasn't finished.

The wheels screamed as she braked; she made a U-turn and soared back toward the vampire, hitting him at eighty-five. The hit lifted the creature off the ground and onto the hood—knocking the vampire that was on the front windshield onto the roof of the car where both vampires smashed into the one on the back windshield. All three hit the concrete. Kayla was ecstatic. "One more to go," she said, grinning and bringing the car to a stop. But Kayla had made a drastic mistake; she had sat too long gloating. "Where did he go?" She looked around frantically for the fourth vampire—the one that was in the front driver's window. Straight away, a crash from behind startled her, but before she turned to see what it was, the vampire was on her—his rotting flesh and foul, cold breath felt like ice on her face. She covered her neck just in time and suffered a bite that was meant for her throat. The two-inch fangs sunk into her arm like hot daggers. Kayla screamed and tried desperately to pull away from the creature—scratching and digging her fingers into the vampire's eyes, which caused him to lose his grip long enough for her to open the door. She had gotten free of the car when the vampire pulled her back and slammed her down hard on the front seat with such force that a light flashed in her head when it hit the seat. The vampire leaped on top of her and sank his fangs into her throat. The stabbing pain took her breath away. Kayla lay paralyzed as the creature's lips drew the blood from her throat like a babe nursing at her mother's breast—the vampire's eyes dancing in ecstasy while the sweet liquid filled his gut and dribbled down his chin. The other three creatures jumped through the back window, eager to join in the feast. One bit into her leg and another drank from her wrist. Kayla's body trembled as she stared up at them through blurry eyes. The car filled with their euphoric moans and the smacking of their lips. Her eyelids fluttered then she lost consciousness from losing so much blood so quickly. The fourth vampire leaned over her, and his eyes rolled to the back of his head when he drew back his lips, but he stopped short of biting into her exposed breast when the roof of the car suddenly flew off. An unseen force lifted the vampires into the air. The demons hissed and growled as their bodies rose fifty feet over the roofless car. The vampires hovered helplessly, twitching and howling like crazed dogs, then suddenly burst into flames.

"Kayla! Kayla!" Beatrice yelled, slapping her face. "Come on, honey." She grabbed Kayla by her shoulders and pulled her to a sitting position. "Kayla! Come on, honey."

Kayla slowly opened her eyes. "Grandma," she slurred, then fell forward, her head falling against Beatrice's chest. Beatrice held her for a moment then helped Kayla to her own car, an SUV that was parked in the middle of the road. She walked Kayla around to the passenger's side and fastened her seat belt. Then Beatrice got into the driver's seat. She pulled from her pocket a potion she'd brought with her and handed it to Kayla who was still woozy.

"Here, drink this."

Kayla felt too weak to lift her head, so Beatrice placed the glass tube to Kayla's lips. She watched as Kayla swallowed the potion sip-by-sip. After a few moments, the color returned to Kayla's face and the puncture marks on her neck, leg and wrist slowly disappeared. Regaining some of her strength, Kayla immediately complained about the smell and aftertaste of the potion. "Ew, what was that, dog piss?" she asked making an awful face.

"Oh, a little dog piss never hurt anybody."

Kayla's eyes grew wide. "You mean that really *was* dog piss?"

Beatrice chuckled.

"Grandma, tell me that wasn't dog piss," she blurted frantically.

Beatrice grinned and glanced over at Kayla.

"Grandma!"

"All right, it wasn't dog piss. But witches never reveal the ingredients in their potions or the spells in their magic. Our abilities are what make us special and different from one another." Kayla didn't seem taken with that explanation. After seeing a worried look on Kayla's face, Beatrice said, "Oh, come now. You don't really believe grandma would give the love of her life dog urine?"

"I don't know. I don't trust you," she snapped, pouting.

Beatrice laughed loudly and playfully ruffled Kayla's hair.

Kayla smiled, realizing Beatrice had been only joking. There was a short silence then Kayla frowned and thought a moment. "By the way, how did you know I was on the road?"

"Veronica called...told me about your stupid plan. I came as quickly as I could. There was no time to wait for the wolves, so I left them a message and set out alone." Beatrice paused then looked at her sternly. "What the hell were you thinking? I told you to stay inside where it was safe."

"I know, Grandma. Don't be mad. I was frightened and I just wanted to be with you."

Beatrice's face brightened and all the middle-age wrinkles fell into soft lines around her eyes and mouth. She reached over and gently stroked Kayla's pink cheek, then started the car. Minutes into cruising along, Kayla looked over at Beatrice and smiled. Beatrice's face darkened as she flashed her eyes up at the rearview mirror. She slammed on brakes and yelled for Kayla to run. Before Beatrice could perform a spell, a vampire shot up from behind the driver's seat and sunk his teeth into her throat.

Kayla ran from the car screaming; she banged her fist on the hood of the car. "No! Grandmother! Stop! Leave her alone!" Kayla was struck from behind, and everything went black.

*****

It was daylight, but no sun had ever invaded the darkness where Kayla lay. "Ah...where am I," Kayla slurred as she regained consciousness. She tried to raise her head but it thumped like a hammer was hitting it. As her eyes cleared, she saw Gunner, Holly, and Amber standing over her and flashing their godawful smiles.

"Not bad looking for a human. What do you think, Gunner?" Holly asked, turning to him.

"Hm, I've seen better," he joked.

Kayla sat up and grabbed her head. "What have you bastards done with my grandmother?" She looked around at her dim, cold surroundings. It appeared to be an ancient dungeon of some kind—the walls and floor were made of dark stone with lit torches mounted on the walls. "Why am I here? Where's my grandmother...what have you done with her?"

"Oh, you'll see her soon enough," Amber said grinning.

"Relax, you and granny are about to be united," Gunner said. Holly and Amber chuckled at his remark.

Holly clapped her hands twice and two undead guardsmen rolled in a cage with a dead Beatrice lying on the floor of it.

Kayla's eyes widened as she jumped up from the floor—ignoring the pain still thumping in her head. "Grandma! You killed her."

"Guilty," Gunner said, pretending to look serious. "She is and she's isn't. You see, witches are quite unique. When they are bitten by a vampire, they die like everyone else. But...and there's always that but," he said, prancing before her as he spoke, "witches, after an hour or so, mysteriously come back to life. But...awe...there's that wonderful but again...they lose their magic and become vampires." He finished and folded his arms across his chest as Amber and Holly stood grinning and waiting for the grand finish. Kayla shook her head. "I...I don't understand."

"You will," Gunner said. He nodded to the guards and ordered them to take Beatrice out and chain her.

Kayla, frowning, watched the guards drag Beatrice's limp body from the cage and chain her hands above her head. Beatrice's clothes were soaked in blood. Her head was resting on her chest. A chunk of her neck was gone, and her long hair was loose and covering her face like someone had draped her head with the bloody end of a mop.

"You see, my dear Kayla, your grandmother is dead, but in about forty minutes she won't be...and chains, I'm afraid, can't hold vampires very long."

"Here, you'll need this," Holly said, throwing a machete down at Kayla's feet. The pinging sound of the metal hitting the floor sent an echo throughout the underground chamber.

"What's that for?" Kayla asked, looking puzzlingly at the blade.

"You're going to need it dear," Amber said.

"What for? My grandmother would never harm me."

Amber pretended to look surprised. "Oh…Gunner, you naughty boy. You forgot to tell her that granny won't recognize her while she's tearing out her throat and drinking her blood."

"Awe, did I forget that little detail? Granny won't remember you while she's tearing out your throat and drinking your blood." He turned to Amber. "How was that?"

"Superb," she said.

The trio turned their backs and climbed the spiraling stone steps. "We'll be back to check on you," Amber said. "If there's anything left to check on."

Holly stopped midway up the stairs and turned to Kayla. "Oh…whacking off her head. That's the only way to kill her…just thought I'd mention that." She caught up to Gunner and Amber, and all three disappeared into the darkness at the top of the staircase.

Kayla crossed her ankles and lowered her body onto the stone floor. She reached over and grabbed the machete while keeping her eyes on Beatrice. Then, thinking better of it, she stubbornly straightened herself and tossed the blade aside. "You won't hurt me. Your love for me is stronger than any vampire urge," Kayla mumbled to herself. She sat looking at the bloodied body of Beatrice as the minutes ticked away.

*****

"Wayne, we can't stay in here much longer. The people are hungry…babies are fretful, there's no water. I'm telling you…we've got to make a move."

"I haven't just been sitting here daydreaming, Bob!" Sheriff Tilbert snapped. "You haven't exactly told me anything I don't already know."

"Awe, then you've come up with something?"

Bob hadn't given Sheriff Tilbert any reason to think that Bob questioned his ability to protect the people. Yet, Tilbert still suspected Bob of feeling that way. Perhaps it was Tilbert's own guilt that had him suspecting Bob. *So many depending on me, God, help me,* he thought. "I've thought of a few things," Tilbert said.

"Well, can you think out loud? We'd all like to hear them," Bob asked with a bit of sarcasm.

"It's not rocket science. We just storm our way to the kitchen area, blasting them as we go…gather what we need and blast them all the way back here." Tilbert knew his plan fell short of being a brilliant idea. He held his breath, watching for any signs of disappointment on the faces of his men.

One of the deputies weighed in. "I think all of us thought of that one, but just needed you to give the okay, Sheriff."
Sheriff Tilbert exhaled with relief.

"What do we do about all the people who are hiding throughout the building?" another deputy asked.

"I'm afraid they're on their own," Tilbert said. "Our concern right now is for the people here, especially the children."

"We haven't heard any cries for hours," said yet another deputy. "Either they're hidden pretty good, or they're all dead."

"We'll just leave them to God," Tilbert said. "Our focus now is to get food and water." Tilbert looked over at another one of his deputies. "Do we have enough ammo?"

"Yes, sir, I made sure of that," he said, pointing to the supplies stacked in the corner. "It was the first thing I grabbed when all hell broke loose."

"Good," Tilbert said. He looked from face to face. "Okay, who wants to go? Who wants to stay?" Every hand, including Bob's, went up. Sheriff Tilbert pointed. "You, you, you, you, and you…stay here," he said, pointing lastly at Bob. "The rest come with me."

The deputies poured over the ammo with rifles and shotguns clicking. Pastor Randall came down from the pulpit and made the sign of the cross on each of the men's foreheads with blessed oil, and he prayed over them. The pastor returned to the pulpit, anointed himself, knelt, and began to pray. He was joined by several church members. The children snuggled up to their parents and watched as Sheriff Tilbert and his deputies silently filed out of the sanctuary.

*****

The rattling sound of chains startled Kayla. She watched as her grandmother lifted her head, her bloody hair still covering her face. "Grandma," she whispered and crawled over to her. Kayla brushed aside Beatrice's hair from her face and gasped when she saw only the whites of her eyes and long fangs peeking from her slightly parted lips. Beatrice shot forward, snapping her jaws and barely missing Kayla's face as Kayla jumped back in the nick of time. "Grandma, it's me, Kayla," she said with hope gleaming from her eyes. But all Kayla got were snarls from the woman who had loved her so deeply for all of her young life.

The thing that once was Beatrice stood, snarling and pulling on the chains so hard that the metal began to give. Kayla panicked and looked around for the machete. Spotting it, she picked it up and held it out, pointing it at the creature. "Grandma, please recognize me. Please...it's me, your granddaughter, Kayla," she said, backing up and looking around for cover. The creature continued to pull at the chains. "Remember this song. You used to sing this to me at bedtime." Kayla began to sing, her voice cracking at every note. But the hideous thing with her grandmother's face continued to snarl, showing the full length of two-inch fangs with saliva streaming down her chin. Kayla could see that one more hard pull would set the thing free. After spotting a door, she ran inside and locked it. She pushed chairs, tables, and old, heavy antique furniture, anything she could find to shove in front of the door.

The rattling of the chains and snarls became louder as Kayla waited with the blade in her hand. Then came thunderous pounding on the door. "Go away!" Kayla cried out. Tears streamed down her face, and her hands shook. The door burst open, scattering furniture every which way and causing Kayla to jump; a crazed creature with the distorted face of her beloved grandmother stood in the doorway, her white eyes peering at Kayla, her lips drawn back

255

and fangs as pointy as needles in full view. "No. Don't," Kayla begged. Beatrice slowly walked toward her. Kayla kept the blade in front of her as she backed up pleading. Beatrice snarled loudly and moved swiftly toward her. Kayla swiped at her with the machete, cutting off several fingers, but Beatrice just looked at the hand with the missing fingers with a strange curiosity. It was as though she didn't need them. She bolted toward Kayla, knocking her to the floor and hopping on top of her. The blade Kayla was holding went straight through Beatrice's body, but Beatrice never flinched. Kayla pounded the creature with her fists and tried to pull the blade free so she could behead her. Kayla finally realized this wasn't her grandmother anymore. Now all she thought about was pulling the blade free from the thing's body and cutting off its head.

Kayla struggled to protect her face and neck and paid for it with numerous bites on her arms and hands, losing the tip of her little finger in the process. Finally, she drove a thumb into Beatrice's eye and pushed the creature off of her then hopped to her feet. The creature recovered quickly, but Kayla had pulled the machete from her body and stood with it in a battle stance. Kayla backed up while swinging the machete, but nothing seemed to deter the creature from advancing. With a look of determination, Kayla swung hard but missed. The creature advanced again, and Kayla swung, cutting off the tip of the creature's nose. Kayla suddenly realized that the only way she might live was to go on the offensive. She leapt forward swinging and cutting at every part of the creature's body. A hand, fingers, and an ear fell to the floor. She backed the creature into a corner and, with one hard swing, decapitated it. The horrid thing fell, and its head rolled across the floor. Kayla sunk to her knees panting, trying to catch her breath. She watched as the decapitated head that was lying face up slowly became Beatrice's wholesome face again. Her blue eyes wide open looking like two stars—her smooth, slightly aging face and soft pale lips that looked so inviting. Kayla put aside the machete; she crawled over to the head, bent, and kissed the cool lips. "I'm so sorry, Grandma. It was my fault. It was all my fault," she whispered tearfully.

Kayla heard clapping behind her and whirled around.

"Bravo," Corina said, applauding. Behind her the trio stood applauding as well with wide smiles on their faces.

"Good job," Gunner said, still applauding. "Oh...we have it on tape...in case someday you have kids and they get curious about whatever happened to great granny."

"Just get it over with, Corina. Killing me should be quite easy. I'm not even going to defend myself," Kayla said, rising to her feet.

"Kill you? Why...I have no intention of killing you."

"Then what do you want with me?"

"A message, to Jewel. Tell her I'm going to tear down that flimsy barrier and destroy them all."

"You...you're saying I can go?"

"Well, the message isn't going to deliver itself, now is it?" Corina said.

Kayla hurriedly walked around Corina and scurried out of the room. She ran up the stone stairs. Kayla had been brought in unconscious so she wasn't sure of the way out. Entering a large room, she looked around for an exit. Discovering it, she ran outside and passed Beatrice's SUV. The sight of her grandmother's car put a lump in her throat. Then she remembered that her own car farther down the road had no roof. She ran back, got into the SUV, and drove off.

Speeding down the highway, Kayla fought back tears. Through her blurry eyes, she thought she saw Matthew's truck pass her going in the opposite direction. Matthew braked and made a U-turn to catch up to her. She pulled over to the side of the road, and Matthew pulled over behind her. He and a couple of wolves got out of the car and began walking toward Kayla. Matthew was surprised when Kayla bolted from the car, ran to him—almost knocking him off balance—and threw her arms around him, crying hysterically. Matthew could barely make out what she was saying.

"Baby, slow down...I can't understand what..."

"She may...made me do it. I had to. I...I didn't want to. I had no choice. It...it was all my fault. I should have listened, Matt...I should have listened."

Kayla, still crying hysterically, became weak in the knees. Matthew held her up then turned to the wolves that were with him. "You guys follow me in the SUV." Matthew put his arms around her and walked her back to his truck. After putting her inside, he got into the driver's seat. Kayla was still crying and trying to catch her breath.

"Honey, what happened and where is Beatrice...why are you driving her car?"

The sound of her grandmother's name made Kayla break down even more and weep uncontrollably. Matthew waited patiently, rubbing her back and smoothing her hair away from her wet face. Finally, she took a deep breath and told him the full story. Matthew gathered her in his arms and held her. "Honey, I'm so sorry you went through that, but you'll see your grandmother again."

"But...but she's dead."

Matthew hesitated while trying to put together the right words. "Witches don't really die...they kind of transfer from one state of being to another."

"What?"

"Look, when we get back to Falcon Haven, talk to Naomi. She can explain it better...okay?"

Kayla appeared confused but said okay. Matthew leaned over and kissed her on the forehead. Then he drove off to deliver the message to Jewel and the witches.

Chapter Thirty-One

Jewel swallowed a hard lump in her throat after hearing the horrible way Beatrice had died. She shook her head, then pulled a distraught Kayla to her breast and held her tight. Jewel fought to hold it together for Kayla's sake. "No sense in blaming yourself, honey," she said.

"But if I hadn't—"

"Stop it now. After we deal with Corina, one day soon Naomi will take you to the Mystic Souls; when you see how happy your grandmother is, you won't feel so badly," Jewel assured her.

"Go on home, honey, and get some sleep," River urged. "Goddess knows you've encountered enough in one night to last you a lifetime."

"Yes, go on, sweetheart," Jewel said, gently pushing her toward the door. Matthew put his hand around Kayla's waist and walked her outside to where several wolves waited to escort her safely home.

Kayla stopped and turned to Matthew. "You...you won't leave me?"

"Not for a second baby. I'll ask your mom if I can sleep on the sofa, okay?"

Kayla nodded and climbed into the front seat of Matthew's truck. The night was still haunting as the full moon lit the top of the tall trees; Kayla watched tree limbs as they appeared to dance to the rhythm of the wind.

After watching Kayla, Matthew, and the wolves drive off, Jewel closed the door. She and River slowly walked back into the family room where River stood by the cold fireplace with his head down—Jewel flopped down on the sofa.

"River, what the hell are we going to do? She kidnaps Becca, kills Rick and now Beatrice...not counting all the wolves." She looked up at him. "River, Corina's winning... I can't believe it...my best friend, gone."

River sighed hard. "The world won't seem the same without Beatrice."

"Great goddess, who's next?"

River stood speechless and looked off.

*****

The distant sound of gunshots rang out from the two-hundred-year-old church.

"Wayne, look out!" a deputy shouted.

Wayne swung to his right just in time to blast several vampires that were almost on top of him. "Hurry up in there," Wayne yelled to the deputies who were snatching supplies as quickly as they could. Wayne and three other deputies stood watch near the pantry. Wayne turned and shouted, "What the hell are you guys doing, milking cows...laying eggs? Let's go!"

"All right!" a deputy shouted back.

But straight away, Wayne's mouth dropped opened when he looked down the dark hallway and saw several vampires crawling on the ceiling and both sides of the walls like huge spiders. "Damn!" Wayne shouted. "You guys take the walls, I'll take the ceiling." Rifles and shotguns exploded upon the creatures as they dropped to the floor and limped away only to be replaced by more vampires.

"Okay, I think we got enough," the deputies with the supplies said. Wayne and his group that had been standing watch were at a disadvantage because the deputies who had helped them fight the demons on the way to the pantry now had their hands full with supplies.

Wayne turned to the men with the supplies. "All right, stick close to us."

"Wayne, we're not going to make it...look." The walls and ceilings were crawling with vampires. "Man, we're done for," he said, his eyes bulging.

"Maybe we can call for backup," said another.

"No!" Wayne said. "I don't want the women and children left alone."

"But Wayne, those vamps won't go near the sanctuary. You saw what happened."

"Oh, yeah, right." Wayne dialed Bob.

"Yeah, Wayne," Bob answered.

"They've got us trapped. We need backup."

"Sorry. Got our own problem," Bob said, staring into the faces of nearly fifty vampires all crowded in front of the main sanctuary door. The creatures had deliberately cut the men off from one another. The three deputies stood with rifles aimed as Bob told Wayne his dilemma.

"Can't you blast them?" Wayne asked. "We're low on ammo."

"We'll do what we can."

Wayne and his men stood their ground as their gunshots roared throughout the building and smoke filled the air. But when the smoke had cleared, there were twice as many vampires as before, and Wayne and his men only had a few bullets left. The deputies dropped their supplies and kept blasting away until only clicks came from every rifle and shotgun.

"Run!" Wayne yelled. The men left their supplies and ran to a large walk-in freezer that was locked. Looking through the glass at them were several terrified people who had been hiding there for days. The people let Wayne and his men in and aided them in stacking large sides of frozen beef and anything else they could find in front of the door. The vampires pressed their faces against the door window, snarling and showing off their deadly fangs. The hinges of the door began to give as the massive vampire crowd pressed against it.

"This is it!" One deputy said, backing into a corner and sliding down the wall to the floor with his empty rifle across his knees.

"No. No. Don't give up," Wayne said. "Bob and the boys will be here, you'll see."

"I don't think so, Wayne," the deputy said, looking at the window cracking.

"Heaven help us," Wayne blurted. He turned and saw his men on the floor, their faces lined with fear. "Get off your asses...we're lawmen, damn it!" Wayne faced the door, held his rifle by the barrel like a baseball bat, and stood in a fighting stance—the men hopped to their feet and followed suit.

"Come on, you demonic sons of bitches," Wayne shouted. He watched wide-eyed as the glass broke and the door hinges popped out one by one. The door fell like a descending drawbridge, and the massive crowd of demons stormed the freezer. Wayne and his men backed up while swinging. Wayne swung and whacked one creature on the side of its head, but the demon kept coming. He swung again, and the same vampire snatched his rifle and whacked Wayne on the side of *his* head. Wayne staggered but pulled a bowie knife from his waistband and held it out while backing up and gritting his teeth. But to Wayne's surprise, the vampires suddenly froze and turned around like they were afraid of something; and Wayne wondered what the hell could frighten vampires. Some of the vampires turned and walked out of the freezer while others remained a few feet from the men and stared out into the hallway. Then Wayne heard cracking sounds coming from the outside of the freezer. He frowned when he saw a great number of vampires bolt past the freezer like scared rabbits as the cracking got louder and echoed throughout the building.

Wayne, who was in front, stretched his neck to see over top of the small group of snarling vampires that had their backs to him.

"Wayne, what's going on? Why are they just standing there?"

"I don't know."

The cracking sound and thumping like heavy things being thrown about went on for several minutes with the vampires in the freezer just staring as if they feared the source of the sound. The men who were still holding their weapons like baseball bats looked at each other puzzled, not knowing what to do.

Three men—all wearing long dark leather coats, steel-tip boots, and dark shades with blue lights on the ends of the frames appeared in the doorway. They were carrying whips. They raised their whips, and the vampires snarled at them while looking around frantically for an escape route, but there were none. One of the men—Wayne could swear he'd seen him before—cracked his whip and the silver ball at the end of it circled the vampire's neck several times before the whip took off its head. The creature melted into the floor and disappeared. The other two men followed suit; each crack of a whip counted for a headless vampire. Then there was silence as Wayne and his men observed several headless vampires lying on the floor—their heads like hideous, masked bowling balls scattered about. The decapitated demons melted and disappeared into oblivion.

The three strange men stood in the doorway with their whips in their hands, steel swords in shafts on their backs, and Smith & Wesson M&P 9s in their holsters. "You can come out now," one stranger said to Wayne and his men.

"Hey, you guys are good with those things," a deputy said, nodding to the whips.

Wayne squinted and looked at one of the men. "Don't I know you?"

"Campbell...Warren Campbell," he said, stepping forward and extending his hand to Wayne.

Wayne shook it. "I'm Sheriff..."

"I know," Campbell interrupted. "And these are my partners, Roy Carson and Ham Williams."

Both Roy and Ham nodded as Wayne introduced his deputies.

"Well, I don't believe it," Bob said, walking up behind the three men. "So, you're the Shadow Hunters? Sure took you long enough."

"Bob, please. These men just saved our lives." Then Wayne frowned and said, "Wait, did you say Shadow Hunters?"

"I did."

Wayne's surprised expression turned into a frown when he looked at Bob. "The sanctuary...are the people safely inside?"

"The people are fine. Those creatures are long gone," Bob said grinning. "Boy, you guys are good." Bob reached to touch Campbell's whip. "May I?"

"Sure," Campbell said smirking, "if you want your hand to melt and disappear."

Bob snatched his hand back and noticed a grey mist surrounding the whip.

"We've been fighting these damn things for weeks," Wayne said. "You guys come along and poof...they're gone."

"They're not gone," Campbell said, pointing to the daylight through the window. "Quite a few escaped. They become invisible during the day. You can't kill what you can't see."

"How did you know to come here?" Wayne asked Campbell. "Did Bob call you?"

Bob spoke up quickly. "No. Not *me*."

"Do you know someone by the name of Naomi?" Campbell asked Wayne.

"No. Is that who called?"

"She said you guys were in trouble...said something about a witch name Corina?"

"I don't know anything about a witch named Corina or anybody named Naomi." Wayne said. "But hey...I don't care who contacted you. I'm just glad you came."

Campbell folded his whip and slid it into a long, slender metal tube.

Wayne continued. "You seem to know a lot more about those creatures than we do. Let's head back to the main sanctuary, I need to hear more about this."

The Shadow Hunters, Bob, Wayne, and his men walked back to the main sanctuary and joined the people. Others who had been hiding throughout the building, learned it was safe and followed them to the sanctuary as well.

Campbell held everyone spellbound as he told of how long the hunters had been chasing the vampires. The hunters knew everything there was to know about the demons. Campbell was also fascinated hearing about how the pastor had kept the vampires from advancing on them. He explained to the pastor how vital he would be in helping them kill the creatures while they were invisible and hiding in plain sight. "We know where they are. Our devices tracked their origin to an ancient castle in a region called Ironforge. Anybody know that location?"

"Too well," Bob said. "Maybe that's where that witch lives."

Campbell went on to say that vampires hated the word of God. Repeating the words from the Bible weakened the spell that kept them invisible until nightfall. The Shadow Hunters were the only ones with the ability to kill them. But you could only destroy them while they were visible in the daylight. "We'll have to flood where they're hiding with sunlight," Campbell said. "Then Pastor Randall, you speak the words, and we'll do the rest."

The pastor said he was all too eager to help them. "I have to warn you though," Campbell said. "It's dangerous. They'll come after you to shut you up."

"Can't live forever," Randall said.

"Hey, a badass man of God...I like that," Bob said.

"Bob," Wayne called to him, frowning.

"Oh...sorry pastor. I...I do have a bit of a potty mouth at times."

"I've heard worse."

"Well, we'd better get going reverent," Campbell said. "We don't know how many of those demons are wandering around that castle. And we'll need to get started as early as possible to destroy them all by nightfall."

"You sure you don't want to think about this some more?" Wayne asked the pastor.

"As I said, I'm only too happy to help."

"I appreciate it, reverent," Campbell said.

"I'm referred to as Bishop Randall. But, you can call me John."

Campbell smiled. "Okay, Bishop John."

Wayne turned to Bob. "You want to stay here and..."

"And what...miss all the fun? Oh no."

"Miss all the...now I see why I stay friends with you, Bob. You're an idiot and you need me."

"We're all idiots. Look where we're going," one of the deputies said.

Bob chuckled as he, Wayne, and several deputies filed out behind the Shadow Hunters and Bishop Randall who was clutching his Bible. Several other deputies stayed behind passing out food, water, and candy bars to the children.

Chapter Thirty-Two

Entering Corina's dark castle undetected was impossible even for the supernaturally inclined shadow hunters. Because of the demon guards' keen senses, statues that had been enchanted to attack and eyes in every wall and staircase, leaving that demonic hellhole would take the act of a deity. And no one knew if biblical words worked on statues, walls, and staircases. Nevertheless, Bishop Randall wasn't just along for the ride.

Campbell peeked around one of the great columns and spotted two guards. "Bishop," he whispered. "Is there anything in that Bible about making us invisible?"

"God doesn't quite work that way," Bishop whispered back. Bishop Randall, a talented former college quarterback, took off his shoe, shot from behind the column, and threw it as hard as he could past the guards. He ducked back as the shoe soared through the air—covering the entire length of the extremely long hallway. When the guards ran to investigate the sound of the shoe hitting the wall, Bishop scrambled across the hall with Wayne and the others following as quickly as possible.

When the guards suddenly stopped and turned around, the hall was clear.

"Sometimes God just gives us guts and common sense," Randall whispered.

"I hear you, Bishop," Campbell said. "But I still think invisible would have been better." Checking his locator device, Campbell saw that the red arrow was flashing like crazy while pointing to the descending staircase. "This way," Campbell said, starting toward the stairs.

"You sure?" Bob asked.

Campbell gave Bob an, are-you-questioning-me look. Bob, embarrassed, raised his eyebrows and followed Campbell, Wayne, and the others down the stone steps. "Whoa!" Campbell said, freezing in place. Well over a dozen guards waited at the bottom of the stairs, their ruby-red eyes gazing up at him. "Go back!"

Campbell shouted. But they all turned to see the same guards Bishop thought he had tricked with the thrown shoe at the top of the stairs.

"Oh, God, we're trapped," Wayne said, aiming his rifle. "You guys take the ones at the bottom…me and Bob will take the top."

"Forget it, sheriff. Guns are no good against *these* demons," Campbell told him. The Shadow Hunters pulled their steel swords from their sheaves. A greyish mist continuously poured from their blades like rapidly evaporating steam. Alone, Campbell took on the guards at the bottom, while Ham and Roy shot up the steps and were more than enough to handle the nearly fifty guards with their swords drawn at the top. The hunters made short sport of the guards—cutting them down and leaving them headless on the floor.

"Come on," Campbell yelled to Wayne and his men.

"You sure know how to leave a mess," Bob said, making a face and stepping over the spread of decaying flesh and scattered red eyeballs Campbell had turned the guards into.

Bishop, descending the stairs, brushed past Bob. "You and your shoe," Bob spat.

"Well, it got us across the hall, didn't it?" Bishop grinned, leaving Bob shaking his head.

Once in the hallway, Campbell was the first to feel a chill in the air—a sure sign that the vampires were near. "We're close," Campbell said, nodding toward French metal doors a few feet at the end of the hall.

"How close…you mean that door there?" Wayne asked.

Campbell didn't answer, instead waving the men to follow him. The closer they got to the door, the colder the air became; by the time they reached the door, vapor was coming from their noses and mouths. The door wasn't locked, and the huge room resembled a warehouse full of empty coffins. "This is it. Ready, Bishop?"

"Yes, of course," Bishop answered with a bit of uncertainty.

Campbell told Ham to open the curtains to flood the room with daylight, which he did. Then the hunters, Wayne, and his men opened the fifty coffins.

"They're empty," Bob said.

"Somebody wasn't listening," Ham said, looking at Bob.

"They're not empty…everybody stand back," Campbell ordered.

Campbell took out several small packets and handed them to Wayne and his men. "Sprinkle this over your clothes," Campbell said. "But don't let it touch your skin."

Wayne opened his packet and sprinkled the brown dust over his clothes then watched his deputies do the same. Some of the dust got into Wayne's nose and made him sneeze. "I guess this is some…some kind of protection?" Wayne stammered, twitching his nose like he was about to sneeze again.

"You can't use our weapons, and yours are useless," Campbell said. "That's the best I can do."

After the men were covered with the substance, Campbell called for Bishop to start reading from the Bible. Randall opened the book and read from a half-sheet of paper that had a list of commands that reminded demons that God was greater than them. As the bright sunlight bore in and lit up the black satin that lined the insides of the coffins, the words spoken by the Bishop greatly disturbed the vampires. Although the vampires had not yet materialized, deafening snarling rose from the coffins and echoed throughout the underground chamber. Suddenly, an invisible force sent Bishop crashing against the wall, knocking the book from his hand. Bob rushed to Bishop, picked up the Bible, and placed it back into his hands. Randall scrambled to his feet and resumed reading only to have the book ripped from him by unseen hands and thrown across the room. Bishop stood in defiance and spoke Scriptures from memory: "Greater is he who is in me than he who is in the world; No weapon formed against us shall prosper; the earth is the Lord's and the fullness there of; Get behind us demon! For it is written: we shall serve the Lord thy God and Him only, If God be for us, he is more than the world against us; For, we are more than conquerors; Do not fear him that can destroy the body, but God who can destroy the body and the soul."

As the Bishop shouted the Scriptures, the vampires became visible one by one; they popped into view like stars twinkling in a dark sky. The vampires were blinded by the sunlight, and their skin burned. One of the vampires rushed Bishop to shut him up, but Wayne jumped in front of Randall and the vampire accidently grabbed Wayne's dust-covered garment instead. The substance set the demon's hands aflame, causing the creature to scream in pain before letting go of Wayne.

The vampires, in agony, held their ears as if the words shouted by Bishop were setting their brains on fire. Fully visible, the demons dropped to their knees as the sunlight fried their flesh and set the coffins ablaze. The Shadow Hunters pulled out their swords and whips to finish them off: driving the swords through the vampires' black hearts and snapping off their heads with their whips.

"That was quick work," Wayne said. "I thought we'd be here for hours."

"I told you there were only a few left," Campbell said. "We got most of them at the church."

"All right, now where's that bitch of a witch?" Bob blurted, looking around.

"She's not here. Naomi said something about a showdown at some place called Falcon Haven," Campbell said.

"That's where the good witches live," Bob said, ignoring Wayne giving him the eye.

Campbell raised his eyebrows. "Did he just say…*good witches?*"

Ham and Roy chuckled. "I see why your town was full of vampires," Ham said. "There's no such thing as good witches."

"Thou shalt not suffer a witch to live. Exodus 22:18," Bishop angrily reminded Bob.

"Now, wait a minute," Bob said. "These witches, not Corina certainly…they saved our lives when the werewolves attacked us a while back."

"Are you believing this?" Campbell said, turning to Ham and Roy. The two Shadow Hunters shook their heads. Campbell looked over at Wayne. "You're not saying anything, Wayne. Surely you don't agree with your partner here about good witches?"

"Let's get out of here. This place gives me the willies," Wayne said. "Then we'll talk more about this."

"What's there to talk about, Wayne? Do you or don't you believe this shit about good witches?"

Wayne didn't answer but walked out of the room and down the hall with his deputies following behind him. Bishop, not knowing what to make of Wayne's attitude, pressed his lips together and walked out ahead of the Shadow Hunters. The men filed down the long hallway, went up the stairs, and crossed the hall, passing the large column where they had hid earlier from the demon guards. As they continued to file down the hallway to exit the castle, a whooshing sound caused them to stop and turn around. Hovering high beneath the hundred-foot ceiling was a stone dragon statue flapping its giant wings. There appeared to be no fire coming from its animated mouth, but just one swipe of its ceramic wing could kill a mortal instantly.

"Holy crap!" Bob yelled. He aimed his rifle at its head and shot. When the men saw that the bullet penetrated the stone and a piece flew off, they looked at each other and smiled. Then Wayne, Bob, and the deputies fired on the concrete beast—blasting and shattering the giant statue into multiple rock-size pieces. The Shadow Hunters stood around amused with their weapons still in their encasings while Wayne and his men gave a short victory shout.

"It's about time these guns had some use in this godforsaken place," Wayne said grinning. "I was starting to think we were just hauling around hunks of dead weight."

Once outside, the men piled into their trucks and cars and headed to Falcon Haven. Wayne and Bob rode in Campbell's van, sharing the backseat with Roy while Ham occupied the front passenger seat and Bishop Randall rode with the deputies.

Right away, Campbell started in on Wayne and Bob. "I'm really surprised at you, Wayne. I thought you and Bob were men of faith. I don't pretend to be religious, but I know there's nothing in the Bible about good witches."

"I can't really say I blame you," Wayne said. "Up until the night of the werewolf attack, I pretty much felt the same way. I know this sounds weird, but I feel like I owe them. They saved our lives. And they've never caused any trouble. But, this Corina…she's the evil one."

Roy looked over at Wayne, chuckled, and shook his head.

"All right laugh," Wayne said, looking irritated. "But all the Falcon Haven witches ever do is take care of the land and sell us their produce."

The Shadow Hunters froze then suddenly roared with laughter. "So, that's it," Campbell said. "For a while there I thought you guys had insects for brains. I see why you're protecting them. You're bewitched…something in their produce no doubt."

"We're not bewitched, damn it!" Wayne snapped.

"How can you be sure? People don't know when they're bewitched," Campbell said.

"Our children eat that produce and they're doing just fine," Bob weighed in angrily. "Besides, the town thinks witches are just a childhood rumor."

"The town doesn't know…really?" Campbell asked.

"No!"

"Hey, it doesn't matter," Roy said. "Just stay out of our way when we get there. We're taking them *all* down."

Wayne shook his head and turned his face to the window. "You're making a big mistake," he mumbled.

The remainder of the ride to Falcon Haven was in total silence. Wayne felt bad that during him and his deputies' time of desperation, the witches had come to their aid, but now he feared that he couldn't return the favor. The words "I suffer a witch not to live" made Wayne sick, but doing nothing to prevent their demise made him even sicker.

*****

Corina stood transparent in a mystical cocoon that floated in the air. The outline of her demonic frame was barely noticeable. Watching her sister, Holly, and friends Gunner and Amber match spell for spell with the covenant witches put a smile on Corina's face as she stood enjoying her imagined superiority. The sky lit up with arcane energy from the ongoing battle between the covenant witches and the trio. Whenever the witches got the upper hand, Corina would summon a spell that put the odds back in the trio's favor. The witches and the trio threw deadly waves of energy at each other. Each wave from the witches' extended hands was matched by a stronger one from the trio. Then a continuous stream of energy flowed from the hands of the witches, but *their* stream suddenly became significantly weaker while the trio's stream grew stronger. The witches' faces strained as they fought the power of the trio's superior wave of energy. The witches' hands burned because their own spell was being forced back on them.

Naomi turned sharply to Jewel and shouted, "The ancestors are weakening against them!"

"No! Corina is helping them!" Jewel said.

"But I don't see her!"

"Trust me, she's somewhere near!"

With the witches' stream of energy all but gone, the trios' superior waves of energy burned the witches' hands and sent them tumbling to the ground—their palms blistered from the intense heat. Gunner and Amber laughed and raised their hands to finish the witches off, but an accumulation of black smoke appeared above them. All eyes were upon the smoke as it suddenly swooped down upon Gunner and Amber and rendered them paralyzed while the smoke poured into the corners of their eyes, nose, ears and mouth—turning them into a soft solid mass that melted into the earth to become twin tar pools. The black gas became a thin stream that Campbell, who was standing nearby with the other Shadow Hunters, sucked into a long tube. Bishop, Wayne, and his deputies stood farther away.

"Who the hell is he?" Jewel asked.

Naomi smiled. "That's him…the man I told you about, Warren Campbell. I called him."

"You called him…you fool…the powerful one who hates witches?"

"I…I think we need to go," Naomi said, scrambling to her feet.

Corina stepped out from her invisible space. "You meddlesome idiots!" her voice boomed. "You'll pay for this!" She waved her hand and a bright orange blaze of light appeared—from it evolved a bald, nude man made of fire. It grabbed at Campbell but missed. Instead, the fiendish inferno picked up one of Wayne's deputies and held him tightly in his fiery arms. The deputy screamed as the fire-demon held onto him while he burned to death. The deputy's death happened so quickly that not even magic could have saved him.

Wayne's instinct was to shoot even though he knew bullets were no match for a being made of fire. Hundreds of bullets peppered the air as they all cut through the demon like pebbles jetting through water.

Campbell struck back by pulling from under his long leather coat a white ball the size of a baseball and throwing it into the air where it burst into a grey mist. It shrunk the fire-demon down to a tiny spark that vanished.

Then Holly looked down at herself and yelled, "What...what's happening to me?" as she too began to shrink.

Corina uttered a spell, but Holly kept shrinking. Corina made a ball of her own that materialized in the palm of her hand. She tossed it into the air where it burst into green mist, but her sister continued to shrink.

"Corina, help me!" Holly shouted, her voice growing fainter as she dwindled.

Corina spoke another spell, then another, and then several spells after that, but nothing worked against the grey mist. Corina's eyes grew pale with anger—tiny red veins showed in the dull whites of her eyes as she watched her sister shrink to the size of a housefly—as Holly's high-pitched voice pleaded to save her. Then the voice faded only to be heard in a dog's ear as Holly's physical being joined forces with the billions of micro-organisms in the atmosphere.

Corina was so full of rage and hatred that she trembled when she spat obscenities at Campbell. She rocked back and sent an electrical charge that hit Campbell in the gut, lifting him off his feet and driving him into a tree. Wayne and his deputies knew this was no fight for them, so they ran and took cover behind the vans, peeking out at times.

Campbell wobbled to his feet; he felt light-headed and dizzy with blood dribbling from his mouth as he spoke. "Is that all you've got?" he said, straightening his face to disguise his pain.

Bob poked his head up from behind the van and shook it at what he thought was Campbell's act of stupidity, then ducked back down for cover when he saw Corina positioning herself to perform another spell.

She lifted both hands and sent a blast of wind that knocked Ham and Roy sideways. Though in pain, they scrambled to their feet and pointed their swords at her; the swords spat two bolts that sped through the air like spiraling purple ribbons, hitting Corina in the chest and causing her to skid across the ground on her back.

Campbell raised his sword at Corina to attack, but she shot a stream of energy at Campbell that hit his sword, knocking it from his hand—it sailed across the dirt surface where it broke in half. On her feet now, she sent another spell that caused him to dive across the ground as the wave of energy shot toward him; the wave skipped over his shoulder, missing him by inches. Campbell, like an acrobat, did three low, overhead flips and scooped up his sword that had repaired itself and restored its pouring grey mist.

Ham and Roy pulled small explosive devices from their belts and tossed them at Corina. The blasts hit Corina in the middle of her chest and sent her flying fifty feet into the air. Before she hit the ground, she said a spell that caused her to float the rest of the way down—her feet making contact with the ground like a feather. She flashed a sinister smile and sent one of her most deadly waves of energy that missed them but struck a tree, setting it on fire. Corina sent another wave, but the hunters aimed their swords and sent a freezing wave of energy that rendered her spell useless.

Corina and the Shadow Hunters lit up the sky with their ongoing battle. The waves of energy looked like extremely long lightsabers striking each other with such speed that the sparks became blurred. Birds flew out of burning trees but got caught in the crossfire—

with many falling to the ground, burning and twitching in agony. Others continued flying with their tails aflame.

Wayne watched Corina lift her hand to produce a spell, but Roy's whip bound her right wrist, resulting in a cracking sound and her exclamation of agony. She lifted her other hand only to have it also bound at the wrist with the cracking of Ham's whip.

The whips, which had been soaked in salt that was harmful to witches, burned Corina, turning her wrists black.

"What do you think you're doing? You can't kill me," she said, her words slightly slurred. She felt weak and dizzy like all her fight was gone, but she still acted defiantly.

"Even if we could, we wouldn't," Campbell told her. "For all of your evil, Corina, death is too good for you. We want you to have a long time to think about the dark deeds you've inflicted on innocent people." Campbell pulled a fist-size globe from under his long leather coat. Inside the globe floated a grey mist. He held it out and aimed it at Corina, who laughed.

"So, that's it? That little misty ball is supposed to destroy me?" But straight away, a worrisome look crept upon her face when she felt a strong pull at the lower part of her body. The globe acted as a vacuum: first, parts of her clothing were ripped from her body and soared across to the globe, which sucked them in. Then Corina's legs shot from under her and she began to inch toward the globe. She twisted and shouted obscenities while flailing her arms about. She hissed and snarled like an animal. As her demise approached, she momentarily took the form of each evil creature she had ever assumed to perform her demonic deeds: first, a serpent, then a hideous clown, a live scarecrow, a wild dog, an evil ancient queen, and one that surprised the hunters—a normal-looking young man—and many others.

Campbell signaled for Roy and Ham to release her wrist as she began to fade while floating towards her prison of uncertainty. Wayne watched and wondered how her whole body could fit inside that little round globe. However, it was not a globe, but a mystical world that held the most evil creatures that had ever lived. The globe was just an entrance point that magically sucked them in and held them. Corina screamed at the top of her lungs before disappearing, and then she quickly reappeared inside the globe. Her miniature-size face mashed against the inner glass—her mouth wide open and yelling something, but no sound came from the globe. Campbell smiled down at the globe before putting it back inside his coat. He would transfer it to a special place that only he and the Shadow Hunters knew about. Corina would be trapped for eternity. No one but the hunters knew how to release the entities from that dark world, which, of course, they would never dream of doing.

Wayne, Bob, and the deputies came strolling out from behind the vans. Bishop Randall had prayed and watched the entire battle while kneeling behind a distant tree. He too came and joined the others. But his eyes were fixed on the covenant witches; they had made themselves invisible to watch the battle. Being visible now, they wanted to thank the hunters, but Jewel told them that would not be wise. Wayne looked over his deputies and frowned. "Where's Chris?"

Bob and the others looked around. Then Ham spotted a body over near a burnt and uprooted tree. "Over there," Ham shouted, pointing.

Wayne and the others ran to Chris who lay with his face and hands blistered, smoke seeping from his clothes. He was near death and barely breathing with blood pouring from his nose and mouth. Jewel ran over to Chris and knelt down beside him to cast a spell, but Campbell shoved her aside. "Get away from him you witch!" he said.

"I only want to help him," Jewel said.

"He doesn't need your hellish help," Pastor Randall said.

"But, he'll die," Jewel said.

"Better to die and be in the hands of the Lord than to be saved by the devil," Randall said.

"Let's get him to the hospital," Campbell said, looking around for someone to help him lift Chris.

"He's not going to make it to the hospital. Let her help," Wayne pleaded. "I know his family, and I refuse to bury another one of my deputies."

Pastor Randall's words boomed from his mouth. "Where is your faith, Wayne?" Randall knelt by the dying deputy, poured oil over his face and hands then prayed. The deputy's body jerked when the oil touched his skin. After a few minutes of prayer, the deputy trembled for several seconds. He calmed down then opened his eyes. The bleeding stopped and the deputy breathed more freely. His face brightened and the color returned to his skin. The deputies cheered and smiled widely. "*Now*, take him to the hospital," Randall said with unshakable confidence.

"I didn't know humans could do that," Jewel whispered, not knowing Pastor Randall had heard her.

"Humans can't. It's the God we serve," Randall said, squinting at her from under his lashes.

"Why do you hate us? We've done nothing but show kindness to humans."

"God suffers a witch not to live," Randall repeated forcefully then looked over at the hunters. "Well, what are you waiting for…isn't there room for them in that little globe of yours?"

The hunters took giant steps forward, but Wayne stepped in front of Jewel. "You weren't there the night she and her friend saved me and my deputies' lives. If they are to be destroyed, let God do it. I won't have their death on my watch."

"Why are you protecting them?" Campbell asked. "Okay, let's say you're right and they are harmless. Can't you see they draw evil wherever they are? Corina only came here because of them. And look at the harm they've caused just by living in this area. If you let them live, what's to keep other horrible creatures from coming here and doing God knows what to your citizens?"

Jewel stepped from behind Wayne and spoke up. "What do you think we were doing before you showed up? We were fighting Corina…trying to protect everyone in this region, including humans."

"Yeah, and you were losing," Campbell said.

"Listen, Campbell," Wayne said. "I really appreciate you, Ham, and Roy saving our town. But I'm telling you…if you try that on these witches, I know I can't beat you, but you're still going to have to come through me."

"Man, what is wrong with you?" Randall asked. "You know what the word of God says about letting witches live. You're going to put this whole town under a curse."

"You may be right," Wayne said. "I don't know why God allowed these witches to save our lives that night. But I owe them. What God does with them after this payback is his business. But you will not harm them today." Wayne stood in front of the witches and gazed at the hunters.

Campbell sighed. "All right Wayne, if you want to live among witches...so be it." Then Campbell squinted at Wayne. "But if we're ever called back here again, we're going to wipe this region clean of everything that's not human. And if you or your deputies get in the way, there'll be collateral damage, I can assure you." Campbell turned and thanked Pastor Randall for his help then the hunters got into their van and drove off with a mysterious cloud of grey mist trailing behind.

"Wayne, you're a fool," Randall said. He turned and walked toward the van he rode in.

"Like I said, I owed them a debt and it's now paid. Whatever happens to them from this point on is none of my business." He looked over at the covenant witches that were standing on the lawn. Jewel fondly smiled, but Wayne didn't smile back even though he wanted to. He climbed into his van and drove off—the truck containing Randall and the deputies following closely behind.

*****

The ancestors returned to their resting places and the covenant witches returned to their homes—what was left of them. The Falcon Haven houses stood in dusty and dreary contrast to the brightly colored homes they were before the battle. The once healthy and green lawns were brown and charred. The automobiles looked as if they'd been in a train wreck, and many were flipped upside down in driveways. Trees were burnt, ripped up from their roots, or cut in half. But all would be restored to its former glory through a few months of tilling, replanting, painting, and repairing.

Several months later.

One morning, the sun rose like a yellow-haired goddess ascending from her throne. Jewel and River sat on a swing in the backyard with the sun on their faces. They watched little Merchant who sat upon the green grass and played with his colorful toy truck. Jewel had kept her promise to get rid of the grimoire, and the covenant witches had dropped the necromancy charges against her, noting special circumstances. River and Dex remained very close, causing the Northern and Southern wolf packs to unite as one once again.

Matthew and Kayla became engaged. The wedding was set for June, and Veronica and Christa were excited to be the bridesmaids. Naomi took Kayla to the Mystic Souls to visit Beatrice. Jewel was right; Beatrice was very happy and said she wouldn't come back to the living even if she could.

Matthew continued to keep an eye on Russell Sooner, who had recently turned eleven. Werewolves didn't usually start their transformation until age thirteen. Matthew planned to break the news to Russell in a way that would keep the boy from freaking out and exposing himself and the pack. Then he'd take little Rusty under his wing and guide him into his strange new life.

Wayne, Bob, and the Sheerfield community had long mourned their dead and repaired the church. Nothing more was ever said about the covenant witches; it was as though they didn't exist. Bishop Randall moved to Ohio and became pastor to a large congregation. He vowed never to step foot in New Berwick again.

Way across town, Ward Burgess was home taking a well-deserved nap when he was awakened by a knock on the front door. He staggered to his feet and was a bit incoherent as he walked to the door. Peeking through the peephole, he smiled at the sight of his nephew, Karl. After Jessie Carter had disappeared, (Ward never told Karl what really happened to Jessie) Karl had asked his uncle

Ward to put Jessie's furniture and other belongings in his basement. Karl would have them picked up and taken to the Salvation Army at a later date. Ward opened the door half-smiling.

"Hey, Unc, you forgot I was coming over?" Karl greeted him, closing the door behind him.

"I sure did," Ward said, yawning and scratching his chest.

"Only really old people take naps, you know that don't you?" Karl teased.

"Oh, shut up. *You* should live so long. Want some coffee?" Ward turned and walked ahead of Karl toward the kitchen.

"Nah, I'm going down to take a little inventory before I have the stuff picked up," Karl said, opening the basement door. "I might want to keep some stuff as mementos," he said.

Ward heard descending footsteps as Karl scurried down the staircase. Ward yawned widely and walked over to the coffeemaker to pour himself a cup. He sat down and sipped on the hot brew. Several minutes later, he heard Karl loudly stumble up the stairs. It startled Ward, making him turn too quickly and spill hot coffee on his lap.

"Shit!" Ward jumped up from the table and wiped the hot liquid off with a cloth napkin. He turned to yell at Karl but froze when he saw the expression on Karl's face. "Karl, what's wrong?"

Karl stood with his mouth gaping—the windows to his soul were unfocused. He looked as if he'd seen something terrifying. His legs wobbled, and Ward had to catch him and set him down before he hit the floor.

"Karl, you're white as a sheet."

"Uncle Ward, you...you need to go in the basement," he stammered.

"What? Why? What's in the basement?"

"I...I pulled the sheet from over it and—and there it was."

"There who...what was? Good heavens, you're not making sense."

Karl didn't answer, but sat stiff, looking off like his thoughts were trapped in another world.

Ward left Karl's side and slowly, reluctantly descended the basement stairs. Once in the basement, he looked around, down at the floor and up at the ceiling, but saw nothing unusual. "Karl, I don't see anything!" he shouted. Ward looked behind furniture, pushed aside articles that were stacked on top of the chest of drawers, and looked under some piles of clothes in a corner. "You sure it wasn't your imagination? You know you spook easily!" Ward yelled up to him. He searched the closet and under the bedding, backing up until his butt bumped into a floor-length mirror. Ward turned around, jumped, and gasped. "Holy Mary mother of God," he whispered. Ward nearly fell when his feet got tangled in the sheet Karl had pulled from the mirror and dropped to the floor. He backed up, stumbling over a suitcase, then ran up the stairs—passing the kitchen where Karl still sat looking into space—and grabbed his phone off the night table. Ward touched the screen and listened impatiently to more than ten rings.

"Hello," the voice finally said on the other end.

"Jewel, come quickly. There's a problem....... No! I...I can't. You need to see this." Ward clicked off and flopped down on his bed to regain his composure.

When Jewel and Naomi arrived, Ward let them in. Karl, who looked disheveled, had not moved from the spot where Ward had left him.

"Is something wrong with Karl?" Jewel asked, squinting at Karl.

"No. It's down in the basement," Ward said.

Ward led the way to the basement. Naomi glanced over at Karl as they passed the kitchen and descended the staircase.

"Why the secrecy? You're freaking me out," Jewel said.

But Ward didn't answer. He led them over to the mirror, pointed, and stepped back. Jewel and Naomi walked and stood in front of the mirror. "Oh, great goddess of the universe," Jewel blurted.

"Who is he?" Naomi asked.

They stood stunned as Jessie Carter's reflection screamed and pounded on the inside of the mirror. Yet no sound emerged. Jewel read his lips as he silently screamed, "Help me! Please get me out of here!"

"So, that wasn't Jessie after all," Jewel reasoned. "Jessie must have resisted. So, Corina created his double, trapped Jessie in this mirror then took over the double's body."

"Another one of Corina's sad victims," Naomi said, shaking her head.

"Can you help him?" Karl asked, standing off to the far side. His face was flushed and he still trembled from the shock.

Ward's face lit up. "Now that I think about it, this might be a good thing, right?"

"Good how?" Jewel asked, frowning.

"I mean, he's not dead. You just have to get him out."

"I can't get him out of there."

"Of course you can. I've seen you do harder things than that. This is a cake walk for *you*."

"Ward, when I did those things, I was practicing black magic. I can't do that anymore. I got rid of the grimoire and had necromancy charges against me dropped because I vowed on my witch's honor not to practice the dark arts ever again."

"Bu…but you just can't leave him in there. He's my friend. You've got to help him!" Karl demanded.

Ward moved closer to Jewel and looked deep into her eyes. "Jewel, please."

"I can't Ward. I just can't. I wish I could. I'm…I'm sorry." Jewel dropped her head, turned, and walked quickly up the stairs. Naomi looked at Ward and Karl like she wished there was something she could do. "I'm so sorry about your friend," she said before mounting the steps.

Ward's shoulders slumped when he heard the front door close. Karl walked over to the mirror and placed his fist against it. Jessie put his fist in the same space from inside the mirror. The two just stared at one another sadly. Karl spoke loudly as if Jessie could hear him, "We're going to get you out! I promise!" Jessie read his lips and nodded. Ward eased down on the sofa and watched sadly as Karl and Jessie tried to console one another.

On the road, Jewel and Naomi were silent during the drive. Occasionally, Naomi would look over, wanting to say something, but Jewel seemed preoccupied with her thoughts. Turning her face to the passenger window, Naomi noticed a strange wooded area. "Where are we? I've never seen this place before." Jewel pulled into a patch of grass in the darkest part of the woods.

"Why are we stopping here?"

"Just get out!" Jewel walked around to the trunk of the car and Naomi met her there. Jewel opened the trunk and took out two shovels, handing one to Naomi.

"What's this for?"

"The grimoire. We have to dig it up," Jewel said, walking swiftly over to a patch of black dirt with Naomi right on her heels.

"But Jewel, you promised."

"I can't let Ward down. He and I go back too far."

"This is dangerous. They'll find out."

"I have to take that chance." She turned to Naomi and spoke softly, "You don't understand…Ward is like family."

"Yeah…and what about me? You're dragging *me* into this."

Jewel nearly choked. "Dragging you int'a… You've always been a part of this. I was the one who took the blame and kept you and Beatrice out of it. Or have you forgotten?"

"So…this is blackmail."

"No. This is you being my new best friend. Now dig!"

Naomi placed her foot on the back of the shovel and pushed it down into the earth; she lifted it and tossed the first of many shovels of dirt to the side. The two women worked feverishly as the noon sky suddenly grew dark with thick clouds. Neither Jewel nor Naomi had brought umbrellas. Maybe they had missed the day's forecast. Or maybe this sudden darkness was a sign of some sort; perhaps a reality that everyone in this strange little town knew but never spoke: That regardless of how normal life appeared on the surface—deep within the crevice, there was always something brewing in New Berwick.

***

284

About the Author

H. L. Randall, born in Baltimore City and a graduate of University of Baltimore, still lives in Maryland near the fabulous Inner Harbor overlooking the Maryland Science Center.

She is a fervent fan of paranormal and likes to bring to life worlds where the unlikely co-exist with one another in a small region of a mystic town—where her villains, who are colorful, intelligent, skillful, and deadly, frequently gain the upper hand.

Interesting still, are her heroes who sometimes must resort to those same attributes when forced into precarious situations, either to save loved ones or guard a most precious secret.

Just like the real world, there are problems and problem solvers; her character's weapons of choice include: crafted blades, treated bullets, mystical dust, religious ornaments, spells, grimoires and potions.

H. L. Randall's books are listed at Amazon.com and Audible.com.

Please visit the social pages below to learn more about her background and works.

https://www.youtube.com/watch?v=1QxJhDPliJ4&feature=youtu.be

https://www.facebook.com/pages/H-L-Randall-Books/888941771173410

https://twitter.com/HLRandallBooks

http://www.universalbattles.com/the-glass-cat-eye

http://www.amazon.com/Glass-Cat-Eye-fantasy-thriller/dp/0986292850/ref=sr_1_s

http://www.hlrandall.com/

www.ingramcontent.com/pod-product-compliance
Lightning Source LLC
Chambersburg PA
CBHW031258170626
46807CB00001B/213